Ritual
of
Proof

Ritual
of
Proof

Dara Joy

WILLIAM MORROW
75 YEARS OF PUBLISHING
An Imprint of HarperCollinsPublishers

RITUAL OF PROOF. Copyright © 2001 by Dara Joy. All rights reserved. Printed in the United States of America. No part of this book may be used or reproduced in any manner whatsoever without written permission except in the case of brief quotations embodied in critical articles and reviews. For information address HarperCollins Publishers Inc., 10 East 53rd Street, New York, NY 10022.

HarperCollins books may be purchased for educational, business, or sales promotional use. For information please write: Special Markets Department, HarperCollins Publishers Inc., 10 East 53rd Street, New York, NY 10022.

FIRST EDITION

Designed by Kathryn Parise

Printed on acid-free paper

Library of Congress Cataloging-in-Publication Data

Joy, Dara.
    Ritual of proof / by Dara Joy.—1st ed.
      p. cm.
    ISBN 0-380-97834-2
    1. Man-woman relationships—Fiction. 2. Feminism—Fiction. I.
Title.
    PS3560.O853 R57 2001
    813'.54—dc21

00-054619

01 02 03 04 05 QW 10 9 8 7 6 5 4 3 2 1

For Cabbycat,

MY ANGEL

MY THREAD

MY LITTLE HEARTBEAT

AGAINST THE DARKNESS

MY LITTLE SMILE

IN THE STORM

AS THE RAIN BEATS US DOWN

AND YOU HUDDLE WITH ME

BECAUSE YOU BELONG

AND WOULD BE LOST ELSEWHERE

WARM IN A COLD DOORWAY

TOGETHER WARM

TEARS WARM

LAUGHTER WARM

TOUCH LIKE TEARS

HOLD ME

I WILL LOVE YOU FOREVER

I WILL.

We don't see things as they are.

We see them as we are.

—ANAÏS NIN

Ritual of Proof

T he shadow moved with precision.

Controlled savagery guided the ruthless sequence of forms, creating an heroic abstraction across paving stone.

Hushed movements in low predawn light mimicked the rustle of wind.

With a deadly snap, a weapon echoed through the trees. Expertly slung, its fatal trajectory gathered speed and momentum. If not controlled precisely, such a weapon was as dangerous to its wielder as it was to its potential target.

Corded ropes arced and spun out, passing within a hairbreadth of the shadow. Like lovers, they moved together as the first rays of day crested the horizon.

The perimeter rustled, sighing to the same pulse-beat. Flora quivered with expectation as dawn approached.

The shadow, the master, the environment—

The weapon.

Over and over the rite went, building into a dance of lethal beauty.

Until all seamed into one.

Whereupon, shadow outlined the heart of day and day ignited the heart of shadow with fire. . . .

omplexity had taken a seat at her table.

She did not want to go to the soiree this evening.

The trip from her properties on the southernmost tip of the continent had been long and fraught with one disaster after another. She wondered how many of those incidents had been accidents.

Luck had been with her.

Luck and the skill of her protectors—fierce women, highly trained in the art of defense.

Green Tamryn sighed; her auburn hair shifted about her shoulders, framing her face. Claudine D'anbere had ever been a thorn in her side. From the time they were children, the woman cultivated an unnatural jealousy of Green. Throughout the years, she had constantly sought to undermine, steal, disrupt, and annoy.

Green supposed it went back to their tutoring days. They had been schooled together as learning partners. Whereas Green was a quick and curious student, earning the affection of their teacher, Avatar, Claudine had been slower to learn, constantly picking fights with their poor, beleaguered instructor, a woman from the southern tribes who eked a living for herself through her teaching skills.

Claudine had ruined that for the woman.

Constantly causing trouble, she had aligned a group of the problem girls against both Green and Avatar. Even though Green possessed an extremely sweet nature, she had within her an enormous core of inner strength. Claudine had never been able to get the better of her.

Which drove the other girl mad.

As they grew older, it only got worse. Claudine constantly opposed her in the House of She-Lords; she tried to woo her friends away; and, she actively pursued any man in whom Green had shown the slightest interest.

She had even approached Green's pleasurer, River. He had the good sense to turn her down flat, recognizing that she was simply out to use him and discard him.

Of course, River was under Green's exclusive protection.

There had been too many mysterious mishaps on the journey home!

Not to mention the appalling condition of her southern estates. The new caretaker had let the place run to seed. The fields were overrun by jakakoos—nasty little beasts—and the house was almost in ruin, with many of its treasures plundered. The crops were almost destroyed and could barely be harvested. They ended up having to burn several fields and replant, which set her back at least five seasons in profits.

Altogether, it had taken her almost two seasons to straighten out that tangled mess. With only the briefest of interim trips back to Capitol Town to take care of her main businesses, her social life had been pared down to sporadic visits with friends and River.

Every time she left, the pleasurer had begged her to take him with her but she had refused. The wild South Land was no place for a man who was used to sleeping on the luxury of spun Ramagi silk sheets.

She rubbed the back of her neck.

Now her southern lands were back in good condition, the estate cared for by an able midwoman. So she had returned once more to her life here.

Green had no doubt that Claudine D'anbere was behind every disaster. The She-Count was making a bid for her southern property. It had been a very close battle to stay afloat; Green had been almost forced to sell. It had not helped when an anonymous offer had been placed with her main crop creditor just when the figures were at their worst. Fortunately, the creditor had faith in her and her family name.

Idly, Green picked up the scented invitation, which was hand scrolled on the finest jinto leaf parchment. It would be her first soiree in almost two seasons. She wondered what the new "come-outs" would look like this year. Eager, fresh-faced young men, nervous and excited, carefully aiming to snag the best title while leading all on a merry chase.

She shook her head, smiling slightly.

Thank sense and sensibility that she had removed herself from that tedious nonsense! Still, it would be important to make an appearance as she reentered society. Besides, Claudine was sure to be there and Green wouldn't let herself miss the look of horrified shock on the She-Count's face when she realized that Green was back and still holding on to her southern properties.

She arched her back, trying to work out a kink.

"You've worked too hard! You need a rest—a *real* rest." An elderly woman bustled into the room with a tray of jinto tea. Placing the tray on the sideboard, she came up behind Green. Brusquely slapping her hands away, she massaged the younger woman's lower back.

"Thank you, Avatar."

"Hmmmph!" the gruff woman replied. "You should have a name-bearer to do this for you."

Green's lips turned up in a soft smile at the familiar gibe. "And why would I want all that grief when you do it so well?"

Avatar harrumphed and chuckled at the same time. The elderly woman treated her more like a daughter than a She-Lord. Back when Claudine had succeeded in having Avatar removed from her post, Green had rescued the woman from sure poverty by bringing her into her own household. Another thing Claudine hated her for . . .

"I was speaking to Duchene Reynard's kitchenkeeper today, down at the town center—"

"You see quite a lot of him, don't you?" Green teased.

Avatar blustered. "He was on his way to the marketplace, and I to the library. It is only natural that we should meet on occasion."

"Yes, especially at the crack of dawn when he does the household shopping for the day."

Avatar put her hands on her sturdy hips. "Do you want to hear what he said or not?"

"Do I have a choice?" Two dimples curved her cheeks.

"No, so listen up. Seems he overheard the Duchene having quite a row with that wild grandson of hers. She wanted him to attend the soiree this evening and he was having none of it."

Jorlan Reynard. Green smiled in fond remembrance of the Duchene's handsome, strong-willed grandson. On several occasions, as a mischievous youth, he had caused havoc at the poor Duchene's social gatherings. One time, he had come into the solar, strutted over to She-Count D'anbere and kicked her soundly in the shin. Everyone was appalled except Green. Having just reached her majority, she found the antics of childhood not that far from her memory. Besides, she would have liked to have done the very same thing. She had laughed long and hard.

Until she found out that he had seen Claudine abuse her mount. He had reacted from emotion without thought for the consequences. Word had it, as a child, he had grown up much the same—letting his passionate heart rule his choices.

He had been punished that eve.

Later, Green had found him sniffling pitifully on a high limb of a Dreamtree. He had tried to hide his tears from her, bravely wiping his face with the back of his sleeve and sticking his chin defiantly in the air.

He was unforgettable. The beautiful dark-haired boy was a strange combination of youth and maturity, even at so young an age. She had told him that it was not a bad thing to have such heated opinions, but one needed to know the most opportune time to vent them. In this way he could create the effect he wanted while maintaining control of himself and the situation.

He had blinked those incredible aqua eyes of his and thought carefully about what she was saying.

Then he surprised her by telling her she was very knowledgeable and wondered if she would take him for a name-bearer when he grew up. He told her he would like that because she was so smart.

She had laughed again, shook a finger at him, then cautioned him to crawl inside the window to his bedroom before the screech wings came out to feed.

His eyes widened and he scrambled quickly back indoors.

In the ensuing years, he had been much talked about by the Top Slice. In fact, the enigmatic fil-Duchene was a favorite subject for their gossip. It was said he was aloof and difficult, yet charming when he wanted to be.

And sinfully handsome.

There was not a damselle in the Select Quarter that didn't think of offering a bed price for him. Some new-breeds claimed he walked on the edge of propriety, although that was strictly rumor and probably wishful thinking on their part. Green could only surmise that, over the years, Jorlan had learned to guard himself well.

"Jorlan . . ." Green mused out loud, wondering what he actually was like now.

"No other," said Avatar. "The word is that he is quite the handful! The Duchene has gone completely white from dealing with him."

"Come now—the Duchene has been whiting her hair for ages."

"Nevertheless! He's a difficult one, that's for sure. Will give some poor woman a run for her time with the trouble he causes."

"Some trouble is worth the effort, Avatar." Green arched into the wonderful therapeutic pressure and sighed.

"You've been working too hard and long these past two years, Marquelle. You need a rest."

"I agree. I intend to stay here in residence at Tamryn House, for the most part, from now on. Now that the crisis in the South Land is past, I am looking forward to resuming a normal Town schedule again."

"I, as well. Traveling back and forth to that forsaken land every few months has not been easy on these old bones."

Green tried not to laugh. Despite her age, Avatar was a stalwart woman, well equipped and often eager to handle the hardships of the road. But she agreed with her. It was going to be nice to take trips only by choice or for pleasure.

That is, as long as Claudine stayed clear of her property.

"Perhaps now would be a good time for you to settle down?" Avatar slyly insinuated, bringing up a favorite topic of hers. "After all, you are the last of the Tamryns. Be a fine shame to end such a noble line simply for the lack of trying."

"Lack of trying?" Green grinned, knowing exactly what the woman was doing. "Surely not for lack of trying?" She teased the straitlaced servant who was more like a devoted family member.

"None of that now." She waved her hand through the air as if to dispel what she considered "cit ways." Avatar had been raised in the country and had never lost her colloquialism. Kept pleasurers did not sit well with her.

Green snickered, shaking her head. She loved to tease people who begged for the privilege. Avatar's austere ways and tendency to take everything at face value made her the perfect foil for lighthearted banter.

"Perhaps I'll find someone to interest me at the soiree . . ." she began, innocently enough.

Avatar's mouth dropped open. This was the first time Green had even hinted at doing such a thing. "I think that's an excellent idea!" she sputtered.

Green blinked guilelessly into the mirastone in front of her. "Who knows? Maybe even that delightful . . . Jorlan?"

A rough, squealing gasp of air sucked into the older woman's mouth. She clutched her heart. "Not that *outwolf*! Not in this house! Never, I say! What are you trying to do to me in my old age, kill me off sooner? Forget what I said about taking a name-bearer; you have plenty of time!"

Grinning, Green shook her finger at her. "Always be careful what you wish for, Avatar."

The old woman harrumphed.

M *arquelle Tamryn was a rare danger.*

Jorlan Reynard's eyes narrowed with a concealing sweep of jet lashes as he keenly scrutinized the woman. The protective strategy shaded his high cheekbones. His strong viewpoints and resolute self-discipline had always warred with this taste for risk.

The dichotomous brew was an indication of his complex character. Yet the exclusive traits that comprised his enigmatical nature were often overlooked in light of his breathtaking appearance.

And if not overlooked, surely forgiven.

Stunning beauty was always pardoned.

As the woman made her way through the throng, many of the guests leaned toward her—reminding him of sycophantic sunpods swaying in the hope of capturing a succulent morsel of moisture.

Of course, the Top Slice always reminded him of sycophantic sunpods.

Especially in the presence of someone who was of primary port.

He exhaled. He hadn't wanted to come tonight. He despised these organized galas of the Season where the Top Slice paraded their eligibles in the hope of garnering the "catch." It sickened him. He had no interest whatsoever in settling down. Ever.

Before he had left for the soiree, he had gone out onto his balcony. A multicolored blanock had landed on the edge of the railing. Its exotic plumage proclaimed it the male.

But of course, he thought. *Even blanocks were forced to show their array! Blame it on the Season. It's male-strutting time.*

He recalled that the blanock had gracefully lifted off the twisted railing, its wings flapping as it gained flight. Jorlan had watched its trail to freedom until it was out of sight. And a good deal longer.

Then he had squared his shoulders and prepared himself for a long, tedious evening. On his way to the soiree, he had vowed that this would be his last Season. The last.

His final cycle of galas.

Then he would be free—

Or as free as an unclaimed male was likely to get.

She brushed by them all, laughing gaily, making quips, patting familiar arms, and winking at several of the men who vainly tried to hold her attention for more than a few moments. Normally such a display would repel him. It did repel him.

He couldn't look away.

Her presence had "activated" him. Completely. He had no explanation for it and he was a man who sought explanations.

"She is captivating, isn't she? Quite the woman of the world. Do you think she'll dance with you?" His friend Lymax had observed where his attention was riveted. Lymax had to be surprised by his unusual interest. Jorlan had never been one to engage in the idle flirtation or pleasant frivolities expected at these gatherings.

"What makes you think I would want that?" he responded dryly.

Lymax snorted in disbelief. "Who wouldn't want to dance with her? And don't look at me like that—I've known you too long, Jorlan; although, truth to tell, I wouldn't claim to *know* you."

Jorlan raised an eyebrow. "And what is that supposed to mean?"

Lymax sighed. "You are my closest friend, Jorlan, and you have been an exemplary friend throughout the years—none better, I say. I have confided in you my entire life. You have aided me through my griefs and sorrows, laughed with me over the joys, never once failed to offer a supporting hand. What's more, you have never behaved like a nog-twist. In addition to that, on many an occasion, you have displayed a genuine concern over my welfare. . . ."

"Why do I feel there is an end point to this mack-mock that I am not going to like?"

"It's no mack-mock!"

Jorlan gave him a look.

"Very well, perhaps a wee bit o' mack-mock." Lymax grinned up at him. "But there is a valid point to be made here. The two people that you have permitted yourself to care for—me and your grandmother— you would willingly face death for. Yet, this extraordinarily brave spirit has never truly taken the risk to give itself to anyone. *Ever*. Have you, Jorlan?"

"What do you speak of?" he asked quietly, while continuing his observation of the woman.

"You keep yourself to yourself. I have seen it within you since we were boys. Since you came to live with the Duchene. I think that was the start of it, although, over the years, your zeal for privacy has grown into its own strange passion."

"Mmm . . ." he responded, distractedly.

"What I have never understood is *why* you cut yourself off so from society. You know you are getting a reputation as dark matter."

The corner of Jorlan's mouth lifted in amusement. "I am only inscrutable to those who cannot read me."

Lymax rolled his eyes. "And what a wit!"

Jorlan chuckled softly.

"Are you not going to shed a flamelight for the rest of us mere mortals?" Lymax threw his arms wide in exaggerated pique.

Jorlan smiled but, true to form, he did not sate Lymax's curiosity. As was his wont, he remained silent as he continued to observe the woman indirectly. The unusual reaction she engendered irritated him.

Intuitively recognizing the threat she posed, he turned away. The Marquelle moved slightly just then and momentarily caught his eye.

For a fraction of time, it seemed as if his heart stopped beating.

In that moment his existence became the pause between breaths wherein forbidden possibility is sired.

A heated tremor passed quickly through his groin. There was no way to describe the odd effect she had on him and he wasn't sure he wanted to describe it, even if he could. Instantly, he shook his broad shoulders to slake off the intense desire welling within him. The maneuver was an old trick he had been taught as a youth by one of his mastery teachers. It worked nominally, but the action brought her attention to an acute focus. The opposite of what he wanted.

He felt her speculative gaze travel the length of him. An enigmatic smile suddenly donned her lush lips as she watched him.

She knew! Knew of the tricks he had been taught! Tricks they had all been taught.

And why shouldn't she know them? It was said she knew a great deal more than the simple tricks of men. It was said she was a powerful, strategically brilliant Marquelle. A woman who knew herself and that which she sought from life. A woman of the town.

If a situation arose, she could be trouble for him.

Immediately, as the warning thought occurred, he turned from her again, only this time he completed the act with his accustomed detached mask of indifference.

In front of him the mirastone walls perfectly reflected her dynamic image. Made out of thin sheets of indigenous mira rock, the exclusive building material surrounded the entire inside of the greeting room. Its exorbitant price, along with its copious use in the hall, bespoke of the affluence of their host, a friend of his grandmother.

The Marquelle's exquisite amber eyes widened slightly at his aloof demeanor, then deliberately took in his measure. He gritted his teeth, hating to be examined like this.

As if he were nothing more than an inconsequential possession for a titled woman's bed.

At least she did not scrutinize him greedily, as had so many others.

When she observed him it seemed as if she were seeing straight through to the very essence of him. He had heard that Green Tamryn was a brilliant orator in the House of She-Lords. As a member of the ruling class and a titled Marquelle, she had a permanent stand on the governing Septibunal. Word had it that she chose her causes wisely and with great care, so when she did take the floor of the chamber the effect was spellbinding. Of the nine issues she had brought before council, all nine had been universally adopted with a sweep tally.

Marquelle Tamryn was generally well regarded and sometimes envied for her reputation, a reputation that did not include her council successes alone. Males vied for her attention and it was bandied about that she was a knowledgeable, sensual lover who spoiled her men for any other women. Seeing how the men here were reacting to her, he could well believe the kloobroth. She was not simply beautiful; there was a rare quality to her.

She continued to observe him with interest.

Glancing in the reflective rock, he noticed her gaze slowly scanning the length of him again. She paused slightly in her perusal to judge the tensile strength of his buttocks—something women had a tendency to do.

Much to the distress of his grandmother, the Duchene, women often remarked that her grandson was a man who could inadvertently cause wars by the solidity of those round, tight globes.

Through no fault of his own, he already had caused a few major skirmishes.

Just this past year, the daughter of an Earlene threatened to fight a duel with the daughter of a Marquelle over the right to him. Fortunately, his grandmother had put an end to the foolishness by refusing them both.

Strangely, Marquelle Tamryn's effect on him was quite different from the others'. . . .

He rolled his shoulders again to release the odd buildup of tension.

Lymax broke into his speculation. "They say that the Marquelle has shown no interest in taking a name-bearer whatsoever, despite that she is the last of her line, titled, and fabulously wealthy to boot."

"Perhaps she shows some sense, then."

Lymax scoffed. "She can afford to be 'sensible,' my friend—you cannot."

"I do as I choose."

"Not in this case. You won't be able to control her like the others, Jorlan. They are all made brainless by your looks and form; she won't be. Marquelle Tamryn is her own woman. She is nothing like the new breeds you are accustomed to. She will not be led on a merry chase to nowhere. If you play with her, she will make sure she collects the zip."

"Rut-bid." Jorlan's lips curled seductively at the enticing thought of such a challenge. *Could* he lead her on a merry chase? It was the side of him that loved to take risks that considered the prospect.

"And you can get that idea right out of your head."

"Mmm, what idea is that?" Jorlan asked in mock obtuseness.

Lymax wagged a finger at him. "I know you, Jorlan, and that expression means trouble. You are a torque, when the mood strikes you. Do not think to tease her. Even the Duchene will not be able to protect you from her—it is said she has powerful alliances in the Septibunal."

Jorlan scanned the voluptuous feminine form in the reflective mira-stone, his sights concentrating on soft, slightly full lips as she laughed with a companion. He wondered what they would feel like pressed against his. . . .

"I will need no interference from the Duchene," he murmured, totally absorbed.

With effort, his aqua gaze broke from Marquelle Tamryn—but not before their glance met once again. Her light auburn eyebrows arched, almost daring him to continue. He turned his focus away from the direct invitation in a deliberately slow movement that somehow became rejection and challenge at once.

"They say she has a housed pleasurer in town." Lymax whispered. "Lucky chum. Of course, that isn't the fate for us, is it?"

"Be glad of it. It is not a life you would welcome, Lymax." He grabbed a goblet from a passing servant's tray.

Lymax sighed. "I suppose not. Fate for the likes of us, noble as we are, is to be bartered to the highest bidder and title that our families can secure."

"Perhaps for you—not for me." Jorlan sipped his hameeri liquor, letting the rare liquid hit his tongue and slide down his throat. Cool and slow. Their she-host was generous tonight; hameeri was prohibitively expensive. Here, in this gathering of the Select Quarter, the Top Slice, as they were called by the lower sets, nothing was too good. These nobles enjoyed their station in life. Most could trace their ancestry back to the commanders of the Seed Ship. A millennium ago, the moon called Forus had greeted the settlers with the warm, loving embrace of a new father—trying desperately to comfort his infant.

The outfit had thrived under the protection of such a loving shield.

Jorlan frowned as perennial questions surfaced in his mind. Not much was remembered about Originpoint. Nothing was ever spoken aloud or handed down in their folklore regarding that time before. As a child, he had often wondered about their shrouded past, how they had come to be where they are, what life was like in that prehistoric time.

In his youthful imaginings, he had dreamt of a world where things were different for men. Where men weren't either bartered about for the pleasure of women or expected to be content in the only role open to them—that of name-bearer. He had dreamt of a place where males had an equal part in society and their name-givers respected them as true partners in all things.

He had even fantasized that men would have a say in how the society itself was run.

One night, when he had made the mistake of voicing his adolescent viewpoints in his grandmother's drawing room, he had been laughed at by the titled women present as a precocious child. Later, the Duchene had counseled him that, although his thoughts were entertaining, he would do best to keep them to himself, as such talk would alienate him from a good match.

Right then he decided that he did not want a "good match," or any match for that matter.

He wanted to be able to live his life on his own terms. Years later, he had managed to extract a promise from the Duchene that she would allow him to approve of his own choice.

Naturally, he had disapproved of every single caller.

Much to the Duchene's dismay.

Jorlan's brow furrowed with slight annoyance as the full import of Lymax's statement registered on him. *She kept a pleasurer.* He was not overly surprised; yet, it annoyed him for some strange reason. In training, he had heard fevered whispers, voices full of longing regarding Marquelle Tamryn. She was well-learned in the ways of men. Rumor had it that she was a legendary lover. Most of the men present tonight almost begged for her attention.

It had nothing to do with him.

"I'm not interested," he murmured aloud.

His friend laughed. "Oh, you're interested all right! Just like the rest of us. The silent, to-himself, outwolf Jorlan just doesn't want to admit that he is finally interested. I saw the way you looked at her."

"I can look. It doesn't mean—"

"That you're ready to forsake your secret vow of never becoming a name-bearer? Perhaps not, but in all the years I've known you, I've never seen you even glance more than a cursory moment, let alone appear speculative at the same time."

"She's . . . different."

"She is that. And they say she has quite an afterburn. I wouldn't care if she was a lowly She-Lord; I wouldn't refuse an offer from her house, I'll tell you." He sighed deeply. "Unfortunately my offering will probably be a very titled, very rich, and very *staid* noble, whose only interest in me will be the continuation of her line."

Jorlan glanced over at his friend. "Why do you say that?"

"My mother has five sons and no daughters. I'm the oldest. The first decent offer that comes along is sure to be accepted posthaste."

Jorlan exhaled, knowing the truth of his friend's words. "You can refuse."

"And shame my family with scandal? No. I am not like you, Jorlan. I am not one to forge my own path by breaking with society's mores, nor do I have an overly indulgent grandmother from a great house to cosset my whims."

Jorlan clenched his jaw. "It is no whim to desire the right of personal freedom."

Lymax shrugged. "It is a man's duty to fasten and produce heirs. Such is his ordained place."

"*Ordained?* Ordained by whom? Do you really believe this to be spirit-law?"

Lymax blanched. "You speak sacrilege! Fortunately, I am used to your wild ways, my friend, but I caution you to hold your tongue. It would be better for all concerned if you let go of these radical ideas of yours. No good can come of it."

"Why is it considered extreme to want to choose the direction of your own life?"

"Face it, Jorlan, we are the lesser sex. That is why our name-givers take care of us. Left alone, we would fall to ruin. We are intellectually inferior. Left unmonitored, our innate male aggression would destroy this world."

Jorlan snorted. "Intellectually inferior?" He pointed to an intoxicated She-Lord who was singing and spinning with several young swaggers across the far end of the room. "I'll wager that She-Lord cannot speak the intricacies of sam'on talk, nor recite from all of the sixty-three books of the bair-tin, nor draw plans for entire cysystems." Cysystems were used by Forus architects to construct everything from simple abodes to entire cities. Jorlan loved working a complicated cysystem.

"True. Your zest and aptitude for learning is well-known, Jorlan—

even though the Duchene has tried to downplay that particular *attri-bute* of yours." Lymax smiled at him. "That swagger over there does not need such abilities, as she is fabulously wealthy and extremely well situated."

"Which is my point. She has a stand on the Septibunal floor strictly on the basis of her inherited title. Even a nog-twist gets a vote on the laws that govern us as long as she is female and titled."

Lymax expelled heavily, not wanting to verbally admit that Jorlan was right on that point.

"As far as what you say about our aggressive tendencies, Lymax, I do not subscribe to that belief, either. Do we not train our minds as well as our bodies in control? In any case, you are right about one thing. My grandmother has given me her word—she will choose no name-giver for me without my consent, and I will *not* give my consent."

Lymax looked at him, bewildered. It was obvious he could not understand his friend's rebellious attitude.

"It won't matter soon, anyway," said Jorlan.

"Why do you say that?"

"Soon I will be past the prime age for such an alliance. Then neither I nor my grandmother will have to be concerned over the matter."

Lymax scoffed. "Have you looked in a mirastone lately, Jorlan? The offers will not cease. In some strange way that none of us hopefuls can understand, your continued refusals have only increased your desirability. The Top Slice sees you as the ultimate challenge and the ultimate prize. Instead of putting them off, it has only drawn them to you more."

Jorlan frowned. That hadn't occurred to him.

"In addition to your stunning appearance, my friend," Lymax went on, "it is speculated that a long-ago ancestor of yours was actually a pleasurer. The nobles have wagered bets on whether or not you have inherited the passion that is so inherent in many of them."

The sharp aqua eyes narrowed ominously.

Lymax put his hands up in a defensive gesture. "Do not blame me— it is what is bandied about. It makes you all the more of the rare prize: grandson of a Duchene and, thrown in for good measure, the blood of a pleasurer in your veins. You have them wild. What woman wouldn't want such a combination in her legal bed?"

"I am no woman's prize! Nor will I ever be."

"That may be true," a melodious voice concurred from directly behind him. "Such a dour expression denotes you more penalty than gift, although it does make you look quite brooding and interesting."

Despite himself, his lips curved in wry amusement. There was no mistaking that melodious voice, nor the infamous wit behind it. He pivoted about to face Marquelle Tamryn. "May I take that as a compliment, Marquelle?"

"Absolutely not." She grinned up at him. An engaging, full-dimpled smile that literally took his breath away.

She was not simply beautiful.

She was incredibly . . . *lovely.*

There was a certain lilt in her voice that seemed to withhold alluring secrets. There was the most beguiling curve to those luscious lips that bespoke of an uncommon knowledge. There was no doubt in his mind that this woman knew what pleased her in a man and what she expected of him. It was in her aware aspect. In her amber eyes.

And yet her name had never been linked with the Kloo Balcony set, the spoiled wealthy new breeds of the Top Slice who frequented the Neon Night part of town. Centuries ago, it had been deemed fashionable for the Select Quarter to meet at an establishment called Almacks, the Later. Despite some competition from other establishments, over the centuries, it had never lost its appeal.

Or its exclusiveness.

The name of the club had been derived from an obscure page of ancient text found in the personal belongings of one of the first settlers from Originpoint. The old text was still in dispute—as some believed it referred to a religious cult of some kind, while others postulated that it was part of an instructional manual. The words "historical" and "romantic" were repeatedly noted. No one was exactly sure in what context the terms were used, although it was known from portions of surviving personal log entries that there were many of these concealed volumes on board the all-female ship.

Some of their historians went so far as to postulate that these volumes might have had some type of a formative effect or influence on their emerging civilization. But that was strictly speculation as well. Whatever ancient pages had survived were kept in a special storage facility, open only to the head of the Septibunal and no other.

But Almacks, the Later had always been a smashing success.

The wildest, elitist band of new-breeds held court daily by the curved Kloo mirrors. Named after the native Kloo, the mirrors seemed to change color the way the Kloo variegated its plumage. And like the ever-changing Kloo, these women seemed to change opinions hourly of what was fashionable. They set style and could shift trends for months with a single disdainful glance at unacceptable garb.

The swaggers who reigned supreme over the mirrors got whatever they demanded from Almacks, the Later. They often demanded the impossible. They were wild, glinty new-breeds used to being spoiled by their wealthy families.

It was not unknown for them to hazard entire family fortunes on the turn of a disc on the beta-baize tables.

"You know who I am?" Green sipped at her drink, glancing up at him over the rim of the filigreed chalice. She had always heard he was magnificent. He was *more*. A spicy blend of insolent dignity and un-tutored vulnerability. Yes, his stares contained a brash challenge, but the glitter in his eyes did not completely hide the unprotected heart within. *And the arresting color of those eyes . . . !*

Except on him, Green had never seen such a mesmerizing shade before. They were a perfect green with a translucent overwash of blue. Aqua eyes. The color was so like the Great Fathomless Sea, which cov-ered over half of Forus's surface. Unforgettable.

And so very penetrating. There was a remarkable faculty behind that contemplative gaze.

An indented slash of amusement slowly curved his cheeks. Green observed the contained reaction. This was no simple, pampered son of the aristocracy. Jorlan Reynard, she was sure, was an enticing receptacle of trouble.

She liked him already.

Unlike most of her peers, she preferred her men to be less biddable than was widely held to be the accepted notion of the epitome of male perfection. There was a blaze-dragon in this one.

And that blaze-dragon wanted to be set free.

She knew how to set him free. Her pulse pounded.

She inhaled slowly to steady her beating pulse as she gazed once again up the tall length of him. His features were utterly beautiful. Firm lips—the lower one slightly fuller than the top—were smooth and sen-sual. They were shaped and sculpted by the finest hand. Tiny grooves at the corners of his mouth seemed to indicate a teasing sense of humor. His nose was straight and perfectly molded.

Like his lashes, his hair was jet-black, thick, and trimmed to just above his shoulders. The silken ebony strands caught the glimmer of flamelight and played riotously with it. Only the slightest of waves saved his hair from being altogether straight. Those subtle ripples added incredible interest. Not enough wave to give any real curl, they created a resplendent texture to his hair. She observed that the jet strands slid languorously when he moved.

It would be difficult to remember that he was the son of a noblewoman. Especially with those looks.

They were far better suited to the bedchamber than the salon.

Green made a mental note to see who was responsible for his progenitor line. By his look, she would say Santorini. No one had ever been able to match Santorini's work in over a thousand Forus years. The methodologist had a master hand and was considered one of the finest genetic artisans of all time. With one hundred and twenty thousand genes in her palette, her genius had been in taking the naturally occurring propensities, or "gifts," within a specific code and embellishing them, thus allowing the individual to then expound upon this talent as he so desired. All he had to do was bring it into focus. Choice and directional pathways augmented the optimum outcome. Talent, according to how Santorini defined it, was a drawing of desire extracted from the broth of genetic and environmental conditions. The unique picture that resulted formed her art. Santorini introduced to Forus the science she called Sensitive genetical environment or selective gen-en.

If a child had a natural disposition to create music, the facets of this talent could be magnified, if he so desired, to explore and maximize that talent in whatever direction he chose. The propensity for these talents were, of course, passed on to his progeny. Green had heard that the gift lent itself to other, more interesting areas as well.

Few women had the great fortune to benefit from a Santorini.

Living examples of her work were extremely rare.

It would up his bed price considerably.

Had she been interested.

Then again, the men of the Reynard line were known for being naturally sensuous—perhaps he was not a Santorini. Perhaps, this was simply him.

In any case, he was a rebellious package of stimulation. Just what she adored. And so very rare. Too bad she was not on the Season circuit. She might be tempted to offer a fasten bid for him.

"No wonder your grandmother always hid you from me when you got older." She smiled secretly into her glass.

"You know the Duchene?" He seemed surprised. She was much younger than his grandmother's usual friends. He guessed her to be about thirty-four or thirty-five Forus years.

"Quite well. We are good friends—our familial relationships go back to the Seed Ship."

"I haven't seen you at the house."

"No. I suspect Anya kept you well removed whenever I arrived." She laughed softly, a lovely pure crystalline sound. "How old are you now, Jorlan? Twenty-three? Twenty-four?"

He watched her through veiled eyes. "Twenty-five."

She arched her eyebrows. "Are you contracted for?"

"No." His response was clipped. "Nor will I be."

A slightly elusive smile edged her lips. "Why not?"

"I do not see my future as such."

"Really? How do you see your future?" Her question was asked purely out of curiosity. She was not mocking him. And for that Jorlan answered.

"I am not sure yet, Marquelle Tamryn. I simply know what I do *not* want."

She seemed to think over his words. "The Duchene has agreed to this?"

He glanced to his right, clearly irritated at being in the position of having to answer. Green was fascinated by his rebelliousness. It was so rare. Such defiance belied an ardent nature.

"She has promised me she will not sign the contracts unless I agree to the offer first."

Green's lips parted slightly. "Unusual."

"Perhaps."

"She indulges you. She must be flooded with offers for you."

"I have turned down all of them."

Green smiled teasingly. "Take pity on her, Jorlan Reynard. Poor Anya must be going out of her head with the annoyance of it."

Her jesting comment made him grin wickedly. "Only when they interrupt her reading." It was well known that Anya Reynard was something of a recluse who loved her vid-tomes. She had passed that love of reading on to her grandson.

Green laughed. "Yes, I have borrowed quite a few from her in the past. Did you know she already sent a parcel over to my estate and I have only just arrived back in Capitol Town? She included a note to the effect that I would need something to dilute the heathen countryside from my blood. A number of them were quite stimulating." She winked up at him.

"Hmm. . . . She won't let me read those."

"And a good thing, too. They are much too corrupting for such sweet . . . eyes."

A soft bronze highlighted his cheekbones. "Do not toy with me, Marquelle Tamryn."

"If I don't, who will?" She gave him such a mocking look that he had to bite back his laughter. How had she managed to turn him around like that? His eyes gleamed with silent appreciation of her. "Yes, who will?"

he drawled in feigned agreement. His voice was low, smooth, incredibly sensual.

Again, she wondered: Santorini's touch? Many of her great works had legendary voices. The kind of voice that made the female awaken.

And stay awake.

Oh, yes, she liked him very much.

No wonder the Top Slice was mad to get him. There were very few surviving Santorinis. In Forus's past, many of them had been fought over to the death. A work of art but never pristine. Sensual, raw, dark, and compellingly exquisite. With intricate personalities to match. Each of the offspring had been unique to himself and different from all the others.

But was he a Santorini?

There had been rumors about his father. The men of the Reynard line were known for their uniqueness and their passion. Green often speculated that was why the Duchene had been so lenient with Jorlan. His parents had died in a transport accident. Theirs had been a rare love, still talked about in the salons today. Loreena Reynard had been an unusual woman who had flaunted convention—not for principle's sake but simply to be different. She had been a willful, stubborn damselle and Daret, with his stunning looks and tendency toward wildness, completely captivated her.

Jorlan had been young—seven Forus years at the time of their deaths. An impressionable age. It was noted that Jorlan had inherited the best and worst of their characteristics. He was impassioned, incredibly intelligent, willful, wonderfully witty, occasionally brooding, and sometimes hot-tempered. In addition to all that, a few of the more respectable members of the Slice, who had had an opportunity to converse with him, had reported that he was unexpectedly complex and inscrutable.

In short, a blaze-dragon.

The musicians struck up the first dance of the evening—a slow joined septille in soft muted shades of pink.

"Will you dance with me?"

She held out her hand while placing her crystal chalice on a nearby table. As soon as its base rested on the masoglass surface, it began to chime softly, resonating with all the other chalices in the room that had been set down in similar fashion. The combined chimes created a beautiful sound of continually blending notes that signified the formal beginning of the evening's festivities.

The large hall was lit with the tapers of a thousand jacama branches. The flamelights were hung upside down from the vaulted ceiling where they burned clean.

There was no way Jorlan could politely refuse. Lymax gave him a look that plainly said "I told you so." Reluctantly, he took her small hand in his and let her lead him onto the middle of the floor.

The dance area filled up quickly as eager young veils accepted hands for the opening septille.

They joined in the dance.

Green's right arm encircled low on his trim waist, her left hand resting on the curve of his left hip. He was taller than she had originally realized. Amazingly tall, in fact.

He tried to hide the slight tremor in his loins, but Green was aware of it. Her nearness was affecting him. She decided that she rather liked affecting this handsome, brash young man who was too opinionated by half for his own good.

So she decided to tease him.

Just a bit.

She knew it was wrong of her, but he was almost asking it of her by the visual challenges he had thrown down this evening. Perhaps it was time someone taught him a little of the ways of women.

Not too much, a warning voice said. He was still the grandson of a Duchene—and a Duchene Green respected. *But enough to show him that it was not wise to spark unless you meant to have a fire.*

As the Marquelle led him into the steps of the intricate, slow dance, which mimicked the rite of courtship, Jorlan felt distinctly uncomfortable. He had not wanted to attend this soiree, the first of the Season. His grandmother had insisted. While she had given him her promise to acquire his consent, she had in no way agreed to his stubborn refusal to entertain offers. Of course, he hadn't mentioned that part to the Marquelle.

Not that he thought she would offer for him. Her mode of living and own reputation for avoiding the Ritual of Proof was affirmation of that.

As they continued on with the dance, the Marquelle glanced up at him through dark auburn lashes. There was a sudden sheen of mischief behind that gold-tipped fringe. Her amber eyes flashed an inviting message to him.

Instinctively, he responded. The blood in his veins thickened. Yet he gazed down at her with the sure, steady look of a man who has been trained to wait for pleasure.

Green's mouth parted. She had not been expecting such a schooled reaction from him. In that moment she knew positively that Jorlan Reynard would be an extraordinary lover.

Too bad he is the grandson of a Duchene. She would have loved to explore his depths. However, she liked her life the way it was—no ties and no complications. Involving herself with the grandson of a Duchene could only end in one way. Fastening.

"Just what are you thinking, Marquelle?" The rich voice drawled teasingly at her, flutters shivered down the center line of her back to pool at the base of her spine. Against fashion, he was direct and supremely confident. She liked that, too.

The finger at his waist played a circle. "What do you think?"

Immediately she felt his back muscles stiffen at her touch. Despite the aloof demeanor, Jorlan Reynard was physically aware of her. He studied her through half-lowered eyes, silently estimating her. "I think you are a woman who is used to getting what she wants."

Her hand slipped from his waist to trail lower, curving slightly over his very firm buttocks. "Is there something wrong with that?"

He arched his eyebrow. Reaching behind him, he lifted her hand firmly back to his waist.

She smiled at him.

Her incredible amber eyes twinkled laughter at him. Laughter and an unspoken challenge. For behind the laughter was a blaze of desire.

That desire seemed to reach out to him, tease him with the lick of its flame. He didn't know how she did it, but he was taken. His breathing ceased and his lips parted slightly. Blood pooled between his thighs, throbbed in his groin.

Her breath seemed to stop, too, in that moment; she placed her palm on his chest and stared up at him.

He is all that is desirable. She looked away for a moment. *He is also Anya's grandson. Remember that, Green.*

He felt her shake slightly as she gazed into his eyes. He wondered what she saw. He wondered why he could not look away.

"Is there something wrong with that?" she repeated in a whisper.

The baiting comment worked. Instantly his nostrils flared in irritation, both with her action and his reaction.

He never allowed himself to be this affected! His focusing masters had all remarked on his phenomenal ability to control and to centralize.

One master had even joked that his future name-giver would be well-pleased with such a talent—especially when that talent was turned onto *her*.

Jorlan had stormed from the class that day.

His mastery was not *for* a name-giver; it was to avoid one.

Control and focus of his desire, he had; but with his passionate nature came a hot-blooded disposition that needed to be steered with an iron will.

"I am not a Santorini," he hissed in a whisper near her ear, causing her to start.

"No?" she whispered back, shaken. How had he known she had been thinking that?

"No." His warm lips brushed the folds of her ear. Tingles shot down her neck.

"Then . . . what are you?"

"I am not very complicated, Marquelle. I am no one you should concern yourself with." Contrary to his words, his hot breath feathered her lobe as his low voice caressed her.

"Of course." She turned her head sharply causing their lips to brush together as if by accident.

Jorlan's eyes flamed.

"But you taste quite complex to me."

Chapter Two

Yes, she was a rare danger, he acknowledged as they continued the dance.

He glanced down at the mouth that had just briefly and boldly caressed his. The small touch had riveted him. One taste of her had seemed to heighten all of his senses. He focused on the feelings she had aroused in him. Focused and expanded and delved.

He breathed deeply, then exhaled.

"I met you once when you were a boy, you know." Green watched his face carefully for some sign of recognition.

"Really?" He stared back at her.

"You don't remember?" Of course he would not remember such an insignificant incident in his childhood. Somehow, she was slightly disappointed, though.

"Was it at my grandmother's?"

"Yes. You had run into the salon like a hissing ball of fury."

He acknowledged her accurate description of his youthful demeanor, his white teeth flashing in the flamelights. "I often entered rooms like that."

"Not much has changed, has it?"

He smiled secretly. "Probably not."

"You seemed such an angry little boy."

"Not always," he responded quietly.

"Just after your parents died?"

Her astute insight surprised him. "Yes, probably. For a while, anyway. I hated the injustice of it."

"They died in a transport accident, didn't they?"

"Yes. Unnecessarily, I found out much later. They were traveling to the western horizon and an arc storm took them."

Her brow furrowed. "Didn't their guide see the signs?" Arc storms were always preceded by an definite series of phenomena.

His nostrils flared. "She saw them; she just didn't heed them. They think she may have eaten a Banta psillacyb. I hear they grow freely along the western routes."

Psillacybs were groups of indigenous Forus plants that caused extreme hallucinogenic effects in humans. They had been adopted by some fringe tribes to the far west for their religious practices. Except for medicinal purposes, they were generally frowned upon by society, although they often made their way to the soirees of Top Slice swaggers.

Those kind of parties generally were not talked about in polite society.

"I'm sorry, Jorlan. I know how hard such a loss can be."

He looked at her curiously.

"I am the last of my line as well."

"May I ask what happened to your family, Marquelle?"

"They were poisoned by a bad crop of hukka grain. It was back during the drought years. You are probably too young to remember that time—I barely remember it myself."

"What happened?" He pivoted effortlessly with her, perfectly matching her steps as they swirled about the floor. The grace of his movements belied the extraordinary martial skill that Anya Reynard had fleetingly remarked on on more than one occasion. The men trained in very basic forms to stay fit, but Green wondered how deadly he could actually be. There was something about his movements . . .

She gathered her thoughts to answer him. "Most of our usual crops were failing so we were forced to experiment with others. It was not known then that hukka must be harvested before it flowers. If you wait too long the stalks become highly toxic."

"I didn't know that."

"Why should you?" she smiled faintly. "I can't imagine your cook lets you into the kitchen much."

"True. Whenever he does, I have a tendency to cause havoc."

She grinned. "I have no doubt of that. And of course, you would not be allowed anywhere near the crops."

"You don't think so, hmm?" His eyes twinkled as he remembered a youthful prank. And then he remembered the brush of her lips against his— He focused on her mouth again.

"No."

He blinked. For a moment he was not sure what she was responding to. "I suppose at one time I enjoyed causing a certain amount of trouble."

His grandmother had regaled half the Top Slice with stories of his boyhood escapades. He had been a mischievous, difficult child. But she knew that he had also been an incredibly sweet child, with a sensitive heart.

"Really? Who would guess?" Green teased him. "And you did say 'enjoyed,' as in past tense?"

He cleared his throat. "We will not pursue that."

"Why not?"

"It is probably best not to." He arched his eyebrow.

"I would venture to say that on some days you arose with a mission to see just how much trouble you could cause in one day."

An engaging dimple curved a line in his cheek. "You wound me, Marquelle. I assure you I am much too serious of nature even to contemplate such a thing."

"That is what you would have us believe. I, however, know better."

"Do you?" He dipped his head and almost, but not quite, brushed her mouth.

It was a daring, bold act on the dance floor. It was mischievous and certainly begged trouble. Thankfully, no one realized what he had almost done. She pressed her hand into his waist. "Behave, Jorlan Reynard."

"Is that what you recommend?"

"If you wish to be safe, yes."

"Perhaps I don't wish to be entirely safe . . . Marquelle."

She sucked in her breath. "You like to play with danger, I see. But be forewarned: Should you play this game with others, they might not be as mindful as I am."

"Then perhaps I should play this game just with you."

He knew what she was about! Her initial plan to teach him a small lesson was backfiring on her. The veil was toying with her! She arched her brow. In the arena of games, he was a novice compared to her mastery. If the Duchene's grandson wanted to experiment with his limits, she would be only too happy to oblige him. "Is that what you really desire?"

"And if I do?"

"Then I would say, come take a walk with me."

"A walk? Where?" He asked her cautiously.

"Just outside to the gardens."

He hesitated for only an instant. Then his gaze fell on her mouth once more. The heat in his glance told her his response before he answered.

"Lead the way, Marquelle."

"Always," she murmured low.

Turning, Green noticed her archenemy, She-Count Claudine D'anbere across the room.

She was standing in the corner surrounded by her sycophants, lesser nobles of shady reputation who followed the She-Count about for whatever favors she could dispense.

She was watching them intently.

At first, Green assumed that it was her usual fixation on Green that was at the root of it. But the more she observed her, the more Green realized that Claudine was for once not focused on her—but on Jorlan. "Claudine D'anbere seems to have a tendresse for you, Jorlan."

He glanced the She-Count's way. Unconcerned, he turned back to Green. "Then she wastes her time. I have already rejected her suit."

"She doesn't seem to realize that."

"Then that is her misfortune. I have made it quite plain that besides not wanting a name-giver, I do not like her. There is something about her that chills me."

"I agree, but a word of warning: Be careful of her. She does not take rejection well. In fact, she does not take rejection at all."

He raised his brow. "What do you mean?"

"Ask her past three name-bearers. They initially refused her, only later to change their minds." And they all died in rather strange accidents, but Jorlan didn't need to know that. "Just heed my words. Do not toy with her as you have me tonight. You might find yourself in a situation you would not like."

"I see, although I'm not tempted to do such a thing. None of these newbreeds holds any interest for me. You are the only one I have ever been—" He stopped when he realized what he was saying.

Green smiled, somewhat stunned. "Thank you, Jorlan, that means a great deal to me."

He was surprised. "Why should it? I have heard you—"

She placed her finger over his lips. "It does, Jorlan. Leave it at that."

He nodded curtly once, his trust warring constantly with his maturity. No longer a youth, not yet a tried man, Jorlan Reynard was an intriguing blend of both. While his demeanor and reactions were that of a seasoned male, on occasion she caught the vestiges of innocent surprise on his features. She suspected that was part of his nature and would never change, no matter the circumstance of his life.

What a compelling, mystifying personality! And what a shame it was that she was not interested in procuring a name-bearer or she would surely be tempted to make a bid for him.

She only hoped that his eventual name-giver would appreciate his rare qualities and allow him the room to develop his potential.

She sighed morosely. Knowing the Top Slice, the chances of that happening were extremely remote. Most women would see him as a beautiful ornament to dress their table and father their heirs. He would be cosseted, left in a gilded cage, and stifled.

It depressed her.

Taking his hand, she led him across the floor to the arched doorways and out onto the terraced logia.

There were several pairs already strolling the inlaid stone logia. Most of the first-seasoners were closely dogged by their retained scinose.

"How fortunate we are that you are not in your first season," she remarked drolly as she led him past the potted plants and down the few steps that led into the shrouded gardens.

"Why is that?" he whispered low and close behind her, bending near her ear. The action made her aware, once again, of his unusual height.

"Because then your scinose would be trailing our every step— almost before we took it." Men in their first season were required to have a scinose. It was feared that a youth's first outing into society, with its rich offerings, might turn a lad's head and the better judgment he had been taught would be in danger of leaving him. No family wanted to take that risk. It was imperative that a son make the best match he could. Any smear to his reputation became a threat to the family.

Generally it was reasoned that if he showed good sense his first year then he should be able to withstand any untoward influences, although many a family retained a scinose until the son was safety fastened.

"I never had a scinose," he responded smoothly.

She stopped and gazed at him over her shoulder. "Never?"

"Never. The Duchene knew I would never tolerate it."

"It is good that she trusted you so. It speaks highly of the relationship between the two of you."

"Yes." One corner of his sensual lips lifted. "But there was something else involved, too."

"What is that?"

"Do I seem to you the kind of man who is easily led astray?"

No, he did not. "You seem like the kind of man who makes choices based on dangerous pretexts."

"Really."

"Yes." She resumed leading him deeper into the hanging shred-moss.

Why was he following so readily then? Did he not know the danger he could be in?

When they reached a secluded spot under the branches of a massive shredder plant, she motioned to him to take a seat on the carved bench.

In front of them the water of a placed pond lapped against some rocks. Once, long ago, she had read that Forus had partially been formed to resemble the Origin place. For some reason, the natural rhythm of Forus had allowed such reshaping only to a certain extent. The innate charm of the mysterious moon yielded just so much before reclaiming its own wild beauty.

Parts of the land were rugged and exotic still—even after a millennium of colonization.

She stood before him, looking down at him. "You are not worried that you may lose your control, Jorlan?"

"No."

That was a challenge if ever she heard one.

On the one hand, she was impressed with his confidence; on the other hand, she was surprised that he had so underestimated her.

"I haven't, you know," he said in a low voice.

She arched a brow. "Haven't what?"

"Underestimated you."

That was the second time. "How did you know what I was thinking?"

"I don't know what you're thinking. . . . I just felt to say it."

She wondered. "Why are you out here with me?"

"Perhaps I'm simply curious."

She laughed at her own expense. "I can't tell you how wonderful that makes me feel."

"No . . . no . . . I did not mean it like that. . . . It's just . . . I don't know."

But she did. She was too experienced not to. The ever-aloof Jorlan Reynard had finally found himself attracted to someone and he wasn't quite sure what to do about it.

Again, she did.

She sat next to him on the bench.

"Why do want to live your life alone?" She faced him and reached up to smooth back his hair. It felt incredibly silky and supple. Even more luxurious than she had imagined. He flinched slightly at the touch of her fingers.

"Why do you?" he rejoined softly.

Her lips twitched. Yes, he was a handful. Smart, angry, with a wildness just barely under control. Green really liked him. He was a rare combination. He might even be a true treasure.

Right then and there, she knew she was going to regret this evening.

Regret having her taste of Jorlan Reynard.

Regret leaving him to the whims of society.

Despite his wishes, she knew that the Duchene would eventually accept a bed price for him. A man of his beauty, wealth, and family position would be fastened. It was the way of the world and a man's lot in life.

Actually, she was amazed he was still on the link circuit. He was a great asset to the Reynard family, in a sense, he was their greatest asset. The alliance he would make would seal their fortune and well-being for generations.

And guarantee the continuation of the Duchene's line—in blood, if not in name.

"What do you seek in life, Jorlan Reynard?" She moved closer to him, letting her lips come very close to his ear. His dark hair shifted slightly with the cool breeze of night and the sultry whisper of her breath. His eyes, those incredible eyes, changed focus to gaze down at her.

Under the planetlight of Arkeus, the unique aqua color—so like the waters of Forus—shone with hidden lights and depth. Hidden intelligence. Hidden wildness.

He exhaled lightly. "I seek the monastery of my spirit, Marquelle."

"What is that?" Her mouth now barely brushed his ear, a light touch of velvet skin against lips, that somehow muddled her. Blood pulsed through her entire body, rebounding to her limbs.

Surprised, she paused a moment. Was she having some kind of abnormal reaction to the hameeri liquor she had drunk earlier?

She glanced up at Jorlan. No, not the hameeri. Whatever it was, he felt it, too. His eyes had closed and his nostrils flared as he inhaled deeply. It was almost as if he were inhaling the experience itself. Bringing it deep inside himself to savor and treasure. . . .

Surely she was misreading this!

Could he possibly be a Sensitive? The thought slammed her. It might explain both their reactions. Her heart sped with the idea. If it was so, why was his family hiding it? Sensitives were worth a fortune in the negotiation stage of a fastening contract.

No sooner had the thought occurred, then the answer came. Jorlan did not willingly seek a name-giver. To appease him, temporarily, the doting Duchene might have agreed to keep his special nature hidden.

It was discovered centuries ago, that certain Forus males were born Sensitives. It was not known what caused it, but it was believed that it had to do with the waning and waxing of Forus on Arkeus and how it acted on those with higher-than-normal sensory abilities. Sensitives were naturally extremely intelligent and extremely passionate. They all seemed unnaturally affected by the rhythms of Forus.

So far, that was the only connection their researchers could come up with. Sensitives heard more, saw more, and felt more. Sometimes, in rare cases, they could convey a small sense of their experience to their partner. They were said to be exquisite lovers. In fact, those not of the noble houses usually became pleasurers. Sensitives in general were extremely rare; Sensitives from royal houses were almost unheard of.

She looked at him, stunned. She was not convinced he was not a Santorini. What if he was *both*? If it was true, he would be the only one known. . . .

She reined in her thoughts. While a Sensitive's disposition seemed to favor the selection of Santorinis, the combination had never been viable. There had been only two male babes ever born with both characteristics and neither of them had survived his weaning stage. It was believed they could not withstand the sensory overload. Her imagination was running away with her.

But she would wager he was a Sensitive.

Of course, no one would have discovered his secret till now—she was positive she was the first woman to touch him with a lover's caress.

"Marquelle, you should know that I seek a destiny wherein I can know the full measure of my strength—not simply feel it resonate within me, but decide upon its fate. This is what dwells inside me and will not be silent."

She clasped his strong chin with her hand, turning him to face her more directly. "It is not considered becoming for a man to speak of such strong control. It is expected of a man that he will always defer to his mother or name-giver to decide what is right for him. Men must be cared for, for their own protection. It is not considered healthy for a man to have too many opinions."

"Do you believe that, Marquelle?" His low voice became husky as he bent toward her.

"What I believe is of no importance." Her lips covered his.

A small, rolling sound of pleasure escaped him. It reminded her of the growl of a fierce lexa beast when it resented the tameness that befell it when offered a balum fruit. The lexa could not resist the tempting fruit that grew high on branches, so far out of its reach. So, too, Jorlan Reynard seemed to resent yet revel in his reaction to the press of her mouth.

Once again, the odd shivering sensation assailed her.

It was him, she realized. The texture of him. And more.

The kiss was a powerful catalyst between them.

He sighed hotly into her mouth. Green felt the awakening twitches skipping through his trained body. Despite his unorthodox persona, Jorlan had a reputation as a man of the strictest control. Yet with her he was battling himself.

She smiled slightly against the firm masculine lips, thoroughly enjoying his taste, and that she was the one unnerving him.

Did he even realize how precarious a situation he was in? With a few expert moves, she could break through every defense he thought he had.

But she would not do that. She would not go that far.

Not just because of what he was—but because of *who* he was. Green discovered that she liked the Duchene's grandson. Very, very much.

"Open your lips more for me, Jorlan," she instructed against his mouth.

With a low moan, he did what she asked. Her tongue slipped sweetly into his mouth, dipping in to sample his nectar. The breath of his desire scorched into her throat, traveling deep inside her, filling her. She closed her eyes to further experience the sensation. To treasure this first, incredible tang of him.

His hands came up, lifting her hair. His fingers sank into the long strands, sliding into the abundant mass until his hands came together cupping the back of her head. Surprised at his uninhibited action, for men were generally compliant in these matters, especially untried men, she opened her eyes to observe him.

Deep in concentration of the sensations he was experiencing, Jorlan's eyes were closed. Long, spiky lashes made crescents on his cheekbones, shielding them in a way. *A beautiful mysterious shadow,* Green thought, *just like the man himself.*

She slid her tongue over his. A ragged growl vibrated against her. He was completely submerged in the experience.

In the pleasure.

He was a Sensitive!

Green blinked at the astounding discovery. She glanced up at him only to discover that his eyes were now open and glittering down at her. A sizzling heat emanated from him.

"What?" he murmured low against her mouth, silken lips playing with the corner of her lips.

Does he know? Jorlan might have no idea that he is different from most other men. She looked at the beautiful man before her, saw his fire and intelligence, and knew he was not simply different—he was unique.

The Top Slice might not know that he was a Sensitive, but his other stellar attributes were readily observable—which explained the never-ending round of offers for him.

What a pity she did not want a name-bearer. She sighed. With Claudine D'anbere causing her no end of trouble and several key issues coming before the Septibunal, she could not even consider such a thing.

Regretfully, she released him.

He gave her a quizzical look that was slightly wounded. For all of his mature disposition, he had not yet begun to master the art of concealing his raw emotions. In the jaded society they lived in, Green thought the trait a particularly charming one.

Somehow, she thought it a part of Jorlan. He would never shroud his true emotions. The ones that burned deeply inside him. The bold trait might cause him trouble in the future.

He would need an exceptionally strong name-giver.

Someone who could protect him from the vicious judgments of the Slice while at the same time allow him to experience the high emotions he needed to channel.

Her shoulders dropped slightly. There were very few women in the Select Quarter who would allow him that kind of freedom.

"Do you never want to experience love, Jorlan?"

His hand came up and stroked the side of her face. The aqua eyes softened to a shade she had never seen before on a human. But she had seen it echoed in the early mornings of Forus as the mist rose off the waters. It took her breath away.

"Do you offer me love, Green?" he asked in the smoothest of tones.

It took Green an instant to realize that his heady senses were getting out of hand. He was igniting them both and he was also deliberately playing with the flame. For his sake, she needed to douse his fire.

She observed him coolly through lowered lids. "What if I was?"

His lips teased at her mouth, sipping at her bottom lip with an innate talent. "I do not wish to be a name-bearer. I have told you this."

"Who said anything about being a name-bearer?" she whispered back.

She knew the exact instant the insinuating remark registered on his passion-drugged brain. Her offer was highly insulting to a man of noble birth. She might as well have slapped him.

At his stunned look, she rose from the bench and returned to the salon.

And yet her thoughts remained back with him.

Green was shocked to discover that she *did* want him.

Really wanted him.

No other woman would be able to handle and release him at the same time. Jorlan Reynard would be the perfect father for her heir.

But right now she did not need a troublesome veil to contend with, no matter how alluring his qualities. She needed to focus on her house—not her bed. Besides, she still had her pleasurer, River, who more than took care of all of her needs.

Yet the simple sweet embrace of Jorlan affected her more than anything she had ever experienced with River.

She decided to leave the soiree, and, regretfully, the compelling Jorlan.

Somehow on the ride home in the Kloo-driven coach, she could not get him out of her mind. The idea of making Jorlan her name-bearer settled firmly in her mind and would not leave.

With the swift decisiveness she was known for in the House of She-Lords, she instantly changed her mind and decided she would make an offer for him.

In time.

He would be the one she fastened.

After all of these years of being a woman-about-town, she would finally take a name-bearer. The Slice would be gleefully shocked with the delicious bus-bit. The kloobroth would spread quickly.

Who would have thought that, with all of the young men vying for her attention and the myriad of invitations from fathers beseeching her to call, she would choose a most reluctant veil, who in all probability was going to object vehemently to the idea?

It was not going to be an easy task.

Still, Jorlan could not hide his reaction to her. The man wanted her.

She would begin by slowly encouraging him without him even realizing it. The veil was keen to experiment—she would give him what he wanted.

Just not in the way he expected.

In time, he would eventually come to her on his own.

His passion was the key.

In surrendering to it, he would surrender to himself.

She hoped.

The Reynard estate was vast.

It bespoke of countless generations of Duchenes, rich in heritage and wealth. Jorlan's ancestresses went back to an Origin officer, of course.

And not just any officer.

Captain Cybella Reynard was considered to have been the Founder of their civilization. How ironic that her progenitor son eschewed the very foundation she had set in motion.

Although most of the prehistory of Originpoint was lost, or kept sealed in dusty vid-tomes, it was known that no living males had accompanied the all-female crew on the *NEOFEM*'s maiden (and only) voyage across the dark reaches of space so long ago.

The innate aggressiveness of the male and his tendency to revert to basic action was not deemed conducive to a long, dangerous trip across space.

Presumably, the female crew had not taken name-bearers, for no name-bearers were allowed on board. Green had often wondered about that condition, thinking it odd—but as it was over a millennium ago, who could say what had really occurred? Perhaps they reasoned that the journey would be less disruptive to the women aboard without males being present.

In all likelihood, the robust female crew might very well have been distracted by them. Who knows how many fights would have broken out over bidding rights?

What was known was that soon after Landing Day—when a secured encampment had been set up and the settlers realized just how welcoming Forus was going to be—they were able to impregnate themselves with sample specimens they had brought with them. Some women were even surrogates for introducing entirely new genetic material into the society gene pool.

The one-sided way proved very successful.

Almost too successful.

Male children began to be culled for the seed they carried and only the best specimens had any real worth. The House of She-Lords had wisely stepped in to outlaw the barbaric practices, stating that they were returning to the methods of Originpoint. The self-impregnation technique had been meant for short-term use for transport of civilization, and not for long-term implementation.

Technical impregnations were outlawed completely and without debate in 318 AL by the Septibunal, who feared that the sole use of the technique would ultimately endanger their society.

So they reverted back to old way.

Since that time, over seven hundred Forus years ago, males were highly contested for, generally cosseted, and usually well taken care of by their name-givers. Some were even loved.

Green approved.

She had never liked hearing about the beginning years; it had always made her uncomfortable.

She also knew that the Septibunal had been very careful with the level of technology in their lives. And yet women benefited greatly from many advancements, the natal accelerator being foremost in her mind.

Maintaining the health of Forus, the moon that sustained them, was a first priority. Natural means were always chosen over manufactured ones. Transportation, for instance, was strictly governed.

The beautiful native Kloo, who were perfectly adapted for transport, were widely used.

The enigmatical animals seemed to form an immediate alliance with the humans, almost craving their proximity. No other specie on Forus except the Klee had formed a similar alliance. Oh, there were numerous other tamed beasts, but the Kloo loved womankind. Sometimes Kloos even sacrificed themselves to save a beloved owner, although they often tried to pretend like they did not care a whit about whatever one was doing. Only it was too easy to see through the lovable grumps. They were terminally nosy.

Green patted her own sweet mount, Kibbee, who prawked appreciatively at her gesture. The flesh vents between her collarbone and chest trilled. Kibbee's flesh vents bypassed the primary intake chambers of her nose and mouth, allowing oxygen to feed directly into her oversized lung sets. A secondary muscle group diverted the excess air to two chamber ducts under her ribs, which expanded at varying rates, depending on her activity. Another set of flesh vents between her hips and under her ribs acted as outtake. This natural adaptation allowed oxygen to pump at a very quick rate through her. Since the Kloo loved to roam the high plains where arc storms were sudden and severe, their survival often depended on their quickness. During a run, both the

Kloo and their sister species, the Klee, displayed remarkable endurance and speed, respectively.

Kibbee had been purchased especially for her loving disposition.

While there were other Kloo that had greater endurance than Kibbee, Green knew that Kibbee would be a faithful mount and a sweet companion on her long trips to oversee the vast Tamryn holdings. Kibbee would never run off and abandon her to the elements, as some of the more high-tempered Klee were prone to do.

Besides, Green thought Kibbee was exceptionally pretty with her pastel-hued plumage that varied according to her mood.

Green rode up to the front portico of the estate and dismounted, handing Kibbee's reins to a door servant who had come out to greet her.

Another servant, Billings, the Duchene's majordoma, met her at the door. "Marquelle Tamryn, good to see you again!" The majordoma greeted her warmly. Green was well liked throughout the Slice.

"Billings." She nodded to the servant woman. "Is the Duchene receiving?"

"I'm sure she'll receive you, Marquelle; come into the morning room and I'll have some refreshment brought to you. The Duchene will be down shortly."

Green followed Billings into the brightly lit morning room. Several ponderous pieces of furniture of a style popular during the six hundreds graced the room. Green preferred a lighter decorating touch, even though she admired the lines and workmanship of the heavy antique pieces known as Arkeus Seize.

One of the drawbacks of being heir to a title was the furniture that came with the position.

Green smiled to herself as she recalled her own attics, bursting with the decor of past ancestors. Unlike other people, who simply divested themselves of unwanted bequests, the aristocracy were bound to keep the moldy things in the name of heritage. Case in point: Her great-great-grandmother had the most hideous sense of color combination, but deep in the recesses of her attic the evidence stayed, gathering dust for future generations of Tamryns to deal with. She was sure there were belongings hidden within the warren of passages that could be traced all the way back to her ancestress from the *NEO-FEM*, who had been first officer and a close friend of Captain Cybella Reynard.

Future generations of Tamryns . . . The thought made Green smile.

It was the reason she was here today.

If all went as she hoped, that future generation would have already made an appearance by this time next year. She touched her flat stomach as a tingle went through her at the prospect.

"Marquelle Tamryn, this is a surprise." Jorlan's deep voice held genuine pleasure at finding her there. Apparently, he had decided that her last comment to him had been in jest.

Foolish lad.

He entered the morning room looking—if possible—even more handsome in the clear light of day. Dressed in black breeches and a loose black overtunic with black boots, he was the picture of indolent grace. There was the same smooth flow to his movements that she had noticed last evening.

His body language spoke of the deliberate, steady nature of one who had the patience to observe. It was the glittering aqua eyes that revealed the banked fire in him.

"Yes, I decided to come visit you, Jorlan."

His brow furrowed for a second as if he couldn't figure out why she would do such a thing. It occurred to Green that he truly had no idea how desirable he was in his own right. He probably thought his attitude was enough to discourage most.

His response confirmed her suspicion. "I don't understand . . ." He hesitated. "Although, it is nice to see you again."

"I would like to begin visiting you, Jorlan."

As soon as her meaning became clear, his face darkened. "I have told you, Marquelle, that I—"

She had anticipated his reaction and was prepared for it with a little strategy of her own. The corner of Green's mouth lifted in a secret smile. "Do not be foolish, Jorlan. Surely you do not think I have come to offer for you?"

He stopped and looked at her warily. "I don't understand."

"You did indicate that you wished to—how did we put it?—play with danger?" She arched her eyebrow.

He glanced down at the carpet, his black lashes stark against his cheeks. When he looked up, his eyes were narrowed in suspicion. "Are you saying what I think you are saying?"

She wasn't going to let him out of it that easy. "What is that, Jorlan?" She purposely gave him a confused look.

"That you will help me . . . explore areas that I have a curiosity of but do not wish to necessarily . . . delve into. . . ." His cheekbones bronzed slightly. Charmingly.

She viewed him through half-lowered lids. "That is exactly what I am saying."

He chewed his lip as he thought it over. "You will not use this to coerce me in any way?"

She snorted. "Of course not. I am not the type of woman who would coerce a man in such a manner. I have no need to do such a thing."

She was referring to her pleasurer. Jorlan truly flushed now and looked away, a muscle ticking in his cheek.

She came up behind him, placing a hand on his arm. "It is my belief that should someone want me, they must come to me of their own accord."

He glanced down at her small hand on his arm, then slowly raised his sights to her. The expression in his eyes captured her. She fell into their depths. Like twin pools of the purest crystalline water, they opened in some way for her. The magnetic light called to her.

Her heart jumped.

The room spun, and the next thing she knew he was righting her with his arm on her shoulder. "Are you all right, Marquelle?"

"Yes." She rubbed her forehead as the last vestiges of the strange sensation faded. Had she been in the glare of Arkeus too long? The ride here had been particularly pleasant; she couldn't recall any discomfort.

"Perhaps a drink would help?" He gently led her to the settee and poured her a cool glass of fresh limo juice.

"Thank you." Gratefully, she took the glass. "Jorlan, did you feel anything str—"

"Marquelle! How delightful to see you!" Anya Reynard's cheery voice filled the room slightly ahead of her bustling frame. She speedily glided over to Green, her grav assists aiding the elderly woman's progress.

"Anya!" She kissed the older woman's cheeks, genuinely glad to see her. Anya Reynard was a kind woman. Some said too kind, as her wayward grandson constantly seemed to get the better of her. "When did you start using grav assists? The last time I saw you, you seemed to be getting along fine without them."

"It's this old injury—remember that time I fell off my Klee? I never seemed to heal right. The repairer thought it was time I stopped being so stubborn and started using the assists. Jorlan finally talked me into it and I must say I do feel a lot better, even though I hate the way they look. Not very fashionable, are they?" She gestured to the metal devices attached to her ankles. "Fashion dictates that it should never be anything less than . . . than what is fashionable!"

"They look fine. I'm glad he talked you into it, although it must have taken some doing, knowing how stubborn you can be about fashion, Anya."

The Duchene laughed. "What can I say? I must have passed the trait on." She looked pointedly at her grandson's casual day attire. That was another argument that had gone nowhere.

Jorlan grinned unabashedly at her, displaying a captivating dimple.

Green rolled her eyes at the two of them. "It's those mounts the Reynards have always insisted on. I don't understand how you all gallop about the countryside on those things. They seem terribly dangerous." The Reynards raised and bred Klee that were specifically selected for their speed. Klee were sleek, powerful, handsome creatures that were very unpredictable. While they were stealthy and moved with a fluid, sensual grace, many an inexperienced traveler had been left to the mercy of the elements when their "faster" Klee mounts had unexpectedly bolted during an arc storm.

"It is only a matter of knowing how to ride them hard, Marquelle—whenever they wish to be ridden . . . hard," Jorlan drawled.

Green raised her eyebrow at him, deciding to let *that* suggestive comment pass. Outrageous for a veil!

"The lad is right!" Anya rested back into the cushions of her favorite chair. "It takes a certain temperament to handle the beasts. I confess I've never quite mastered it as some of the other Reynards have. Now Jorlan here is brilliant with them. Scares me sometimes, the way he tears about the countryside on them." She opened her holofan with a snap and began to fan herself vigorously. Tiny botanicals danced about the spines in a virtual windstorm. "I realize I shouldn't encourage such wild behavior, but I can't bring myself to stop him. He enjoys himself so."

Green laughed. Then stopped abruptly as a certain dreaded voice filled the chamber.

"I shouldn't allow him such reckless pastimes, if it were up to me. Really, Duchene, you risk your most valuable commodity."

Claudine D'anbere strode into the room like a woman well used to giving orders and having them instantly obeyed. Anya's majordoma rushed in after her, apologizing profusely to the Duchene for not having time to announce the ill-mannered woman. Green grimaced in distaste. Of all people, she did not wish to see Claudine D'anbere!

A muscle ticked in Jorlan's jaw, but he did not respond to the She-Count's abrasive, insulting comment.

Anya waved Billings off with her holofan, frowning at the She-Count. She had never liked Claudine D'anbere. "To what do we owe the *pleasure* of this visit, D'anbere?"

"I thought I would come and see how you and the fil-Duchene are faring," She gestured to a seat. "May I?"

The Duchene nodded curtly. Anya Reynard detested those who dispensed with formalities before liberties were granted. After all, her ancestress was the Captain. It was terribly rude of Claudine to arrive unannounced! The nog-twist.

Green looked over at the woman who had made herself her enemy.

On the surface, Claudine D'anbere was a beautiful woman. Her black hair was worn in an uplifted fashion, in a style generally accepted by the Slice as stylish for day wear. By contrast, Green preferred to wear her waist-length hair loose and flowing; she had never subscribed to the almost slavish devotion the damselles of the Select Quarter had for following the Kloo Balcony set. By the admiring looks the come-outs cast at her, they seemed to approve of her choice.

Claudine D'anbere's eyes were light gray. On anyone else, the color combination would have been captivating, imbuing a sense of warmth.

Not on the She-Count.

Her pale eyes were as cold as the frozen ice slabs on the peaks of the Inez ranges. There was no warmth at all in the glinting stare. In fact, Green had often wondered if a touch of madness sparked in their depths.

Of a certain, there was something dark and cruel within her.

Something unforgiven.

Jorlan seemed to sense the same, for he took a seat on the far side of the room, close to Green. Claudine's hard eyes narrowed for the briefest of moments as she registered the silent rejection in his action.

"And how are you faring today, comely Jorlan?" Claudine sat back in her chair, letting her arm drape down over her crossed legs in a studied pose of fashionable nonchalance. Green thought the affectation utterly absurd.

"I am quite well, thank you, She-Count," he responded in a clipped tone that was barely civil.

Claudine ignored his scorn. "I saw you at the soiree the other evening, but you disappeared before I had a chance to come by and say hello."

Green watched the She-Count carefully, worried now for Jorlan. *Had she seen them leave to go out to the gardens?* He would not want Claudine as an enemy. If Claudine realized that Jorlan had been with her . . . !

But Claudine was focused strictly on Jorlan. It suddenly struck Green that Claudine had assumed Green's presence in the Reynard house was simply in visiting her friend, the Duchene.

Green almost laughed out loud. Claudine rarely made mistakes, especially when it came to Green. Due to Green's renowned penchant for remaining unfastened, Claudine did not even consider her as a rival for the man. It was an irony she welcomed.

She knew exactly how Claudine would react when she found out the truth. Enraged. But she could deal with Claudine. Soon Jorlan would be willingly under her protection—if all went as she planned.

"I left the gathering early." Jorlan informed the She-Count.

Claudine raised a thin eyebrow. "Really. Were you ill?"

"No."

Jorlan's curt answers were nothing short of rude. The Duchene gave him a warning look out of the corner of her eye. As far as she was concerned, there was never an excuse for bad manners.

Claudine avidly watched Jorlan with the expression of a gluttonous jickne right before it dines. "I was rather surprised to see you at the soiree in the first place, Jorlan. We all know your dislike of such social events."

Jorlan's lips thinned. His dislike of the social season was well known. He had gone to the soiree to appease his grandmother, who had insisted he attend. He was so disgusted with the position he was in that he did not even bother to comment on the She-Count's prodding remark.

An awkward silence filled the room.

The Duchene spoke, alleviating the strange tension.

"Was it a good time, She-Count?"

"Not really. Let us say that my interest was quickly lost in the evening." She smiled coldly at Jorlan. "Although I had a better time later on. A group of us went over to the Gardens in the Neon Night part of town. Ended up at Number 99. You know the place, don't you, Tamryn? I could swear I've seen you there."

Green knew the place. It was a dank, seedy pit hole that catered to the exotic tastes of damselles for wagering . . . and other more sordid pursuits. Although Green had been there in the past, she had never availed herself of those dubious pleasures.

She glanced over at Jorlan, who was looking at her with something akin to revulsion. She returned his look with a steady one of her own. Green never explained herself to anyone. The veil could make his own judgments—whatever they were.

"I have been there, yes," she answered truthfully.

Claudine smiled. "Although I've never seen you in the *special* back rooms. I suppose you don't have the gall for that kind of zip."

Jorlan's eyes widened slightly. Claudine had set out to insult her. Little did she know that she had inadvertently elevated her in the fil-Duchene's eyes.

The Duchene fanned herself vigorously, distressed by the outré topic. The holo fan depicted Klee racing wildly across the plains. "What a dreadful place that is! Surely you will catch all kinds of illnesses there, She-Count. I've heard horrendous stories about the men they keep in house. They say they are nothing more than street urchins, some of them there against their will! One wonders what—" The Duchene stopped when she realized her words were not for mixed company. Jorlan should not be hearing this.

"It is nothing of the kind, Duchene. Besides, the sparks are thankful for the touch we give them—and well they should be. If it wasn't for us, they'd starve. 'A touch for some touch,' as they say!" Claudine grinned evilly. "Touch" was a slang term that the Slice coyly favored when referring either to coin or a bit of the velvet veil. They thought the play on words terribly clever.

"How fortunate for them that they have you," Green returned coldly. She detested the conditions in the Gardens.

"It's easy for you to talk such," Claudine sneered. "You with the finest pleasurer on Forus! When are you going to tire of River and give him over to the rest of us?"

"She-Count D'anbere, I will remind you that my grandson is in the room," the Duchene sputtered. "You will cease this talk immediately. It is entirely improper!"

Claudine glanced over at Jorlan; he returned her look with a stony expression. It was obvious that the veil hated her, which aroused her further. Claudine loved to deal with hate. She had a special gift with hate. Just the thought of showing Jorlan her talent with the emotion excited her.

She patted her hair and cleared her throat to steady herself. Now was not the time to let her fantasies run wild. She would have him soon enough. She had already made sure of it. "You are right, of course, Duchene. My apologies to you and your grandson."

The Duchene snapped her holofan shut. She wasn't appeased by the apology, although politeness demanded she accept it.

Billings brought in a refreshment tray and placed it on a table near the She-Count. She left the room with a disdainful sniff aimed in the She-Count's direction.

"How are your lands to the west, Tamryn? I heard you had some trouble there these past months." Claudine availed herself of a sweet from the tray.

"I can't imagine how you could have heard such a thing." *Especially since you were the cause of it.* Green tried to contain her ire over the woman's statement about her pleasurer. *No matter what happens, Claudine, I promise you will never touch River. Never.* Green knew she would never let the vulnerable pleasurer come to harm from such a woman.

Claudine bit into her treat, making a great show of letting it dissolve on her tongue. "Really? That was not the talk among the Slice. The kloobroth has it that you almost went bankrupt trying to save the place.

I would have just let the fool thing go. Why risk everything on some backward plantation?"

"That plantation has been in my family for ages. The workers have been with my family for generations. They depend on me for their livelihood, although I don't expect you to understand that."

Claudine waved her hand. "Silly sentimentality if you ask me."

"I didn't ask you."

Claudine paused in the eating of her treat. "Too bad. I'm sure if you had, you would have avoided months of grief." She popped another piece of the sweet into her mouth.

"I'm sure. But since everything is perfectly fine and running smoothly, the topic is moot, isn't it?"

Claudine bit off the final piece with a snap. Green Tamryn had somehow managed to pull her estates out from the brink of ruin! How the Marquelle had done it was nothing short of a miracle, since Claudine herself had set the strength of the trap. The entire scenario was irritating in the extreme, but there was always next time.

Her purpose in this visit had nothing to do with Marquelle Tamryn, who was undoubtedly here to visit her old friend the Duchene.

"I was wondering if your grandson and I might take a ride together, Duchene. There is a Klee I am interested in purchasing and I thought he might advise me."

Jorlan spoke up for himself before his grandmother could answer. "Surely you do not need the advice of a *man* to make such a purchase, She-Count."

"It is well known that you have a gift with the beasts. Your input might be very useful."

As an invitation it was rather insulting. But Claudine would never see it that way.

"I am sorry to disappoint you, She-Count, but I have made other plans this day."

Claudine bristled, seeing through the pale apology. "Perhaps some other time then," she said icily.

"Perhaps."

"Definitely." Claudine stood, wasting no time in further formalities now that her target was out of range. "I'm afraid I must be on my way, Duchene."

"So soon?" The Duchene could barely keep the glee from her voice.

"Yes, I'm afraid so. I will see you before long, Jorlan."

There was a slight threat laced in the promise that seemed to unnerve the Duchene. Green looked at her curiously.

Claudine curtly nodded once at Green, as politeness demanded, before grandly exiting the room.

"By the Slice! That woman is terribly rude!" Anya frowned at the empty doorway.

Green and Jorlan smiled secretly at each other. As if rudeness were the worst of Claudine's offenses.

"I thought I might take a walk in your lovely gardens this morning, Anya; that is, if you don't mind lending me your delightful grandson as guide?"

Anya Reynard glanced over at the "delightful" grandson, who, she assumed, in all probability was about to bolt from the room. She was somewhat surprised to see him nonchalantly examining his toe, apparently in no hurry to leave or in any objection to the Marquelle's request.

The Duchene met Green's eye. She nodded. "I think that would be an excellent idea." Claudine D'anbere's visit had obviously shaken the older woman. A slight tremor shook her blue-veined hand. Green speculated on whether Anya's distress was due to more than just simple dislike for the brash She-Count.

"Come, Jorlan, show me the wonders you have to offer." Her amber eyes twinkled with double meaning as she held out her hand.

His expression was equally subtle as he took her proffered hand and led her out into the bright sunshine.

The gardens at Reynard House were breathtaking.

The Duchene had always had a fondness for flora and had consistently cultivated rare, exotic plants for the garden. There were even a few extremely rare Origin plants whose stemmings had been carefully grafted on to existing plants on Forus. The resultant plants had been gorgeous hybrids—huge roseyal blooms and fragrant lillacia. They had never been able to figure out why Origin plants wouldn't grow directly in Forus soil. It *seemed* as if they should—but they wouldn't germinate. Only one plant had ever been able to, and that had been something of an accidental discovery.

Green inhaled deeply of the lovely morning scents.

"Mmm. How lovely! You are fortunate to be able to enjoy this beauty, Jorlan. Although my mother would have been furious with me for admitting to this, your grandmother's gardens are the best in Capitol Town." Green's mother and Anya had often engaged in a friendly rivalry as to who had the better garden. Green had nostalgically continued the bi-play.

Jorlan smiled, the edges of his lips curling up in a provocative way. "Your secret will be safe with me." He gazed down at her out of the corner of his eye with a gleam. "That is until we return and I just happen to mention to my grandmother . . ." He left the implication unsaid.

"You wouldn't do such a thing! Not about the gardens!" This had been a long-standing and well-loved feud.

"Mmm-hmm." He nodded to put more emphasis to the unpardonable deed.

Her lips twitched. "You scoundrel! I can't believe you would—"

He laughed, a rich, alluring sound, which showcased gleaming white teeth and curved dimples. He was a *charming* scoundrel.

She shook her finger at him. "I'll owe you for that one, be sure."

He arched his brow. "I'm counting on it, Marquelle." The hoarse tone was pure seduction.

Despite her age and experience, Green blushed. Jorlan Marquelle was an engaging package. Every indication she had was that the man was more than even she had surmised. And she rarely underestimated anyone.

He was certainly more playful than she ever would have guessed.

And, for some reason, a reason she could not name, there was the sense that under it all he could be very, very dangerous. *How could a man be dangerous?* She viewed him askance.

"What?" he mouthed.

"I'm wondering about you."

He stopped and crossed his arms over his chest. "And just what are you wondering?"

"I'm wondering what is going on behind those aqua eyes of yours."

He blinked slowly. Purposefully. "Perhaps nothing."

"I sincerely doubt that."

"Perhaps I am wondering just what it is you think to 'show' me out here."

"I thought you were showing me."

He stared at her expectantly.

"The gardens?"

"So I am. What do you think?" He spread his arms wide, indicating the landscape, but his inquiry was not about plantings.

So she answered in him in kind. "I think it is a beautiful place, rich in detail, and layered with complexity. Vibrant, with subtle tones, and altogether individual in nature."

"You flatter my family," he responded evenly, giving nothing away.

"The Reynards have always been known for their leadership abilities; surely that trait is evident even here in this . . . garden."

"Yes, they have often paved the way where others have followed." He watched her carefully.

"And is that what you wish to plant in your garden?" she asked pointedly. What he was implying was so radical, it would surely ostracize him from decent society, especially if he spoke of it to others.

He watched her steadily. "Yes."

She sucked in her breath. "And how do you hope to accomplish such a thing? Surely such seeds would not grow in this soil and might in fact end up poisoning your entire house."

"One never knows what can take root when the proper conditions are met."

"Have a care, Jorlan." She put all pretense aside. "It is one thing to entertain outlandish notions, quite another to attempt to act upon them."

" 'Outlandish'?" His nostrils flared.

"You would disgrace the Duchene for a youthful whim?"

"This is no youthful whim. But you needn't concern yourself, Marquelle. I assure you, I would never hurt my grandmother."

She breathed a little easier at that statement. For a minute, she wasn't sure if he did not have some foolish escapade in mind. "I suppose not; you do realize that you are more apt to cause wagging tongues by our walk last night than by anything else?"

He shrugged. "I do not think I am that interesting a topic to the Slice."

"Then you underestimate your charm."

"Charm?" His lips curled in a sneer of disgust. "Is that what you call it?"

"Among other things." She let her gaze travel the length of him. It was ironic that one so blessed with natural attributes should be so opposed to the appreciation of them by the ladies of the Select Quarter.

Unlike other come-outs, Jorlan did not get flustered or nervous at her blatant regard. Instead he met her perusal with a steady regard of his own that made *her* slightly uncomfortable. With his looks, she supposed he was used to women trying to chase a "bit o' the velvet."

What was it about this young man that gave him the maturity and the *knowing* not usually found in men twice his age, if ever?

A disturbing thought occurred to her. Surely he had not . . . ?

No, she had tasted him herself, experienced firsthand his initial trembling, his slightly hesitant touch. Whatever made Jorlan different was inherent in *him* and had nothing to do with any outside influence or experience.

They walked by a mesh-pond. Tiny crisscrossed fibers covered the liquid underlayer of the plant, forming a red ripple fading out to pink on the edges. The mesh-pond was in bloom; several tiny pink-and-white buds dotted its surface. It was a charming sight.

As they strolled by, the mesh-pond croaked slightly, begging Jorlan for a tidbit. He leaned over to snap off a cilia twig from a nearby bush, tossing it into the fibers as they passed.

Gurgling happily, the mesh-pond absorbed the treat.

Green smiled to herself. Despite his insolent stance, there was a hidden kindness in his heart. Again, she remembered the incident with Claudine's Klee when he was a boy.

"What are you thinking?" he murmured.

"I was remembering something from a long time ago. . . ."

"About your family?" He smoothed away a strand of auburn hair that had flown into her eye.

"It's not important." She looked up at him. He was shadowed; beautifully shadowed. "Kiss me," she breathed. "Right now."

He paused only a second, then simply reacted. He bent forward, brushing warm, smooth lips over hers. It was an incredibly tender kiss. At once sensual and sweet.

Standing on tiptoe, Green's hand reached up to cup the back of his head. Even though he was bending, he was still towering over her.

Green's hand clasped his shoulder and upper arm, noting the muscular strength concealed by his black sleek-cut layer coat. Her fingers sank recklessly into the depths of the silky black hair. Its texture was finer than any she had ever touched. Softer. More luxurious. The strands slid between her fingers, twining about her hand. *Have I ever felt such hair?* She marveled at the sensation of it. There was something incredible about touching Jorlan, the feel of him unlike anything—

Again, she felt him tremble.

Jorlan tried to stiffen himself against the sensual assault but could not. Against his will, he felt himself give over to the awareness. Felt his body come alive as the tremors shivered down his length and throughout his body.

Green felt his initial resistance followed by the reaction he could not contain. Somehow, the fact that he had lost a bit of his rigid control in the essence of the moment pleased her.

She was going to love awakening this man.

Teaching him of the passion within himself. Watching it rise slowly until it overtook him. And her.

A picture of him sprawled across her sheets came into her mind. His golden skin warmed by flamelight, flushed with a slight sheen of moisture, dry and hot to the touch as he waited for her to come to him. For her to ignite him. His eyes were illuminated with his heat.

Jorlan jolted suddenly, breaking off the pure kiss to stare into her eyes. Shielded, his expression became inscrutable.

"Wh-what is it?" She tried to control the pace of her breaths, which had sped up with the press of his mouth and her unaccountable thoughts. It was a mystery to her how this untried veil had managed to get to her like this.

A muscle ticked in his jaw. "Nothing, Marquelle." He pulled back from her abruptly.

She regained her composure with his distance. "Do you not like the taste of me?"

"I like the taste of you just fine."

"Then what is it?"

"As I said, nothing." He snapped a boomerang leaf from the branches of an overhanging Dreamtree, setting it in flight. The small V-shaped leaf spun back and forth through the air, riding the currents as it gently cascaded to the ground.

Had he somehow picked up a glimmer of her impetuous fantasy? She glanced up at him through the fringe of her lashes. *It was possible.* Who knew what he was capable of? The boy had been a mystery; the man was an enigma. And yet, he had spoken the truth. He could not hide his reaction to her. The slight warm flush of his golden skin, the husky tone of his voice told their own tale.

"How long have you known that you are a Sensitive?"

His shoulders stiffened. He looked back at her. "What do you mean?"

"There is no sense trying to hide it, Jorlan. You might have gotten away with it with another woman, had you chosen someone else to experiment with. I, however, know better. I am too experienced not to. You knew that as well, which makes me wonder why you chose me to explore with."

He looked up at the tallest branches of the Dreamtree where a Ramagi was spinning its matrix. "Yes, I know of your experience. And you're right, I am curious where perhaps I shouldn't be. I have never had such a curiosity with anyone before—" He stopped, unwilling to say more.

Green watched him carefully. *What was he weaving?* He wanted her. Only her.

It was not simple experimentation. Not with this man.

She stored this incident away for later contemplation. "And what of being a Sensitive?"

His brow furrowed. "I do not know what you are saying."

"You . . ." She hesitated. Perhaps he did not know. Perhaps he had no idea that he was very different from most men. That he experienced the senses on a completely different level. Being brought up in a proper way in a proper household, he would not have been exposed to the term "Sensitive."

"Why did you break away, Jorlan?" she said carefully.

He rubbed the back of his neck as if he were releasing a building tension. "I'd rather not delve into it, Marquelle, if you do not mind."

"I do mind." She approached him once again, placing a hand on his forearm. "Tell me what it was. And my name is Green."

"Very well . . . Green. I cannot put a name to it. I had this—this vision, you might say. . . ." He glanced up at the bank of clouds on the horizon. "It sounds strange, I know."

"No, no it doesn't. What did you see?"

He looked her way; a muscle beat in his jaw, and then he stared at the clouds again.

"Yes?"

"It was a rather erotic image."

"Go on." She was sure now what he was going to say, what he had seen. The same thing she had. Him, in her bed. . . .

"I saw you lying across my bed. Your skin was lit by flamelight, your hair was spread across the pillows. It caught flames of light. Your eyes were closed as if you were dreaming or thinking of something or someone.... Something caught your attention and you rose up on your elbow and looked my—" He stopped, as if sensing some danger.

She watched him speculatively. His description of his vision was not just like hers—it was an exact *reflection* of hers. *What does it mean?*

His words interrupted her thoughts. "It appears as if a storm is coming." His aqua eyes scanned the horizon.

He glanced down at her. "Shall I tell Billings to have a room prepared for you for the evening? I would not want you to be caught in an arc storm on your journey home."

"Thank you, Jorlan, but I shall be fine. There are plenty of places to take shelter on the way."

"There are no places to take shelter between here and your estate. It is all open land."

"It doesn't look like an arc storm to me. In any case, I never said I was going directly home." At his angry, resentful look, she turned and headed to the coops to retrieve her mount.

It was only the slight hurt in his eyes that made her add, "I have a business appointment in Town. Unfortunately. I expect I'll be tied up late into the night going over dreary account ledgers."

"I'm sure you'll be up very late doing *that*, Marquelle," he replied cynically.

A small smile graced her mouth. Jealousy was an excellent mood for a brash, independent male who wanted no name-giver. Perhaps she should point that out to him?

"Your untoward *concern* is touching, Jorlan, but you may sleep easy tonight knowing that I am in the arms of my ledgers and nothing else."

His azure eyes narrowed dangerously. "What makes you think I care, Marquelle?"

"I had a vision." Her soft laughter trailed after her as she left.

Come-outs were not the only ones who could be mischief-makers. With the right incentive, a seasoned Marquelle could easily develop a yen for it.

Her progress to the coops was reflected in his pale eyes.

Whatever lay beneath their contained, hidden depths remained a mystery.

Chapter Four

lthough the arc storm never came that night, it did arrive several nights later.

Green's business in Capitol Town had taken longer than she had estimated. Since she had been tied up on her western properties these past months, the accounts were behind and had to be brought up-to-date. Instead of one night of dreary ledgers, she had dealt with four nights of tedious accounts.

The one bright spot was that she and her solicitor had finally put the books to right.

The strange part was that she had been in town all that time and had not once gone to see River. In fact, she had not been with the lusty pleasurer for several months. Since she had met Jorlan, she did not seem to have the desire to visit him. Her brow furrowed.

The rain began to pelt her and Kibbee as the Kloo plodded its way through the muddy roads of the country. She was headed back to her estate, not wanting to spend another night in town. Her thoughts wan-

dered to Jorlan as she tried to get her mind off of the cold drenching she
was getting.

Tomorrow, she would see him again; maybe offer to show him her
estate. His eyes were really the most unusual color. . . .

A rumble sounded above and Kibbee shied on the path.

Green tightened her hold on the reins and patted her mount's side.
"There, girl. Guess we didn't see that arc-er coming, did we? If you can
put some wind to it, I believe there is a tavern not too far down the
road. We can take shelter there. They have a nice warm Kloo coop."

At the magic words "warm" and "coop," Kibbee expanded her vents
and with an inhaled gust of intake significantly increased her speed.

Green smiled, shaking her head. There was nothing Kibbee liked
more than a warm bed of soft tilla leaves. Coops usually provided nice
tilla beds for the Slice's Kloos and Klees.

Green galloped into the courtyard a short time later just as a second
arc flashed across the sky. She was already sodden to the skin. It
wouldn't be long before the storm was directly overhead and the only
safe place to be when that happened was inside shelter.

Arcs were attracted to ore-rocks. If one could stay clear of the ore-
rocks, one would be fine. Unfortunately, the black stones littered the
natural landscape. When building a structure of any kind, the first thing
one did on Forus was clear the area of ore-rock. It had not taken the
original settlers long to figure that out, although many lives have been
lost to the vicious storms.

A coop-keeper ran out to meet her, taking Kibbee's reins and leading
her off to her tilla bed.

Green pulled open the door to the tavern, gratefully stepping into
the dry interior. The inside was dark and musty. Not even the large
flamepit that roared at the back of the room could dispel the gloom.

A few patrons sat sipping brew and passing secrets. Her saturated cape dripped across the floor as she made her way to a rear table in the far corner.

A barboy immediately came over to place a warmed brew in front of her.

"Thought you'd be wanting this right off." He winked at her, taking the opportunity to flirt. He had an adorable expression that softened some of his coarse edges, but Green knew that in another five years that adorable quality would be entirely destroyed by the life that had been chosen for him.

She glanced over at the bar and noticed an older man cleaning the counter. He bore a strong likeness to the barboy. A heavyset woman, presumably the older man's name-giver, came from the direction of the kitchens. She snapped at him to go help the cook. Wearily, he trudged back there.

"That's perfect, thank you." Green smiled warmly at the barboy, feeling unaccountably sorry for him.

He was smitten; his eyes almost popped out of his head. Green was an uncommonly pretty woman. "If you need anything, just ask!" He grinned sweetly at her and trotted off to join his father in the kitchens.

Green was about to throw the cowl of her hood back when the front doors burst open and four sterling examples of new-breeds reeled drunkenly into the room, immediately demanding to be served. They were all thoroughly intoxicated.

Green did not recognize two of them, but she did know Claudine D'anbere and Angela Farthenwright. Angela was Claudine's little pet. The lower She-Baron followed Claudine about, trying her best to imitate the She-Count's debauched ways. This was a perfect example of like attracting like, Green rued.

She quickly pulled her cloak closer about her face, hiding herself in its voluminous depths. She had no desire to talk to that reeling group. They were sure to cause trouble. Thankfully, the dark corner hid her from view. They didn't even notice she was there.

The barboy rushed out with a tray of warm drinks, squeaking when Claudine pinched him roughly on his thigh. "He's a comely one, eh, Farthenwright?"

"If you don't mind the stench of brew on him." Angela belched loudly.

The barboy tried to extricate himself quickly from the group but they all got a good feel before he was able to. Green shook her head and went back to her drink, trying to shut out their obnoxious ruckus.

And she was able to do just that—until she overheard a certain name.

"To Jorlan Reynard!" Claudine raised her tankard high in the air to make a toast.

Green covertly glanced up. *Why was Claudine toasting the Duchene's grandson?*

Angela asked the very same question. "D'anbere, why should we drink to that high-held veil? He's not about to give anyone a taste."

"Ah, there's where your wrong, my lovely. By this time tomorrow, Jorlan Reynard will be offering it to me on a solid platter."

Green snorted at the ridiculous statement. The brew had gone to Claudine's head! The woman was obviously hocked.

"Rut-bid," Angela scoffed, guzzling her brew, again reflecting Green's viewpoint.

"I have to agree with Farthenwright on that. No one has been able to get near that rare prize!" the Lordene on her right stated. "What makes you think you bagged the brilliant lad?"

"Very simple," she gloated. "I have spoken to the Duchene. Let us just say that I have pled my suit most admirably to her. She will sign the fasten contract tomorrow morning." She clinked her glass with Angela's.

"You sly glove," Angela smirked. "Whatever do you have on the old girl, hmm?"

Claudine snickered. "Just enough, it seems."

They all laughed raucously and started a long round of toasting and drinking. The woman who owned the tavern pushed the barboy toward them, chastening him to make sure their tankards were kept filled. Presumably, he was to fill whatever else the Tops wanted as well.

Hidden in her corner, Green was horrified. *Could it be true?* Was the Duchene going to give Jorlan to Claudine? It had to be true; Claudine would not be bragging to her friends like this. *What would make Anya do such a thing?* The Duchene was not fond of the She-Count. Green could not imagine the elderly woman giving her beloved grandson to *that . . . ! D'anbere must have coerced her!*

Green closed her eyes, feeling a pain clutch at her heart just at the idea of such a unique, gifted man under the controlling hands of that woman. Why, her last three name-bearers had died! *Inexplicably.* She swallowed and broke into a cold sweat.

She couldn't let this happen! Not to Jorlan.

She thought of the way his eyes wrinkled at the corners when he laughed, how intense he became when he had his first taste of her lips. She remembered the soft sound he made at the back of his throat when she ran her fingers in his hair.

Could she let that beauty be destroyed? *No.*

She would not let this happen!

Pivoting about on her bench, she noticed a small doorway behind her to her left.

As soon as she could get the barboy's attention, she signaled him discreetly. He rushed over to her, glad to be away from Claudine's set. "What is it, my Lordene? Another tankard?"

"No." She kept her voice low. "Does that doorway behind me lead outside?"

"Yes, but surely you do not wish to leave? The storm is raging and will probably go on for most of the night. There are a few rooms here. . . ." He paused. "Upstairs." His offer was plain.

"That is quite all right. I must go, but I don't wish to be noticed leaving—do you understand?" She reached into her waist pouch and extracted a plat-coin, flipping it over to him.

The barboy swallowed, obviously never having seen one before. "I will get you some change, my Lordene."

"That won't be necessary. Just make sure that their attention is focused on you for the time that it takes me to leave. They are so hocked, they won't even realize it. Can you do it?"

The barboy grinned as he pocketed the plat-coin. "I can do it."

Green nodded. "Good. And a bit of advice: Do not go with them later or you will sorely regret it. They are not the kind that will leave you smiling in the morning and they might not even pay you for the torture."

The barboy paled. "Thank you for telling me, my Lordene. I think I will get lost in the coop tonight after you leave."

She nodded to him.

The barboy did not waste any time in doing as she had asked. Soon, all their attention was focused on him as he outrageously flirted while serving them brew. Green slipped out the back door and dashed across the yard, the darkness of night and the rain aiding her. Her luck held when no arc traversed the night to illuminate her path.

She quickly entered the coop, finding Kibbee right away by the Kloo's delighted snores of happiness.

To say that Kibbee squawked at being awakened to go out into the storm was an understatement. It took all of Green's persuasive powers to convince the recalcitrant Kloo to let her saddle her.

Mission accomplished, they galloped out into the arc-laden night, heading for her estate. She needed to retrieve the lineage scrolls kept locked in her study before she rode over to the Reynard estate.

An arc zigzagged through the sky, connecting with an ore-rock on the other side of the road. The hum of unstable current vibrated along her skin. It was close. Kibbee glared at her over her shoulder, curling the edge of one thick lip in sheer disgust at the foolhardy venture. Green firmly told her to keep going.

The Kloo obeyed, but only after she had spit a huge wad of saliva into the wind as commentary.

Green wrinkled her nose. It was going to be a long, dangerous ride.

Even if she survived the storm, she was still going to have to convince the Duchene to go along with her plans.

Knowing Claudine's threats, it was going to take all of Green's persuasive abilities. On top of that, Claudine had hinted that the Duchene had already given her consent. Anya never retracted her word. Never.

Green steeled herself for the confrontation she knew she must win.

And she would win.

She was not known in the House of She-Lords as a brilliant orator for nothing.

*G*reen pounded on the door of the Reynard estate.

It was well past the middle of the night.

Miraculously, she had made it through the arc storm. How, she had no idea. Three times she had almost been fried to a crisp. The edge of her cape was singed in two places and still smoking slightly. Poor

Kibbee's plumage had stood straight up in the electrified air. They would probably both reek of smoke for a week. But the faithful, steady Kloo had not bolted. She had stayed by her. They were rightly called woman's best friend, and Green had already made sure she was well taken care of for her valiant efforts.

A sleepy Billings cautiously opened the door until she recognized the bedraggled Marquelle on the stoop. "Marquelle Tamryn! What has happened to you? Did you get caught in the arc storm? Oh, dear me! Come in! Come in!" She all but dragged Green into the foyer.

"Go and awaken the Duchene at once. I must see her!"

Billings's jaw dropped. "But—but I cannot awaken the Duchene at this hour! She will have my head!"

"Tell her Marquelle Tamryn is here and that it is of the utmost urgency. I will await her in her study—go!" Green was already striding off to the study down the corridor.

As she waited for the Duchene, she poured herself a tumbler of hameeri liquor, both as a fortifier and a warmer. She was almost at the point of exhaustion. She had been tired at the start of her journey from town, but after riding through the storm for hours, constantly staying alert for the arcs, she was near collapse.

Thankfully, she had been able to get what she needed from her study without awakening her household. It had not been easy to go back out into the stormy night again to ride here. Now she needed to draw in her real strength—to convince the Duchene she must take back her promise.

The large doors opened and a pale Anya Reynard entered. She closed the doors softly behind her. By her haggard look, Green was not sure the older woman had been sleeping at all. And she knew why. This entanglement with Claudine must be killing her. Anya loved Jorlan dearly; she would never want him to be so despoiled.

"Green, wh-what are you doing here? Is there an emergency called by the Septibunal? My goodness, look at you! *Did you ride through an arc storm to get here?* Please, sit down immediately! You look near to collapse, my dear girl." Always considerate, she drew Green to a chair in front of her desk.

Anya took the seat behind the desk. "Is it the tribes to the south? I warned them about—"

"No, Anya, OneNation is fine. The reason I've come is of a more personal nature."

Anya poured herself a glass of water from the carafe on her desk. Green noticed that her hand shook slightly and she seemed to have aged several years overnight.

" 'Personal nature'? What might that be?"

Green sighed. "I know about Claudine's bid for Jorlan. By the sheerest stroke of fortune I overheard her in a tavern on my way back from Capitol Town."

*U*pstairs in a far bedroom, Jorlan lie sleeping. Suddenly, his aqua eyes opened. Deep in a dream, he stared at his own vision.

"*H*ow could you do this, Anya? You know what she is like!"

Anya Reynard covered her face with her hands. "I cannot tell you why. It is done, Green."

Green took a deep breath. She reached across the table to place her hand on the older woman's arm. "You cannot. You have promised him you would not—not without his consent."

Anya wiped her eyes and stared at Green. "He told you that?"

"Yes."

"I never promised him that, exactly. I told him that I would *try* to allow him his consent. I realize I might have misled him, but Jorlan knows he is the future of this family. I could never promise him that."

"But why Claudine? She's so horrible! You don't even like her."

"True, but I must." Anya looked away sadly.

"She has something on you, doesn't she? I know her too well. What is it? Do you owe her?"

Anya seemed to crumple before her eyes.

"I should have realized." Green was heartsick over this new twist. "Why didn't you come to me?"

"You were away seeing to your own problems; I couldn't burden you further with mine."

"Let me guess: Your distant estates began to have trouble. Funds were being channeled out and mysteriously disappearing? Crops weren't yielding their price?"

"How do you know that?"

Green closed her eyes. "Because it was what I experienced. I barely managed to bring the Tamryn holdings back from the brink of ruin."

"D'anbere offered to lend me the funds to see it through. I foolishly accepted. Now she is calling in the note in full. It is an affair of honor, Green."

"There is no honor with that woman! Don't you see that she was probably the one responsible for your troubles in the first place? She set you up as she did me—only for different reasons. Nonetheless, there are ways to stop her—as I have discovered."

"It matters not. She is coming tomorrow for the signing of the contracts."

"Does she offer a fastening bid?"

"The price she offers is clearing the debt I owe in exchange for my grandson."

"How much do you owe her?"

"Four hundred thousand plat-coins. Green, it is a fortune."

It *was* a fortune. Yet nowhere near what Jorlan might have brought in on open bid. Not only had Claudine created the Duchene's problems, she had neatly found a way to acquire her grandson for a fraction of his true bed price. Green acknowledged it was a fiendishly clever plot, if abhorrent.

She took a deep breath. "I will treble the amount. She will have to accept that amount as payment in full."

Anya gasped. "What are you saying? No one has that kind of money available."

"I can get it."

"It will bankrupt you!"

"Let me worry about that." She reached into her pouch and withdrew a small locked box. Taking a key from her chatelaine, she unlocked her ancestral chest and withdrew a rolled parchment, which bore the names of all of her ancestresses since the *NEOFEM*. By tradition, a mother must place her son's name on the familial scroll of the name-giver, along with her seal.

Once etched there, the contract was irrevocable.

"Give Jorlan to me, Anya."

The Duchene looked at her, stunned. "*You* want him? But—but I thought you were opposed to taking a name-bearer."

"Not anymore. I want him."

A tear fell from Anya's eye. "I am so sorry; I have given my word, Green. I cannot. Had I only known . . ."

Green drew herself up, gathering her courage for the final plea. This would be her only chance to save him. "Anya, Claudine is a cruel, twisted woman in ways you cannot even fathom. Surely you would not want to deliver Jorlan to someone like this?"

Anya began to sob. Green got up and came around the desk to hug her. "I will cherish him. You will never need worry for his welfare. Sign the contract, Anya. For his sake."

"She will never allow it."

"The fastening price I offer will be sufficient to satisfy honor in the Septibunal's eyes. Claudine will not be able to refuse it and she will know it. You will have bested her but made a powerful enemy."

Anya steadied herself, the color coming back to her face. *Clever, wonderful girl!* "So be it, then. If the Tamryn name protects Jorlan, then I am not afraid of anything Claudine D'anbere might try to do to me." She picked up the Tamryn gold pen and scrawled Jorlan's name onto the Tamryn ancestral line with a flourish. Then she took her seal and placed her mark.

Green released her pent-up breath. *Jorlan was safe.*

"There is one thing I ask of you, Anya."

"You may ask anything of me. I will forever owe you a debt of gratitude for saving him; I am aware what has happened to her other name-bearers, though nothing has ever been proven."

"Did Jorlan know about this matter with D'anbere?"

"No. I thought it best to keep it from him for as long as possible."

"Good. Then I ask you not to tell him at all."

"But why? Surely he will be as grateful to you as I am."

"No. He must only know that I have contracted for him because I desire him. He must never doubt that I want him. If he learns of the role Claudine had in this, he will always doubt my reasons. You see, Anya, I had already decided to bid for him before I learned of this."

Anya smiled wanly. "That is the first thing I have heard that has made me happy in two days."

Green returned her smile. "I truly want him, Anya. I meant it when I said I would cherish him."

"You cannot know how grateful I am to hear that. I had always hoped it would be so."

"Really?"

"Yes, since you must know. Perhaps in the long run D'anbere did us a favor."

Green chuckled and shook her head. "Somehow it is hard to think of Claudine and favor in one sentence. You realize Jorlan is going to be furious with us both."

"Perhaps now he will abandon these foolish notions he has about male equality. Honestly, I don't know where he gets these ideas of his— certainly not from my side! Can you imagine *men* standing in the House of She-Lords? The next thing you'd know we'd be at war with everyone!" Anya shook her head, clucking under her tongue.

"I don't know, Anya, perhaps it wouldn't be quite as bad as that." Green winked at her.

"*Hmf!* It's just not natural. Men belong in the home raising the children and that's that! At any rate, I'll leave the soothing of him up to you. I can guarantee you will have your time of it."

"Oh, I have no doubt of that."

"You are staying the night, aren't you?" Anya rose and walked around the desk. "I can't let you leave in the condition you're in, dear girl. You look ready to drop. Imagine, braving an arc storm for a fastening contract! Quite the story to tell your children."

Green winced. "Ah, let's keep that between us, shall we? I do not want to look too much like passion's fool."

Anya looped her arm through hers as they walked into the foyer and up the stairs. "Sometimes it's good to look the fool, especially when it is for those we hold dear."

Green patted her hand. "I'll face D'anbere with you in the morning."

"Somehow I knew you would."

* * *

*U*pstairs, the translucent eyes of Jorlan Reynard stared seemingly at nothing as the storm spoke to him in the language of endless rhythm. Then, as the wind abated, they drifted shut again, taking him deeper into sleep.

"*W*hat do you mean, the bid is off!*" Claudine D'anbere hissed at the Duchene. "Might I remind you that you have already accepted my terms?"

"On the contrary, She-Count," Green said, strolling into the sitting room. "She has accepted mine."

Claudine was stunned to see Marquelle Tamryn. She blinked rapidly, trying to digest what was happening. It must have been difficult considering the amount of brew she had consumed the night before.

Indeed, her eyes were red-rimmed and bleary from a night of debauchery.

"What fantasy is this?" She sniggered crudely. "Surely you do not expect me to believe that *you* have the bid on him?"

Green did not answer; she simply stared at Claudine with a steady, confident look.

Claudine sucked in her breath with a hiss. "This is not legal! You have agreed to my fasten bid, Duchene!"

"But I have trebled it." Green took a seat by the tall window.

"*Trebled it?*"

"I think all will agree that more than meets your terms for the note to the Duchene Reynard."

"I should say not!" Claudine flung back. "There is the question of her grandson, whom she has given—"

"As collateral to the note. The note is now paid back to you in full." Green nodded to Billings, who handed the She-Count a Tamryn account chit. "Twelve hundred thousand plat-coins. In turn, my *accepted* bid price on Jorlan. I'm sure the Septibunal will agree all parties are satisfied."

Claudine stared at the chit in disbelief. "You do not have the funds to cover this."

Green raised an eyebrow. "If I did not, I would not have written it."

Claudine's temper flared. "Do you think I will not have him? As far as I am concerned, this pays the monetary debt of the Reynards only."

"Then you better think again." Green removed her ancestral scroll from her pouch and opened it. Slowly she turned the scroll around to face the She-Count. Jorlan's name along with Anya's crest was plainly entered on her family line. Once a son's name was entered on the scroll, the act was irreversible. "He is already mine."

Furious, Claudine flung the scroll aside. "You may get his veil, but you will never keep him. *That* I promise you!" She faced the Duchene with a sneer. "And you, Duchene Reynard, have made an enemy this day. Be forewarned."

The old woman drew herself up with the dignity of centuries of Reynards. "Are you threatening me, She-Count?"

"Take it as you will." With that she stormed from the house, slamming the door behind her.

It took several moments for the reverberations to settle down.

In the sudden silence the Duchene turned to Green. "Well, I thought that went rather well."

A bark of laughter came from Green. "Oh, splendidly!"

"Do you think she'll cause much trouble?"

"Does Forus revolve around Arkeus?"

"*Hmf.* We shall take her on together, then."

Green got up and walked across the room to hug the elderly Duchene. "No, Anya. I will take her on. Alone."

"But I—"

"Shhh. No objections to this, now. It is up to me; surely you see this? I know her ways."

"Are you saying I am no match for that screech wing?" She raised a haughty noble eyebrow.

"In mind you are more than a match for her, but this might go beyond that."

Anya's shoulder's sagged. "You are right. I have confidence in you, my girl. Always have. I will aid you in any way you need."

"I know. And by the same token, I am counting on you to tell me if she bothers you in any way."

"Done."

"Good." Green straightened and bit her lip as she realized what came next.

"What is it?"

"Now I must tell Jorlan." She did not appear particularly thrilled with the task.

Anya chuckled at her expression. "Hmm. If you think Claudine was difficult . . ."

"I can handle Claudine. Your grandson is another story altogether."

Anya laughed. "Come now, I've seen you take on the entire House of She-Lords single-handed and win."

"As I said, your grandson is another thing altogether." Anya's chuckle followed her out the door as she went in search of her soon-to-be name-bearer. Otherwise known as the blaze-dragon.

She wondered if the arc storm was going to turn out to be the lesser of the two challenges.

She was soon to find out it was not going to be even a close second.

Chapter Five

Green found him dismounting his Klee by the water fountains in the back of the house.

Anya had told her that he often rode his Klee, Sabir, in the morning. She had taken the time to bathe and change into some clean clothes Billings had procured. At least she didn't have to face him in half-burnt, smoky clothing.

Jorlan alighted, clearly surprised to see her at the Reynard estate so early in the day. There was no way for him to know she had actually arrived in the middle of the night.

He wiped the sweat from his brow before patting his still-winded Klee.

He had ridden Sabir hard. Jorlan's reckless, wild rides were a favorite topic of the Slice. The man took unseemly risks that most thought of as bordering on indecent. Yet the words of chastisement were often laced with sighs of longing.

"Marquelle . . . Green, it is good to see you here." He gave her a broad smile of greeting, his perfect white teeth flashing in the daylight. One naughty dimple curved his cheek, making him altogether too alluring a sight for such an early hour.

He won't be smiling much longer, Green thought.

He stripped off his shirt and hung it over his Klee's saddle. Bending over the fountain, he ducked his head under the spray. He flung his head back as he straightened, letting the droplets slide down his neck and chest. Then he turned to her as he ran his fingers through his wet hair, slicking it back. Water glistened off of his lashes; the black crescents framing the pale azure color of his eyes.

Green had never seen such natural beauty in her life.

And it was now hers.

"I must speak with you about something, Jorlan. May we go somewhere out of the view of the servants?"

Jorlan arched his brow, giving her a sensual look from beneath his jet-black lashes. "Of course," he whispered.

Obviously, he had completely misinterpreted her request as her desire for them to experiment some more. And he was not opposed to it in the least, she noted, taking some comfort from the reaction.

She hoped she had the strength to guide him in the ways he needed.

"We can go over to the mesh-pond again. Come." He took her hand in a natural gesture and led her through the gardens. Green marveled at how warm his grip was, how sure. His large hand completely surrounded her smaller one, but the hold was not overbearing. It was comforting and right.

He brought her to the same bench they shared the other day and sat them both down.

"Now, what is it that is so important that you need to speak to me about?" He leaned forward, getting closer to her.

A droplet of the cool water fell on her mouth. His pupils flared as he noticed it. Slowly he reached up to let his fingertip glide across her lower lip, wiping it away. "Excuse me," he murmured in a raw voice.

Green's hand captured his wrist, stopping his action. "I have something to show you."

His mouth lifted at the edges. "Really?"

"Yes." She reached into her pouch and retrieved the scroll. His brow furrowed in confusion as he watched her.

Unwinding the ancient pattern, she showed him his name next to Anya's seal.

At first he did nothing but stare silently at the parchment.

Then he raised his eyes to hers. He tried to hide the hurt shadowing them, but could not. "Why?" He spoke hoarsely. "Why did you do this?"

She observed him coolly, shielding the truth from him. "Because I can. And because I want you."

Jorlan flinched as if slapped.

"And because I want you, this is the only way I can have you." She finished succinctly.

He clenched his jaw. "I made it plain to you that I did not want to be bid on! I ask you again: Why did you do this?"

"You knew it was only a matter of time. Your grandmother had to accept a bid for you eventually. Surely you realize this? You are the last of the Reynard line. You have a responsibility not just to your family but to our community. Your ancestress was the Captain. Your line must continue."

"*No!* It was to be my choice—not hers! I never wanted this, Green. You must release the bind. It is not that I don't . . . care for you; it is simply not the path I see for my life."

"I'm sorry, Jorlan, I cannot. You know as well as I that once the scroll is signed, it is irrevocable for you." She placed her hand on his arm in a gesture of compassion. "Perhaps in time you will see this is for the best."

"I will never see it that way, Marquelle Tamryn." He yanked his arm away from her hand.

"Think again. There will be much you can gain from this alliance. My name will protect you always and, in some ways, you will have much more freedom than you do now to pursue your pastimes. I am not as conventional as your grandmother. We already know that we are compatible in *other* ways. I can promise you will have great pleasure in my bed."

Jorlan leaned forward, resting his forearms on his knees. He gazed pensively into the mesh-pond. Green gave him some time.

"What if I tell you I know of this pleasure already?" he spoke quietly.

"Are you saying what I think you're saying?" Green blanched.

He nodded silently as he stared over the flower-strewn lattice.

Green trembled and turned from him to gather her thoughts. A man without a veil could not go through the Ritual of Proof! The aristocracy held great store by the Ritual. It was the only way to know that his seed was a name-giver's alone. Such a thing became crucial in matters of inheritance. One never wanted an unscrolled child in one's household, making claim to a line. It just wasn't done.

Green's thoughts tumbled over one another as she sought a solution to this dilemma.

Regardless of what transpired, Jorlan was in grave danger from Claudine D'anbere.

"So you see," he spoke softly, "you must cast me aside and have me stricken from the scroll. I'm sorry, Green."

Green paused in her frantic thoughts and glanced at him out of the corner of her eye. *What if he is misleading me so I will revoke the contract?* She viewed his features carefully as he stared straight at the pond.

A tiny, tiny muscle twitched in his jaw.

I don't believe it. There was no way he could feign his innocent response to her touch; to her instructions. *Am I willing to gamble my house on him?*

Yes, she was.

In fact, she already had. The price she had paid to save him had almost emptied her coffers.

Nevertheless, even if she had read him wrong, she would still take a chance on him. She could never live with herself if she let him fall into Claudine's hands, which is exactly what would happen if she revoked the contract. She had promised the Duchene that she would take care of him. And she would.

If what he said was true, there would be no future for him in the Select Quarter. He would be ostracized from polite company. Even though Jorlan thought he wanted that, Green did not think that he realized what such a life entailed. He was condemning himself to loneliness and sorrow.

After Anya was gone, he would be open game for every unscrupulous social climber looking to secure the hefty Reynard estate. Since he was the last of his line, conceivably the estate might come under the jurisdiction of the Septibunal to govern for him in his behalf. They would not hesitate either to control him, order him to fasten, or send him to the monkery.

Jorlan's passionate, sensitive nature would not fare well in a monkery.

Despite his opposition to the idea of the binding, he wanted her. Every intuition she had told her so.

Once he secured her name, he would never have to worry about those things, regardless of what happened to her. She would make the proper provisions for him.

"Your grandmother will be ruined by this; you do realize that?"

Jorlan inhaled deeply, and stared unblinking at the mesh-pond. The corner of his eye moistened, but he held firm. Green couldn't help but admire the strength of his beliefs. It was unusual in a man. He was unusual. Most men were led by other things.

It made her decision all the easier.

"It changes nothing, Jorlan. The fastening will occur as contracted."

He sucked in his breath. "You will let me shame you at the Ritual of Proof?"

She viewed him speculatively. "Will you shame me?"

The muscle in his jaw pulsed. He would not answer.

"We shall see then, won't we, fil-Duchene Reynard."

"Think it over, Marquelle. We can avoid all this if you cast me aside. I will get my grandmother to forgo the insult barter."

"No, Jorlan. The contract will stand. You will be my name-bearer."

"Once they initiate the Ritual, they will never *allow* me to be your name-bearer." He spoke low, through gritted teeth.

"We shall see."

"In either case, you will get no pleasure from me."

"As I said, we shall see."

That night Jorlan rode his Klee over the hills and vales of the Reynard estate. Both man and beast were wild in the night.

Despite their reckless regard for safety, each of them was confident—for two very different reasons.

Sabir, in love with the freedom of the run, knew that the man anticipated each of his moves. He rode with him in flowing synergy, matching his rhythm. This man was as untamed as a Klee; he would never seek to master him.

And so Sabir was confident.

Jorlan, spirit flying, felt the same way. He would never be mastered.

He was confident Green would back down before the Ritual of Proof took place.

She would not risk the disgrace.

"*I*t is for the best, you know."

Anya found her grandson later that evening sitting in the far corner of the solar. Since Marquelle Tamryn had left earlier in the day, he had been nowhere to be found.

She had expected that.

Since he had been a child, whenever he was troubled, he sought solitude. Only when he had worked through what was on his mind would he fully rejoin the life that was around him.

She had often wondered if the solitary life of a monkery was not more suited to him. It could never be, for two very important reasons: He was the last of the Reynard line, and his own nature would never survive it. Jorlan needed to experience all of the physical world.

There was something *different* about her grandson.

Something untapped.

"The best for whom?" he said quietly.

"For you and for us." She glided in front of him, her grav assists whirring lowly. The sound mingled with the shushing sway of the plants, the calming gurgle of the fountain. This had always been his favorite room. She knew why: It brought the outside in.

He stared directly at her. Not for the first time, she wondered where those aqua eyes had come from. No Reynard as far back as she knew had eyes that color. Nor had his father's side.

She remembered when he was born. . . .

Loreena had said his birth was almost rhythmic. Her contractions did not follow the normal pattern. They followed the sound of the waves outside the oceanside cottage where she had gone to give birth. He flowed into life like a gentle wave upon the shore. There had been very little labor.

Her daughter had remarked that he had the dark slate eye color so prevalent in the Reynards; indeed, her own eyes were such a color. But, over the following month, they had started to change in hue, mystifying everyone. By the time he was a year old—the time of Forus's revolution around Arkeus— his irises were the brilliant aqua color so reminiscent of the waters of the moon. They remained so to this day.

Naturally, the family had kept *that* bit of oddity to themselves.

Lately, she had begun to wonder if there was any significance to it. Jorlan seemed to have *deepened* in these last years. He had always been inordinately mature for his age; there was a natural wisdom in him that did not speak of a twenty-five-year-old come-out who had lived an almost totally sheltered life on her estate.

He was an enigma. He constantly warred with his emotions. Anya knew that there was an enormously caring heart inside of him; a heart he shielded as if he were preparing himself for a heroic storm.

She inhaled deeply. Green Tamryn was the one to unveil him—in every regard. She had placed her faith as well as the person she loved most in this world in Marquelle Tamryn's capable hands.

The girl would not disappoint her. There was something of valor within that small frame.

"You will fasten with the Tamryns, it will ensure our lineage," she reiterated with conviction.

"And what about my happiness, Duchene?" He spoke so low she had trouble hearing him. "Does that not mean anything?"

Anya gave him a superior look. "You do want her. I am not blind."

He shot her an angry glare.

"You cannot hide much from me, my boy. You never could."

A muscle ticked in his jaw.

"It will be better than you think."

He clenched his teeth. "My freedom will be gone forever!"

"Listen well: There is no such thing as freedom that is sought outside oneself. We are all bound by convention. While it is true you will be under the rules of the Tamryn household, you can still make your own peace within yourself."

"That is not all that I seek and you know it!"

"You must put aside those ideas. I have told you time and time again, they have no place in this society. You will only bring unhappiness upon yourself and others."

He sat silently in his chair.

Anya spun on the assists to leave.

"I disagree with what you have said about freedom, Grandmother," he remarked in a soft tone. "For I do not have the freedom to decide my own destiny. You have decided that for me."

"You would have chosen the same on your own."

With that she left the room.

*D*ue to the situation with She-Count D'anbere, both Anya and Green thought that the waiting time for the Ritual of Proof and subsequent vows should be brief.

They arranged for a special meeting of the Septibunal, who were not scheduled to convene for another month, at the close of the Season.

Jorlan was not in agreement, but held his own council. He was certain that Green would renege on the bind when they faced the Septibunal. She would not risk the potential disgrace that would follow if she went ahead.

*T*he day of the Ritual of Proof dawned bright and cloudless.

Green arrived in the special chamber designated for the rite. It was a large room. At the head, the seven members of the Septibunal sat on a dais. A quorum of seven was always needed—seven woman to swear to a man's pure name.

Green was dismayed to see the room so full. Normally, when a special session was called, the chamber was empty except for the families involved. In their case, word must have spread rapidly. The woman who had forsworn a fastening and the man who had refused to be fastened were coming together in the most talked about ceremony of the century. Everyone wanted to see it.

Green glanced over the sea of faces, noting the prurient curiosity. Jorlan was the catch of the town. Many watched Green with envy, others with good cheer. All in all, the event had taken on the atmosphere of a spectacle.

She noted that only six Septibunal members had taken their seats. One was missing. So she was not overly surprised when Claudine finally took the seventh seat as a named stand-in for the absentia member, Marquelle Harmone.

Green now knew that Marquelle Harmone was in D'anbere's pocket. An important bit of information for later reference, when the lines were drawn.

Claudine caught her eye and grinned smugly. Three of the seven members would examine Jorlan. *Think again, She-Count.* Green was about to stop her nemesis cold. She wouldn't be getting her fill of Jorlan this day. Or ever.

A hush filled the room as the clerk rang a tiny glass bell seven times denoting that the Ritual of Proof was to begin.

Jorlan was brought in.

He was garbed in the formal Ramagi gold robe of the initiate-into-fastening, and nothing else. The brilliant red sash of the Reynard family was draped over his left shoulder and pinned to his waist with the Reynard insignia. His gleaming black hair brushed lightly against the silken fabric at his shoulders.

In stark contrast, his extraordinary azure eyes flashed in rebellion.

He was utterly breathtaking.

Many of the onlookers inhaled sharply at his appearance. Strangely, it was the fire in him that captivated the Slice. Rarely had a come-out been seen with such spirit! There was not a woman present who did not imagine what it would be like to fasten such a man.

Jorlan met Green's look with an insolent glare of challenge. Several women gasped.

The corners of Green's lips curved. She should have been angry at his behavior, but in truth she couldn't help admire his come-and-get-some attitude. Oh, she was going to come and get some all right—later that night, when they were alone.

The veil still thought he had outsmarted her. Well, he was in for a shock, as was everyone else.

The head of the Septibunal, Duchene Hawke, issued the beginning statement calling for proof. "We gather here, women of fine standing, to witness the induction of a man, Jorlan Reynard, into the line of Tamryn. Marquelle Tamryn, do you have the scroll of your family?"

Green stepped forward. "I do," she said in a strong voice.

"Show the assemblage the seal of Reynard affixed to yours."

Green pulled out the scroll and held it up for the Septibunal to see. Murmurs of approval rang through the assemblage.

Green began to put it away.

"Wait," Claudine called out. "I did not see it clearly enough to check the seal."

Murmurs rang throughout the hall. She-Count D'anbere was just short of calling Marquelle Tamryn a liar before the Septibunal.

Green's amber eyes narrowed. She was about to issue a challenge when Anya, standing at her side, forestalled her. "Careful. That is what she wants."

Duchene Hawke frowned down the dais at the She-Count. "Marquelle Tamryn, might you be so good as to show the scroll once more to our *temporary* member?"

The set-down from Duchene Hawke caused many to titter. Claudine bristled.

Green unrolled the scroll once more and approached the dais, leaning over the long table to shove it in Claudine's face. "Have a care, D'anbere," she said under her breath.

Claudine snorted. "I am shaking in my boots." She fingered the meteor-blade she always wore at her side. There were not many who could wield the deadly weapon. It was said Claudine had been designated a platinum-class warrior. While the meteor-blade was highly regarded for the discipline it took to wield, and generally revered for the Gle Kiang-ten level of form, martial skills were regarded by many women as necessary but uncivilized. The She-Count commanded her own army and had a rare love of brutal military tactics. Aggressive qualities reminiscent of rampant male testosterone were not generally lauded on Forus—even when the skill itself was appreciated.

But the meteor-blade was not about military skill. She-Count D'anbere would not know that, though.

Claudine waved her hand, brushing the scroll away in a dismissing gesture. Under other circumstances, Green would have been tempted to kill her for the insult to her family. But then, *she* was a stateswoman. Such actions were not her norm.

Duchene Hawke nodded at Green, indicating that the scroll was acceptable to the Septibunal. "Jorlan Reynard of the House of Reynard, step forward."

Two escorts on either side of Jorlan led him forward. It was clear his step was not lively.

Duchene Hawke raised her eyebrow at his insolence, shaking her head with a slight smile of her own. "Do you, Jorlan Reynard, grandson of Anya Reynard, direct descendant of our revered Founder, come before this council free in body and soul?"

Jorlan seared Green with a warning look. "I do."

"And do you now undergo the Ritual of Proof with a clear mind and body?"

Once he responded to this question, he would be led into a small private chamber where he would be made to disrobe so that three council members could verify that his veil was intact. The small membrane, which had a tiny break in it and grew over the head of his penis, could be ruptured properly only by the internal muscles and fluid from a woman's body.

And the first time, the act was quite painful for the male.

Jorlan hesitated, staring at Green.

He was actually going to call her bluff! Green shook her head. *I don't think so this time, my Jorlan.*

Claudine leaned forward in her seat, watching the small byplay with interest. Her cruel eyes glimmered.

Green spoke up, loud and clear, shocking everyone. "The House of Tamryn forgoes the Ritual of Proof!"

Pandemonium broke out.

No one had forgone the Ritual in over four hundred years! The forgoing of the Ritual of Proof was a great boon to the House of Reynard from the House of Tamryn. Green was clearly stating that she relied solely on the honor of the Reynards as all the proof she needed. And their history books would say as much.

Jorlan's mouth parted in astonishment as he realized how she had bested him.

Anya's eyes filled with tears. "Green, I do not know what to say. . . ."

"You do not have to say anything, it is what I want to do." She looked straight at Jorlan. "It was what I decided to do as soon as you signed the scroll."

Jorlan's nostrils flared in anger. She had outwitted him and he could not withdraw now. She had left him no way to withdraw.

Knowing that something was afoot, Claudine stood up. "She cannot forgo the Ritual of Proof! The Law demands it!"

"Only when the one to be fastened refuses to forswear his virtue." Duchene Hawke faced Jorlan. "Do you, Jorlan Reynard, pledge your virtue?"

Jorlan exhaled brusquely, hating this demeaning ceremony and everything it stood for. Why should he have to prove his worth by some thin piece of skin? "Yes," he ground out. "I pledge it."

"And how do you come to the House of Tamryn?"

Before he answered, Jorlan looked at them one by one, letting them know clearly his hatred for this travesty. "I come to Tamryn House pure, as is the honor of my family."

The assemblage murmured approval but Claudine overspoke them. "He is lying!"

"She-Count D'anbere! Impugn my family again and I will call a vote for an Honor Forfeiture." Anya pinned the She-Count to her chair. By the Bair-tin, the books of law and civilization, and depending on the severity of the forfeiture levied by the Septibunal, the She-Count could stand to lose a significant amount of property, wealth, and maybe even her title.

Claudine swallowed. Perhaps she had gone too far—for now. But there would come a time later . . . and she knew just how she was going to do it. She nodded curtly to Duchene Reynard and sat down.

"Green Tamryn," Duchene Hawke called out, "Do you have something to say?"

"Yes!" Green called out. "Let me leave this room . . ."

Everyone held their breath for this was the last opportunity the Marquelle would have to refuse the Reynard seed.

". . . and go on to the next! There, you may bring him to me dressed in the garb of his house—for the last time!" The crowd let out a raucous cheer. The coveted, resistant Jorlan Reynard had been bagged by the notorious damselle, Marquelle Tamryn!

The female escorts took Jorlan to another room where he would change into black pants, a loose black shirt, and black boots. His family sash would be draped once again over his shoulder and he would be paraded to the Tamryn estate for the final ceremony that evening.

Green watched them lead him off. The piercing look of loathing he gave her over his shoulder did not bode well for a happy fastening night.

She sighed.

His body she could win over. But his mind and heart were another story.

He did not have to love her to give her an heir . . . but it never hurt.

In the meantime, there was something she had to do before the ceremony that evening.

Outside, she retrieved Kibbee from the Kloo hand and headed in the direction of the western part of town.

An exclusive section, where women of means kept their personal pleasurers.

Chapter
Six

Green let herself into the tastefully appointed town dwelling off of the Rue de la Nuit.

The discreet abodes in the center of town, with their enclosed rear courtyards, were the lodgings of favored pleasurers. Only the cream of the crop reached this private status. They were kept exclusively by their patronas and afforded every luxury.

In exchange, exclusivity was not only expected, it was demanded.

Green found River out in the courtyard, resting on a lounge chair. The magnificent pleasurer was fast asleep.

A light wind gently tousled his dark golden locks. Green took a moment to watch him as he slept. There was something about River that was very different when he was asleep—

The alluring sculpted features, normally guarded with a distrustful wariness, softened into clear, uncluttered comeliness. That he was a remarkable-looking man was never in dispute. It had been his sensational looks that had been his salvation.

But Green had always known there was more to River than his appearance. While his inner emotions mostly remained closed off from her, there had been times over the past few years when she'd had glimpses into his protected, hidden self.

The man was more complicated than he ever let on. Green often wondered if the smooth, even nature he affected was just that—an affectation. There was no way of knowing, for he zealously safeguarded his inner realm.

Only some things could not be hidden.

River had a wounded heart.

Despite the ordeals he must have experienced in his youth, Green knew he had never lost the compassion and intrinsic goodness within him. Even when he tried to cover it over by assuming the laconic attitude so favored among the Slice, it was evident to her.

He was a skilled, considerate lover. A few times, he had almost lost his control and shown her his real passion, but he always seemed to be able to pull himself back from that precipice. River knew *never* to cross that line. It was what made him such a valued pleasurer.

He was also a decent human being—in some ways far more honorable than his "betters." Many She-Lords cared for nothing but their own gratifications and used their stations to achieve whatever they desired, regardless of the price or cost in human terms.

Green would miss him.

She quietly walked over to the couch and stood over him. He was an extremely light sleeper; she was surprised she had been able to cross the courtyard without him hearing her. Once, during a nightmare, he had curled up so tightly that it had taken her hours to get him to uncoil and relax his body again. He had shaken the entire night while she held him. He would not speak.

The next day, he acted as if it had never happened. In all the time they were together, he never once mentioned the incident to her. River hid his personal horrors.

Brushing her fingertips gently over his forehead, she smoothed back a few locks of hair that had fallen over his face. The color always reminded her of golden sunlight on heliotrope, the only Origin plant ever to take root directly on Forus soil.

His lashes flickered at her touch. Instantly alert, he snapped his lids open.

He stiffened slightly as he always did when awakened suddenly, but relaxed when he recognized Green. Deep forest-green eyes focused on her with genuine fondness.

"Green . . ." The smooth voice rolled sleepily from his throat. "It's been so long, I thought you'd forgotten me."

Green smiled easily. "Who could forget you, River?" She sat down next to his hip. He rose up on his elbows, bending toward her for a kiss.

Green placed her fingers against his mouth, stopping his forward motion. "We need to talk."

He did not even blink, but something in his eyes changed. A shield dropped down over them, shuttering their depths. "Of course. Would you like a cool drink? I have some limo juice in the library."

Green nodded.

River lithely rose and headed for the double doors that led to the library. His motions would have seemed perfectly fluid to any other observer, but not to her. Green had a gift for reading people. The slight hesitation in his step as well as the tightly curved fist of his right hand told her that he already knew what she had come to say.

He must be used to this, she realized sadly. How must this be for him?

Green decided to follow him indoors. River strolled over to a side table and poured her a tall glass of the sweet-tart juice. He handed it to her, then walked over to the opposite windows, which looked down on the busy thoroughfare below.

He gazed through the sheer curtains to the street and waited. A pulse ticked in his throat.

"I'm afraid I must end our agreement, River." Green spoke softly.

River closed his eyes, trying to collect himself. "Give me a moment."

Green gave him that time, remaining silent.

Pain *and* fear hit River together. *How could he start over again?* He was twenty-eight years old. *Too old.* He was well past the prime age for a special secluded pleasurer.

He could not go back to the way it had been before! He could never make himself do it. He had no more to give. Nothing. *I will die inside.* He took several silent breaths to steady himself.

When he could speak, his voice was dry and slightly rough. "I had heard of the Reynard bid, of course. The whole town is talking of it."

He wondered what it would be like to know your ancestresses and to have someone think so much of you and your name that they would inscribe it to their family scroll. His name had always been worthless. It was only his body that had any value to the Slice.

Green nodded. Kloobroth spread quickly among the pleasurers, who usually had plenty of time on their hands between visits from their patronas. They often met in the courtyards to discuss snippets they had heard from their lovers.

River cleared his throat. This was very hard. A pleasurer could not afford to have pride. Especially not a twenty-eight-year-old pleasurer. "Many, that is, most of the other patronas are fastened, Green. I would not be a distraction for you, or interfere in any way with that. I can still be here for you when you need me. This need not change our arrangement."

Green sighed. "I'm afraid it does. What you say is true; the practice is an acceptable one to the Slice—but not to me. I could never do that to Jorlan; I would not feel right about it. It is not my way."

River was not surprised by her answer. Her code was one of the things he admired about her. She had turned his whole life around. He was incredibly grateful to her, and perhaps more. He watched a young spark dash around the corner to enter the back door of a house. The scene was so familiar that ice pooled in his stomach. He swallowed. "Have you no feelings for me at all, Green?"

"Of course I do . . . just not those kinds of feelings."

River turned and stared at her. "Is it because he can give you a veil and I cannot?"

"You know me better than that."

He looked at her inquiringly.

"Jorlan is remarkable to me; there is something about him that sings to my spirit."

Incredibly, his eyes filled with moisture. He turned from her.

Green rushed up to him, placing her hand on his arm. "It is not as if you love me, River."

He swallowed again to regain his composure. "I could have loved you."

"It is not meant to be. I am sorry. . . ."

He knew that was true. Well, what did he expect from her? She was a Marquelle and he was nothing but a pleasurer whose favors were sold to the highest bidder. He could not be unfair to her. She had been more than kind to him. She had saved his life and was never less than honest with him. Whatever happened in the future, he must make his own way and not blame her. She had kept him in the lap of luxury for several years, denying him nothing. And she had been so sweet at night. . . .

He gazed down at her and smiled poignantly. "I know that, Green.

And I want to thank you for . . . everything. If you hadn't come along, I would have been passed from woman to woman among the Slice."

She lightly grazed his forearm with her hand. "You did what you had to do to survive. I always understood that."

His gaze shifted away from her. "There were many more than I ever allowed you to think."

She was not surprised. His stunning looks and the lack of the protection of a title would have made him fair game for the aristocracy.

"You must find someone rich and of a good nature, perhaps a childless, older woman, who can give you the protection of a moderate title in return for an heir. You will be well taken care of and she might even come to dote on you to distraction." Green winked at him, trying to lighten the atmosphere.

River laughed. "And how am I to secure this miracle? Have you forgotten my lack of a certain, shall we say, item, that would be required for the Ritual of Proof? Not to mention my complete lack of family name?"

Green wagged her finger at him. Reaching into her pouch she extracted a passage chit and a letter, which she handed to him.

"What is this?" he asked hoarsely.

"The letter is an introduction by Marquelle Damus, which states that you are a distant cousin of hers."

River gave her a disbelieving look.

Green shrugged nonchalantly. "The Marquelle owed me a favor. The travel chit is to take you out to the farthest colonies west." *Far away from Claudine D'anbere.* "It is an untamed land, barely civilized, but I somehow think it might suit you. The colonists are mostly plantation owners. Men of good breeding are in low quantity because of the rough conditions. The planters will not be so particular about the likes of veils. They will not look into your story too deeply. Simply stick to the tale and you will be greeted with open arms." She wagged her brows at him. "Literally."

A huge grin spread across his artistic features, lighting his entire face. His expression contained the ray of hope. This was the first time Green had ever seen him show such unguarded emotion, and it transformed him.

"You will have to wait until the end of the Season to begin your travel, as it is too dangerous this time of year for such a journey. And be careful whom you choose; don't give yourself too easily. Make them all work for you. I predict you will have them all slavering over you. Lead them on a fine chase!"

"Ha! *That* would be sweet recompense, wouldn't it? What a delightful prospect!"

Green chuckled.

His face became serious. "I cannot thank you enough, Marquelle Tamryn. You do not know what this means to me."

"I think I do."

River took his final look of the woman before him. The incredible woman who had shared his bed for many years. She was unusually strong, intelligent, and compassionate. She had her own inner sense of justice and always lived her life on her own terms, with an uncommon wisdom. It would not surprise him if she was named the head of the Septibunal one day. He cupped her soft cheek tenderly. "Don't teach him everything you've taught me. You might shock his aristocratic sensibilities beyond repair."

Green snorted. "I think with you it was the other way around, River."

He gave her an intent look. "One more time?"

She shook her head reluctantly.

"You really do care for him."

She inclined her head and turned to leave.

"I hope he appreciates what he is getting," he murmured as Green let herself out.

*A*t that very moment, at Tamryn House, Jorlan was being dragged to the Marquelle's chamber to await the fastening ceremony.

He had already blackened the eyes of the three male servants who had been assigned to serve him.

He squared his shoulders as he sought a way to escape directly after the vows were spoken.

Marquelle Tamryn would have no fastening night!

*W*hen Green approached her estate, she was astounded to see the number of tethered Kloo and coaches littering the drive. It was so cluttered that servants were dashing here and there trying to find places to lead the Kloo to. The coops were obviously full to brimming by the disapproving squawks coming from that direction.

It seemed that the Top Slice had taken it upon themselves to issue their own invitations to what was supposed to have been a private event!

Disheartened at the commotion, Green decided to enter her estate by using a secret portal around the back of the house. She was sure the poor servants were frantic trying to accommodate all of these unexpected guests, and because it was the Select Quarter, they were bound to be extremely demanding.

As she took the backstairs, she idly wondered how many were attempting to stay the night. Gossip was the Slice's lifeblood and for a certainty they were slavering to see how Jorlan was going to react on the morrow.

Green's mouth firmed. *No one was staying.* If she had to throw them all out personally, she would! Regardless of how rude it seemed.

Their life together was not going to be mack-mock for the salacious appetite of the Slice!

She slipped into a darkened hallway, moving surreptitiously to a back door, which led to her chamber. She was grateful to see Avatar waiting for her there.

"I thought you'd show up back here, what with that spectacle down below."

Green stormed over to her wardrobe, yanking out a plain white robe. As she yanked off her clothes, she let Avatar know exactly how she felt about their guests' prurient interest. "Filthy voyeurs, the lot of them! If I had wanted witnesses, I would have asked for them!"

"True enough, girl, but you got them just the same. And they'll be expecting a fine show of it, too."

"Well, they're not getting it!" Naked, Green dipped into her bubble-pool, letting the warm water lap up to her chin. It was traditional to bathe before the ceremony in front of a witness—in this case, Avatar. She would have to dip under the water three times to cleanse her spirit for the union. Likewise, she assumed that Jorlan was also being bathed in front of a witness.

A crashing sound from the next chamber—which sounded suspiciously like a body being hurled against the wall—made her jump.

"By the Founder! What in the blazes is that?"

Avatar chuckled. "I'd say it's your demure soon-to-be name-bearer. He doesn't take kindly to being told what to do, and he likes even less anyone assisting him in the matter. He's already done considerable damage to three servants. You're going to have trouble with that one. I hope you know what you're doing."

Avatar had *not* been happy with her choice of name-bearer. She had groused on, constantly asking Green if she had lost her mind, if she was sure she knew what she was doing, and did she realize that the veil had a reputation for being extremely difficult?

Green had smiled patiently and replied yes, yes, and, again, yes.

"I really think you secretly admire my choice, Avatar. Be honest: You like the fire he shows. It appeals to your tribal spirit." Avatar's people had originally hailed from the far southern tribes whose origin ancestresses were in the *NEOFEM*'s maintenance division. It was only in the last three hundred years that that branch of tribes had been incorporated back into OneNation.

Avatar harrumphed. Although Green did see the slightest smile grace her stern features.

Green ducked her head beneath the water again.

"One more time and that'll do it, Marquelle. Roseen has prepared the bed straps. Made them extra strong. We all know you'll be needing them that way," Avatar said pointedly, referring to Jorlan's reluctance.

"Mmm," Green dunked down, coming up with a splash. "That's three, Avatar." She flung her wet hair out of her eyes and grumbled, "I have no idea where that ridiculous custom came from!"

Avatar chuckled. "Who knows why people do the things they do? All I know is that it's a ritual and that's that."

Green made a face as she exited the water. Another crash-bump came from next door.

Avatar snickered. "It appears your loving name-bearer really does not like that custom."

"It's probably more that he doesn't like being assisted to it." Green chuckled with her.

Once out of the bath, Avatar helped Green dry her long hair with the bristles of a newi plant. The small appendage branches were snapped off the mother plant. The spiny bristles were highly effective moisture extractors and were used for a variety of household applications.

Next, Green donned the white semisheer robe traditionally used in fastening ceremonies. The robe had a very special sash tied around it. Her family sash, which had been used by the Tamryns for generations.

"You look lovely, Green." Avatar theatrically dabbed at a tear at the corner of her eye.

Green frowned over her shoulder as she went out the door. "You can stop the overly sentimental act, Avatar, it does not suit you at all."

Avatar grinned broadly, not in the least repentant. Even though she questioned Green's choice of name-bearer, she could not contain her genuine happiness on her fastening day.

Green marched down the stairs to the formal room, a determined stride to her step. The room was a sea of people.

Jorlan had already been brought down. He awaited her in the center of the room.

Green's lips curled with amusement as she realized that his hair was still damp and slightly dripping onto his black shirt. The aqua eyes narrowed at her in icy defiance. Apparently all they could get was his head dunked underwater. He still wore the same clothes he had on at the Ritual of Proof.

She snorted. *Ah, Jorlan, what am I to do with you?*

The noise level of the crowd increased markedly at her appearance. Half of the guests she did not even recognize. Discreetly, she motioned to her majordoma, Mathers. The staunch white-haired woman, who had been with her family for as long as she could remember, strode over to her with a forceful gait. The distinct sniff of utter disdain for the rabble of the crowd was obvious on her florid face.

"Where did they all come from?" Green hissed to her.

"I don't know, my Lordene. They seemed to arrive consistently, like a plague of popular sentiment." Mathers was the mistress of droll humor.

"They are *not* to stay the night. Is that clear, Mathers?"

Mathers's chilling grin spread across her face. "I dare say not, my Lordene."

Green gave her a look. The woman was enjoying her work far too much. She was going to absolutely adore tossing out the rarefied gentry. To confirm her summation, the servant literally rubbed her hands together in glee, and there was a slight gleam in her squinty eyes.

Mathers said simply, "Before or after the ceremonial meal?"

Green bit her lip. "After, I suppose."

Mathers chortled with anticipation.

"Have the kitchens prepared a—"

"Don't worry about that now. We've taken care of everything for you, Marquelle. This is your fastening day, you just enjoy it."

Green's eyes moistened. Her people were very good to her. She loved them all and would never give them up—not one of them—without the best fight she had in her. And they knew it.

"Thank you, Mathers. Has the Septibunal arrived yet?" As a high-ranking member of the aristocracy, the Septibunal would oversee her fastening rite.

"Yes, Lordene. They are ready to observe the vows. Should warn you, that snip-butt D'anbere is here with them."

Green frowned. "I don't want that woman in my house. Show her out immediately. And please don't refer to her as a snip-butt, Mathers; she is a She-Count."

"Yes, Lordene," Mathers intoned by rote. Both of them knew Green might as well be talking to the wall. Mathers always referred to anyone she did not like as a snip-butt, and that was that.

"You can't remove her, Green." Anya came up beside them. "She is here in an official capacity as a stand-in council member. She must oversee the fastening."

"I have no doubt that she arranged that. Watch her closely, Mathers; under no condition is she to leave the formal room."

"Too late for that, I think." Anya nodded to the grand stairway. Claudine D'anbere was strolling down the stairs from the upper floors and there was a very self-satisfied smirk on her face.

"What do you think the snip-butt was doing up there?" Mathers's beady eyes got beadier.

A small worry-line furrowed Green's brow. "There's no telling."

She sighed. Whatever Claudine had been doing upstairs, she supposed she'd find out soon enough.

"Mathers, just in case, have my room thoroughly searched, especially the bed. She might have placed something between the sheets."

"The snip-butt!" Mather blustered.

"Warn the servants to be careful, Mathers," Anya cautioned the faithful majordoma. "Being a venomous sort, she might have loosed a coil-winder or something like it."

Mathers nodded gruffly and marched away, intent on making sure her Lordene's chambers were scoured from top to bottom while the ceremony was going on.

"Shall we, my dear?" Anya held her hand out to Green to lead her to the center of the room to begin the fastening. "Or should I say 'daughter'?"

"I rather like the sound of that, Anya."

"So do I, daughter, so do I." Anya patted her hand as they reached the cleared circle where Jorlan awaited them. When she released her hand she backed out of the small space.

The Septibunal members came forward and formed a circle around the two of them. Green ignored Claudine, who was trying her best to catch Jorlan's attention.

Duchene Hawke nodded at Jorlan, indicating he should go on his knees in front of Green. When a full minute had gone by and Jorlan still did not kneel, several guests began buzzing.

Green nodded to his two attendants, who not so gently placed their hands on his shoulders and forced him down. He was strong enough to stop them, of course. Instead he made just enough of a display to show rebellion.

He stared mutinously at her.

Green sucked in her breath. With his pale aqua eyes, black hair and outfit, his sheer determined defiance, she had never seen him more beautiful. She knew she would never forget the way he looked at that moment.

Slowly, Green leaned forward to remove the familial sash of Reynard from his waist. Her fingers were remarkably steady, considering. She could feel the heat of his skin beneath the cool satiny texture of the Ramagi fabric. Accidentally, she brushed the hard muscle on the plane of his stomach as her fingers grazed the knot. The slight intake of breath told her that he was not immune to her touch. A good sign.

Avatar came through the circle, bearing the Tamryn sash on a pillow. Green switched sashes, taking the Tamryn one in her hand. She held it aloft and, with her voice clear, spoke directly to Jorlan and not the Septibunal as was custom. "With this sash, Jorlan Reynard, I give to you my name, the protection of my house, and my honor. I will accept in return your seed to bear my children, whom I will entrust to you—the most precious of my life—into your care." With that, she deftly tied the Tamryn sash around his trim waist.

Now it was Jorlan's turn to respond.

Except the new name-bearer remained silent.

A muscle ticked in his jaw as he watched his Lordene. The guests would later attest that the force of his displeasure was palpable.

Despite everything, Jorlan must accept the vow for the fastening to be legal. Green met his challenging look with her own strength of will. Suddenly, surprising everyone, and in a highly unorthodox manner, she seized Jorlan by the chin and fastened her lips to his in a brand. "Do not shame your grandmother," she hissed into his mouth.

Jorlan started, stunned by her bold action.

When she released him, she waited for what he knew he must do.

"I will bear your name," he bit out angrily.

Green arched an eyebrow, waiting for the rest of the acceptance. "And . . . ?"

He gritted his teeth. "And I will . . . *obey* you in all things."

Green nodded slightly to him in acknowledgment, then held the Reynard sash high in the air. "Arise, Jorlan Tamryn from the House of Tamryn."

In a doubly symbolic gesture so beloved by the women, she rent the Reynard sash cleanly in two. Originally the action symbolized that the male's ties to his old house were torn asunder. Over time, the meaning had become blurred with the rending of the veil.

A great cheer filled the room as the damselles celebrated the symbolic rupture. "My servants have prepared a repast for you in the dining hall; please avail yourselves." Green went to take Jorlan's arm so that they might lead the way.

He yanked it away from her. "You have what you want from me in name only, Marquelle Tamryn. I suggest you be satisfied with that."

Green gave him a look that questioned his sanity. "I hardly think so, *Marqueller* Tamryn. I suggest to you that you eat a hearty meal—for you will surely need it."

His cheeks flushed bronze both from anger and . . . something else.

With that, she all but dragged him into the dining hall.

Chapter
Seven

Jorlan was conspicuously silent during the ceremonial feast.

He sat next to her, glowering down into his plate of roasted tasteslikerooster with an expression that Green was surprised did not sear the cooked creature to cinders. Tasteslikerooster had been a favorite on Forus since the time of the *NEOFEM*, and was the first indigenous bioform the settlers had encountered. Since it had no intelligence to speak of and they were in need of an additional protein source, tasteslikerooster was the difference in that first year between struggling to survive and full stomachs.

Since that time, schools of them were raised specifically for consumption. It had a marvelous taste that lent itself to literally thousands of recipes. No one could recall why the Origin crew had given it such an odd name. Some of their researchers believed that "rooster" was a slang term among the crew for a particularly sensual male.

In any event, Jorlan's attitude was starting to cause comments.

Green leaned toward him, brushing her lips across his cheek. At least it looked that way to their guests. In actuality she was speaking to him in a low voice. "Are you going to sulk all evening, my wilding?" she whispered in his ear, giving the fold a little lick.

He started at the delicate touch. Giving her an angry glare, he remained stubbornly silent.

"I see. Perhaps you would rather go upstairs and prepare yourself for tonight then?" Her mouth brushed lightly at the soft skin under his lobe. He swallowed, twitching slightly from desire. Pointedly, he looked away from her down the length of the long feasting table.

Green raised her eyebrow at his blunt action. "Very well; I shall signal for the waiting-servants now." She lifted her hand to snap her fingers.

Without looking at her, Jorlan's hand came over hers, capturing it in his grip. He placed both their hands on the tabletop, firmly holding hers down.

Green gasped. He had her neatly pinned. What was he doing? Name-bearers never disobeyed!

The guests were watching them very closely. If she tried to extricate herself they were sure to notice his behavior and she would be forced into doing something she did not want to do. Especially on their fastening night.

Name-givers had the right to discipline their name-bearers if they so desired. Although the practice was not generally applauded by the Slice, it was deemed a woman's sole right to decide what was proper for her name-bearer and her household. When a man fastened, whatever property he had, all of his belongings, and his entire future welfare belonged to his name-giver. Even the sons of aristocratic women did not have any say in the direction of their lives or their land.

It was a woman's world, after all.

Nevertheless, Green was not about to start their life together by having him disciplined. She wanted him to come to her willingly. She knew that wouldn't happen initially, but it was a span she was willing to endure. The end result would be worth it.

Her viewpoints were not going to stop her from taking a stand, though.

"Are you going to release my hand or do I—"

"What? Have me beaten?" He turned to her, aqua slits of challenge burning into her.

"I like your passion, Jorlan; it will be all the more enticing for me to turn it to a different direction later."

His mouth firmed. "If you think that to happen, than you had better think again."

Green met his look head on. "Do you really think I will allow this fastening to go unrent? Perhaps there is a psillacyb in the hameeri liquor you've been drinking?"

He glanced at his goblet, his complexion paling.

Green rolled her eyes. "Do not be foolish! I have no need to mesmerize you to my bed; you will be there willingly, soon enough. What's more—if past experience is a teacher—you will enjoy it."

"*No.*"

Green shrugged. "Then that will be your choice, but somehow"— she ran her fingers along his rock-hard thigh, feeling the muscles instantly bunch—"I doubt it."

He exhaled noisily, refusing to respond.

"Are you going to release my hand?" Green's tone was clipped and direct. Discipline was out of the question, but displeasure was not. Jorlan needed to realize that *she* was firmly in control of her house. "I will not ask you again."

He watched the musicians.

"Ava—" Green began to call out an order.

"If I release you," Jorlan interrupted, "will you agree not to summon the waiting-servants?" The waiting-servants were to escort him up to her chambers and prepare him for her.

"I do not bargain in my own house. You have two choices, Jorlan. You can either release my hand and see what I will do or you can remain as you are and you will surely see the consequences . . . and so will your grandmother."

Jorlan's nostrils flared. He released her hand.

Green stared him in the eye. He was testing her. Inwardly, she sighed; but she had known it was going to be like this with him. Difficult. If she had wanted a demure name-bearer, she would have bid on any number of young men. She wanted Jorlan. Spirited blaze-dragon behavior included.

He watched to see whether she would stand down in what he considered an agreement between them, since he had released his hold.

Without breaking eye contact with him, she lifted her hand and snapped her fingers three times, summoning the waiting-servants.

Instantly, the rowdy crowd went silent.

"Bring him to my chambers," she announced concisely.

Jorlan flinched as if he had been struck. Then a look came into his eyes. . . .

And Green, experienced in the ways of the world and people, recognized that look.

The guests banged their goblets on the table, applauding the directive in the bawdy good-natured cheer that always accompanies such suggestive statements.

After all, the guests knew what the command signified and the event that was sure to follow. Bedding was, for some reason, always an eagerly thought-of event. It didn't matter who was doing it, who was thinking of doing it, or who had done it. The subject was endless mack-mock for the Select Quarter.

The waiting-servants, three of them, came forward to escort the name-bearer to his new bed.

Jorlan stood abruptly, almost knocking over his chair. Without giving her another look, he stormed off with them.

Green watched him knowingly. She signaled Mathers over to her.

The elderly servant immediately bustled over. "Yes, Lordene?"

"Assign extra guards over him. Have them stand sentinel outside the room and outside the windows and balcony as well." She spoke in aside. "He has the look of a Klee just before it bolts."

Mathers chuckled. "That he does. I'll get right on it!"

Green nodded. Lifting Jorlan's goblet to her lips, she drank deeply of his hameeri liquor.

He was going to give her a difficult night, but, by morning's light, the veil would be calling her name in ecstasy.

*U*pstairs, tied spread-eagle to her bed, Jorlan was calling her every name he could think of—and none of the terms he used was even close to ecstatic in nature.

Somehow, the waiting-servants had overpowered him.

He was angry, although to be fair to himself, there were *a lot* of them.

Initially, he had tried a quick escape over the balcony. He soon discovered that that route was heavily guarded. They had caught him forthwith.

But not before he had taken down five of them.

Then he had tried a secondary door, which led from the bathing chamber. Again, he had been forestalled.

Green.

Somehow she had intuited what he was about to do. The woman was uncanny! Still, he had caused quite a bit of damage before he went down. Especially to one, a wiry orange-haired snip-butt, who kept taking any chance he could to get a kick in.

Jorlan almost smiled at the snip-butt's dazed expression when he had expertly flipped him directly onto his tailbone. The dazed expression was followed by a howl of pain. Men generally did not know the secret forms of Gle Kiang-ten.

Unfortunately, they had been able to throw a sheet over him, drag him up onto the bed, and bind him before he could get free. The bed straps were amazingly strong.

They would have to be.

His nostrils flared again as he realized he was caught well and good.

Marquelle Tamryn could do whatever she wanted with him and there was naught he could do.

After they had him bound, the snip-butt had told everyone to leave. That's when he had taken his revenge. He had sneered down at Jorlan and struck him hard once in the face.

Defenseless, Jorlan could only tense for the punch he knew was coming. The force of it rocked his head back but he did not let out a sound.

"Good. Keep silent," the orange-haired servant jeered. Then he paused, seeming to think over what he had done to the Marquelle's new name-bearer. "It's simply a payback for what you did to me."

Jorlan stayed silent, staring at him with loathing.

"If you say anything, I'll deny it—remember that. Opper's been in this household a long time; she'll believe Opper before she does you."

"Who's Opper?"

The servant sniggered gutturally as if Jorlan had uttered the greatest witticism. "Who's Opper? I'm Opper, you dim-nit!" He got off the bed and retrieved a large, sharp-looking blade and began shining it suggestively on his pant leg.

Jorlan watched him carefully, wondering what he was going to do with it. The possibilities didn't bear thinking about.

Opper approached, leaning over Jorlan threateningly. "I could cut up your perfect face with this, you know. She wouldn't want you so much then, would she?"

Probably not. Jorlan was almost tempted to tell him to do it.

"However, that would be more difficult to explain away. I don't think I could talk my way out of that one."

A light of understanding came into Jorlan's pale eyes. He sucked in his breath. "You hate her."

The servant's eyes widened. He stepped back. "Guessed that, did you?"

"Why do you hate her so much?"

Opper blinked rapidly. "Why, the usual reason for the likes of someone of my station. She ruined me, she did! Took my veil! Made me pretty promises, then cast me aside."

He's lying. I wonder why? Jorlan's voice became deeper, softer. "Tell me more. . ."

"She promised me a fine house on the Rue de la Nuit, but did I get it? No! I'm stuck here waiting her table and taking roughhouse from you! It should be me lying there, bound up—not you!"

It seemed Opper had a fancy for his Lordene. The corners of Jorlan's lips curled. He couldn't help it. The irony was too much.

"Feel free to take my place," he quipped sarcastically. It would almost be worth hanging around to see the look on Green's face when she found this disheveled orange branch in her bed.

He had been joking, but the orange branch actually seemed to be thinking it over. Jorlan held his breath.

Suddenly the servant's eyes darkened as if he remembered something. "What do you think I am, a nod-bod? She'd be onto me right quick then, wouldn't she? And I'd be on the streets faster than you can say it."

Jorlan exhaled in annoyance.

The servant took the blade and sliced down his shirt, careful not to nick the golden-bronze skin. As he pulled the fabric away, he said matter-of-factly, "So you best keep your mouth shut about the tag and I'll keep my trapper closed about your little offer."

Jorlan did not even deign to respond.

The servant Opper tugged off his boots, none too gently. Taking the blade he began slicing Jorlan's pants.

"Most wouldn't care for a blade around these parts, would they?" He taunted Jorlan with the blade, bringing it right alongside his member. Jorlan did not even blink. He just watched him steadily.

Opper glanced down. "Well, look at that now, would you?"

Jorlan was puzzled. *Look at what?*

He glanced down at himself, then back up at Opper. The servant seemed giddy all of a sudden; he began humming a strange tune. That's when Jorlan began to worry. *What is he doing?*

Opper got up and retrieved the Tamryn sash, placing it horizontally across Jorlan's hips and groin. It was a normal thing to do on such an occasion, but nothing about this man's actions seemed normal.

Opper shook his finger at him. "You'll remember Opper now, won't you?"

With that he gave a strange little cackle and left the chamber.

With dread, Jorlan awaited Green. His beautiful, sensual, oh-so-talented name-giver. The only woman he had ever wanted from the instant he had set eyes on her.

The woman he was forced to fasten.

He would never forgive her.

But could he resist her?

*G*reen entered the chamber soon after Opper left.

At least she hadn't left him to wait too long. He didn't know whether to be relieved or not.

She ignored him at first.

Walking around the chamber, she lowered the flamelights one by one to a softer glow. As she passed one of the urns that had been knocked over in the tussle earlier, she clicked her tongue, bending to right it.

All the while Jorlan watched her from under lowered lids. Finally, she approached the bed. Standing by his side, she stood there deliberately taking her fill of his near-naked form.

Covered only in her sash, he was quite a sight.

Perfectly portioned muscular thighs and long legs. A lean waist. Beautifully formed chest and broad shoulders. Well-formed arms. And hands that were a woman's fantasy—strong, long-fingered, powerful. Flamelight danced a sheen on his golden-bronze skin and illuminated every highlight in his silken black hair.

His sensual features took her breath away with their intensity.

They were the kind of features you could never look away from; the expressions as subtle and ever-changing as a complex dream.

Jorlan Reynard—no, Jorlan *Tamryn*. What layers dwelled beneath the translucent aqua eyes that glittered so brightly between black lashes?

She wasn't sure.

But she was going to have a lifetime to find out.

"Do you like what you see, Marquelle?" he hissed, breaking their silence.

"Yes, I do."

Her immediate and forthright response confounded him briefly. Without hesitation, she untied her sash and dropped her robe. The white, sheer material pooled at her feet. Unable to stop himself, Jorlan allowed his burning gaze to travel the length of her nude form. She was beautiful, womanly full, and narrow in exactly the places he preferred. The sash that covered his hips shifted slightly but he refused to outwardly acknowledge his reaction.

Green reached over and ran her fingertips lightly over the plane of his lower belly, directly above the edge of the sash. Every muscle in his body tensed, locking in preparation for the battle to come.

"This is not going to be a fight, Jorlan," she promised him.

"So you say."

She bent over and placed a soft kiss on the tender skin she had stroked. The sweet touch became a scalding caress. His breath hitched. The muscles in his belly drew up. A faint shimmer of sweat dotted his forehead.

Green smiled knowingly. "So I say."

"If you take me . . . to your house," the husky voice tried to forestall her, "you risk your name and the names of your children."

Green did not believe it for a heartbeat. "I'll make you a wager, Jorlan."

"Wager? What wager?" His raw tone was clipped.

"The moment I remove this sash the truth will be upon you. Our private Ritual of Proof. Am I to believe the tale you tell or what my intuition knows? Are you the man I think or not?"

A muscle ticked in his jaw.

"Remaining uninformative as always, I see. I guess we shall just have to find out for ourselves."

Would his honor remain? Was he still intact? Or had he given in to his desires and shamed both their houses? Had he really cast aside the mores they lived by? No one would ever know but the two of them.

She removed the sash, tossing it over a nearby table.

Slowly she glanced down at what she had bared.

"Well. Well. Well." She looked up, meeting his eyes.

He immediately looked away from her, staring at the far wall. Green thought there was a sheen of moisture in his eyes but she could not be sure in the low lighting.

A sudden compassion for him filled her. She knew this was hard for him. Sitting down on the bed next to him, she gently cupped his chin, turning him back to her. "Jorlan, you don't have to— *Who did this to you?*" Her finger traced the bruise on his cheekbone, the only mar on his arresting face. "I will have them removed from the house at once!"

"It is not important." Once again, his thick lashes shielded his emotions from her.

"It is important to me." Her gentle lips carefully swept the discolored area.

Jorlan closed his eyes. That touch always felt like magic to him! *Why?* "Green, do not . . ."

"Do not what?" Her lips moved over his beautiful face, feature by feature, adoring each sculptured line with tiny sips.

Jorlan's heart began a quick beat; his breath came noticeably faster. "No," he whispered.

"Yes," she whispered back, letting her mouth pull across his lips slowly, enticingly.

She nibbled delicately on his bottom lip, then suckled sharply on it.

An out-and-out attack he could withstand. A slow seduction he could not.

She tortured him by teasing him with her mouth. Her lips pressing once, twice, against his. A tiny sweep with the tip of her tongue over his upper lip. The faintest drawing at the edge of his mouth.

He tried to ignore her caresses. He couldn't. In spite of his hostile attitude regarding the accepted taking of a name-bearer, he still desired her. Now he was warring with himself.

As her mouth played over him, her lips teased him into responding back. "Kiss me the way I taught you, my wild one."

And he did.

Without realizing it, his lips responded to hers. Sought hers. Followed hers.

Every nerve, blood vessel, and pulse in his body came alive. The feeling, the indescribable perception, surged through his body. The strength of it staggered him. She had kissed him before and it had been incredible, but not like this.

It was as if his entire body knew that there was going to be more and more and more. *How can I fight this?*

"You can't." Green answered him. He hadn't even realized he had spoken out loud.

"You don't know that." His voice was already roughening with desire.

"I do know it." Her tongue sank into his mouth, slipping deep into the warm, wet channel. He groaned in the back of his throat—half growl, half moan.

"How—how do you know?" Unconsciously, he was kissing her back, his mouth reaching for hers, hot and deep.

"I'll tell you later," she rasped and moved down the strong column of his throat.

He shivered as she laved the skin there, catching a tiny piece of it between her teeth, letting him feel the small sting of a soft bite, before her open mouth slid down the side.

"*Merde!*"

"No swearing in ancient familial tongues," she quipped as she nipped sharply against his collarbone.

Jorlan lifted his head slightly and narrowed his focus on her. "That is not close to swearing. I can show you swearing if you—*Sweet Cybella!*" Her tongue took long, slow laps back and forth across the centerline of his chest as she worked her way down his flat stomach.

His breath was very ragged now.

Green purposely undulated down farther, allowing his member to scrape along the downy skin of her stomach. A sound between death and ecstasy rolled from his lips.

He became rock-hard to bursting and very large.

Her breath came in hot tantalizing puffs very close to his velvety skin. Her mouth almost touched him. Almost.

"What are you doing, Green," he panted raggedly.

"I'm making you mine, Jorlan." Her luscious mouth covered him then, completely. Dewy, warm, slippery. It was the most incredible thing he had ever felt. *Yet.* Then she moaned low in the back of her throat, letting the resultant vibrations skitter along his encased shaft.

Jorlan reared up off the bed, pulling at the tethers, yelling at her to release his bonds at once.

And the man could yell.

Green had never in her life heard such a creative diatribe.

She ignored him, of course, and continued to pleasure him. "Do you know how good you taste, Jorlan?" Her tongue flicked over him just before her mouth slid down the length of him.

"Green, please!" He gritted his teeth, positive he would die of this Tamryn torture.

Again she ignored his plea. "I could taste you and taste you and taste you all night and never tire of it. . . ."

A very loud growl came from him. He threw his head back and clenched his fists, tugging them sharply against the binds.

Green knew he was close to breaking; she had purposely pushed him to this point, past the edge of his control. It would be easier for him this way. His innate passion would overtake his reason, and for now, that was a good thing. His broken moans and hoarse cries—torn from him against his will—were driving her wild as well.

On this night, however, she needed to maintain her focus.

A few droplets of dew moistened her lips. An intoxicating sample. She rubbed her mouth around the sticky fluid, savoring his rich flavor.

With one last pressing lick, she moved up his body. "Taste yourself," she breathed into his mouth. Her lips fed his.

Jorlan cried into her mouth, seizing her lips in a rough, untamed kiss. He became wild for her and all he could think of was having more of her. "Release me from these bonds! Let me up. I will not fight you; you have my word."

Green sighed regretfully. "I cannot, Jorlan. The pain of the breaching will be violent; especially so for you. It is too dangerous."

He closed his eyes and rested his damp forehead against her cheek. "I will control the pain." His incredible lips played expertly against her skin, the inborn passion within him coming to the surface. "Release me, Green. I want to touch you."

She took his compelling face in her palms and stared down at him. "You cannot control this pain. I know that you do not wish to be bound, and I do not wish you to be bound, either. But to do otherwise is too dangerous for the woman. Normally, it is the rule that we are to keep the binds on until after completion. I will not do that. I will release you as soon as the rending is over."

He realized it was the best he was going to get. Still, it was a concession. He nodded curtly at her.

"Good. I'll make it the best I can for you. . . ." She placed her hands on his shoulders and rocked back on him slightly.

Jorlan glanced down their bodies, watching her poised over the tip of him. Her hand cupped his face and she brought his focus back to hers. He gazed at her inquiringly.

"I want to see your face as I breach you. I always want to remember the look in your eyes as you first experience pleasure. I want to remember how you felt at this moment." Her own eyes filled with tears.

Jorlan's mouth parted slightly, stunned that she would treasure this so. She was so experienced, he assumed that it would mean nothing to her except claiming him to her house.

But it meant something to him. It always had.

"Thank you," he whispered. For the first time he looked at her and exposed some of his heart. He scanned every delicate, interesting feature on her face. The very face he had dreamt about since he had been a child of six. Yes, he had remembered her when she had come out to the garden. How could he ever forget?

Upon seeing his unguarded expression, Green's mouth parted in wonder at the heart-stopping radiance emanating from him. He was so enchanting! Why did he hide this part of himself?

Green pressed her mouth to his in a fast kiss. Then she watched his expression as she abruptly lowered herself down on him. Green gasped as his pulsating fullness wholly filled her. The rapid entry was to instantly break his shield in as uniform a way as possible. The pain would be severe but, hopefully, of less endurance.

At first, Jorlan felt nothing but unbelievable pleasure. It was so incredible that he cried out with it. Her warmth and moisture coated him everywhere. He felt as if he had glided into a cushion of slick, pulsing comfort so—

Then it hit.

The first burning wave of agony. It seared the tip of his manhood, spreading throughout the entire head and down the shaft.

"Get off!"

Green shook her head.

He tried to buck her off of him. Green wrapped her thighs around his hips and stayed where she was, firmly seated. His entire body lurched under her. He clenched his teeth as the waves of pain continued to slam him. His body became coated in sweat.

And yet, in the curious phenomenon of the piercing of the veil, with its resultant constricture, his erection did not falter. It was a physiological quirk that puzzled yet delighted women the world over.

Although there was nothing delightful about seeing your namebearer in pain.

Green smoothed his dampened hair off of his forehead. "I know. . . . I know. . . ." She tried to comfort him. "It will be over soon. No one knows why it takes so long, it just does. The membrane must dissolve completely. We have to stay like this until it is complete or you will feel pain the next time."

He opened his eyes and tried to catch his breath. He was very pale. "This—this is horrible! I will die of it!"

Green covered her mouth with her hand to hide her smile. She realized Jorlan had no idea what the fastening was to be like. Most gently reared young men did not. They came to their fastening beds completely mystified.

She was not sure that was a good practice.

"You will not die of it, I assure you. There; see? It's getting better now, isn't it?"

He glared at her mutinously.

"Isn't it?" she repeated.

"Slightly," he reluctantly admitted.

"Mmm-hmm." She rocked very easily on him. He sucked in his breath. His pupils dilated at the sensation.

"No pain?"

"Not too much . . ."

"How about this?" She rotated her hips slowly.

He coughed. "That is . . . not too bad. . . ."

"I don't think we need these anymore, do you?" She reached up and quickly untied his wrists.

"No. We don't need them." Without thinking Jorlan immediately sat up, determined to undo his ankles himself. He stopped when he came face-to-face with Green.

He had slightly pushed her backward on his lap. The angle was different. Much more pressure. Jorlan blinked. "Ah, this is . . . very . . . that is . . ."

Green chuckled and wrapped her arms around his neck, bringing him closer. As she did this, her hips slid and rotated against him.

A puff of air escaped his lips. "I . . . need to . . . untie . . ."

Green drove against him a little harder.

"I mean . . . I . . . to . . . get the . . ." He gave up. Closing his eyes, he simply let the sensations carry him away. His arms wrapped around her tightly, surprising Green a little.

She rocked him with a very definite rhythm now. Hard. Swift. Deep.

"That . . . is . . . so . . ."

Her mouth covered his. He groaned; the sound moved through her throat. Through her body.

"Jorlan," she breathed. "You are so incredibly beautiful. Let me feel you more. . . ."

"How . . . ? Tell me . . ." His mouth caressed along her jawline, his hot breath ragged puffs against the folds of her ear. He trembled in her arms even as he lifted his hips into her thrusts.

"Flex in me," she whispered.

"How so?" He captured her mouth before she could answer, sinking his tongue into the depths.

"Mmm." She broke off from him. "Pull your muscles up . . . inside."

He did. They both moaned.

Green paused, worried that he was hurting. "I'm sorry, did that hurt?"

"*No.*" He was breathing unevenly. He groaned. "I—"

She kissed him. It was too much for the first time. Too much perception all at once for a Sensitive. "Jorlan, come peak with me now. . . ." She began to guide him to that end. Her hand reached down between them, circling the base of him with a steady pressure. She worked her hand up and down on him easily as she moved with him.

Her contractions came first by design. "Now, blaze-dragon. *Now.*"

The rapid pulsations sent him over.

"Green . . . I . . . *Green!*" He poured into her. Endlessly. She continued to release around him, her strong contractions adding to his.

Spent, Green reclined on top of him.

Jorlan tried to catch his breath. He could not. *Never* had he felt anything like that! He opened his eyes languidly. Like a sated outwolf.

Green's auburn hair was draped over him like a coverlet. A rosy flush from her exertions dusted her cheeks. Her skin was incredibly soft against his sensitized body. She was so pretty.

Many different emotions tumbled through him. She truly was his name-giver now.

He was not happy with what had occurred—

Yet he was not altogether unhappy with it, either.

One thing was certain.

He still ached for the feel of Green Tamryn.

Chapter Eight

ilken lips played pleasingly with the muscular ridges of his
abdomen.

Jorlan's eyes drifted shut as Green lazily teased him with her mouth.
Her loving little caresses and nips seemed to him especially nice.

The action showed an honest caring. The Marquelle had gotten
what she wanted from him, she did not have to make him feel treasured
into the bargain. He supposed he appreciated that, even though he was
nowhere near to accepting his circumstances.

All in all, it could have been worse.

Much worse.

She could have taken him without any regard for his feelings or
inexperience.

She hadn't done that.

He wondered why. Most Lordenes would have.

From what he had heard, they cared only about their own pleasure.
Some of them actually believed that the man should have as little

pleasure as was possible. Men often spoke of the rending of the veil as something best not thought about. It was generally dreaded. Yet she had taken her time to give him as much enjoyment as she could.

The part of Jorlan that was acute to reactions of the flesh acknowledged her kindness.

The part of him that railed against being in this position in the first place, he temporarily suppressed. He knew he was going to have to reassess the path he took in view of what had transpired. He could not lie to himself. He wanted her. Admittedly, he was captivated by Green Tamryn.

In all ways. His brow furrowed.

This was something he was going to have to work through. He could never forswear his ultimate goal of personal freedom and equality of choice. Men were human beings who had every right to control their own lives and property! Tomorrow would be time enough for him to regroup and formulate a new plan in that direction.

There was something intrinsically wrong with the synergy in One-Nation. It was something he sensed but could not thoroughly define.

For the time being, it probably wouldn't hurt him any to wholly enjoy this new experience.

And he was enjoying it.

Too much.

Every time her fingers stroked him, he shivered. When she stopped, he felt bereft of her touch. She was like an arc storm to his senses— bright, thrilling, intoxicating. And he *burned* to touch her everywhere. She had not allowed him to do so yet, but he vowed he would.

At that moment he was so deliciously languid, so perfectly spent, that he did not care what she did to him—as long as she kept doing it. In light of that, perhaps it would be wise of him to take some time to explore this unique relationship with her.

His thoughts drifted lazily with her ministrations.

His veil was gone. He wondered if he would seem different. He wondered why men had to go through such an ordeal the first time.

"They say that women might once have had veils . . ." he murmured drowsily.

Green smiled softly against his ribs. There was something about seeing the rebellious Jorlan dreamily sated that was highly satisfying.

"Do you believe that could have happened, Green?"

"I think it is a story that servant men tell at night in the sleep houses to hoodwink mischievous little boys who are eavesdropping on them," she chortled.

Eyes still closed, Jorlan grinned broadly, showing white teeth and dimples. "How did you know that?"

"It seems exactly like the kind of thing you would have done. You were a very precocious child."

"Really?"

"Very much so. I seem to remember the Duchene telling me that you were forever getting into mischief."

"You must have me confused with someone else."

"Ah, yes, that other Jorlan Reynard."

He laughed.

Green loved his laugh. It was so complete. Unlike the other comeouts who snickered genteelly at anything a damselle said that might be interpreted (with a huge measuring cylinder) as witty; Jorlan's laugh was outright and textured. The kind of laugh that made one want to join in.

It was a shame he did not do it often. Green vowed she would get that laugh out of him at every opportunity.

Her hair tickled his thighs. He lifted his head. "What are you about down there?"

She smiled against his curls. "Should I show you or tell you?"

The edges of his lips curled up. He rested his head back on the pillow, folding his hands behind his head in a waiting posture.

Green chuckled. "I see."

"What?" he drawled. "I am merely resting. Which as you know I need after the ordeal you have put me through."

"You're right. You do need to rest." She stopped her ministrations and scampered up the length of him.

His face fell. "I was teasing." He paused. "You need not stop, Green."

"Yes, I do. You are sore and raw. It would not be right of me to continue."

"I'm fine, I assure you. Do not stop on my account," he offered graciously.

Green gave him a look.

"And what brought about this change of attitude?" She rested her chin on his chest, waiting.

He stared at her, realizing what he had just admitted. Not only had he liked what she had done to him, he liked *how* she had done it. In fact, he was hungry for more. Even so, he wasn't ready to admit that. Especially since she had bid for him against his will. He was not going to get over that so easily.

"Hmm? I didn't hear you."

He fumed. "I think you heard me very clearly awhile ago."

"Yes, the entire estate and probably half the countryside heard you, my wild one." Her finger played with his nipple, circling and rubbing. "I liked it."

He narrowed his eyes at her. "I was not referring to that." He paused. "I don't think half the countryside heard me."

"You may be correct."

He gave her a cautious look, waiting for the other boot to drop.

She obliged. "No doubt the *entire* countryside heard you."

He snorted. "You mistake your own yells." The look he gave her was so engagingly sweet that Green felt her heart warm.

"Tomorrow, I'll make sure they hear you all the way to Capitol Town."

He sucked in his breath. "You think you could do that?"

"Oh, yes." She pressed her lips to his in a deep kiss. This rare part of him was so sweetly artless. She realized that he had become vulnerable with their lovemaking. It surprised and moved her.

"Mmm," Jorlan breathed into her mouth. "I like your kisses, Green; I always have."

"I know." She slipped her tongue inside, tasting him.

Jorlan's pulse speeded up. "That does not mean I am any less disposed to this situation."

"I know." She suckled on the tip of his tongue.

Jorlan hardened instantly. "You know, I am not that sore, Green . . . ," he assured her again. Just in case.

She pulled back. "You are more sore than you think, and if we continue in that way, you will be very uncomfortable tomorrow."

"Perhaps I will endure this soreness if—"

She placed her hand over his lips. "There are other ways. I will show you."

His pupils flared. "More than what we have done?"

"Oh, much more." She grinned.

"What ways?" He laved her fingers, letting his tongue curve around and between. "Tell me."

"Tell you?"

"Show me," he mouthed.

She rolled off him and left the bed, heading for the bathing chamber.

"Is this something we are to do apart?" he joked, calling after her.

She laughed. "Nooo. I am getting a basin of water."

A basin of water? His agile mind played with the possibilities. What could his name-giver do with that?

She returned, carrying the water bowl and some cloths.

He looked at her skeptically. "What do you do with those?"

She chuckled. "Well, nothing too serious. We need to clean you off, blaze-dragon. There is always blood the first time."

He hadn't realized that. He glanced down, seeing the smears streaking the length of his manhood.

He paled. "I did not realize."

"No, of course you didn't. Men are worried enough about the fastening. There is no sense in scaring someone silly with talk of blood." She carefully dabbed the smears with the water-soaked cloth. The cool liquid felt good on him. Her soothing care felt better. She was being very thoughtful. Again, he realized most name-givers would not be so.

"Will the bleeding continue?"

"No. It is from the membrane. Once it is ruptured, it is over." She finished cleaning him up. "There; good as new."

"Maybe better," he drawled. "Thank you, that was . . . kind of you."

She looked at him surprised. "You are my name-bearer, Jorlan. I will always take care of you."

He was not happy with her response. "I see."

"I doubt you do, but I hope you will in time."

"Green?"

"Yes?" She placed the bowl with its pink-stained water on the table beside the bed.

"What did you mean earlier when you said it would be more painful for me than others? Why did you say that?"

Green walked back to the bed and sat down on the edge. She took his hand in her own. "Jorlan, have you never noticed anything different about yourself?"

His brow furrowed. A sudden angry expression clouded his features. "I have told you—I am not a Santorini."

She was not sure about that, but decided to let that go for now. "Perhaps, but I am speaking of something else."

"What?"

"The way you respond to touch, for instance. . . ."

"Not all touch." He gazed at her. "You do not have to tell me I am acutely susceptible to your touch; I have already learned this."

Green paused. He had just admitted something to her that he was not even aware of. He was not just affected by her touch, he was *susceptible* to it. She put the revelation away to contemplate later, when she was alone.

"What?" He watched her carefully.

She took a deep breath. "I believe you are a Sensitive."

"A Sensitive. You have mentioned this before. What, pray tell, is that?"

"We're not sure, exactly . . ." she hedged.

He waited. Silently, patiently. In control. The very qualities that many had observed in lyrical exposition about Forus. The enigmatically beautiful moon they lived on had often been cited as having mystical, arcane depths. The methodologists had indulgently agreed—in the poetical sense only.

Green wondered. It struck her that Jorlan was a strange combination of naïveté and ancient wisdom. In certain practical matters of life, he seemed to have little or no knowledge; yet in deeper things, he seemed to have an abiding intuition, an almost uncanny sense of the collective consciousness. He reflected attitudes beyond his years.

There was true, innate strength within him. She was not sure if he recognized it—or, was well aware of it yet hid it from others.

"There have been very few Sensitives that we've known of to study."

His expression froze at that and she reassessed her earlier supposition. *He knows something is different about him. He protects himself.*

She cleared her throat. "We do not know why, but on rare occasions a male is born who seems to have certain extrasensory abilities."

"What are these abilities?"

She shrugged. "They appear to be completely different for each individual. One was seen to have a preknowledge of the coming of arc storms. . . ." She watched him carefully. No hint of expression crossed his features to give away his thoughts.

"Another," she continued, "knew where the underground rivers flowed across the desert plains to the west."

"These seem like very innocuous abilities, as you call them. Why the interest?"

"Regardless of their particular areas of strength, there are three attributes all Sensitives seem to have in common. One is a superlative receptive ability with anything involving aesthetic perception."

His eyelash flickered.

"They also have an elusive beauty about them."

"So?"

"So this makes them a very rare and sought out—you'll excuse the expression—commodity by the Top Slice. Such males have urgent, profound desires; they are entwined with all things sensual. Once introduced to pleasures of the flesh, they become master and slave to passion at the same time. In short, they are phenomenal lovers."

A strange smile played about his lips. "And you think I am like this?" He laughed softly.

Green arched her brow. "I think you have the capacity for this, yes."

A flash of white teeth showed her what he thought of that. "I'm not sure whether I should be flattered or not."

"It is not about feeling flattered. It is about what is. Your bed price would have been enormous, if it was believed you were a Sensitive. I might not have been able to afford you."

His face darkened.

"Sensitives from aristocratic families are seldom seen. Ironic, isn't it—if you thought to hide this attribute to prevent the bidding. You probably would not be here right now. In all likelihood, you would have gone to the House of a Duchene instead."

"I was already in the House of a Duchene."

Green viewed him thoughtfully. He wasn't as opposed to this fastening as he would have everyone believe. She wondered if Jorlan was more opposed to the concept of the fastening itself rather than the idea of being with her. He had more than enjoyed the coupling. "Yes, you were."

He rubbed his lower lip with his forefinger. "What was the other trait you spoke of regarding these Sensitives?"

"They all have a strange connection to Forus. It almost appears transcendental, really; it is not well understood."

"How is this transcendence displayed?" He sat up in bed and rested back against the twining columns of sheensui bark that made up the crafted piece. The sheensui had been twisted and formed around the bed. Over the years, it slowly continued to grow, taking its moisture directly from the air. Eventually, the columns would bend and meet, forming a lovely latticed arch over the bed; a cocoonlike haven for its occupants.

"We've only observed fragments. Their ambient mood cycle mirrors the path of the moon around Arkeus. Intense introspection at apogee, illuminating insight at perigee."

"Perhaps it is coincidence."

"No, it is more. The observations have been too profound. There are some methodologists who have gone so far as to say that Forus seems to *respond* to these people in some arcane—"

Jorlan snorted.

"I know it sounds absurd, but I tell you the phenomena have been observed on more than one occasion—and with different Sensitives. The methodologists have no explanation for it."

"And you think this describes me? A deviant who enigmatically resonates with the spirit of Forus moon?" He laughed hollowly.

Green gazed at him sharply. She hadn't said anything about the "spirit" of Forus. "What I think is that if there existed a Sensitive of strong attributes, who was also powerfully *linked* in some way to Forus, he would do his best to hide it. After all, he would be constantly walking a dangerous line."

Jorlan's lids lowered. Aqua sparks glinted between black lashes. "Perhaps you simply wish to think you got an exceptionally good bargain for the bed price, Marquelle."

"Perhaps. Time will tell."

"And if you are correct in your assumptions—what then?"

Green toyed with the edge of the coverlet. "If such a person were also of strong temperament, then it could be argued that he could be a threat to our way of life."

"Would you see it that way?"

"No. Such a person would need a strong name-giver to temper his rash emotions while guiding his strength to its full potential."

"Are you such a person, Green?" He spoke softly.

It was as close as he would come to revealing himself and she knew it. "I am such a person, Jorlan. But, regardless of what may or may not be, know this: I will allow you freedom here on the grounds of my estate, where you may explore your own thoughts. However, I expect you to behave civilly and always to respect the traditions of the House to which you now belong."

His nostrils flared; he hated to be hemmed in by these foolish rules of society! *Hated it.* "How could I not keep your blessed traditions?" he snapped.

"Jorlan," she said in warning.

He folded his arms across his chest and gazed up at the interlocking branches above. "How like these sheensui we are, Green. Entwined by another hand, we now grow inexorably together. What final pattern will we make?"

"What, indeed, Jorlan."

It did not escape her that he had neither committed to the rules set before him nor admitted to anything of a more personal nature. He was a shrewd, astute debater, better than many so-called masters on the floor of the Septibunal.

A tiny smile graced his face, an acknowledgment of her own cleverness. He interlaced his fingers and stretched his muscular arms out. "So, name-giver, what were these 'other' ways you spoke of? To experience pleasure differently?"

"Didn't forget that, did you?" She gave him a wise look.

"I simply am curious to seek knowledge." He attempted to appear innocent.

"Of course."

His eyes gleamed with amusement. "Show me how it is we can achieve pleasure 'other ways,' " he whispered, "or I will forever doubt that such a thing is possible and—"

He lost his voice because Green's mouth was already showing him and had come very close to his oversensitized manhood in the process.

He could feel the heat of her breath on him. Moist and searing.

All she did was breathe over him, yet to that tender skin it became so much more. Hot streams of air embraced him like a sultry breeze, stimulating the responsive tissue. *Like Forus breath . . .*

Jorlan closed his eyes; his private vision one of connection and continuity with cycles of rotation and life.

Then she suddenly blew on him, cool, moist puffs that contrasted sharply to the steamy heat. Uninhibitedly, he moaned as his responding arousal invigorated every pleasure center in his body. Shivers coursed through him. "You can do this to me without physical touch," he rasped. "How is it so?"

"You are a Sensitive, Jorlan. Your ability to feel is not rooted simply in the tactile perception, it is more, deeper. This pleasure I will give you will awaken many responses."

"I am not what you think," he groaned hoarsely, already losing himself in the erotic stimulation.

She ignored his denial, paying more attention to his response. "This will not irritate the tender area, for there will be no handling or rubbing."

He was surprised. "You think to bring me to release without touch there?" His breathing deepened, thickened.

"Yes." She pressed her soft mouth to his groin, kissing and laving him everywhere but where he most wanted to feel her lips. As expected, his response was stellar. The low sounds rolling from deep within his throat told her what she needed to know. Jorlan was giving himself over to the passion.

She slid up the side of his body, her warmed skin like the finest, supplest coverlet over him. Jorlan's entire body shook with his awareness. He lifted his head to kiss her. She pulled back, lifting her breast for him, sweeping it against his mouth in invitation.

His pupils blazed with desire and he quickly took her into his mouth, suckling greedily on the sweet, hardened tip.

He was an adept novitiate. Soon his drawing actions changed, became subtler, his tongue flicked over the hardened peak, he let it skim over his face, his eyes, and to his lips again. It was as if he had delved into the sensation and lost himself in it.

And by his wanton actions, he was drawing her right along with him.

Now it was Green who cried out in pleasure.

She ran her hands through his hair, feeling the soft strands slide between her fingers. Never had she experienced such an exquisite sense of response!

He called out, a low, rumbling ache of sound that vibrated to her toes. The outcry was so erotic, so sensualistic, that she cried out with him.

"You taste intricate, Green. Like the variations in a Ramagi web. . . ." Imitating her earlier actions, he pulled back to gently blow a stream of cool air over the protruding, moistened tip. Green trembled in his arms.

He glanced up at her through his lashes and smiled slightly. A combination of age-old knowledge and new delight.

Emboldened, he breathed hotly over the same spot, making her sigh his name.

That was when Jorlan discovered three very important things. He discovered that he loved provoking this response from her; he loved watching her as he showed her *his* response; and he loved the sense of power all of it made him feel.

In that moment, Jorlan Reynard broke free of a thousand years of male sexual conditioning.

He became the aggressor.

Shocking her, he wrapped his arms tightly about her waist, bringing her down on top of him on the bed so that they were flush against each other. His fingers skimmed along her sides, brushing back and forth, up and down as his mouth once more laved her breasts. Taking the tip and a good portion of the plump breast into his mouth, he drew heavily upon the globe. He experimented by flicking his tongue across the swollen peak. And then his teeth.

Her moaning reaction was all he needed. He feasted on her then. Showing no mercy, he laved and flicked and suckled and bit. His hands cupped her under her arms, easily lifting her higher so his mouth could find better access to her chest, the underside of her breasts, the satiny plane of her torso.

"*Jorlan*," Green gasped, placing her palms on his shoulders. She tried to think, but it was impossible! A familiar dizziness assailed her. Something about what he was doing was . . .

She blinked. He said she was as intricate a Ramagi web, but he was spinning it! "You—!"

He quickly interrupted to shift her focus. "Do you not like what I am doing, name-bearer?" His teeth captured the tiny bud in an abrasive graze. He tugged sharply, slowly letting the firm tip slip from his grasp.

She lost her breath completely and tried to wiggle away from him.

He held her fast.

He discovered his revenge. He rediscovered his capture. In a sense he felt as if his true shield had been broken, and with it, he felt himself come alive. It was strange yet wondrous. Powerful yet humbling.

For he was neither hunter nor prey yet both at the same time. She had pierced him, but he thought he just might have the ability to *shatter* her.

Sexually, at any rate.

Jorlan came to the revelation that what he had initially viewed as his surrender may in fact become his release.

In this one area, at least, he would find his equality with her.

He would demand it.

But not verbally. Physically.

Green sighed over him, her breaths coming in tiny shivery gasps.

Jorlan's mouth opened over the plane above her stomach and drew on the skin there.

She quivered against him, lost. "Ohhh . . . Jorlan, I think we—"

"*Mmmmmmmm.*" He rolled the sound, letting the vibration slice through her. He could feel her dampness against his chest now. She was excited for him. She wanted him, he knew.

Oddly, the idea of that made him groan. He swelled even more and felt himself begin to throb against the downy softness of her legs.

While he did this, his fingers slid into her auburn curls, tangling in the short strands that wrapped around his fingers. Tugging gently, he immediately felt more of her dew; it covered his hand. Just the feel of that hot, slick substance made him tremble.

Suddenly, he wanted to feel the velvet channel hidden between her nether lips. So he slid his fingers between her folds. He had never felt anything so perfect; so wonderful! It reminded him of the hameeri flower, whose soft pink petals shielded a honeylike bud; its sweet nectar so highly sought after.

Her scent covered him along with the dew and was just as sweet. It almost made him wild.

Without thought, he slipped his long middle finger inside, going deep into the passage. Her muscular walls surrounded him with tiny contractions. Her body trembled and he thought he felt a small bite behind his shoulder. His lips curled at that. *You like that, do you, name-giver? Perhaps you will like this even more. . . .*

He stroked inside her, long, deep, even thrusts that mimicked what she had done before. He watched her eyelids flutter shut. Then he stopped being aware of what he was doing and simply reacted, giving over to something deep and elemental inside him. An instinct unmined until that moment.

He did not even stop to wonder how she would react to what he was about to do.

He just did it.

He moved her up on him to just the right place.

Green's eyes shot open. "What are you . . . ! *Sweet Cybella!*" His mouth covered her and that was the last rational thought that Green was to remember.

Jorlan's tongue delved between her folds, flicking and sampling, sending her already inflamed pulses to the sky. Intuitively, he knew exactly what would give her the most enjoyment, where to press, when to suckle.

The first time his tongue found that extrasensitive hidden spot, Green reared back from him. Jorlan knew the pleasure was so intense it was almost pain for her. His palm planted flat against her rounded buttocks and pushed her firmly against him. His other hand reached between her legs and squeezed the folds of her lips tighter against his mouth and tongue as he stroked the delicate tissue, flicking the spot he had discovered, over and over—until he knew she couldn't stand it anymore.

Her soft mews were exciting him beyond his own rational thought.

Jorlan did not seem to know where he was or who he was or what he was doing. With a raw growl, he gave himself over to this new, enticing sense. The heady taste of her intoxicated him and all he wanted to do was scrape his tongue inside her. It was a shocking idea, but once it entered his head, he knew he was going to do it. Wanted to do it. *Had* to do it.

He dipped inside her. Carefully at first, absorbing the sense of her.

Green sobbed, clutching his strong shoulders. Shocked senseless, she tried to wiggle free of him.

His response was to sink his tongue in her as far as he could go. He began stroking her. . . .

Green started screaming. She did not even recognize the sounds she was uttering.

Then he did the unthinkable.

He withdrew from her, spread her lips with his fingers and blew coolly. Right on the hidden spot he had discovered.

"*Arc-it!* Stop this, Jorlan! You're killing me!"

His tongue flicked rapidly against the now throbbing spot, sending her higher. She spasmed repeatedly against his lips, choking and sobbing and moaning his name.

He did not stop.

Jorlan felt her contractions and felt himself respond. The pulses resonated through his body, gaining as hers did, matching them in strength and frequency. When she screamed her release, he roared his but a few seconds later.

Green collapsed over him.

Jorlan took deep breaths, trying to regain his equilibrium. *What had happened to him?* He had set out to show her something about himself. He had ended up falling prey to his own revelation. That worried him. He could still smell the scent of her; it was all over him now and he knew in his heart it would always be over him.

He sighed against her, even now loving the texture of her rubbing against his face.

Green slid down the length of him until his lips pressed into her throat.

She circled her arms around his head, burrowing her face into his hair. Her warm breaths teased him as she tried to regain her normal breathing.

"Are you all right, Green?" he drawled huskily. His hand idly stroked her back, simply enjoying the sensation of touching her. The gesture was somewhat possessive.

She shook her head, still stunned by his actions. "Men are not generally so aggressive," she panted unevenly.

"You did not seem to object to it, as I recall."

She laughed softly. "Oh, I objected all right, you simply chose to ignore it."

He nipped the side of her jaw playfully. "I know." He grinned, nibbling on her cheek.

"Mmm. I probably should caution you—"

"It won't do any good," he revealed truthfully.

"Probably not." She smiled sleepily. "And right now I am too tired to instruct you on proper deportment."

He laughed. "If you were interested in proper deportment, you would not have taken me as your name-bearer."

"Got that figured out, *hmm*?" She yawned and began to drift off.

"Yes, I have that figured out," he whispered.

Green mumbled something incoherent, falling into a deep slumber on top of him.

"Among other things," he murmured enigmatically.

The only response was a gentle snuffle.

Jorlan drifted off to sleep, having no idea that he had flaunted every convention of society on his first fastening night.

The next morning, Green would begin to have concerns about the wild side of his nature.

Chapter Nine

*J*orlan awoke perfectly.

He felt a complete warmth nestled in the soft coverlet. An unbelievable sense of comfort pervaded every cell in his body and he couldn't recall ever waking up feeling this wonderful.

His eyes still hadn't opened, but a small, satisfied smirk curved his firm lips. Residual aftereffect of being well used and well pleasured.

Green.

His name-giver had cuddled into him as they slept. She had held him to her all night. Again, making him feel cherished and not simply a commodity for her bed.

Once he had awakened to her kissing his throat while she slept, her hands skimming down his sleep-warmed sides. He had whispered something to her then—he had no idea what—and she had whispered something back.

He thought she might have murmured, "I know . . . ," but he couldn't really be sure. She had fallen back asleep then.

He had, too.

Jorlan stretched languidly on the silken sheets. He was enticingly erect; it seemed he had been so all night. The slight scrape of Ramagi cloth against his swollen member was sheer torture.

His thoughts went to the previous night.

The experience had been incredible to him. Utterly overwhelming. Surely, he would not have experienced this with anyone else. He remembered Green's tiny cries, her deep-throated moans. The beguiling sounds made him want her more and more. The feel of her and then the *taste* of her . . .

With a low groan he turned onto his side. If he rubbed against her as if he were still asleep, maybe she would turn to him and—

His hand stretched out across the sheet as if by accident.

The place was empty.

He blinked and opened his eyes.

She must have already gotten up. He scowled, strangely hurt that she hadn't stayed with him.

He glanced down his length and scowled again.

This was the horrible affliction his training master had warned him about when he was being disciplined for the fastening bed. His master said that the frequency of the dilemma would increase with use, yet the more relief he was given, the more he would probably desire the affliction.

He said it was called Male Tragedy Paradox.

Jorlan sighed mournfully.

All he had to do was think Green's name, hear her voice, remember her touch and MTP assailed him. He inhaled deeply, beginning the grounding meditation of the Gle Kiang-ten. Few could master the technique, but it had always come naturally to him. The discipline emptied the mind and channeled his root energy back into Forus.

Just as he was reaching total calm, the door to the chamber burst open.

"Up at last, are you? And its about time, too!" An elderly woman with a slightly maniacal look about her bustled into the room carrying a tray laden with food. She was followed by another woman, also somewhat elderly but with a more solemn look to her.

"Now don't be getting use to this! The Lordene had this sent up to you today. Said she wanted to be sure you awoke to a hearty meal. She'll be spoiling you if you ask me!"

Jorlan sat up in bed. The sheet fell to his waist. With his disheveled hair and sleepy-eyed look, the new Marqueller was quite a sight to behold against all that Ramagi silk. Both women gawked.

"Who is asking you?" he drawled, smiling slowly. He ached all over but he had never felt so *good* inside!

Avatar snorted. Down in the Southern Regions, where she was from, it never hurt for a man to have a bit of the juice in his belly—especially between the sheets.

"Troublesome snap-branch! None of your rut-bid, now." Mathers plopped the tray squarely on his lap.

Jorlan tried not to wince.

"And in case you forgot, I'm Mathers and this here is Avatar. I'm the Marquelle's majordoma." She puffed up her sagging chest to a formidable display. "I don't normally deliver dining trays so don't get any fancy notions!"

As if he would dare.

Jorlan viewed the tempting tray. It was laden with all manner of delicacies from snogglehound pudding (which wasn't really made of snogglehounds, the beasts just had a fondness for it) to baked lumpies. His favorite morning hukka biscuit was there and a small pot of Dreamtree jam. A little pitcher of cool fuzzle-muzzle cream sat beside a hot pot of sunpod tea. Someone had thoughtfully placed a magnificent aqua roseyal bloom in a bud vase for him.

"Yes, it was herself." Mathers gleefully informed him. "The Marquelle seems to have developed a fondness for that green-blue color these days. Must have pleased her well and good."

"My Lordene couldn't stop smiling and humming silly tunes this morning." Avatar added, a knowing leer on her face.

Jorlan's cheekbones bronzed.

Both woman laughed uproariously.

He gave them an odd look. He wasn't sure what they found so humorous, but it was obvious that they adored the Marquelle. She was rather adorable, he supposed. Especially when she viewed him with that forbearing, exasperated expression. He grinned at the memory of it. Yes, sometimes he enjoyed putting that look on the Marquelle's face. Of course, sometimes he didn't intend to—it just happened.

"He's smitten," Mathers whispered loudly behind her hand to the other woman.

"And why shouldn't he be? He got the best name-giver in all of OneNation! Go on, then, lad, eat." The one called Avatar motioned to him.

"You must be famished, eh?" Mathers elbowed Avatar in the side with a leering wink.

A dimple curved into Jorlan's cheek.

They all laughed.

Jorlan dived into the food, devouring it with a hearty appetite. The two woman just stood there staring at him. Midway between a spoonful of lumpies, he paused in question. "Why are you two staring at me like that?"

The women seemed uncomfortable then.

Avatar cleared her throat; Mathers pulled out a white rag from her back pocket and began sweeping at nonexistent lint on the nearby tabletop.

Jorlan arched his brow. "Well?"

"Beggin' your pardon, Marqueller, it's just that we've never seen anyone as beautiful as you up close and bare as a side of tasteslikerooster."

Avatar elbowed her sharply in the side.

She coughed. "Beneath the coverlet, that is. Cybella help us, but we're women! We've got imaginations, you know."

His mouth parted in shock. What was he to say to that? "Oh."

He quickly went back to polishing off his tray, doing his best to ignore the goggling servants. Was it going to be like this every day? He didn't think he was going like being stared at as if he were a ripe balum fruit.

"Ah, did Green, I mean, the Marquelle, have her morning meal yet?"

"Oh, lad, she's been up for ages!" Avatar waved her hand. "It's past the midday."

"Is it?" He glanced out the window, surprised to see the high angle of the sun along with the rising Arkeus. He had never lost sense of the day before. He chocked it off to his extraordinary, sensual night. Somehow it must have impaired his internal cadence.

"Mathers will draw you a fresh bubble-pool and lay out some clothes for you. The Marquelle apologizes for not having a personal man for you yet. Would you like Opper to come and assist you again?"

Jorlan's lips firmed. "No."

"I don't blame you," Avatar concurred. "He is something of a nog-twist."

"Snip-butt," Jorlan and Mathers simultaneously intoned under their breaths.

Surprised, they grinned at each other.

"You'll do, lad." Mathers gave her stamp of approval. "I can see you're a man who likes to get creative with the language—just like old Mathers."

Avatar harrumphed. "Don't be teaching him any of your foul-tongue ways, Mathers. He's a gently reared lad. The Marquelle will have your head."

Jorlan and Mathers beamed at each other. One promising, one daring.

Avatar rolled her eyes. "When you're finished we'll take the tray. The Marquelle is waiting for you out by the coops at the rear of the house. I think she has a surprise for you." She winked at him.

"A surprise?" He was not sure he liked surprises. He had enough of surprises these past few weeks. His eyes narrowed suspiciously. "What kind of a surprise?"

"Ooo, look at that expression of distrust in his face! It's a beautiful thing, isn't it?" Mathers crowed.

Avatar frowned at her. "You'll find our Mathers has a strange sense of the world. We all suggest you don't adopt it. As for the surprise, you'll find out soon enough—that's what a surprise is, in case you don't know." With that she took the tray from his lap, hooked Mathers's elbow, and dragged her out of the room.

At the door, Mathers turned around to give Jorlan the "ain't she a tight one" hand sign: thumb and index finger joined in a circle with the three middle fingers fisted downward.

Jorlan chuckled huskily as they closed the door.

He shook his head. They were quite different from his grandmother's servants. Although he liked Billings well enough, the woman was stuffy and straitlaced. She was an absolute tyrant about protocol, and as majordoma she had run the house with an "atomically calibrated" precision.

This entire household was very different from the Duchene's.

Still, he was shocked to feel a sudden, deep pang of homesickness.

He shrugged it off, refusing to acknowledge it. Life in the Duchene's house had not been easy for him. While his grandmother had treated him with the utmost love and devotion, due to her high position in society and his eligibility to the Slice, she was generally forced to hide him from view until he came of bid age.

Jorlan's extraordinary looks and position made him vulnerable to every swagger looking to improve her station. The Duchene could not take the risk that a woman would try to coerce or lure him to impropriety. So, he had been forced to lead a secluded life.

Well, that portion of his life was over now. He was a fastened man.

Jorlan wondered for the first time what freedoms would come with his new status. Surely more than he had enjoyed in the past?

Exhaling, he threw off the coverlet and padded nude across the carpet. He stood in front of a large, ornate mirastone on the far wall of the bed chamber. His gaze scanned the length of his naked body.

Except for the loss of his veil, he didn't look any different. At least, not to his eyes. Would women be able to look at him and *know* that he was no longer a veil?

Somehow, he thought they might.

*J*orlan strolled around the balum hedges by the front of the coops.

The bushes were adorned with the tiny infamous fruits that made their way onto almost every table of the Select Quarter. The oval-shaped, sweet balums were believed to endow one with prolonged physical stamina. The Slice was mad for them.

As he passed by the thick row of plantings he snapped a ripe fruit off one of the branches.

Green turned at the sound and grinned. "Do you really think you need that?"

He smiled, shaking a finger at her. "It's not for me." He picked up her hand and playfully deposited the fruit in her palm.

"Oh, you think I'm going to need it?"

His eyes flashed with a wicked gleam.

She laughed. "In your dreams. You have a ways to go to keep up with me, my fine name-bearer." Standing on tiptoe she placed the sweet balum in his mouth.

Jorlan swiftly captured her fingers, sucking on each one before he would let her pull her hand back.

"But you've made an excellent start," she breathed somewhat raggedly, moved by the stimulating act.

His arm swiftly came round her, shocking her. "I am willing to make an even better ending. . . ." His lips lowered to hers.

Green placed her hands on his chest to forestall his action. She looked uncomfortably around the yard.

Fortunately, no one from the Slice was present to observe his untoward behavior. "Jorlan, what are you thinking? It is not seemly for a male to make such blatant overtures."

Jorlan flushed and pulled back from her. By his expression, Green could see he was hurt. The last thing she wanted to do was stifle his budding sensuality. He was just beginning to open to her.

Chum-off to the Slice! She liked him the way he was—as long as he didn't take this too far. Green placed her arm around his neck and pulled him down to her. "Personally I find it quite charming." She lightly kissed his mouth.

Jorlan hesitated but gave over to the kiss, if a bit reluctantly at first. Green felt his lips tremble under hers and knew he was having a hard time holding back. One part of her was delighted that he was so taken with her.

The saner part of her was worried.

His unrestrained responses of the previous evening had shaken her. Without any prior sexual experience, he had lost himself in a pleasure-seeking act of unbridled eroticism.

Not for the first time she wondered what complications would arise due to the fact that he was a Sensitive. And not just any Sensitive. Jorlan coupled the trait with an almost reckless disregard for decorum. The combination was dangerous.

He definitely needed her to guide him. That was certain.

And she needed him for the fire he brought to her life.

Last night had proven that for both of them.

"You were wonderful last night, you know. I thank you for such a beautiful and meaningful gift, Jorlan."

"It is I who must thank you, Green. Despite my initial reluctance, the experience was more than I had ever thought. I am sure it was due to your kind patience and expert tutelage. You made it memorable for me."

She smiled warmly at him. "Then I am forgiven for fastening you?"

His expression hardened. "No. But since it is done, and there is naught to be done about it, I will try to make the best of the circumstances."

He saw by her crestfallen face that there was no sense in trying to deny the obvious. He was just causing her unnecessary distress.

Unsettled, he ran his hand through his hair. She deserved more from him. He gave it to her. "In truth, I enjoy your touch—as you well know."

It was not what Green had hoped for; however, considering how he had been only yesterday, it was a vast improvement.

"We can explore more of that 'touch' later, if you like," she punned. Touch was a popular slang term, referring to torrid sex.

His dimples showed. "I would like that very much, but . . ."

"But what?"

"Need we wait for later?" He viewed her through that thick fringe of black lashes.

He was not going to step down on his attitude. Somehow, she knew he wouldn't. Somehow, she liked that.

"Not too much later," she promised him. "Meantime, I have something for you."

"Yes, so Avatar said. What is it?"

Green called out to the coophands. Two young women led a very frisky Klee out of the building. The energetic animal almost broke rein several times as they tried to bring it forward.

A huge grin spread across Jorlan's face. "*Sabir!*"

At the sound of Jorlan's voice, the buoyant Klee paused in his bucking. He prawked a loud greeting. Then he rushed pell-mell toward his master, dragging the poor coophands behind him.

Jorlan heartily embraced the Klee around the neck. Sabir bleated in ecstasy.

Behind her, Green heard a suspicious *pharunk!*

She turned and saw Kibbee watching the whole scene. Disgust was evident in every flesh-fold of her neck. She turned her back, showing the Klee her raised Kloo backside and dismissively fluttered off. But only after she made another terribly rude noise.

For some reason, Kloo and Klee often got into what appeared to be competitive mock battles for human attention. Strangely enough, the trait was mirrored by humans, who were vehemently divided into either Kloo or Klee camps.

Jorlan grinned at her as he patted Sabir's neck. "Thank you for bringing him to me, Green. I think your Kloo is jealous, and well she should be." Sabir trilled a happy agreement.

Green put her hands on her hips. No one insulted Kibbee! "Oh, really. I wonder if you would be saying that during an arc storm when this fine fellow left you to roast!"

"If he did such a thing, I would deserve it, for I would not have the ability to ride him and I would be endangering us both. But that is not the case. Sabir knows he can race the arcs with me if he wishes. He knows I will stay with him all the way."

"*Race the arcs?*" Her face showed her confusion. "What do you mean?"

Sabir bleated. A shutter came over Jorlan. He shrugged. "A figure of speech. Klee are not the undependable mounts that people make them out to be. The problem is most do not know how to ride them—they only think they do."

"Most name-givers would not see it that way, they would not allow you to ride one. At least not until they have had their heir from you," she quipped.

Jorlan snorted. "Sabir and I understand each other, don't we?"

Sabir prawked.

"But you, my name-giver, cannot ride a Klee." Jorlan grabbed the reins in his hand and expertly slung himself up onto Sabir's back. The Klee pranced playfully.

Green's jaw dropped. "Who says I can't ride one?"

Jorlan bent over the pommel. "I do," he whispered provocatively.

"*You* do! You can't be—"

"In any case," he interrupted her, "you don't have to worry about an heir just yet, Green, for I have no intention of giving you one."

"*What?*" Green was staggered. "What do you mean?"

But Jorlan was already racing out of the yard and into the Tamryn hills. The way man and beast moved over the terrain it was a wonder they both didn't break their impossible necks.

Green clenched her fists.

She was going to have to talk to him about judging risk.

She was also going to have to find out what he meant by that last cryptic statement.

As far as she knew, no man had control over such things. It was strictly a woman's decision. Perhaps he did not understand that.

She shook her head. Anya really should have schooled him better in fastening matters. She sighed. She supposed it eventually would fall to her to enlighten him.

She laughed to herself. Maybe she could make the lesson instructive and pleasurable at the same time.

She called one of the coophands. "Lida!" The girl came running over.

"Yes, my Lordene?"

"Take a mount and find the Marqueller. Remind him that he must return within a few hours so he can get ready for the postfastening meal at his grandmother's."

"Yes, Lordene, but it may take me that long to catch up with him." Lida looked doubtfully at his dust trail.

Green nodded in commiseration. "His Klee will wear out long before your Kloo is even winded. And, while you're at it, follow him at a distance to make sure he doesn't break his fool neck."

The girl went to saddle a Kloo. "I don't think that beast is quite tamed, Marquelle."

Green was in complete agreement. "No, I don't think he is."

Only she wasn't referring to the Klee.

*G*reen heard Jorlan's boot heels clinking on the flooring as he made his way into their chamber.

She had taken the opportunity to do some reading, a favorite pastime of hers and one she hadn't had very much time for lately. Her vidtomes were stacking at an alarming rate! The small window in the corner of her airscreen was already blinking a warning that she needed to do some thinning of stock.

She sighed.

How was she to do that? The stories were too captivating! Maybe she could purchase another wristview? She bit her lip. She already had three and they were full to bursting, so to speak. Collecting is a nasty habit, she admitted.

Right after, she resolved to get one more wristview.

She looked up from her seat by the window as Jorlan opened and closed the door. He was covered in dust from head to foot. A chagrined smile greeted her. It was rather endearing.

She smiled genially while snapping off the button on the wristview. "Did Lida find you?"

Jorlan rubbed his ear. "Ah, you might say we found her."

Green sat forward. "What happened?"

He chuckled. "Sabir and I doubled back and decided to take that old stone wall down by the—"

"*You jumped the Tamryn Wall?*" The structure had been part of the original wall of the first Tamryn dwelling, built right after the settlers had arrived. It was an ancient landmark. "It's at least three and a half meters in height!"

"Probably higher." He grinned.

"Jorlan!"

He put a hand up. "Klee are excellent jumpers. They can easily achieve the momentum they need to clear—"

"Tell your grandmother that! That's just how she almost killed herself."

She was altogether right on that one. Only his situation was entirely different. "Well . . . that's true about her; but—"

"Sweet Cybella!" Her face paled. "You didn't land on Lida; tell me you didn't!"

"Not exactly." He hedged.

She eyed him. "What do you mean, 'not exactly'?"

"I saw her before she saw us, so I managed to veer Sabir to the left. Unfortunately we were midair at the time."

Green got paler. "Did you have a fall?"

He gave her an insulted look. "No."

"Then how did you get covered in dirt?" She swept her arm, indicating his mussed-up condition.

He chuckled. "Lida's Kloo glanced up in time to see Sabir and me springing over its head—sideways. The Kloo, um . . ."—he looked up at the ceiling—"sort of fainted dead away. I think it thought we were a giant screech wing or something."

Green arched her eyebrow, crossed her arms over her chest, and tapped her foot.

Jorlan's gaze flickered to the left. "After we landed, I rode back to see if Lida was all right. She was, but her Kloo was so angry that it kicked dirt all over Sabir and me."

She tried not to smile. It definitely wouldn't do to smile. "Mathers has drawn a bubble-pool for you. We need to leave for the Duchene's soon."

He nodded and began to head toward the alcove. Green called after him. "Jorlan."

He looked at her over his shoulder.

"No more jumping."

He stopped. "I can't agree to that, Green."

"You must. It is far too dangerous. Everything today turned out fine, but only by the sheerest good fortune. You must see that this is reckless behavior. The risk far outweighs any momentary thrill you get from it."

He exhaled heavily. "It is not about momentary thrill. It is about feeling the wind and heart of the land, it is about moving like one with Sabir. It is about freedom of the spirit."

Touched by his impassioned words, Green held back what she was going to say. Could she take that away from him? But the danger . . . ! "Jorlan, I would not be doing my part as your name-giver if I did not at least try to safeguard you from what is surely trouble waiting to occur. I am only concerned for your safety and the safety of my people."

He noticed her distress; he walked over to her. "I understand that." He cupped her face gently. "I will ride more carefully."

She hesitated. It was in her power, and certainly her right, to forbid him to jump—or ride for that matter. Any other name-giver certainly would.

And Jorlan knew it. He waited to see what she would do.

She sighed softly. "Very well."

His eyes flashed with admiration and more. "I'm glad you feel that way, Green," he drawled huskily.

She lifted her chin. "And if I didn't?"

"I'd find a way to do it anyway," he answered truthfully.

"I figured that."

"Mmm. I figured you figured that."

They smiled at each other. "Go take your bath." She shooed him away.

He held out his hand. "Take it with me."

Her lips parted. The look he gave her was open and incredibly mature. It took her breath away. She placed her hand lightly in his.

As he led her to the bubble-pool, he said in a low voice, "You need not worry, *my name-giver*; I will not come to harm in this manner."

She glanced up at him through the corner of her eye. "You cannot know that for sure."

"Yes, I can."

The water gently lapped against her.

Sitting comfortably between his muscular thighs, Green closed her eyes and leaned back into Jorlan's chest. Mathers had floated scores of lillacia blooms in the pool. The eccentric old servant must have been duly impressed with the new Marqueller to do such a thing. *Now there was an unlikely friendship brewing!* She chuckled to herself. Avatar had already warned her that she had seen the two of them bantering heatedly. There was no telling what aggravation the two would cook up.

Green sighed blissfully in the water. They probably shouldn't dawdle; they needed to get to the Duchene's. Tongues would wag if they missed their postfastening dinner.

Only she felt much too good to move.

She suspected Jorlan felt the same by the low, pleasing sound that rolled from his throat every now and then. His lips nibbled the back of her neck, sending chills down her spine in a superb contrast to the hot water. She arced her neck to give him better access.

Earlier, when they had undressed, he had gathered her long, heavy hair in his hands and helped her pin it up. There was something very sensual about the feel of those capable hands sliding through the locks of her hair. The tender motions he used, his gentle touch and care, told her that Jorlan felt more for her than he wanted to admit.

Conscious of the late hour, she had helped him wash, running the cloth over his body and hair in brisk strokes. It had the opposite effect than she intended. He had dunked his head under the water, flinging his hair back when he broke the surface. Small droplets of water clung to his black lashes and dripped over his golden skin. His azure eyes sparkled, the water reflecting in his eyes. He blinked slowly as he watched her.

"Come rest against me," he had said enticingly.

And so she did.

"*Rrrtttrrrt.*" He placed his lips against the curve at the base of her neck and playfully let the rumbling sound vibrate along her skin.

Green jumped.

He chuckled against the nape of her neck.

It always surprised her when this side of his nature came out.

"I've always loved your hair like this," he drawled as he brushed his cheek aside her throat. "It looks like it is precariously situated and unseen forces could make it fall over at any moment; yet somehow it never does." He caught a lock between his lips and playfully tugged it. "It stays firmly where it is. It reminds me of you."

Green paused. He had a remarkable sense of intuition. Without realizing it, he had sensed her stance exactly. She would never give in to any battle without the good fight. Metaphorically speaking.

"Except it was you who placed it atop my head to begin with, Jorlan. If it makes a picture you like, it is your own doing," she responded ambiguously.

"Not so." He nipped her shoulder. "We both know whose fasten holds the clasp."

A small grin curved her lips. He was clever. "Are you trying to sweeten me, wilding?"

"*Me?* Now why would I do that?" His arms encircled her waist, pulling her very tightly against him under the water. His swollen member jutted against her buttocks.

"I see. Then what is it you are doing?" She raised her eyebrow and peered up at him over her shoulder.

He looked down at her through half-closed eyes. "I am simply adjusting your *attitude* so you can be more comfortable, name-giver."

"How thoughtful."

"Yes."

His hands cupped the fragrant lillacia water, letting the water and some blooms cascade from his palms over her breasts. The rivulet slid between her legs.

"Perhaps it makes you think of something?" He flexed against her. Exactly as she had taught him. Only better.

"Um, no, not really."

He exhaled heavily. "Really."

"Can't say it does."

"Hmm . . ."

"And so subtle." She laughed. He bit her shoulder again. "I suppose you would like to help me wash, as well?"

"Do Kloo irritate everyone?"

She thwapped the cloth back over her head into his face without releasing it.

"I suppose not everyone," he conceded under the circumstances.

"Just remember that. Kibbee is very hurt that you are not paying attention to her."

Jorlan rolled his eyes. *KLOO.* They were the most difficult beasts! Who could understand them? Green, apparently.

She put the cloth in his hand and placed her hand over his. He gazed down with renewed interest.

Guiding him, she brought their wet hands over her chest, rubbing the cloth over her breasts.

He liked this already. The texture of her skin was the softest—

"Kibbee is very sensitive. She's been sulking and you haven't even noticed."

Jorlan grimaced. Why didn't she just splash him with cold water? The image of a "sulking" Kloo face was not what he wanted in his mind at the moment. Or any moment. It was the multifluttering nostrils that finished any sympathetic tendencies one might have—as far as he was concerned. "May we not speak of Kloo right now?"

"Very well." She sighed deeply, but brought their hands down along her stomach and over her taut thighs.

Much better subject, he thought. He slid between her cheeks from behind, letting himself barely tease against the soft folds of her femininity.

So knowledgeable yet still so untutored. His Sensitive's erotic abilities were awakening. Green opened her eyes slightly and smiled knowingly.

"And what are you thinking about?" he breathed in her ear.

"You."

"What about me?" His teeth captured the small lobe, tugging on it.

"I'll tell you some other time."

"Is it good?" His foot slid along her calf under the water, back and forth, stimulating with the luxuriant sweep of skin and warm water.

"Very good." She felt the dampness of his chest above the waterline as it skimmed her back with every deep, silent breath he took.

Then *he* began to move their hands.

He brought the cloth up between her inner thighs, the light scraping motion sensitizing the tender area. "I am entranced by these tight auburn curls."

"Are you?"

"Yesss." The cloth rubbed through them, dipping between her woman's folds beneath the water. He turned their hands, letting her feel the tip of his manhood just resting at her portal.

Then he placed the cloth around his finger and stroked her there with both. It was smooth and rough at the same time.

"Jorlan . . ." Green rested her head back against his chest.

His other hand cupped her chin, turning her gently so that his mouth covered hers as he continued to rub and stroke her with the cloth, his finger, and himself. The lillacia perfume wafted all around them, in steaming scent. Jorlan breathed deeply of the perfume that was mingled with their scents. That deep pleasure sound rolled in his throat again.

He dipped his tongue into her mouth as his finger dipped into her from below.

Green moaned into his lips.

Jorlan's other hand covered her breast in a massaging caress. His palm opened over her extended nipple, brushing back and forth.

"Do you like this?" he mouthed.

"Yesss, yesss!" Green kissed him deeply.

"Green . . . let me feel you . . . like before. . . ."

"You want to come inside?" She pressed back into him, circling her hips against his groin.

"By the Founder, yes!" he hissed.

For an instant she thought to prolong his heightened pleasure by making him wait but then decided against it. There was a part of her that wondered if he *would* wait any longer. She wasn't ready to confront that answer and what it would entail.

She pulled his hand away from her and swung over onto him, facing him. He leaned back against the rim of the bubble-pool. His pupils were hazy, dilated. His wet, dark hair, slicked back from his forehead. The masculinely shaped lips—that felt so perfect when kissed—parted slightly, showing the edges of white teeth.

A pulse beat heavily in the strong column of his throat.

Green placed one of her hands on his wide shoulder; the other she placed over his heart. The rhythm surged strongly, powerfully. She could feel its hammering through her fingertips. Not rapid. *Intense.*

Jorlan's passionate gaze swept over her features. Moisture dotted his brow. "Come to me," he whispered hoarsely.

And she did.

She joined them, sinking down on him. Green threw back her head and bit her lip. There was an incredible sense of connectedness when he was inside! Not just to him. To all things. It made her feel things she had never felt before—elusive perceptions that mingled with her entire being.

Jorlan groaned aloud.

His arm encircled her waist, bringing her closer. He bent into her throat, trailing his lips along her hairline, holding her tightly to him as he did so.

That area was an extremely sensitive spot for Green. She was so over-come by what his mouth was doing that she stayed immobile on him, drowning in the feel of his touch.

Jorlan arched his hips, surging fully into her.

Green's eyes flew open. *"Jorlan."*

She could feel his amused smile on her throat. He lifted into her again, raising her up in the water so she would come down hard on him.

"Have a care, you will injure yourself!"

His palms pressed flat to her back, causing the swollen tips of her breasts to poke into his chest. He smiled at the sensation and rubbed his water-slickened chest against the firm tips.

"Then show me how you can move on me, sweet *lexa*."

The endearment (such as it was, after all, he was calling her a sweet huntress) did not go unnoticed by her. Green arced her back, her hips thrusting tight into his. Whereupon she demonstrated to him that even a person who favored Kloo could ride like the swift, untamed bolt of an arc.

Only last longer.

Soon Jorlan was lost in her lively, penetrating movements. He throbbed inside her as she slid continuously on him. Her thighs squeezed him tightly, causing him to call out. He bit her shoulder and then the side of her neck.

As she slaked their desire, he dragged his nails from the back of her neck to the base of her spine. Not enough to scratch but enough to tingle the raw nerves.

Green immediately released.

Her strong contractions flowed around the entire length of him and he felt himself thicken dangerously.

Pressing his mouth to hers, he captured her screams of pleasure. His palms slid over her rounded buttocks, pressing them taut against him as he ground into her tighter. He had never felt so good! *So alive.*

Visions swam through his head. He found the exact one he wanted as he expelled his fluid into her.

Green rested her forehead on his, trying desperately to regain her breath. The time! "We must hurry or we'll be late for the postfastening meal! Anya will flay us alive if we are much later!"

"Why?" Jorlan gasped, also trying to get his breath back. "Why must we go to this dinner?"

"It is the custom. Your grandmother must see that I have been treating you well."

Jorlan laughed and groaned at the same time. "The proof will be there for all to see, I fear."

Her eyes rolled. "You can't see such things, Jorlan."

"No?"

"No."

"You think no one will notice this sated, sleepy look on my face? Or the slow, halting stride to my walk?"

She laughed. "Perhaps that, yes."

"Mmm. I thought so." He let his head bang back against the wall.

She blinked as something occurred to her. "What did you mean when you said you loved my hair this way? I never wear it like this except when I bathe."

"Did I say that?"

"Yes!"

"Hmm. Then I love to see it when you bathe."

"But you've never seen me bathe before!"

"No?" He plucked her lower lip with his teeth.

"No." She placed her hands on her hips. She was beginning to wonder just how much he was playing with her. Every time she answered his no with her no, his lips twitched slightly.

"Well, if I had done so, lexa, I imagine it would have been quite a vision. . . ."

He smiled secretly.

Chapter Ten

The guests had already arrived by the time they got to the Reynard estate. By custom, the dinner was a fairly intimate one consisting of the Septibunal and Anya's closest friends. The Duchene at first gave them a discreetly disapproving glance. Then she winked at them.

Green started to explain. "I'm sorry, Anya, we—"

The Duchene held up her hand. "Don't bother with an excuse as it is obvious to me why you are late." She gave Jorlan a pointed look. He showed a sudden feigned interest in the floral designed carpet.

The Duchene was not finished. "And I don't have to ask how you are faring, Jorlan, for I can tell by the sparkle in your eyes that you are more than fine."

The postfastening dinner was to alleviate concerned fathers and mothers that their son had not suffered any ill use during the fastening night. Normally, it was a happy, festive occasion—unless the name-bearer was unnaturally glum.

This was not the case here.

Jorlan's cheekbones darkened slightly in embarrassment.

"Don't be shy about it." Anya tapped him with her holofan, causing a miniature arc storm to erupt between its spines. "I'd rather see you this way than any other."

"Oh, but I'd rather see him a somewhat different way," Green jested, starting off the fun as the proud name-giver. She grinned wickedly. Anya snorted.

Jorlan gave them a forbearing look. "You are both disgusting."

They laughed.

"Better get use to it tonight, my blaze-dragon. Tonight is the night you take all the ribbing from the guests."

"Horrible custom. Do I look so different?" He made a dreamy face. The Duchene chuckled.

The guests were going to tease him good-naturedly about his loss of the veil and his introduction to the finer pleasures in life. He sighed. "How bad is this going to get?"

"Pretty bad," Green warned him. "Oh, and they'll cloak it in double entendre to make sure it'll sting worse." She smiled brightly at him. Stepping on tiptoe she kissed his cheek with a smack.

"Then I thank you in advance for coming to my aid—both of you."

"Did we say that?" Anya asked Green in mock seriousness.

"Can't recall that." Green smirked at him.

He sucked in his cheek, trying not to let his smile show. Since his bath, he had been in the most extraordinary mood. All of his senses seemed to be alive and singing within him. He had never anticipated this. And he was wise enough not to ignore it. *There had always been something about her. . . .*

Green handed her cloak to Billings. "So is the Septibunal here as well?"

"Yes, all seven of them, including that—that—"

"Snip-butt?" Jorlan supplied helpfully.

Anya gasped. "Really, Jorlan!"

Green and Jorlan's eyes met in mirth.

Anya continued. "This is the last that—that person is to be allowed in my home!"

"Let's hope she doesn't upset the festivities too much tonight." Green's mood wilted slightly. Claudine was managing to ruin her most memorable occasions once again.

Billings came over to congratulate Green. Anya took the opportunity to speak in an aside to her grandson. "It is as I told you, is it not? You are happy with my choice and the outcome."

Jorlan was silent for a moment. He spoke quietly. "I have always preferred the choice, Duchene, as you seem to know. It is not Green I object to, it is the manner in which I was taken."

"I know you do not object to her. Do you think I did not see you watching her all those years—hidden upstairs whenever she came to visit?"

Jorlan flushed.

"I have always known that you wanted her."

"Not more than my personal freedom," he bit out.

"You cannot tell me you did not enjoy your fastening night; it is there in your face for anyone to see."

"I am not speaking of that," he said in an undertone. "I am speaking about a decision being taken away from me—from all men."

Anya fumed. "Again with that?"

"Always with *that*. Just because I am pleased with my name-giver does not mean I have abandoned my beliefs. It just seems to me the better choice is to fully explore both pathways. I will not shut Green out, for she is meaningful to me and my life. However, I am as committed as

I ever was to my own direction. She bid on me knowing full well my aversion to the practice; I have not forgotten that and she knows it."

Anya was plainly disapproving. "There are things you know nothing about."

Jorlan arched his brow, wondering if there was not some deeper meaning behind the remark. "I am learning and so will bide my time— for now."

What is that to mean? Anya gave him a horrified look. "Cease this foolish talk! I will hear no more of it! You will hurt her, Jorlan."

Jorlan exhaled heavily. "Grandmother, I *care*. I would never . . ." He stopped, unwilling to go on.

The confession seemed to mollify the Duchene somewhat. "Good. I will be optimistic that your good sense and breeding will eventually win out."

A muscle ticked in Jorlan's jaw. "We must never forget male breeding, should we?"

Anya fluttered her holofan, but couldn't quite meet his eye.

Billings left Green. She turned to the pair, curious as to what they had been whispering about. But her curiosity would have to be answered later; there was something she needed to speak to the Duchene about first. "Jorlan, I need to speak with your grandmother for a few moments, privately; do you mind? It won't take long."

"Of course not. I'll go round to the kitchens and scare cook for a while." His expression was one of speculative mischief-making.

Anya rolled her eyes. "Mind yourself!"

"I always do." He strolled off down the hallway toward the kitchens, a distinct stealth in his step.

Both women watched after him with varying degrees of amused wariness.

"He's never been an easy person to figure." Anya remarked.

"I can tell that."

"Shall we go to the study?"

"That will be fine."

As soon as they entered the room, Anya rolled the doors closed behind them with a click.

*A*n alert pair of narrowed grey eyes watched them from the edge of the greeting room. Claudine D'anbere stealthily made her way down the hall and stood by the study doors.

"*N*ow what's this all about, my dear?"

Green picked up a small figurine of a Klee in full canter that sat on the edge of a desk. It was a work of art, capturing the free, unfettered nature of the animal. Somehow she knew Jorlan had given it to his grandmother.

Carefully, she set it back down. "It's about Jorlan."

There was a long pause in the room. Finally Anya said, "What is it? Are you not happy with him?"

"Don't be foolish! I'm mad for him and you know it." She paused. "Why didn't you tell me about him?"

Anya viewed her with a hooded expression. Had she overheard Jorlan's confession? She didn't want to give away a confidence. "Tell you what?"

"Don't pretend you don't know. That he is a Sensitive!"

Anya blinked. A Sensitive? Her complexion paled in shock. "I—I never knew, Green, I swear!"

"How could you not know?" Now Green was stunned.

Anya sighed. "I knew there was something different about him; it never occurred to me that he might be a Sensitive. It is so rare in the aristocracy."

"I know. It took me by surprise as well."

"Did you find out . . . last night?" The old woman blushed, not wanting to hear any details.

"I suspected beforehand; last night it became obvious."

Anya's shoulders slumped. "I am so sorry, Green. I really had no idea." *But it explains so much.* "Does this bother you?"

Green snorted. "Don't be a nog-twist, Anya; of course it doesn't bother me. It's quite a boon, if you must know."

Anya put up her hand. "Please. I do not need to hear this, I am his grandmother."

Green chuckled. "Very well. Although I am concerned should this become common knowledge. It would make Jorlan very uncomfortable. As it is, he is trying to understand what it is himself. I really think he has no idea how different he is." Green's face reflected her impression of those unique qualities of his.

"You like it, don't you?" Anya was astonished.

"Oh, yes." Green grinned at her. "Definitely. It is his differences that fascinate me, Anya. He is a most uncommon jewel."

"That he is. And with a good heart, too . . ." she muttered, lost in thought.

"Yes, he has."

"I have always thought it the key to him," Anya shrewdly clued the younger woman without giving anything anyway.

Green raised her eyebrow. "Perhaps."

"In any event, I agree with you; it's best to keep this information to ourselves. If you should ever have a son and he inherits the trait, you would be besieged with bids from his infancy. Neither of you will have any peace." She sighed. "Sometimes the Slice can be so self-serving!"

"*Sometimes?*"

"*Hmf!*"

"Shall we go and watch Jorlan take his beating? Despite Claudine's sour face, it should be fun."

"Yes, let's! The come-out deserves it after all the trouble he's caused me over the years!"

Chuckling, Green shook her finger at her.

Sometimes on rare occasions, the Duchene became simply Anya Reynard.

*M*oving quickly away from the study doors, Claudine made her way back into the greeting room. *Jorlan was a Sensitive!* Her hunger for him took an exponential leap. Her eyes flashed with victory and something dark.

First, she would have to destroy Green once and for all.

Jorlan would then be bound to her and her bed. She wondered how long it would take her to use him up.

Soon, she promised herself. *But not too soon.*

For this kind of work, timing was everything.

*T*he snogglehound whined piteously for a scrap of pudding.

With its five short legs, barrel-shaped segmented body, ridiculously small head, and perpetually dazed expression, the snogglehound was a favorite pet of the Select Quarter. Some of them were pampered to death.

Literally.

The animals had no sense of when to stop eating. Like the Slice, they positively coveted rich foods. The snogglehound sat up, extenuating his long body so his tiny head sailed by the edge of the table. Whereupon he loudly snuffled the food as he passed.

Claudine D'anbere hissed. "I cannot believe you brought that beast in here to the table, Chamford! It belongs outside."

The snogglehound let out a piteous wail. "There, my pet; here's a piece of pudding for Hugo." Earlene Chamford threw Hugo a bit of food and D'anbere a sneer all at the same time. The Earlene was making it quite plain that Hugo was staying.

"I think he's rather adorable." Green chuckled behind her hand as Hugo caught the snippet, then lifted his chin to sneer at Claudine in an exact replica of his owner. Snogglehounds were brilliant mimics.

Jorlan laughed outright.

Claudine put her drink down with a clink. Anger suffused her face but then she seemed to remember something. At ease, she sat back in her chair and gave Green a look that could only be called gloating.

Now why is that? Green wondered. With Claudine one could never be too careful.

"How bright the flamelights are tonight," She-Count Grier announced as she took a helping of Jacama outlander sausage. "Can one guess what fuels the spark?" she remarked coyly.

The guests at the long banquet table chortled and clinked their glasses with their carved spoons.

Jorlan glanced at Green and rolled his eyes. "It's starting."

Green winked at him.

"Yes." Claudine sat forward. "Although one can say that some of the fire has died down to a smolder." She looked Jorlan right in the eye.

Misinterpreting her real meaning, several Lordenes and their name-bearers called out in good fun, "Hear! Hear!"

Jorlan, however, knew her meaning. He met her look and stared her down.

Green sipped at her drink and casually remarked, "I don't know, She-Count, it seems to me the veil, once broken, is twice as strong."

The guests pounded on the table, thoroughly enjoying Green's saucy wit. Claudine's mouth pursed but she reluctantly raised her goblet to Green.

"I could have done without that one," Jorlan remarked in an aside to her. She flicked him a quick look of amusement.

A volley of servants came from the kitchen with more platters of food. They started placing them on the groaning table, much to the delight of Hugo, whose head was seen popping up all along the edge. The snogglehound was so excited, he scurried back and forth under the table, only to come up on either side between everyone's chairs to sniff at each new plate of food as if it were positioned just for him. It was very comical.

Jorlan's lips twitched as he watched the silly scamp. "Can we get a snogglehound?"

"I don't see why not." Green grinned at the pup.

"Spoiling him, already, eh, Marquelle? That's the way to do it!" As if the fil-Earlene Shazi would know anything about it! The elder man had never fastened, but was a much loved wit in the Slice. Green had always liked him. He was a sharp old nog and a close friend of the Reynards. She had seen Jorlan speaking with him for quite some time before they went in to dinner.

"Did I hear you say you want a snogglehound?" Earlene Chamford paused, her spoonful of crawlsinthedark soup dripping onto the Balinting lace table cloth. "Why, take Hugo! He'll be my postfastening day gift to you both!"

Green blanched. "But, Earlene, he is your pet! We couldn't do that."

"Sense and sensibility! I insist! There, it's done!"

Green's eyes filled with tears, and not because of the generosity of the gift. She simply could never understand the callous disregard the Slice had for things and people they considered beneath them. Poor Hugo looked from the Earlene to them in complete bewilderment, having no idea his entire future had just changed.

The Earlene had already forgotten him. She was conversing with a newly widowed Baroner who had caught her eye. And when she was done with him, no doubt he would be discarded much the same as Hugo.

Hugo made a pitiful questioning sound.

Green wiped her eye to hide her display of sentimentality. Jorlan's hand covered hers. "He'll come to us," he spoke quietly to her. "Watch." He held out a treat to the little snogglehound.

Hugo hesitated at first, sensing that something important had happened.

Jorlan's eyes softened in a way that made Green's heart thump. Hugo came galloping over to him. He took the treat and licked Jorlan's fingers, then sat up straight and waved three of his legs at Green.

"See?" he whispered to her. "He loves you already."

"Jorlan," she breathed in an undertone. "How did you—?"

"I know how he feels." He glanced at her through his spiky lashes.

Her breath stopped in her throat. *What was he saying?* Surely not what she . . .

"About being a pawn of the Slice, that is." His irises glittered mysteriously.

Green exhaled. For a moment there, she had thought he had meant something else.

"What are you whispering about over there?" Marqueller Goodcock leaned forward, his bared chest almost completely spilling free of his shirt. He had been drinking heavily all evening. His name-giver laughed raucously and reached over to tie a few of his laces.

"Nothing like a fine set of pecs to get the appetite up!" General Staunchly quipped, just before she belched loudly and rang for another goblet of hameeri.

"A toast!" Fil-Earlene Shazi lifted his glass. "To whatever gets it *up!*"

Everyone burst into laughter at the bawdy cheer.

Except Jorlan, who blushed crimson.

And Hugo, who snatched a piece of sausage from Claudine's plate.

"Like that, do you?" Claudine smiled evilly at the snogglehound. "Here—why don't you have the rest of it?" She reached over and picked up the whole piece of sausage. Her intent was clear to Green.

"Don't give him that."

"Why not? He seems to want it." She dangled the foot-long piece of sausage over the snogglehound. Hugo sat up and waved all his feet madly.

"It's too much! He won't be able to digest it."

"Nonsense." Claudine lowered the sausage to Hugo.

Real distress showed on Green's face. By the time she got around the table it would be too late. "No, don't," she pleaded.

The snogglehound was just about to snap up the sausage when Jorlan spoke. "Hugo," he said in a low, even tone.

The snogglehound stopped and stared at him quizzically.

"Come here." He patted his side.

Hugo hesitated. On the one hand was a snogglehound's dream piece of food; on the other . . .

"Come, Hugo." Again Jorlan spoke in that calm, even tone.

Unbelievably the snogglehound turned away from the Jacama lowlander sausage and trotted happily over to Jorlan.

Jorlan petted his small head and told him to stay by Green.

Hugo sat by Green.

"I say! That was quite amazing!" Lordene Emiline sputtered. "I have a way with them but nothing like that—you must be very gifted, Marqueller."

Green glanced around the table, worried.

"Should we not ask the Marquelle about that?" Anya bantered, changing the focus back to the usual postfastening ribbing. Everyone guffawed.

Green flashed her a grateful look.

At that moment, Billings approached her. "I have an urgent message for you, Marquelle!"

Concerned, Green took the placardview from her, putting it in privacy mode to read the missive. Her brow furrowed.

"What is it?" Jorlan asked.

"There is trouble on one of my estates on the edge of the Southern Lands."

"Does it say what it is?"

"Something about an unidentified sickness affecting the household. Apparently it is not deadly, but the locals are very superstitious about such things. The majordoma tells me I need to come at once."

"How far away is it?" Jorlan's eyes lit with the prospect of travel. It was something he always wanted to do—only under better circumstances.

"It is three weeks' journey from here. But you cannot come, Jorlan. It is a dangerous route, fraught with peril."

He viewed her silently. There was no way he would let her go into such danger alone. Not now, not ever. He leaned forward as if to whisper in her ear. "I am coming with you, Green. If you refuse, I shall follow you on Sabir."

"Don't be ridiculous! Sabir could never make such a journey."

He arched his brow. "Shall we bet?"

She exhaled noisily. "Please, Jorlan, it is too much of a risk; you know nothing of the wilderness and—"

He laughed, tickling her ear.

"What?"

"Let us just say I know more than you think. I'm coming."

She was getting to recognize that look. "Very well. But you must heed my instructions at all times."

His lips twitched. "Yes, my name-giver."

"And do as I say."

His hot tongue flicked her ear. "Yes, my name-giver."

"And you will have to ride a Kloo. A long trek like this is no place for a Klee."

He paused to sigh deeply. He caught her earlobe in his teeth and tugged. "Yes, my name-giver."

She smiled, but her eye caught Claudine's. The woman was too smug. *She's behind this, I know. The Founder alone knows what we'll find there—if we get there.*

Green sent a message to Avatar to prepare for the journey and to make sure an extra contingent of protector-guards accompanied them. She was not going to put Jorlan at risk.

Jorlan stood. "I'll be back in a moment. There is something I need to get."

"Where are you going?"

"Upstairs to my old room."

"We moved all of your clothing and personal items to Tamryn house. What do you need?"

He bent over and said to her alone, "My meteor-blade."

Green sucked in her breath. "*You wield a meteor-blade?* But how?"

Jorlan placed his index finger up to his mouth, cautioning her to be silent. Then he left.

While Green apologized to the guests for their abrupt departure, her mind was reeling with what he had just revealed to her. As far as she knew no man had *ever* wielded the blade. They were forbidden. The deadly weapon required the utmost skill and concentration. There were very few women who could accomplish it.

But that wasn't the only thing that bothered her.

Whoever mastered a meteor-blade must also master the mysterious forms of Gle Kiang-ten.

Which meant only one thing.

Jorlan was a platinum class warrior.

And if anyone found out, his life would be in danger.

They set out almost immediately upon their return home.

Avatar, the master organizer, had everything arranged by the time their coach delivered them to the doorstep.

Everything, that is, except Jorlan's gear.

"Mathers, have one of the boys pack some of Jorlan's things—he is coming with me," Green called out. She handed Hugo to her and told the majordoma to make a comfortable bed for the sweet snogglehound in the corner of the kitchen. Hugo's whole body wagged.

Avatar gasped in horror. "You're not bringing that snap-branch come-out on a trip like this!"

"I am." She nodded firmly. Jorlan met her eye and smiled proudly at her.

"Have you lost your sense? It is a grueling journey! He has no sense of any life outside of the sheltered care given all veils! It's not right of you to bring him! As your advisor, I must strongly caution you against it."

Green gave the feisty woman a disbelieving look. "Since when have you become my advisor?"

Avatar harrumphed. "Marquelle, the rigors of such a journey, despite any comforts you bring along, will prove too much for him. What's more, he knows nothing of rustic life! He's just as liable to step on a razor rock as to avoid one." Razor rocks were extraterrestrial nonintelligent life forms that were highly toxic when stumbled upon. It was believed the life forms inadvertently "rode" to Forus on a meteorite (or another craft—which had never been proven) eons ago, finding a natural niche on the high open desert where they could slowly munch on the nitrogen-rich sand.

Since they didn't eat much and grew very, very slowly, they were mostly ignored, except if they were inadvertently stepped on or brushed against. Then razor-sharp shards sprung up, forming a shield all around them. The natural and formidable defense mechanism was presumably geared to prevent them from being munched on by predators that had a taste for extremely crunchy fare.

Besides causing nasty slice-cuts, the razor points could, in some rare cases, infect the bloodstream with silicon-based "organisms" that continued to grow inside the human body, turning lethal. The methodologists had developed a rather nasty cure for the nanosites, but one needed to get to them in time.

In fact, the meteor-blade weapon had been fashioned after the razor rocks. Using selective genen techniques on the silicon life forms, methodologists were able to produce a small number of hybridized razor rocks for meteor-blade use. The resultant form was noninfective, but its blades were deadly sharp.

The process was expensive, strictly monitored, and lengthy. Which made meteor-blades nearly impossible to acquire. Usually, they were only given to masters of Gle Kiang-ten by their masters. Only a master of Gle Kiang-ten had the inner stillness and strength of will to work such a weapon. Most never achieved the status.

Green still wondered how Jorlan had been able to achieve this. Especially at his age. She vowed she would get answers to those questions—and soon.

"And that's just one of the dangers!" Avatar blustered on. "Add to that raiders, highwaywomen, and all manner of beasties, and—"

Green put up her hand. "I appreciate your concern for my name-bearer, Avatar, but I am taking him with me. He will be fine. Besides, this is not a journey to the deeper regions. There is just a stretch of high desert on the route, the rest is—"

"Through jungle!" Avatar crossed her arms over her sizable chest, not backing down a bit. Green rather thought the woman couldn't bear the thought of having to lug a man along with them. Some women were like that, believing men truly belonged lounging in the home and bed and nowhere else. Others were just plain superstitious, maintaining that a male on a traveling party boded ill luck. The attitude tracked all the way back to the *NEOFEM*.

Green was very fond of Avatar, but some of her beliefs could be considered rather primitive.

Mathers bustled back down the stairs and into the grand foyer. "He's all set, Marquelle! I packed him up myself. Had one of the lads add his baggage to the pack Kloo."

"Good. Thank you, Mathers." Green went back to arguing with Avatar.

"Threw in some surprises for you, too, lad." Mathers winked coyly at him. "For catching the Marquelle's eye at night, if you know what I mean." She guffawed suggestively and elbowed him sharply in the side, twice.

"*Omph!*" Jorlan gave her an incredulous stare. What was the woman thinking? That he was going to drape himself in a sheer Ramagi robe so that he could . . . Hmmm.

Mathers winked again and nodded her head encouragingly.

Grinning, Jorlan asked Green if she was ready to go.

They left with Avatar grumpily marching beside them.

The protector-guards, six women, highly trained in the art of defense, were already mounted, waiting for them. Their leader, Miara, had not yet become adept with the meteor-blade, but she was fluent with many weapons and was a strong, dependable leader who inspired loyalty in her crew.

Defense squads hired themselves out to the aristocracy for various reasons, ranging from travel escort through hostile areas to general protection from threats. Lordenes accrued them on a regular basis, but Miara was on permanent retainer to the House of Tamryn.

Green had hand-picked Miara to her household, knowing that she would never disappoint. She had been right. Miara had assembled an expert team.

The protector-guards greeted Green and nodded politely to the new Marqueller.

Green mounted a Kloo, as Kibbee was brought around for Jorlan. "I thought this would be a good opportunity for you to get to know Kibbee better."

Jorlan stared at the preening Kloo suspiciously. "You've got to be jesting."

Green cocked her head to the side. "Not really; I told you, she feels you have been ignoring her."

Kibbee's neck folds fluttered, indicating her distaste. The Kloo had figured out who was expected to mount her. She was not overjoyed.

Neither was Jorlan.

He approached the attitudinous Kloo reluctantly. Kibbee shied away and prawked at him.

Jorlan rubbed his jaw. "Could I not take Sabir? You would be surprised by his endurance, Green. He—"

"It is Kibbee or nothing. We need to reach the high desert pass. You know as well as I that a Klee cannot get as sure a footing and he will not have the stamina for such an arduous climb. Now make haste, namebearer; we are wasting time."

Several of the protector-guards snickered at the reprimand. Jorlan threw her a narrowed look. Wrapping the reins tightly around his wrist, he hoisted himself onto the Kloo's back.

Kibbee put up a fuss, skittering here and there, snorting and spitting; but it was just for show. With one stern look from Green, she calmed down and trotted into place behind Green's mount.

They started out with Miara and one of the guards in the lead followed by Green, Jorlan, another guard at his back, then Avatar and the remaining three guards taking up the rear.

"You see?" Green called back over her shoulder. "Kibbee is a dear. You will learn to love her soon, just as I do."

Jorlan glanced doubtfully down at the Kloo's bobbing head. Kibbee turned and curled her fat upper lip at him in disdain.

"Terrific," Jorlan muttered. "I am enamored of you already."

Kibbee squawked and faced the trail but not before she took a playful nip at his boot. *Kloos.*

They rode for most of the night.

After they had left the town limits and were traversing open plains, Green took the lead with Miara. The two women conversed quietly on and off, their low voices muted on the night breeze.

Jorlan leaned back in his seat and gazed up at the sky. Millions of stars twinkled brightly against the black backdrop of space. They reflected in his eyes as he stared in awe.

The Reynard estate was surrounded by foliage; he had never seen such a wide expanse of sky! Occasionally a comet streaked across the sky in a dazzling display. Jorlan slowed his mind of all thought, taking the time to absorb this moment of beauty. The excitement of adventure stirred his blood.

He inhaled the brisk air deeply into his lungs, taking pleasure in the puffs of vapor as he exhaled. The temperature was going down; they had been ascending the mesa steadily. Jorlan pulled his cloak closer about him, wondering how Green was faring. He hoped she wasn't cold.

Avatar pulled her mount up beside him, pacing her Kloo to his. "It is captivating. Where I come from, the sky seems so big, you can almost touch it."

"And where is that?"

"From the deep southern region. The South Lands. You'll only see a taste of it on this trip, lad, for we're only going to Hadley Tip."

"I would like to see it some day, if it is as you say."

"Oh, it is. But it is a rough country. The clans down there have their ways and we have ours."

"Why did you come to Capitol Town?"

"I needed something different. Happens to a person sometimes."

"Yes."

Avatar looked over at the young Marqueller. He was staring at the stars again. It struck her as odd—how knowing he was about the natural things in life, about people. He was sometimes quiet and contained as if he were studying everything around him. Only, it never made one uncomfortable. On the contrary, when he was calm, relaxed, there was a certain solace when one was in his presence.

He was a strange brew of contradictions. All fiery one time and quiet the next. *Quite the package,* she concluded. "The Marquelle would not let you be going to the deep southern regions so easy."

Unconsciously, Jorlan patted Kibbee's forefeathers. The Kloo's flesh vents quivered a low trill. "Why not?"

"She couldn't protect you down there—not a man that looks like you."

"I am fastened."

Avatar guffawed. "That wouldn't matter one bit. You'd be stolen as quick as that!" She snapped her fingers in front of his face.

The woman was trying to scare him out of traveling. He almost laughed out loud at the ridiculousness of it. His teeth flashed in the night light as he gave Avatar a quick smile. "Do not be foolish. Green would never allow such a thing."

Avatar snorted, then chuckled heartily. "All right then, lad, but I'm not exaggerating."

He shrugged.

Up ahead, Green slumped in her seat, then righted herself.

Jorlan watched her in concern. "She's tired."

"Yes, she is—very tired. Seems like ages since she's been able to rest properly what with the troubles she's had."

Jorlan turned swiftly toward her. "Troubles? What troubles?"

Avatar realized she had said too much. She carefully edited her words. "Oh, this and that. Being a Marquelle carries a lot of responsibility."

Jorlan's brow furrowed. "Yes, and she did say she had recently returned from her western properties. . . . Is this connected in some way?"

He is too sharp for his own safety, Avatar thought. Green had expressly forbidden her and Mathers to say anything about her troubles with She-Count D'anbere. She pursed her mouth. "Don't think that would be likely, do you?" she replied noncommittally.

Jorlan gave her a sharp look. "Of course not." *What are they hiding?* he wondered.

Green slid over on the Kloo again.

Jorlan watched her carefully. She was close to exhaustion and there was only one thing that would make her stop. "Avatar, tell the Marquelle I need to stop to rest," he said decisively. "I grow tired."

Avatar arched her brow. The Marqueller wasn't the least tired. But he was a wise one. She smiled secretly at him. "You do look a little peaked around the edges, Marqueller. I'll ride up and tell the Marquelle we need to be stopping."

She pulled forward, speaking low to Green.

Immediately concerned, Green turned to look back at him and wearily called out to Miara to seek out a good spot to rest.

Tomorrow they would not be able to ride at night. They would be in razor-rock country.

Chapter Eleven

They had long since left the high mesa and were now traveling through lowlands where small streams etched their way through the landscape and rainbow trees edged the meadows.

Jorlan was captivated by their multicolored shades. His aqua eyes didn't seem to miss much on the journey, Green acknowledged. Whether he was taking in the pleasures of the surroundings, delighting in the joy of discovery, or simply being alert to his surroundings, Jorlan was *aware*.

Green had noticed it from the moment they had set out.

Another Sensitive trait, she supposed. They had been fortunate to cross the short distance of high desert without encountering any herds of razor rock.

Or any brigands.

Although highwaywomen generally preferred the more traveled and lucrative Ginny trail, which led west, one could never be too cautious. Especially when one had her precious name-bearer in tow. Green glanced over at her blaze-dragon and watched him fondly. Her affection for him grew with every passing hour. He had kept pace on the journey, and then some. Of his accord, he had quietly helped the guards whenever they stopped for rest, taking down supplies from the pack Kloos, helping to prepare meals, and setting up sleepers.

Even Miara, who was impatient with the pampered sons of the aristocracy, had remarked that Jorlan was well liked by her women. He worked quietly along with them and held his counsel.

Green marveled that none of them thought it strange that he was so able to fit in with them.

The sleepers were open to the sky, and on the nights they stopped to rest, he seemed to treasure when she made love to him as he looked up at the stars. It fascinated her to watch his eyes as they hazed over with starlight and desire and he lost himself to his passion. *To her.* On those nights, she would have to cover his mouth with her own to prevent his uninhibited moans from being heard.

It seemed that each time she made love to him, his sensuality deepened. His desire was unrestrained and sometimes uncurbed. Jorlan was becoming bolder and bolder. So far he had waited for her to come to him. She glanced at him out of the corner of her eye. He was going to cross the line soon—she knew that.

She just didn't know what she was going to do about it.

Instead of shocking her, his daring ways excited her.

As his name-giver, she should put more of a firm control on him. Such untamed behavior was not considered proper for men. But she liked his wildness. It arose from deep within him like the unbridled change-of-season winds of Forus—the scorching winds whose airy touches brought defined pleasure to sweltering flesh.

She rode closer in to him.

"I remember the first time I saw the rainbow trees, Jorlan; I couldn't stop staring at them, either." Green reached over to Kibbee and gave her

Kloo a sweet piece of balum fruit from her sack. The Kloo had been especially good with Jorlan, who was constantly trying to get her to pick up pace, being used to his faster Klee.

Kibbee squawked appreciatively, gobbling the succulent morsel.

Jorlan snorted. "She has you at her mercy."

"Of course she does." She grinned at him. "As long as I allow it," she added with underlying meaning.

Jorlan gave her a knowing look. "I suppose there is a message in that for me?"

"I suppose there is." She raised her eyebrows up and down, making jest of the comment.

He laughed and grabbed her reins.

"Jorlan! What are you doing? The guards—"

"Are paying no attention to us."

"But you—"

He sealed her mouth with his. The kiss was hot with promise. It amazed her how *good* he had become at it. He had long since exceeded her instruction and with every press of his lips had been adding nuance after nuance, until he took her very breath away. And it wasn't just with kissing, either.

Not even River, who was an accomplished lover, could kiss like this! Of course, River had always held back. Green often wondered what the expert pleasurer would be like when he finally let go.

Her thoughts left her as the tip of Jorlan's tongue played with the edges of her mouth.

"Sometimes I can be taken away from my thoughts simply by the way the corners of your lips curl," Jorlan whispered huskily. His sultry breath caressed her mouth.

"Is that so?" Did he know what she had been thinking?

"Yesss. . . ." He bent his head, again sealing her mouth with a solid stamp of possession. Green moaned at the feel of him; her hands reached up and clasped his wide shoulders, bringing him closer. His tongue—

Kibbee prawked loudly.

Green heard female laughter. "Hey, you two!" Miara called out. "We'll be stopping soon enough for the night. Make him wait a bit for it, Marquelle, and he'll be dancing prettier in your bed!" Ribald laughter ensued.

Flushed, Green broke off from him, giving him a chastising look. "Now they are giving me intimate advice!"

Jorlan winked lazily at her.

Too bold by half, she rued. Her heart beat a tattoo in her chest. *I'm spoiling him,* she acknowledged to herself.

He slowly licked the taste of her from his lips as he watched her from under lowered lids.

Green sucked in her breath. *And I have no intention of ever stopping!*

"*It's* a little cold!" Green shivered in delight as she dipped into the cool, clear water.

They had found a place to rest for the night near a lovely small pond that was secluded from view by a thick grove of rainbow trees. Green had immediately thrown off her clothes and waded in, desperate for a real bath. They had been cleansing themselves by the streams they passed on the journey. It was adequate, but not the same.

On the bank, Jorlan cocked his head to the side and watched the droplets of water sluice down her pointy breasts. His hands rested on his hips. "I can see that, name-giver."

"Very humorous!" She put her hands on her own hips, which only caused the water-cooled peaks to jut out farther. "What are you waiting for? Are you coming in?" Her breasts bobbed as she talked.

Jorlan clicked his tongue. "You couldn't stop me," he murmured to himself.

"What?" she called out as she splashed water up her arms.

"I said, 'I'll be coming right away.' " He was very good about not smiling at that.

"Can you hand me the cleansing lotion? I left it in my satchel."

He bent to retrieve the lotion when, out of the corner of his eye, he caught low movement on the side bank close to Green. As he straightened, his hands went slowly to his waistband.

"Do not move, Green." He spoke in a calm, controlled tone that seemed odd under the circumstances. She *did* hear that last comment.

"What is it?"

"Shhh. There is a weavermouth behind you."

She froze. Although small in size, weavermouths were deadly. "How many heads?" she whispered.

He untied the hidden knot inside his waistbelt. With an economy of movement, he began to uncoil the meteor-blade he kept hidden from view under his shirt. "Three."

Green closed her eyes. "You'll never be able to get the three heads in time. Perhaps if I stay like this . . . ?"

"It will attack anyway; you know that."

A tear fell from her eye. "Use the blade on me, then. Don't let it get me, Jorlan." Death by a weavermouth was terribly gruesome.

"No." He would not even think it. He unslung the blade's cords.

"Jorlan, please, I beg you!" She tried to keep her voice even despite her rising anxiety. "I once saw a weavermouth attack. . . . I could not bear—"

"You won't have to." Faster than she could register, he snap-slung the coils in transecting arcs through the air.

Green could not believe what see was seeing! *Jorlan was wielding two meteor-blades at once.*

The meteor-blades passed each other in the air. Perfectly thrown, they spun out in opposite directions.

Just as the weavermouth was rearing back to strike, the meteor-blades came at it from two different sides, shearing off two of its heads instantly. The third head was still in its descent strike. Jorlan snapped his left wrist up, bringing the meteor-blade hurling back. At the same time he flung the right meteor-blade in an arc around and over, letting the right side of the cord swing over his neck. The maneuver was almost impossible, yet he had done it. The left meteor-blade sliced back on its path. As it brushed by the weavermouth, the razor spikes extended with a *whoosh!* taking the final head with them.

But the danger to Jorlan was not over. He had to be able to stop the combined momentum of the blades in such a way as to make sure they did not brush by him while they were extended or he would have the same fate as the weavermouth.

It was what made the meteor-blade so difficult to master. You did not get second chances with it. It took years of practice with simulated meteor-blades before one could even begin using the true forms. And years after that before one had the complete concentration and mastery to wield the real weapon. If ever. How had Jorlan accomplished this?

He swung the cords in perfect precision. Easing down the speed, notch by notch, he ran them through a series of the intricate meteor-blade forms of the Gle Kiang-ten. Green had never witnessed the forms used in this particular sequence before. She watched him, spellbound.

Finally he was able to rein in their speed to where he could safely flick his wrists to retract the blades.

She let out a sigh of relief.

Jorlan stopped them altogether and returned them calmly to his waistband as if nothing untoward had occurred.

"How did you learn to do that?" It was said there was once an ancient Golden Master who had the ability. When she had died, it was assumed so had her knowledge. As far as the Select Quarter knew, no one had ever reached that level of the Gle Kiang-ten again.

Jorlan casually began to remove his clothes as if he hadn't just performed a feat of legend.

He shrugged noncommittally. "I mostly taught myself."

Green gawked at him. "Are you saying you taught yourself the meteor-blade? But you would have to know the advanced forms of the Gle Kiang-ten!"

He stepped into the water. Immediately his strong arms embraced her waist, hugging her close to him. "I am glad nothing has happened to you, name-giver." He placed a kiss upon her brow.

"But the skill . . . ?"

"It is fortunate my knowledge saved you." His mouth covered hers. His lips trembled slightly.

Green gave herself over to the heartfelt kiss. Jorlan was not shaken over the battle with the weavermouth, she realized. He was shaken at the prospect that he might have lost *her*.

She kissed him back, deeply.

Right now, something was happening between them that needed to happen. He breathed on her lips. It reminded her of the sigh that a Klee makes when it discovers it can run free. It was the sound of painful joy.

There would be time enough later to talk to him about the meteor-blade. Somehow, though, she suspected that she might not be getting the answers she sought from her enigmatical name-bearer.

His hands stroked down her back with a perfect sensitivity.

And when he groaned into her mouth, she swore she saw the azure oceans of Forus lapping the shore.

*G*reen pulled back on the reins of her Kloo as they neared the edge of a slow-moving river.

They had long since left behind the lowlands and the dangers of weavermouths. Green's face lit up at the sight before her. The banks of the river were lined with jinto plants and Banta psillacybs; they had been navigating through a heavily foliaged area for hours. Several of the lovely, massive jinto leaves were floating on the water, which was steeped in hallucinogens. The river was safe to bathe in for short periods of time—but not to drink.

Avatar chuckled as she watched the Marquelle. She knew exactly what the auburn-haired woman was thinking. "Go on then," she teased her. "You know you want to."

Green bit her lip. After all, she was the leader here. "How would it look?"

"Like you were enjoying yourself?" Avatar smiled fondly at her. "It's not as if we all haven't seen you do these things before, my Lordene."

"True. But what will Jorlan think?" She sighed wistfully at the jinto leaves.

"What would I think about what?" Jorlan rode up next to them, his sights going to the phenomenal scene before him. He sucked in his breath. "I've never seen jinto before, at least not with my eyes . . ." he murmured distractedly, overwhelmed by their lush beauty.

Green glanced sharply at him. What did he mean, *with his eyes* . . . ?

"The Marquelle always gets strange notions when she sees those leaves." Avatar, oblivious to what Jorlan had just unconsciously uttered, nodded at the cascading leaves gliding gently down the river.

Jorlan turned to Green and grinned teasingly. "What kind of notions, *lexa*?"

Green's face colored slightly. She wished he wouldn't call her *that* in front of the others. And she wasn't sure she wanted to tell him about this notion. It wasn't seemly for a Marquelle to indulge in such frivolity, especially in front of a name-bearer who had a tendency toward wildness.

"Come now, Green," he coaxed her. "If you don't tell me, I'll just wheedle it out of Avatar."

Avatar harrumphed and crossed her arms over her ample chest. "And how are you going to do that, you sass-bit! Do you think I haven't been around long enough to be able to see through the wiles of beguiling men?"

Jorlan laughed. "Avatar," he whispered enticingly, purposely modulating his voice to a purring tone, "tell me, please?" He blinked his eyes once at her. Slowly. The effect was stellar.

Avatar reddened.

Green chuckled, shaking her head. He was tying them all around his hand! Even Miara's women were completely taken with him. She gave him a look and clicked her tongue. "Leave poor Avatar alone, blaze-dragon. She doesn't know how to respond to your ways."

"What *ways*?" he asked innocently enough, but the secret, scalding look he gave her shivered her down to her toes.

Avatar recovered from her momentary fluster. "I know all about young men's enticements. I'm not so old as I've forgotten *that*." She paused, recalling a particularly engaging enticement from her past. She snickered wickedly in fond recall.

Green gasped in feigned shock. "Avatar! *You?*"

"Why not me?" She snorted. "Youth always thinks they invented the sport!"

Jorlan nodded in agreement with her, feigning alignment in her corner. "So what is it she is considering, Avatar?"

Not even realizing that Jorlan had simply switched tracks to get his
answer, Avatar replied. "She wants to take off her clothes, and lie naked
on one of those leaves as it floats down the river to Tamryn Lane."

Jorlan arched his brow. "Green! *You?*"

"Stop that," she grumbled, embarrassed.

He laughed. "Let's do it!" He grabbed the reins of her Kloo.

"*We?* I never said—"

He gave her a look so fraught with sensuality and unspoken promise
that she was momentarily speechless.

Even Avatar started coughing.

Green glanced at her, wondering what she could possibly say.

"It's all right, Marquelle. You'd be foolish not to go now, wouldn't
you?"

Green's lips twitched. "Give us time to float around the far trees and
out of sight, then come back and take the Kloo. Leave our clothes by the
bend at Tamryn Lane. We'll see you later this evening at the big house.
Make sure Miara and her women are comfortably settled and tell
Sweeney, the majordoma, that I will arrive shortly after you." She nodded to Jorlan to dismount.

Jorlan glanced at Green out of the corner of his eye as they slowly
floated down the river. Lying side by side, they both stared up at the sky
through the interwoven branches of the giant jinto plants on either side
of the bank.

The jinto, also known as "the veil plant," was revered on Forus for its
amazing properties. The oldest living plant on Forus, it was estimated
to be five hundred million years old. Because of its staying power, many

of the southern tribes regarded it as a symbol of male fertility. The broad, double-rounded leaf was coated in a velvety, supple skin, while the underlying support structure was extremely rigid.

"There is something symbolic in this, isn't there?" Jorlan joked.

Green closed her eyes and smiled. This was sheer bliss.

"It doesn't seem to have the same effect on me as it does you."

"You don't like it?"

"I like it—I just think there is something about the *feel* of this leaf and the sensation of the rocking water that deeply appeals to the female."

She grinned. "Why would you say that?"

"From the look of utter ecstasy on your face. You know, I've seen that look before, Green," he drawled.

"Have you?"

He turned on his side to face her, rocking the leaf gently. "I wonder what I could do to add to this experience you are having?" His fingers lightly stroked down her arm.

She opened her eyes a fraction, viewing him through the slits.

The edge of his mouth lifted in a sensual half-smile. Without warning, he rolled on top of her.

Green's eyes shot open all the way. "Jorlan!"

He chuckled at her expression, the corners of his eyes crinkling.

Green stared up into his sensual face and lifted her eyebrow. "And what do you think you are doing?"

He actually tried to appear as if he was thinking over her question. Green laughed. The ends of his dark hair tickled her shoulders as his head lowered. He smiled down at her, then brushed her lips with his own.

"That's very nice, wilding, but you still haven't answered me."

He nudged her thighs apart with his leg and settled firmly between them, throbbing in response against her mound without entering her. "You tell me, lexa."

Green arched an eyebrow. "This is not a favored position, Jorlan."

"It seems to be so for me," he whispered down to her. He entered her—just the tip of him.

He was too bold by half. He had actually initiated their lovemaking, which was frowned upon as unseemly for men. On top of it—he was on top. This was a very interesting position, she had to admit. Many women liked the man on top, although they only alluded to it at the clubs. And they engaged in the activity only with their pleasurers, if at all. There was something about the illusion of giving over the control. . . . Although even pleasurers were acting at it. Everyone knew who really had the control.

Only with Jorlan, she worried that this might go beyond illusion. Jorlan would not be pretending to lead the situation. He would. Green wondered if she should let such a blaze-dragon . . . fly.

She might have made the decision except that it was taken out of her hands.

His hands framed her face. As he gazed down at her, his fingers delved in her hair, cupping the back of her head. He continued to caress her hair as the current of the water carried the leaf downstream with gentle rolling motions. Jorlan's entire body slid against her in a smooth yet slightly abrading manner. In addition, he did not move within her, but remained barely inside. The rocking motion of the jinto shifted his internal position ever so slightly; the small induced movements were incredibly erotic.

Behind his dark head, Green noticed the entwined branches of the plants overhead. They reminded her of their sheensui bed at home. Soon their fastening bed would grow together, symbolically representing how a woman and man come together into one after they fasten.

She wondered if they would ever be like that: fusing and joining, growing yet blending together. . . .

"What are you thinking?" he asked softly. He bent his head, letting his lips tease the edge of her bottom lip. Even in this he was already being overly bold. He did not hesitate to ask her her thoughts.

"Why should I be thinking of anything? Cannot a Marquelle simply lie back and enjoy the feel of nature and her name-bearer?" She purposefully prodded him with the strangeness of what he was doing. He did not rise to the bait.

"In that order?" he drawled suggestively, playing his hand perfectly.

"Mmm." *He is a clever torque.* She reached up and languidly ran her fingers through his hair, exactly as he was doing to her. Her fingers laced behind his corded neck, letting the satiny fall of his hair glide through her hands.

Jorlan watched her evenly.

"You have an objection, name-bearer?"

"No," he surprised her by saying.

"And why is that?" She stretched against him, letting him feel her motion up and down his body.

His pupils hazed slightly and dilated. The tactile sensation had affected him more than she anticipated. For a moment he almost became lost in the vision of it. *How much of a Sensitive is he?* she wondered. *How can he be so deeply affected by such a simple stroke?*

Green continued to observe him as the pleasure flowed through his senses. His breath, warm and sweet, licked at her lips. *Like the initial wind before an arc storm . . .*

When he finally spoke, his voice was so low she almost didn't hear him above the lapping water. "I have no objection, Green, because I have come to know that I am one with this connection."

Her mouth parted in a combination of wonder at the beauty of his words and consternation at his meaning. It so closely reflected what she had just been thinking. Did he mean the two of them or his connection to something *else*?

She started to ask for clarification, but Jorlan used the opportunity to kiss her thoroughly, sinking his tongue fully into her mouth. Again, the action was unfashionably bold. And yet, it was unbelievably exciting!

Green knew from experience it wouldn't be long before he went wild.

Sometimes he gave himself over to every touch and movement. When that happened, he always prolonged each sensation—for both of them. It was curious, but Green noticed that, often as not, she became wild right along with him.

"It is not just about sensitivity," he murmured, his breath warm inside her. "It is more than that."

"How did you know what I was thinking?" She played with his mouth, loving the taste of him.

"I just did."

She paused. Looking up, she met his earnest gaze with doubt. "What does that mean, Jorlan, that you 'just did'?"

He gave her a look of disbelief. "I am not a mind reader; what are *you* thinking, Green?" He smiled slightly.

"It's just that you've done that on several occasions now—with a higher frequency than is to be expected. In fact, it is almost uncanny."

"Ah." He nibbled her upper lip, delicately suckling on it.

Green nipped his lower lip sharply.

He gave her a patient look. "What is it, my name-giver?"

"Define 'ah.' "

He shrugged. "We have become . . . in tune. That is all. Much like the seasons and the jinto."

"What does the jinto have to do with us?" She watched him intently.

"Nothing . . . and everything. This jinto leaf we are lying on comes from a plant that is countless millennia old. It was here before any of us humans came to Forus. I wonder what secrets of its five hundred million years of species memory are within the solid stalks and veins of its life."

It was a fanciful thought. She viewed him askance.

"If one could 'hear' its unique voice, Green, what stories would it tell, do you think?"

"Hear . . . as in actually hearing a voice?" She swallowed.

His azure eyes pierced her. "No. Hear as in 'viewing.' "

"I'm not sure I understand exactly what you mean by viewing."

"It is not important." He looked down, veiling himself once more.

Her hand cupped his cheek to gently raise his face to hers. "I think it might very well be of extreme importance."

He shrugged. "Perhaps the vision is simply the essence of life seen as a continuity, a progression through time that is ever changing yet ever the same. Perhaps it speaks of forever and only a moment in time."

"That's extraordinarily thought provoking, Jorlan. Do you have a poet's soul hidden within your depths?" She stroked his cheek. "Tell me, do *you* 'view' this way?"

He almost answered her, then at the last moment, his lashes shielded his eyes from her. "Who can say what we intuit from our imaginations?"

It was more than imagination. She knew it. He simply didn't trust her enough to confide in her. It hurt, but she understood his reasons. He was opening up to her sexually, with his passion. In time, he would in this, too. She had the wisdom to wait.

She arched her back and kissed him deeply. "Yes, my blaze-dragon, who can say?"

He gave her a subtle smile. "You are very wise for such a young name-giver, Green."

"Oh, really! And you are calling me young?" She gave him a sideways look.

He chuckled. "Yes. In essence. At times, you remind me of a child, so—"

"A child!" She started laughing. "I am a She-Lord! I preside over the laws of this land; the welfare of countless people rests on me; I run huge estates; I—"

He placed his fingertip against her lips. "I did not finish. It is your constant wonder and delight even in the smallest of things that makes me say this. Where we are right now is proof of it. Who else in the House of She-Lords would glide down a river naked on a jinto leaf— with or without her name-bearer?"

She bit her lip. "You think it foolish?"

"No. I think it *inspired*." He brushed the back of his fingers against her cheek. "You fascinate me, Green. You always have."

She blinked at him, stunned. "Is that how you describe your reaction to our fastening night? Utter fascination? You blackened the eye of every male Tamryn servant!"

He laughed huskily.

"You are the most difficult name-bearer that a woman could ever—"

He silenced her with his mouth. Hot, steaming sensual kisses that stole her breath. And he kept on giving them.

"You seek difficulty in a man," he whispered between fevered presses of his mouth.

"How do you come to that conclusion?" She moaned, responding to his silken touches.

"Look who's on top," he drawled.

At her outraged expression, he grinned broadly. "But you know what, Green? I think I prefer your choice. I like how you react to it." His mouth covered hers again. Strong. Capturing. Demanding.

Over them, in the branches, blanocks soughed their predusk chorus. The vibrational notes they produced were unlike the sounds of any creature on Forus. They would modulate their strange songs, peaking in and out of resonance with varying cadences. None of their instruments could duplicate it, although many tried. The lush call to dusk always struck a deep chord in humans, arousing in them a sense of tranquility, well-being, and connection.

Many of the Slice purposely tried to woo blanocks to their gardens for that reason. Although, like many of Forus's native residents, they went where they willed. Blanocks showed up in some gardens, yet not in others—no matter what the treat laid out before them.

Green had always enjoyed watching the blanocks at the Reynard estate. For some reason, they loved to flock there.

Green's brow furrowed. Come to think of it, just a few days ago, two were newly spotted on Tamryn property.

"I love blanock song." She sighed happily at the pure notes.

Jorlan smiled softly. "I know you do."

"Avatar said a few have been seen by the house. I hope they stay."

"I've seen them. They are already nesting in the Dreamtree next to the balcony of our bedchamber."

"Really?"

"Yes." He dipped his head and fastened his lips to her collarbone, delicately suckling the skin. The moist, warm drawing action sent tingles to her bare toes.

"*Mmm*, that's lovely. . . ."

"The blanocks or what I am doing?" He rubbed his chin back and forth over the curve of her shoulder.

"Both." *Could anything be as lovely as this?* she wondered. The bobbing of the leaf, the gurgling water, the blanocks, the light cooling breeze, and the feel of Jorlan—inside and out. Surely this was a perfect moment.

"I am partial to your waist chain. . . ." Jorlan's hand stroked down her body, skimming over the thin waistlet she had donned that morning. A tiny gold disc, called a T9-disc, dangled from the lock.

"The T9-disc holds the combination code to the secured, protected records of Tamryn Lane. It was not donned for a fashion declaration, Jorlan."

"It certainly makes a declaration to me." His fingertips slipped under the chain and smoothly toyed with it.

For some reason, Green's skin became extra sensitive under that chain. She wondered suddenly what Jorlan's lips would feel like if they played with the chain the same way.

He met her eyes with complete understanding of her provocative thought. His lips widened into a slow, wicked smile. Then his free hand threaded through her hair, twining it around his wrist so that, when he rested his forearm next to her head, she was effectively pinned down. Soon his mouth played at her ear. "What do you wish for . . . ?" he breathed softly, covering the left side of her chest with his palm. "In here."

She covered his hand with her own. He could feel the rapid tattoo pulsing against his fingertips. Beating wildly to blanock song and to him.

The azure eyes flamed. Jorlan made that special sound in his throat. The sound that always resonated through her—*such incredible passion!*

Green lost her breath at the sheer sensuality of his spirit.

Jorlan scooped some of the cool river water into his palms, letting it stream through his fingers. The liquid cascaded over her breasts. Water pooled between the mounds, running in rivulets over the creamy skin. He watched the last rays of the sinking sun glimmer on the clear moisture, watched the firm peaks harden further as the first breeze of twilight lilted over her slightly chilled skin. And she felt so warm inside!

He bent his dark head, ever so slowly, opening his lips over the red bud so she could feel the warmth of his breath in contrast to the cool water. Ever so slowly, he drew the small bud into his mouth. Ever so slowly, he sipped on the sweet peak.

Green sighed, wantonly lifting into his embrace, closer to the exquisite clasp and tug of his firm lips. He prolonged each palpation of his tongue, of his lips. The extracting, seeking motions designed to wring every last bit of pleasure.

Then he flowed over her like the water that carried them away. Smooth. Sleek. Sensual. His mouth meandered in steam trails. Laving her navel, swirling the perimeter. Drawing.

Green had always been especially tender in that spot. Her eyes drifted shut no matter how hard she tried to continue watching him, no matter how hard she tried not to let the stimulation he was giving her overcome her. He caught her waistlet chain with his teeth, tugging on the links, which he used to roughly pull her closer to him.

Green moaned loudly at the exotic combination of the gentle and the primitive.

Jorlan tossed back his hair and stared at her with narrowed, steamy aqua eyes. "Perhaps you are mine after all."

It was a look she had never seen on any man before.

She swallowed.

The fire in his eyes reflected something profound igniting within him. His breathing altered, becoming deeper, stronger.

Spellbound, she watched him come over her. He rested on both forearms, still pinning her down as he came forward to gaze down at her. There was something in his face . . . some inner acknowledgment. . . .

She was curtained by that jet hair. She was curtained by *him*.

Jorlan made sure she could not look away from him as he penetrated her, sure and fast. All the way. Until he could go no farther.

Until his hipbones tunneled into the rounded edges of hers.

Green cried out sharply at the angle of penetration, at the complete fullness. Her uninhibited cry scared a flock of blanocks into flight.

But the sound he wrung out of her had nothing at all to do with fright.

It spoke of sheer elation.

The awareness of him on top and inside made her reckless. He pulsed within, flexing sharply against her inner walls. He covered her mouth with his own, drowning out her pleasure moans only to fill her with his own low purrs of ecstasy.

Green's hands cupped his buttocks, kneading the firm globes, bringing him deeper, closer, tighter to her.

Jorlan groaned raggedly and thrust sharply into the wet channel, over and over. Grinding his hips, his mouth never leaving hers, he stroked stronger and harder.

It wasn't as if his control left him, Green realized, but rather that he had joined his will to his desire.

A Sensitive's desire.

One of his palms slid like flame over her hip, grasping her thigh. He expertly moved her leg up and over to the side in a skillful maneuver that many a pleasurer would never learn. The position allowed him the deepest access. Like everything about Jorlan, he intuitively knew it. He thrust into her, hands cupping her face as he kissed her wildly. Devouring.

"Jorlan, Jorlan . . ." Green could not catch her breath against this sensual onslaught. He didn't want her to.

"Let me hear you, Green," he rasped unevenly. "Tell me what I am doing to you! Do I drive you wild as you have done to me? Do you think about me when we are apart, when we are together, when I lie sleeping next to you? Do you *ache* in the night when you want me but are forced to wait because it has been declared *seemly* that you must do so?"

It was obvious that he did not realize what he was saying or what he was disclosing to her. Caught up in his passion, Jorlan was simply reacting to the sensuality flaring between them. But she realized.

He ached for her.

All the time.

He wanted her. And he was trying hard to control it.

Was this the side of him that was the Sensitive, or was it more than mere desire . . . ?

He caught her lip between his teeth and tugged on it. "Do the tremors go through your entire body because you can forever taste the texture of my skin . . . ?" He groaned and twitched inside. A sheen of sweat glistened over his body.

"Jorlan," she whispered, "I do want to feel you. . . ."

"Green . . ." His eyes hazed over. "And . . . and . . . do you long to hold me because you can remember my scent and love it when it covers you the entire night . . . ?"

"Ohhh, my name-bearer, I had no idea that—" She cried out, arching her back as he thrust solidly in her.

"Then feel me," he cried, hoarsely. "I am not simply someone who bears your name. I am more. I want *more*."

Her hands sunk into his hair, she cupped his head, her kisses covering his forehead, his nose, his eyes. "I never wanted you to think that you were but a part of the Tamryn holdings! Please tell me you do not feel this way!"

"I feel," his voice was breathless. "I feel . . ."

He blinked. All motion stopped.

His eyes seemed to sharpen. He looked down at her, horrified. His mouth parted slightly. Jorlan had not intended to open himself in this way. His Sensitive's heart had stripped his reason, revealing some of his core—the core he forever shielded from everyone.

Green knew that the only way to stop him from shutting her out again was to lighten his mood. "It's all right, my blaze-dragon. There was no one here but us and the blanocks. The blanocks have since left. I am sure they are not too happy with you for making me scream like a screech wing." Screech wings fed on blanocks.

Against his will, Jorlan's lips curved.

"See if you can do it again," she suggested teasingly in his ear. "I think I see a few still hovering about. Besides, you haven't quite finished what you started." She nipped the lobe.

The corner of his lips twitched, although he seemed somewhat chagrined. "No, I haven't, have I?" He moved slightly in her.

"Mmm, wonderful." She smiled at him.

"Yes, it is." He slid full into her and halted.

Green looked at him quizzically, wondering if he would be all right. If they would be all right.

"I meant what I said, Green."

She took a deep breath. "I know."

He glanced away, then back at her.

Chapter Twelve

They arrived at Tamryn Lane later than Green had intended. The river, which flowed past the back of the property, deposited them on the bank. Per instructions, Avatar had left their clothes for them. They were both pleasantly tired.

Jorlan gazed up the sloping land to the big house. Several large-pane mirastone panels glowed in the dark. Flamelights lined the path. Tamryn Lane was more rustic than Tamryn House, but the plantation was still grand—especially by the provincial standards on Hadley Tip.

Green took Jorlan's hand as they walked the path in companionable silence. The warm strength of his clasp lent a certain unaccustomed comfort to her.

"What do you grow here?" he asked her.

"Hukka crop. If it was light out, you would see it all around us and in the fields to the rear." She gestured to the land beyond the estate house.

"Do you think they got into a bad crop, Green? Like what happened to your parents?"

"No." She shook her head. "That was something quite different. We know more about hukka now—how not to consume it after it flowers. My people here live and breathe the crop; they know what strains to plant and when to harvest. It has to be something else. But I appreciate your help, Jorlan."

He smiled softly, inclining his head. Green was so different from other She-Lords. Perhaps that was one reason why he had always been drawn to her. Even as a child, he had recognized it. It was the way she related to him. Not simply as a male—as a *person.*

"Ah, there's Sweeney waiting at the door for us!" Green's words interrupted his reflection.

The majordoma let them in. Green noticed that Sweeney was not her usual robust self. Her complexion was peaked, her eyes dull. Normally energetic, her movements were listless.

"We've been waiting for you, Marquelle. I can't tell you how happy we are to see you here. I know you'll get to the bottom of this. Just as I told the tenants who wanted to clear out—wait 'til the Marquelle gets here, she'll fix us right up! We're all counting on you, my Lordene."

"Thank you, Sweeney." Green's shoulders dipped imperceptibly. The reaction went unnoticed.

Except by Jorlan.

Gone was her lighthearted spirit of just moments ago, replaced by the heavy responsibility of her title. It was the first time he realized how much rested on her, how many people she was responsible for, how they looked to her for leadership. . . .

He wished he could help relieve some of this burden. His experiences in the Ducheen's house must count for something, and he had his own way of solving things. Perhaps he could aid her with just the two of them knowing, just as he had done with the weavermouth.

Only he would be wielding a weapon much different from the meteor-blade.

And yet, so very similar.

"Come into the keeping room, then." Sweeney tried to liven her step, but it was plain she was out of sorts. "You both must be hungry. I'll have cook fix a nice tray for you and bring it in to you myself. Avatar and Miara are awaiting you in there."

"Thank you, Sweeney."

"And may I say congratulations on your fastening? We are all very pleased to have you here as well, Marqueller."

"Thank you, Sweeney." Jorlan smiled in a charming way at the woman, causing her to become quite flustered. She dipped an odd bow and shakily left the room.

"Another conquest," Green muttered under her breath.

Jorlan chuckled. "You must be so proud to have such a fine name-bearer. Are you not, Marquelle Tamryn?" He folded his arms over his chest and gave her a very bland look.

The torque was pushing the line. Green clicked her tongue. "And so demurely modest about it, too."

"But of course." He grinned a slow, wicked smile.

Rolling her eyes, Green took his wrist and dragged him behind her into the keeping room.

Jorlan got brief glimpses of the house. Airy rooms, a much lighter style of furniture than Tamryn House, with plenty of paddle fans on the ceilings. This was a much warmer, humid climate than the one he was used to. The air was thick, and yet he liked it. The rich scent of nightbloomers tinged the air even inside the house. *Exotic sounds and textures . . .*

"It took you long enough!" Avatar groused good-naturedly as she sipped a hameeri liquor by the fire.

Miara rose. "Marquelle. Marqueller," the protector-guard greeted them.

Green joined them by the fire, taking a seat with Jorlan on the settee. "What is the status here, Miara?"

"A little over half the household is sick."

It was worse than she had thought. Green bit her lip, sending a worried glance Jorlan's way. She was concerned about the risk of illness for her name-bearer. "I never should have exposed you to this."

"I will be fine." He gently squeezed her hand to reassure her. "And I am here to make sure you will be, as well."

Green squeezed his hand back in a silent show of gratitude for his support. "What is causing the sickness, Miara? Any ideas?"

"Just speculations, Lordene. They have checked the crops to be sure it is nothing there. The hukka is fine. The crop manager wonders if it is not some kind of microbe that keeps being passed again and again amongst the household. No sooner does someone start to feel better when it comes back again. It has weakened the entire staff and most of the tenants. Several of the tenants have already left, despite Sweeney's valiant efforts. Reports coming back are that the illness does not leave with them. Once away from Tamryn Lane, a complete recovery ensues."

Jorlan arched his brow. That told him much. *The illness was tied to, or was of, the land.* He might just be able to help Green more than he had anticipated.

Green sighed at Miara's assessment. "The harvest will soon be upon us; we cannot afford to lose our people. There will be no one to bring in the crop. There has to be an answer for this. What did the local methodologist say?"

Avatar swirled her drink around in the goblet. "Apparently, she is nowhere to be found. Curious, isn't it?" She caught Green's eye.

Green knew what she was implying. Rural OneNation areas such as

Hadley Tip had an assigned methodologist to the region. Often they were of a sub-par standard and received their posts either as political favors or through connections.

Still, even a poor methodologist was better than none. And they had to take an oath, promising that they would never abandon their posts. Areas could not be left without replacements; rural people relied heavily upon their expertise in critical situations. The penalty for abandonment was steep.

It was too unusual an occurrence to overlook.

Sweeney entered the room with a tray laden with food. Jorlan immediately went over to help the older woman with the heavy burden.

Which flustered her anew.

"Our Jorlan has entranced another one," Avatar spoke low to Green as she discreetly handed her a code-sealed pocket envoy. "This arrived for you via the main house line. It looks serious."

Green glanced down at the small disc and its branded imprint seal. It had been burnt immediately into the small pocket envoy disc, which indicated its confidential status. The Septibunal had sent the dispatch. Only her personal viewer would be able to decipher its coded language. Such messages were rare. While not of an emergency nature, their contents were most often of the direst kind. She did not have a good feeling about this.

Green acknowledged Avatar's concern and slipped the disc onto her waist chain. She would read it later, when she was alone.

Jorlan placed Sweeney's tray on the low table between their chairs, retaking his seat on the settee beside Green.

Sweeney wiped her damp brow with a cloth. "I beg your pardon, Marquelle, this illness has left me drained."

"I can see it has. Please take a seat, Sweeney."

"But, Marquelle! It isn't proper for a—"

Green waved her to the seat, ending her objections, then reached over the arm of the settee for the carafe of water. "Would you like some, Jorlan?"

"Not right now, thank you."

Green poured her drink. "Well, since we are to get no help from the methodologists, we must become our own investigators. I think we should start by re-creating the progression of the disease. Who had it first, where did it initially spread to. . . ." She brought the goblet to her lips.

Jorlan, who had been gazing into the fire, swiftly turned his head. His aqua focus fixed on the water. Before she even had a chance to take a sip, his palm came over the top of the cup.

Green gave him a quizzical look.

Casually, so as not to alarm the others by his behavior, he bent near her ear. "Do not drink it. It is tainted," he whispered.

She glanced down at the water, then back up at him. "Are you sure?" she whispered back.

"Yes."

They stared at each other for a long moment. He offered no explanation, no basis for the conjecture; he simply expected her to trust him without asking why. Should she?

Green placed her goblet back on the table. "This water does not seem right to me, Sweeney. Has the cistern been checked?"

"Yes, my Lordene. There is no cloudiness in the water, nor any odor. Our regular testing methods recognized no harmful organisms."

"This may not be so simple." She met Avatar's knowing look. "The methodologist must have had a molecular analyzer. Where was her station?"

"Up in the Victorias, Marquelle," Avatar answered her.

The Victorias were located just after the next plantation. "Good.

Someone can make the trip there and back tonight. In the meantime, no one is to drink the water."

Sweeney paled. "If it is the water, we shall die of thirst out here without a supply. What do we do then, Marquelle? The river water is not drinkable."

"Perhaps we can make a temporary arrangement with one of your neighbors, my Lordene, at least until the problem is solved," Miara suggested.

Miara didn't know that the neighboring plantation was owned by a branch of the D'anberes. In no way could Green make an arrangement with them. "That won't be necessary. Fortunately my foremothers were smart women. There is an alternate water source secretly hidden in the far eastern slope. It is less convenient, so the water will have to be ported until we can clear the main cistern."

Relieved, Sweeney nodded and rose tiredly to her feet.

She returned shortly with another goblet and additional hameeri for Green. "Drink this, Marquelle—until we know for certain."

"A rather extravagant substitute." Green sipped the expensive liquor.

"What makes you suspect the water supply, Marquelle?" Miara also poured herself another cup of hameeri.

Green pointedly stared at the goblet of water she had placed back on the table. "I never disregard what is right *next* to me—no matter how innocent it appears."

Out of the corner of his eye, Jorlan keenly watched her. His name-giver was too clever by half.

*I*t was indeed the cistern.

The water had been laced with a toxic biocrobe, specifically designed to cause vague yet lingering symptoms. Someone had purposely sabotaged their water supply. And the toxins were from a very sophisticated source.

A source only found in Capitol Town.

Biocrobes were used for targeted purposes—usually they were designed to feed on other biocrobes or on naturally occurring Forus organisms that were dangerous to humans. In terms of illness, they were administered only as a cure—never as a cause.

There was worse news.

Green had read the pocket envoy. The Septibunal was calling her and Jorlan back to Capitol Town for a special hearing regarding her fastening. Jorlan's Ritual of Proof had been brought into question "with substantial evidence to the contrary." The missive went on to further state that such a transgression, if proven accurate, would not be taken lightly by the Septibunal.

Green knew exactly how to interpret that weighty pronouncement.

It meant that their fastening could be dissolved and Jorlan stripped of all his titles and his rank in society. He would be without protection. In addition, there would be a huge forfeiture penalty from both the House of Tamryn and the House of Reynard for their part in conspiring in perjury to the Septibunal. Jorlan himself might very well be part of that forfeiture.

They could all be ruined.

Since she had forgone the Ritual of Proof, only she and Jorlan knew the truth. Her word would be all she had on the floor of the chamber.

All she had against whatever evidence they had to the contrary.

There was only one person who could be behind this. *Claudine.*

Green slammed her palm against the wall of the bathing chamber. It was always Claudine! She never stopped and she was becoming bolder and bolder. If Jorlan hadn't determined that the water was tainted, she might have lost many of her tenants, which in turn would have left most of the hukka crop unharvested. There was an extremely short window for optimum harvesting of hukka—right before it flowered and became toxic.

She was already heavily extended. Jorlan's bed price had almost drained her coffers. Anya Reynard was hurting as well, she had needed Green's money to pay back Claudine. She-Count D'anbere was very aware of their situation—she had caused it. Claudine also knew the loss of this crop would be devastating!

Green suspected that Claudine had arranged for her to leave Capitol Town by tainting the water supply here at Tamryn Lane. While Green was away from Town, she had used the opportunity to stir up the Septibunal.

The woman worked fast, she'd give her that.

Green glanced at the missive again.

Due to the grave nature of your sojourn to Tamryn Lane, the Septibunal is allowing you to complete your business there at which point you must return immediately. There is a rumor you are with child.
                                                    Duchene Hawke

Rumor? What rumor? Green closed her eyes and took a deep breath. Duchene Hawke was subtly giving her a message without violating her position. Green would remember her kindness. Duchene Hawke was telling her not to return until she had a well-laid defense in order.

And that defense included a child from Jorlan.

Preferably an heir.

It would be much harder for the Septibunal to revoke their vows once an heir had been added to the Tamryn scroll. Such an heir would ensure a next-in-line for their houses. Even if Claudine's scheme ruined them, if her heir was already born, the Septibunal would consider her birthright as separate and inviolate.

For the Duchene even to hint at this, the evidence they had must be entirely condemning.

Green glanced into the room, seeing Jorlan; he was fast asleep in the middle of the bed. He was tired. It had been a long day fraught with so many emotional pulls. Their ride down the river on the jinto leaf, their unorthodox lovemaking, and the concern over this troubling illness.

Jorlan. He was still not safe from Claudine! Green passed a hand over her eyes. Their estates were not safe.

She must protect them; it was her responsibility both to her fore-mothers and to all the people who depended on her to survive. She had to produce an heir—and soon! Even if she lost her holdings they would fall to her heir. A Tamryn.

Green sighed, knowing what she must do. Their relationship was just beginning to blossom—this would damage it, she was sure. Jorlan would feel betrayed and forced and utterly controlled.

But there was nothing to be done. She had to act now. She knew that with every fiber of her being.

He would just have to come to terms with it.

She needed to discover why he claimed he could withhold his seed. After what she had seen of his ways, she was not so sure he had spoken out of ignorance. Any man who could wield two meteor-blades at once with the grace of a Gle Kiang-ten master just might know what he was talking about.

Resolved, yet saddened, Green lowered the flamelight and slid into bed next to him.

He immediately rolled toward her, wrapping her in his arms in his sleep.

"Jorlan," she whispered, her lips pressed his forehead.

"Mmm . . ." He cuddled his face into her throat and went on sleeping.

She smiled faintly. He was a contradiction of fire and gentle rain.

Her fingers sifted through his clean hair—still spicily fragrant from his recent bath. The vigorous strands settled softly into place. Even in the darkened room she could see the black, glistening sheen of it.

His warm breath teased her skin, rhythmic puffs that were perfectly relaxing.

Only she could not relax.

Not now.

Too much depended on how she combated Claudine's wiles. There was so much at risk, including her Jorlan.

She glanced down, watching him as he slept, peacefully unaware of all the currents around him. Currents that had the potential to drown the Tamryns and the Reynards.

"Jorlan . . . ?" she spoke low in his ear.

His lashes flickered against her neck as he clung to his sleep.

Her lips pressed against his forehead again. Green wanted to awaken him gently. She wanted his guard to be down.

Or as down as she was likely to get it. She pressed up against him.

He took a few sleepy nibbles at her throat in an attempt to get playful before his breathing fell to an even rhythm once again.

She whispered in his ear. "Wake up, wilding, I need to speak with you. . . ."

Jorlan's lashes flickered again. His mouth opened on her throat and softly laved the tender spot.

Green smiled. He obviously had not understood the word "speak." In his sleep-haze, he thought she had something quite different in mind. "No, sweet dragon. I need to ask you something."

"*Nnnn?*" He didn't remove his mouth, which now moved up her neck and was lightly sucking on her lobe.

"What did you mean when you said you will not give me an heir? Males cannot prevent that."

He stopped nibbling. She could feel his breath hot on her skin as he stilled and tried to awaken.

She immediately began stroking his back in long, light sweeps, knowing that such an action would lull him back into a relaxed mode. It was something she had learned of his Sensitive's nature. When awakened from slumber, he was very susceptible to touch and massage. It seemed to enervate him and all his focus pooled into whatever he was feeling. On a few occasions, he had become drowsy yet unbelievably aroused at the same time. The fascinating juxtaposition was one more facet to his intriguing response to stimulation.

Was it any wonder that throughout the ages, scores of odes had been written about the enigmatical Sensitive?

"I . . ." He inhaled the scent of her skin; a low moan rolled from his throat. Green continued to stroke his naked back, still warm from his sleep. Her foot slid between his legs.

"Mmm, what are you doing with your foot?" He sighed against her breast. Then his teeth scraped sensuously along its edge.

"What were you going to say?"

He took a deep breath. "I can prevent it, Green," he finally admitted.

Green looked down at him in dismay. Did he realize what this could mean? "How?" She tried to keep the worry out of her voice.

He raised his eyes to hers. "I can tell the cycle of your natural rhythms. I know when . . . *how* you are responding to that cycle."

"That is impossible! No one can just know such things."

His palm cupped her breast. "It is possible." He flicked the peak with his tongue.

"But . . . you . . . that is . . . you *do* release, Jorlan."

"Of course."

"Then there is always the possibility that—"

"No. I know you have been off your peak cycle."

Green gasped. He was right. How could he know that? "I have never heard of this!"

"No?" He seemed surprised. Then she felt him grin against her chest. "Perhaps I will teach you something then, my name-giver."

Green frowned at him. "Men do not just know these things, Jorlan."

"Really?" He playfully bit the side of her breast. Without thinking, she brushed her thigh against his. "Ah, I love the feel of you. . . ." Jorlan, so relaxed, almost seemed to fall back asleep again.

Green absentmindedly stroked him as her mind raced for answers. "Tell me how you know this," she prodded him.

"Hmm?"

Green arched warmly against his body. "Your way of knowing?" she asked.

He yawned. "It is simply the cadence of nature. . . ." He yawned again.

There was nothing simple about this. "Are you saying that you somehow *intuit* my cycle?"

He hesitated. "I cannot put it into the correct words exactly . . . but, yes."

"It's never simple," she murmured to herself.

He bit her shoulder and stretched out against her, promptly falling back to sleep. Sometimes it was impossible to wake a man.

Sometimes that was a good thing.

Cadence of nature. He was about to learn something new about a woman's cadence.

The next day, Green took Jorlan on an extensive tour of the plantation, all the while giving him a detailed lecture on the hukka crop.

Jorlan realized most She-Lords would not bother to discuss the intricacies of a working plantation with their name-bearers, believing that their only interests were of the frivolous kind.

She not only explained how the crops grew and how they harvested, but she included a detailed description of the best methods of minimal processing in order to maximize the wholesomeness of the grain. She then went on to teach him about how the grains were priced on the market, and included some secret Tamryn techniques for getting top plat-coin for their crop—which was, by and large, considered by the Slice to be a select variety of grain.

Jorlan listened carefully. As was his wont, he remained quiet while he learned what he needed to know.

Green was amazed at his retention level; she was more than pleased with his acute interest, making a note to herself to begin teaching him everything she could about the Tamryn holdings. She had always believed that knowledge was the best weapon. Too many times she had seen vast estates go under due to poor or corrupt management as the result of something untoward happening to the She-Lord. Most name-bearers did not have a clue as to how to step in and take control; the job usually fell to the nearest female relative. Sometimes unscrupulous relatives would take over the properties entirely, ousting the former name-bearer to a monkery, along with any of his sons.

Green wanted to make sure that Jorlan would be able to carry on their legacy if something should happen to her. To that end, earlier, she had shown him the secret route through the jinto forest to the second cistern. The route was known only to five of her most trusted household members. She explained to Jorlan that if the location of it should ever be discovered, it would mean the Tamryns had a traitor in their ranks.

By the time they checked the silos, night was falling.

"Are you tired, Jorlan?"

He straightened, lengthening his spine in a stretch as he sat astride Kibbee. "No, just hungry." He grinned.

He gave her a smoldering look that left no room for interpretation. Which was just the mood Green wanted him in.

She had plans for her unrestrained name-bearer. Plans he was going to love.

And hate.

She answered his glance with a slow, seductive smile. "You are thinking like a true Tamryn, wilding." She purposely turned her mount toward the big house.

It was going to come down to tonight.

*W*hen they got back, a much improved Sweeney led them to a small dining area in one of the alcove plantrooms. As they took their chairs at the two-seat table, Sweeney informed Green. "The strain of the biocrobe has been identified, my Lordene. You were right. Avatar has already sent to Capitol Town for a neutralizing agent."

"How are the tenants?"

"Well, with the untainted water now reaching them, many are much improved. But then we knew you'd fix it all up right, Marquelle—once you got here."

Sweeney beamed at her, then lit the small flamelight on the table. "I'll tell tonight's serving boy to bring your meal. Looks like you two can have a nice quiet dine. It's right pretty tonight, now that Arkeus is high and the other moons are shining." She gave Green another beaming glance and left.

"She looks upon you as a savior," Jorlan teased.

Green blushed. "They are not used to our cit ways out here."

"Maybe that is not a bad thing. I like it here in the South Lands. It is so open and free." He leaned toward her, resting his elbows on the small circular table.

"Ha! You might think twice before you say that. This is only the Hadley Tip of the South Lands; they are still somewhat civilized here. Go farther south and you would be scooped up by a savage tribeswoman. And she would treat you with less cordiality than she does her Klee. They are nothing like Capitol Towners who know how to spoil their men with comfort and Ramagi silk." She grinned at him.

"Hmm." He rested his chin in his palm. "Avatar indicated as much. I thought she was exaggerating."

Green shook her head. "Hardly. Although I imagine a leader might indulge her name-bearers as a way of showing off her wealth to her sisters."

"*Name-bearers?* As in plural?" Jorlan eyes rounded.

A dimple grooved her cheek. "Oh, yes. It's quite the custom down there even though we in Capitol Town consider it barbaric. But then that is the South Lands." She shrugged.

"You are jesting, aren't you?"

She gave him an innocent look. "The Western Colonies are worse in some ways."

"You won't tell me, will you?"

She gave him a tiny smile.

He gave her a beseeching stare with a slow sweep of his black lashes.

Green chuckled. "I will tell you this—it is worse than you imagine and better than you think."

He exhaled, pretending frustration at her response. "I shall just have to see it for myself then."

Green became serious at once. "No. It is far too dangerous a place for you."

"I can handle myself, as you have seen."

"Not against tribeswomen. I'm afraid you will have to stay out of that region, my name-bearer. I could not guarantee your safety down there. You would be taken . . . in *every* way. Perhaps by many."

His mouth parted slightly at the crude picture she painted.

"I am sorry to shock you, but that is the way it is. It is better you do not harbor any romantic illusions about the place as some young men do. It would be an assault on your nature."

"Mothers let their sons be treated like this?"

"No. That is the fate of outsiders. Their sons are strictly watched over from birth. They are kept cloistered and sheltered in the family home until their fastening day—which in most cases is the day they meet their name-giver. Once fastened, name-bearers must show respect by coming to their name-givers from the foot of the bed. Sometimes they pleasure their name-givers silently under the covers—a symbol of their never intruding upon their name-giver's importance or life."

Jorlan scowled disgustedly. "I do not think I will be asking you to take me there."

"I didn't think you would."

Their meal arrived with a young serving boy, who was so nervous to be serving the Marquelle and Marqueller that he almost dropped his tray. Jorlan caught it just in time and righted it for him. "There's nothing to be worried over, lad," he spoke in the smooth tone Green had heard him use on Hugo and Sabir.

It seemed to calm the poor fellow right down, for he finished laying the dishes in a competent manner and left.

"Does that only work on males and animals?"

"What?" Jorlan paused with his drink lifted halfway to his lips.

"That voice you use to tame."

"The voice I use to— What are you talking about?"

"Don't act as if you don't know. That smooth, silken tone that rolls over one like flowercream."

His aqua eyes flashed amusement. "I don't know—but I'm willing to test out your question later . . . if that is what you desire, name-giver." He looked as if he were enjoying some secret merriment.

"Hmm." Green sipped her hukka brew.

Jorlan snorted and dug into his plate of steamed snob-bobs. "Mmm. They don't taste like this back home."

"That's because they have to be imported from out here." Snob-bobs lived exclusively on the bottom of the southern rivers. Only certain fisherwomen had the ability to dive for them. Their pink flesh was extraordinarily sweet and beloved by the Slice, who thought nothing of paying exorbitant prices for importing them.

Hence the name given them by the fisherwomen: snob-bob.

As they were enjoying their companionable meal, Avatar's and Miara's heated voices, from the other side of the house across the courtyard, peaked and waned over the various shrieks of night creatures.

"Are they having a row?" Jorlan chuckled. "If they are, my plat-coin is on Avatar."

Green laughed. "They are playing shredder. They always do when we come down here. Rural life curtails the night life of Capitol Town. I wouldn't be surprised if Sweeney is in there with them as well, having her wages neatly skimmed by those two."

Jorlan's brow furrowed. "What is shredder?"

"It is a southern game of chance played with small, stiffened pieces of shredder plant. I will show it to you sometime, if you like."

"Might be interesting. Can we wager?" He viewed her through half-closed eyes.

Green sat back in her chair and folded her arms across her chest.

When it came to games of sport, she was an expert. As he was about to find out.

"What would be the point if we didn't, my blaze-dragon?"

She gave him an enigmatic smile.

Jorlan hesitated at that smile. He paused for a moment as he observed his Marquelle.

Then arched his brow in challenge.

Chapter Thirteen

*W*hile Jorlan was bathing, Green went over to her pharmkit. She was in her fertile cycle, but the implant on the underside of her upper arm would prevent a pregnancy. Woman always had complete control over their cycles. Most women simply put their cycles into a latent, dormant state when they were not thinking of having heirs. The phase maintained proper hormone levels while blocking fertilization.

Every so often, a woman came out of the "dormancy" for several cycles. Green was in such a phase now, which was a good thing because she would not be able to do what she was about to do if she wasn't.

She took a handheld out of her pouch and flipped open the top. Then she simply clicked a button and snapped the lid shut. *Sweet Cybella, it was good to be female!*

Already, her hormone levels were rising to complete an ovulation. Without the implant releasing its coded instructions, she had just made herself fertile.

She was about to find out how sharp Jorlan's instincts were.

* * *

*G*reen was already in bed when Jorlan came into the room from the bathing chamber.

She decided to immediately draw him into her sensual battle.

It wouldn't take much, she knew. He had been headed to this point all along. She was simply going to prod him over the edge. And with good reason.

There was too much danger around them for her not to take this step. She had saved his life, now he must save their name and their lines. Regardless of her personal wishes, she had to do this.

"Are you waiting for me, lexa?" he drawled as he eagerly approached the bed. Like most new name-bearers, he became rigid simply from the thought of sex. Once through the ordeal of losing a veil, come-outs usually became quite eager for what they had been missing all those years.

Especially if they had been broken in right.

She purposely baited him. "What makes you think I would wait for you?"

Jorlan stopped advancing and stood at the foot of the bed. His lips parted in surprise at her mood. "I did not mean anything untoward, Green. Surely you realize that?"

"Do I? Why is that? You have been overly bold this entire day."

As she had intended, her jibe flamed the mark. His nostrils flared. "How so?"

"Your comment at the table, for one. The serving boy heard you—I think it was why he almost dropped our meal."

Jorlan blinked. "I—"

"And yesterday, on the jinto leaf. Do you have any idea how you flaunt convention and risk your name? *My name?*"

"What are you talking about?" His pupils flared in anger.

Very good, Green thought. Her name-bearer was a man of hot emotion. In all ways.

The steely azure eyes narrowed. "I care not for convention and you know it well!"

Green crossed her arms over her ample chest and stared at him as haughtily as a Marquelle could. "Yes, I know it well. You should be submissive like other name-bearers!"

A pulse beat in the side of his neck.

Her provocation worked. The one thing guaranteed to raise Jorlan's ire was a reminder of a name-bearer's status. His nostrils flared as he stared at her stonily.

"Do you hear me? I said *submissive*."

"Oh, I will be submissive, if that is what you desire, name-giver." His voice was chillingly low.

Resolutely, he walked over to the foot of the bed. Lifting the silken sheet, he insolently slipped underneath. Whereupon, he slid his way up under the coverlet toward her on his back.

It was a calculated insult to the traditions of the southern tribes. Green prepared herself for what was sure to follow.

When he reached her legs, his untamed touch was anything but submissive.

Green gasped as his strong fingers clamped around her ankles and yanked her down so she was lying flat.

His sharp teeth caught fast at the back of her heel, nipping roughly as his hands roughly pushed her legs apart. Slowly, on his back, he slid up between her calves. Silken strands of hair brushed her leg. She could feel his anger in the rapid, hot exhalation of his breath against her body.

His mouth clamped on the tender skin of her inner calf. The bite he administered was an exquisite blend of erotic fury.

A puff of air escaped Green's lips as she tried to yank her legs free.

Not that she actually wanted them free.

She had set out to provoke him and the tournament was just beginning. The more she invoked his "submissiveness," the more furious he would become. Green was counting on her ability to know exactly how he would react. She had no doubt that she was about to fuel the blaze-dragon out of control.

She also knew that she was the only one who could ever do this to him.

Jorlan had made himself vulnerable to her.

Such vulnerability denoted a high level of trust. His perception of this would be a violation of that trust. She prayed that in time he would realize that his trust in her was inviolate. What she was doing now would hopefully protect them both in the future. It was the *only* thing that could protect them.

His mouth worked along her legs in quick heated bites, sharp presses of his lips. His tongue slid against the backs of her knees. Then he dragged his open mouth behind her thighs, the sting of the edges of his teeth scraping like pinpoint flicks of a needlewing. His breath was coming in short, shallow pants; already he was delving into the passion of his anger.

Green's fists caught at the material of the coverlet, squeezing it between her fingers, steeling herself for this erotic onslaught. Her heels dug into the bedding as his lips moved higher on her, trailing moistly between and behind her thighs. As he worked, his jaw purposely scraped and kneaded against the soft skin. His arms locked tightly on her legs as she pretended to attempt to twist herself free.

"I think you should release me, Jorlan," she hissed, breath catching in her throat as his teeth tugged at the soft exposure behind and under the curve. He did not respond to her directive except to spread her legs farther apart.

She felt his long hair sliding against her buttocks. Then his fiery tongue stroked a molten trail at the juncture of her legs.

"Jorlan!" Green threw her head back against the pillows, upper body arching.

Jorlan's arm tightened across her legs, pinning them to his chest. "Am I not submissive enough for you?" he rasped.

Not waiting for an answer, he spread her nether lips from beneath her and began to devour her. In front of her, his fingers tangled in her woman's curls and tugged sharply.

Green had anticipated a strong response from him; she had just not anticipated this utter surrender to his Sensitive's side. Somewhere she had read that a high Sensitive, if angered, might free fall completely into his sensual responses. Since no high Sensitive had ever been tested, the supposition was pure conjecture.

Green had wondered about the limits of his abilities.

Now she knew.

Jorlan was indeed a high Sensitive. *And she had purposely provoked him.*

She knew it would be best to stop this now, but it was too late. Jorlan was beyond rational choices. He would react strictly to his tactile impulses until he had played out the erotic passion brought out of him. Green closed her eyes as she reared off the bed in response to his ministrations.

His tongue insinuated itself and slid the length of the seam, swirling against the folds in a very dedicated way. The tip of his tongue wriggled up and down, dabbing the throbbing center of her desire. The hardened nub pulsed stronger and stronger.

Green bit her lip to keep from screaming out a release. She needed to hold back.

He flicked the tender, central spot, tapping strongly. A moan escaped her clenched jaw.

Jorlan craved more than that from her.

Strong, long fingers dug into the front of her thighs. With steady pressure, he curved her back into him—so he had the exact access he wanted. *Full access.* His chin rubbed teasingly into her mound, grinding against her opening.

The intense, rotating pressure—an unbearable pleasure—elicited the reaction he sought. Green tried to break his hold, but the odd position made it impossible. He had the upper hand. In more ways than one.

Molten, satin lips covered her entirely. A ruthless kiss of passion. Then he suckled sharply—right where she throbbed the most.

Green screamed. Her entire body convulsed. Without thought, she covered his hand on her thighs, clawing desperately at him, trying to get him to free her. He pressed his tongue inside her and *stroked*. With each slick plunge, he propelled her internal spasms on and on.

The shudders racked her over and over. She had never experienced anything close to this ecstasy in her life. How long could he keep her like this? As long as he desired, she realized.

Hot lips skimmed over her buttock, sultry and wet. A deep groan of unbridled hunger etched along her skin, half plea, half conqueror.

At the base of her spine, Jorlan pressed his mouth, drawing tightly on the delicate curve. Caught fast in his grip, Green emitted a soft cry of wanting.

Swiftly, he shimmied up her back, mouth recklessly laving her backbone, her shoulder blades. She felt him slide totally under her now; the damp skin of his chest grazing provocatively along her spine. Arousing with every contact.

When his lips reached the back of her neck, his arm came around her to firmly hold her on top of him. She squirmed wildly in his embrace.

"Is this submissive enough for you, my Marquelle?" His low voice was rough, breathless.

The tiniest of smiles curved Green's lips. Despite her demeanor, she was still the one in control. She deliberately replied, "Not quite."

Jorlan's pupils flared anew.

"*No?* Perhaps I can be more submissive, then, *just for you.*" He bit her shoulder before flipping them both over on the bed.

He was now on top of her.

Green did not like this position. She was facedown on the bed, while his hips rode snugly against her buttocks. She had never heard of a man being allowed to take such a position! She had never imagined how vulnerable it made a woman.

Green turned her face to the side and bucked against him, grazing his erection with her behind. "Let me up!

He smiled humorlessly against her neck. "It seems to me I asked the same of you once. I do not regret what you did—only the manner in which you did it. Perhaps you will feel the same . . . *later.*"

He grabbed her hands and pinned them over her head.

"This is unlawful—you must obey me!"

He laughed low against her throat. The vibrations of the sensual drawl skittered along her spine. "I do not think a Marquelle who is so unconcerned with proprieties as you are will sound the alarm. It may look bad to your friends," he whispered provokingly.

It was good Jorlan could not see her expression in that moment. For it was an expression of near-victory.

"You will be punished for this."

"Will I?" His wiry curls brushed against the rounded globes of her backside as he ran his member back and forth along the crease of her buttocks. A tiny moan issued from her lips.

"By you, Green?" He stroked against her again. "Are you sure?"

Green sucked in her breath. This was getting perilous! His sensuality was awakening a dangerous need within him to both conquer and enslave himself. The wild erotica of a Sensitive.

"Try me," she responded as coldly as she could.

"I intend to." His manhood, feeling like razor rock encased in Ramagi silk, glided possessively over her back. He rose up on her and traced the back of her neck in the same manner, deliberately letting the pulsing tip of his member skim over the edge of her earlobe and along her jaw line.

"What the rut-bid do you think you're doing?"

"I'm not sure." He wrapped her hair around his wrist and yanked her head back toward him. *"But I like it."* His mouth slammed down on hers. He feasted on her. Wild. Inflamed. Released.

Green knew she was walking a fine line as to what would be viewed as acceptable behavior by the Slice. In firing up Jorlan, she was running the risk of pushing him into areas that might be better left unexplored by a man whose nature was so rebellious. That was, *if* she had the choice. She did not.

"What do you hope to gain by this?" Green spoke around his fevered kisses.

"The question is: What do *you* hope to gain by it?"

Does he know what I am doing? Green gasped as his tongue forced its way between her lips and penetrated her mouth.

Then gasped anew when he immediately penetrated her from behind. He was full and throbbing inside her, buried to the hilt! She cried into his mouth.

Releasing her wrists, his arms tightened about her narrow waist to pull her up, tightly into his groin. Green arched and screamed at the same time, her hands ineffectually pulling at the strong, muscled arms that embraced her. His mouth slid off of hers to feverishly lave the side of her face and jawline.

He groaned a hot ragged breath next to her ear, pressing even more into the wet canal. Wildly, he buried his face in the strands of her hair, inhaling its scent, biting the edge of her lobe right through the mussed-up tresses.

Green had never felt such penetration. It was deep, dark, erotic.

This was what she wanted from him—a Sensitive's uncontrollable desire.

Jorlan was enslaved by his own passion; he surged, strong and deep. Powerful and fast. Lifting to her cadence, her sighs, her cries of "more."

"Yes, yes, yes . . ." Green could feel the ends of his hair flicking her shoulders, the strands shifting along her spine. He rose up higher on her, arching his back to grind into her. Again and again. In that moment he suddenly reminded her of a Forus arc storm. Elemental, raw. An explosion of mysterious force, gathering strength out of nowhere until everything was touched by its magnetism.

Under such a storm, Green clutched the sheet in her hands. "Come, my blaze-dragon! Come to me now!"

Jorlan moaned incoherently and leaned completely over her to bite the edge of her breast.

"Green," he rasped.

The man was lost. It had to be now. Her provocations had held back whatever special sense he had, but it wouldn't much longer. She rotated her hips as she pressed sharply back on him. Her hands encircled his wrists, which he was using for leverage next to her head.

He groaned long and low—somehow holding back. This was not the time to hold back! "Jorlan," she croaked, "Show me your ecstasy . . . !"

Eyes closed, he shuddered violently. Still, he held back. Sweat trickled down his brow. He rested his damp forehead on the curve of her shoulder.

"*I know,*" he murmured raggedly. "I know what you are doing."

Green inhaled unevenly. He knew? Rut-bid!

"What did you do?" he rasped.

Green turned her head and stared into the pale eyes so close to her own. What had she done? She had used his Sensitive's nature against him. The very gift that warned him of her state, enslaved him to it.

Yet he also was a man of his own determinations. She thought it over. Which would ultimately rule him, his logic or his Sensitive's nature?

Green ceased her motions as well and calmly viewed him over her shoulder. A She-Lord in her prime and very much in control. Of her house and of herself. "It is your call, Jorlan. Do whatever you will."

He closed his eyes and the emotion that ripped through him was sublime agony.

With a raw groan he sank into her. He pounded against her forcefully, pulling them both suddenly higher and higher. It was Green's victory. As he rode faster, harder, stronger within her, giving her the child she needed for the continuation of her house, Marquelle Tamryn carried him on the crest of hot desire.

When he yelled his release, he was the captive. Her scent was all over him. *In him.* He had her in his hold, yet it was she who held him.

He had lost.

His Sensitive's nature was hostage to the emotion it craved.

Her love.

"*Y*ou played me."

"As you played me?" Green got out of bed and reached for her robe.

"I know there are things you are not telling me, Jorlan. Yes, I played you. I simply did it better than you. You had a choice. You could have stopped. You didn't."

An angry gust of air exited his nostrils. "A choice! You used my Sensitive's passion against me!"

No, I used it for you. But she could not tell him that. "I met you in a challenge. You lost."

He sat up in bed and furiously kicked the entwined coverlet off his legs.

Green raised an eyebrow. "Take heart. Perhaps you are not as virile as you surmise."

He threw her a look.

Green picked up the hormomitor she had left next to the bed. A series of beeps sounded. A small smile graced her lips. "Then again, maybe you are."

For an instant, Jorlan forgot his anger and stared at her, awestruck. "Are you—?"

"Yes. You have given me a child."

He was unnerved. She could see the warring emotions on his face. Wonder. Trepidation. A flash of speculation. Quickly followed by intense fury.

"I did not give you a child. You took it."

Green's features hardened. He had no idea of the danger they were in. She had not wanted to do such a thing, but after everything he had seen of her, he should have known she had the most important of reasons.

Not that she needed them.

He was her name-bearer; it was his duty and ordained place to give her children. An heir was vitally important to the Houses of Tamryn and Reynard.

Suddenly she was very tired. Tired of every responsibility that had been placed on her shoulders. Tired of having to make choices she abhorred. She pinched the bridge of her nose with her thumb and forefinger. "Perhaps you do not wish my touch anymore?"

His breath stopped in his throat. "No. I did not mean that at all. I—"

She did not let him finish. "Very well, Jorlan. If that is the way you feel, you will not be bothered again."

Her meaning became clear to him. He paled, then flushed in anger. "You—you would seek pleasure *elsewhere*?"

She didn't bother to answer him. Tying the sash on her robe, she left the room.

*J*orlan paced the bedroom like a Klee before an arc storm.

Why? Why did she do such a thing?

Do what? a small voice inside him asked. Act as any Marquelle would have under the circumstances?

He thought she was different! He thought she understood his beliefs. He had even half convinced himself that a part of her agreed with him. He slammed his palm against the wall, unseating an overhead urn from its place on the shelf.

He caught it in midair.

The last thing he wanted was a concerned servant checking on him at the moment. Extraordinary reflexes had been his birthright. He had just never realized why until recently.

Green would bear their child in three months—he was certain she had already taken a natal accelerator, which would shorten the human gestation period by two-thirds. Natal accelerators were the rule rather than the exception. No woman wanted to prolong her pregnancy. The state was draining and at times uncomfortable. For each month that passed, she would pass through a standard human trimester.

The by-product of the acceleration would be extreme tiredness and Green would have to take precisely balanced nutrients to sustain her own health as well as the child's.

He rubbed his forehead.

He was not ready to be a father! How could he ever live his life the way he hoped? How could he effect the changes he sought within the society if he was tied down to his children? Did she not care about his feelings at all? Perhaps he had been fooling himself into thinking he was more to her than simply a man who carried her name and title. More than just brood seed to ensure her line.

Green. A sheen of tears came into his eyes. Did she not know him at all? He loved her with every particle of his Sensitive's soul!

He always had.

There was something in him that recognized the perfect blending of their spirits—like the seasons of Forus, ever changing, yet ever constant. It was something he had only recently come to fully understand.

And it was revealed to him through their lovemaking. Their joinings were powerful and often elemental.

He thought she knew him.

Now they would be estranged.

He sat on the edge of the bed. He did not want that.

Was it so important to her house that she had to beguile him into this at this time? For the first time Jorlan wondered about that. Oh, he knew she had fastened him for that purpose—all She-Lords did.

For some strange reason Marquelle Tamryn had decided that *he* was the one to father her line. He wondered about that, too. Green had never shown the slightest inclination to fasten before meeting him. Could she have fastened him as a favor to his grandmother?

His heart sank.

She might have.

He thought she had some tender feelings for him—the proof of that was the unusual freedoms she had given him. How was he to open her to the complete love he knew they could share if she ended up banishing him to a remote Tamryn estate where he would see her only rarely?

How could he bear to think of her in the arms of another man?

Where would his child go? With him or with her?

A small lump formed in the back of his throat. Despite his objections to this, he would not want to be separated from his child.

He ran a shaking hand over his face.

Wisely, he realized that, despite his beliefs, he did not want to lose his family.

He grabbed the tumbled coverlet in his fist. It was still slightly warm from their bodies. Burying his face in the material, he inhaled the mingled scent of their passion. It covered him like the warm cloak of home.

Once again he was betrayed by his nature.

He could not override the longings of his heart.

That heart would have to trust her.

Green took herself to the farthest reaches of the house.

The topmost floor.

From there, she used her chatelaine to open a private stairwell that led to a rooftop cupola. The round room was open to the elements. In olden days, it had served as a lookout against any unknown indigenous species that might prove hostile to the settlers. None had ever made itself known.

So rooms like this, called visionaries, acquired romantic reputations, for they were often used as rendezvous places by amorous She-Lords. Green had always used her visionary as a place of refuge.

She leaned against the railing and stared out at the expanse of Tamryn land.

The night sky silhouetted the peaks of the hills; Arkeus was setting.

What she had done, she had done, in a sense, for this land. For this land and for her name-bearer. *Jorlan is the Tamryn legacy.*

But had she sacrificed their happiness to protect him from the Septibunal?

She prayed not.

Her hand went tentatively to her stomach. It was flat now but would not be for long. Already the first stirring of the natal accelerator was making itself known in her body. Their beloved child.

A precious life that should have been a symbol of more than the power games of state.

A single tear traced its way down her cheek.

*H*e found her in the study.

She was sitting by the flamelight, perusing a vid-tome. She did not even look up when he entered, although he knew she sensed his presence.

"Yes, what is it?" Her voice was efficient; not cold, yet devoid of warmth.

Jorlan hesitated briefly. He was not a man who generally accepted what was put before him. He took a deep breath. "I would not want you to seek pleasure elsewhere, Green."

She closed her eyes in relief, then held out her hand to him.

He came to her, dropping before her chair on his knees. "Forgive me."

She stared at him wide-eyed, not believing what she was seeing. *This* was a huge concession. He had taken the traditional stance of a contrite name-bearer before her chair.

He embraced her, enfolding her in his arms. As he spoke he covered her face with small kisses. Again, a very time-honored way of apology. "I never meant what I said to you. I can't bear to think of you in the arms of another. I—"

She covered his mouth with her own.

He lifted her out of the chair onto his own lap. *Not* traditional.

Now, that was more like the Jorlan she knew. Green smiled to herself. Her fingers reached up and combed back his long dark hair. He captured her hand in his and brought it to his lips.

"Don't ask me why, Jorlan, for I cannot tell you."

"I will not." His intense aqua gaze bored into her. "I have already reasoned that out."

He had learned to trust her. Somehow he knew that her actions had not been arbitrary. Their relationship had just taken a major step forward.

Green cupped his beautiful face and stroked the side of his firm jaw. "I know you don't like this. You have already told me it is not what you see for yourself. So, if you prefer, you can give the daily care of our child over to a scinose."

Jorlan froze.

"It is often done in the Slice."

"I would not do such a thing, Green," he said softly. "Even though this is not the entire path I seek for my life, I have always felt it the moral responsibility of fathers to care for their own children."

She held back the tears attempting to fill her eyes. He was exactly as she thought. There was a strong, caring passion within him. His rebelliousness was accompanied with a sense of honor. She had seen that when he refused to disrespect his grandmother. "You are my treasure, wilding."

Jorlan took a shaky breath. His palms cupped her face as well. "As you are mine. But, Green . . ."

"Yes?"

"I don't forgive you."

"I know."

The next day, Green and Avatar discussed the best course of action.

While Green wanted to return to Tamryn Hall, both agreed that would not be the wisest thing to do. Word would get out they were there and they would all be called before the Septibunal at once.

So Green elected to remain at Tamryn Lane.

This new Tamryn would be the first in countless generations not to be born at Tamryn Hall.

Green dispatched a missive to Duchene Hawke informing her that she was indeed with child and indicated vague complications. That factor, she wrote, plus the situation on her estate, precluded her return for several months.

Duchene Hawke responded in couched terms that she would indicate such to the Septibunal. The hearing would be postponed.

A later missive followed confirming the postponement with the added note that She-Count D'anbere seemed especially furious with their decision to wait. Again, Green thanked the Duchene for letting her know what was happening. The woman was close to overstepping her impartiality as head of the Septibunal and Green was grateful.

So the weeks passed.

In the beginning, Green was devastatingly tired and slept a good portion of the days, waking only to eat, and to take very short walks with Avatar, who filled her in on what was happening on her estates as well as her business interests.

Jorlan, she had discovered, had an amazing acuity for the workings of the plantation and its systems; he had already laid out several new plans for the irrigation routes, designed three improved storage facilities, which would largely increase their ability to harvest and properly store the crop, thus increasing their profit yield. What was more, he had proposed that they realign their planting cycle to a table he had set forth. He claimed it to be better for the hukka, as it coincided to the rhythms of Forus.

Green had it implemented at once. When Avatar questioned her about it, she simply smiled and said, "Do it."

The crop began to flourish. As it matured under the benevolent eye of Arkeus, so did Jorlan, away from the constrictures of the Select Quarter. The gently rustling plains of the Hadley Tip awakened his sense of being. This mostly ungoverned, open land accessed his deepest nature. In the Marquelle's temporarily diminished capacity, no one questioned his role in overseeing the plantation.

In fact, Green instructed her people to listen to him as they would to her. Jorlan loved her for that, and he quickly came to love Tamryn Lane as well.

Often, at night, he took long solitary walks across the moors. Green watched his silhouette crossing the fields, Arkeus-shine lighting his way. When he returned, late in the night, he would slip into bed, chill and damp from his excursion. He would gather her to him as she slept, letting her heat warm his bare skin.

They had to cease sexual relations until Green entered the next level of the natal acceleration, and even after that such activity would be restricted. One of the drawbacks of the natal accelerator was that almost all of a woman's energy was directed toward the growth of the fetus. Overall, it was not much of a sacrifice, since it cut the time of gestation down so drastically.

Of course, it was vital that Green take acceleration supplements. If not, the nutrients the rapidly growing child needed would be taken from her own body's store, and without such supplements the rapid growth cycle could quickly turn dangerous.

Even so, the waiting was difficult for Jorlan.

When he slept and his control lessened, his Sensitive's nature rose within him. The lightly perfumed scent of her skin and the brushes of her ripe body next to him made him ache. Often at night, he would awaken in a sheen of sweat.

Always hard and throbbing.

A few times Green had awakened as well, and, noticing his state, had relieved him of his misery in a very essential way.

Through their open balcony, his raw moans drifted across the night fields, becoming part of the sultry southern breezes.

The season of the southern arc storms was coming. A band of ore-rock rimmed the mesa they had traveled through. Soon it would be ablaze every night with the dazzling lights of arc strikings. A curtain of ragged fire, slicing the sky. Just one of the dangerous, unexplained beauties of Forus moon.

One night, near to the time of the arc storms, Jorlan went out for one of his solitary walks and returned riding a Klee. Green had heard its thundering pace as it galloped across the land, and she had come to the balcony to see what was happening.

Jorlan was astride the beast. They thundered across the plains, through the fields of hukka. Firewings flitted all around him in tiny bursts of glittering light, their fragile iridescent wings beating in cadence to his unbridled ride. In the distance an arc zigzagged across the sky to the ground, where it connected to an ore-rock with a small explosion. Klee and man raced faster. Wild and elemental.

In fact, the scene was so untamed that Green watched half frozen in fear for Jorlan, yet spellbound at the sheer unfettered beauty of it.

Sabir knows he can race the arcs with me if he wishes. . . . He knows I will stay with him all the way. . . . Green remembered Jorlan's strange words. Was that what he was doing with this Klee? Why? What did it really mean?

She bit her lip as she observed them. Another arc split the sky. The strange Klee reared up and roared in triumph. Jorlan threw his head back and did the same.

What were they celebrating?

Chapter Fourteen

The Klee, which Jorlan called Shringa, made itself part of Tamryn Lane.

In other words, available to Jorlan. It rested on a nice bed of tilla leaves whenever it decided to, and ate whenever it wanted to.

Kibbee was insanely jealous and spent a great deal of time spitting and prawking loudly in protest—to the point where several of Miara's women threatened to take the Kloo out and use her for target practice.

One day, just as Green was beginning to enter her second accelerated trimester, Mathers showed up at their door with Hugo in tow.

Green was shocked. "Mathers, what are you doing here?"

The old majordoma lifted her chin pugnaciously. "I've been present for your mother's birth and yours, Marquelle. That's two generations of Tamryns. I'll be spleened if I'm going to miss the coming of the next heir! I brought the Tamryn sash with me for you to drape over her when she's born."

Green shook her head and smiled at her fondly, hugging the old dear. How had she ever endured such a grueling trip? "Mathers, you shouldn't have."

Hugo was vastly excited to see them. Tails wagging furiously, he scampered over to Green, whereupon his little head bobbed all around her, sniffing and checking. His little head hovered over her rounded stomach, then let out a series of happy yips.

Jorlan strolled into the room, grinning as he saw them. "I thought I recognized those braying yelps." Hugo ran to him, circling around him excitedly. Jorlan obligingly petted the bobbing head.

"Hugo's a noisy thing, isn't he, though?" Mathers watched the pup with patient amusement.

"Hugo?" Jorlan looked over at the majordoma innocently. "I was referring to you, Mathers." He tried to keep a straight face.

"*Phssst!*" Mathers waved her hand, chuckling. "On with you, now, Marqueller. I'm on to your sass-bit tricks."

"Are you?" He stroked his jaw. "Then I suppose I'll just have to come up with some new ones. Can't have you second-guessing me."

Mathers agreed. "Right so, Marqueller."

They both grinned at each other.

"And I suppose I'll have to keep an eye on both of you." Green waddled over to a chair and sank into it.

"What's all this commotion about?" Avatar strode into the room like a general on patrol. Hugo sat up on his hind legs and issued a strange gurgle-plat sound. Presumably a snogglehound respectful greeting of sorts.

"By the Founder! *Not him.*"

Avatar acted irritated by the pup, but Jorlan had caught the irascible advisor sneaking tidbits to him on more than one occasion.

"Ah, he's not that bad, once you get used to his odd ways." Mathers replied.

"*You're* defending Hugo?" Jorlan was shocked.

"I wasn't speaking of Hugo," Mathers shot back.

Jorlan's eyes danced. He threw her one of the hand signals she had taught him.

"Jorlan!" Green was shocked. She turned an accusing look on to Mathers, who looked at the ceiling.

Avatar rolled her eyes and put up her hands to stop the squabbling that was sure to start. "There's enough of that! Tell us, Mathers, what news from Capitol Town?"

Mathers gave a discreet glance at Jorlan, saying, "Oh, the usual nonsense: She-Count Lazara has been making a play for Marquelle Juene's youngest son, much to her horror. The Marquelle can't abide Lazara's drinking ways, but after all, she's also got five other snip-butts to fasten-off, though he be the best looking of the bunch, which isn't saying much." All of the Juene boys had wispy hair and thin lips. "If you ask me, she should take the offer and be glad of it." Mathers loved to gossip.

"True." Avatar concurred.

"Rumor has it that D'anbere is after that pleasurer River Carmel." Mathers gave Green a meaningful look. Green's hand went to her throat. *River.*

"Did—did he accept?"

Jorlan's acute gaze watched his name-giver.

"No. They say he actually tossed her out the door of that place he lives at on the Rue de la Nuit."

"That must have endeared him to the Slice," Avatar grumbled.

Mathers shrugged. "D'anbere is not well liked. Besides, it's known he's under the protection of a powerful She-Lord. Most think She-Count D'anbere was out of line."

Green nodded but knew that River was in grave danger. She needed to send a message to him to watch his back lest he find a D'anbere blade in it.

Jorlan stroked Hugo's head as he listened to the byplay. He was not fooled. He knew that River was—*had been*—Green's pleasurer. He couldn't stop the blister of jealousy that rose in his throat. He hated to think of her with him in the past, although he understood that women had their needs and couldn't be expected to wait for fastening as men did.

Mathers turned to Jorlan. "Your friend, the one that was at your fastening, got himself bid on."

He raised an eyebrow. "Lymax? Who bid on him?"

"She-Lord Baringer." Mathers winked at him.

Jorlan grinned. Baringer was a kindly, quiet She-Lord, who preferred country life and vid-tomes to the mad bustle of the Select Quarter in Capitol Town. His friend had lucked out after all. He was happy for him.

"We can go visit them when we return, if you like, Jorlan. I rather like She-Lord Baringer and her estate is only a day's journey from Tamryn House."

"I would like that, Green." He smiled at her.

"Good. Now, if you don't mind, Jorlan, I want Mathers to bring me up to crack on business matters at Tamryn House. I'll see you at supper?"

He had been summarily dismissed. His cheeks bronzed slightly. It was not like Green do this. "Yes, of course." He left the room with Hugo tracing his steps.

Avatar watched his departure. "I think you hurt the lad's feelings, Marquelle."

Green sighed. "I know; it couldn't be helped. I will make it up to him later. Now tell me, Mathers, what is really going on?"

"Well, that snip-butt D'anbere is stirring up the Slice but good! She's started a rumor that Jorlan lied at the Ritual of Proof and you was a party to it."

"That high-held hock-top!" Avatar bristled.

Green frowned. "I thought she might do something like this."

"Once she found out you were carrying the babe, stories started surfacing that your line could be tarnished by Jorlan's lack of innocence. I tell you, Marquelle, it's a right kloobroth being kicked up. And it's working, too—the Slice is up in arms about it. They want to know why you won't come forward right away to dismiss the tales."

"That's exactly what she's trying to do—make me come forward now, before my child is born! Well, she'll just have to wait and so will the Slice! Once my heir is here, Claudine's position will be weakened."

"Let's pray it's an heir." Avatar gave her a meaningful look.

"I just wish I knew what evidence she has. . . ." Green sighed as she patted her swollen belly.

"You might have to give up Jorlan, Green," Avatar warned her. "The action would probably appease the Septibunal enough so they at least won't strip your titles and lands."

"No! I would never do such a thing. Jorlan is a Tamryn, and a Tamryn he will remain! If we are to be taken down, it shall be together."

"Claudine claims a prior bid on him." Mathers interjected. "Says you stole him from her. The snip-butt even hinted that he was hers in anticipation of the fastening. That waggering She-Lord has set her sights on our lad. She will never let it be."

"Her claim to him was false; I'll never let her have him. I stopped her before—I'll stop her now."

Avatar and Mathers nodded in agreement.

"The night Anya agreed to disregard Claudine's offer and sign my scroll, I promised her I would always take care of him. Despite the threat that Claudine had over her, the Duchene gave him to me, knowing I was the only one to safeguard him from Claudine. His life and well-being have always been in danger from her. I would never let Jorlan down, nor the Duchene. The Tamryns guard their own."

Avatar and Mathers concurred by banging their fists together.

*J*orlan leaned back against the scratchy bark of the Dreamtree, which nestled against the house.

He closed his eyes, exhaling its illusory scent. *Their fastening was being brought into question.* Why hadn't she told him?

Because she hadn't wanted to worry him.

Green. Green. She had been protecting him all along! Why had he not seen it? Her sense of honor staggered him and his heart filled with raw emotion. He had never known such a brave woman. Silently, and without fanfare, she protected all under her title, taking care of him just as she did for everyone and everything under the Tamryn banner. He loved her for that strength.

But he resented her for it, too.

His heart fell.

Green's actions were motivated not by love but by duty. She treated him as she did everything that came under her protection. No more and no less.

She cared for him because she considered him a Tamryn—not because she harbored a special affection for him.

He was not happy with this revelation, yet . . . he also had a belief in himself. He could turn her around. He could make her see him as more. As an equal, vital part of her life.

But only if he took that final step—

Only if he truly opened himself to her.

And that was a big risk.

Despite the outcome, he would never accept the role he had been forced to play in their society, even if he had to come to terms with it.

As the days wore on, and the time of the birthing grew near, Green became more listless. The Southern Region was not the best choice in which to have a child; the climate was much more hot and humid than in Capitol Town. As the sweltering days of summer passed and her time was imminent, Jorlan surprised her with his care. He often rubbed her back in the early morning as they lay in bed together and seemed overly concerned with her welfare.

Although he never spoke of the child, once, when he thought she was sleeping, he lightly ran his hand over the mound of her stomach.

Green wondered what he was thinking. What he was feeling.

Their relationship, while not strained, had changed. Not only did they have to abstain from traditional intercourse, but, since the night Mathers had shown up, Jorlan seemed to draw deeper into himself. It was as if he was wrestling with some momentous decision.

One morning at dawn Green awoke feeling peculiar in a way she couldn't define. She turned to find Jorlan staring at the rising Arkeus, the jet fringe of lashes shielding his eyes. "Our child will come today."

Green sucked in her breath, her hands patting her bulging middle, which seemed to have recently dropped lower. "You're sure?" She never asked him how or why. Sometimes Jorlan just knew things.

"Yes."

"Fine. Then could you send Mathers to me? She'd be terribly disappointed if she missed even a minute of this."

Jorlan smiled faintly, and tossing the covers out of the way, got out of bed. He started to leave, then paused, turning around slowly. "Would you like me to stay with you?"

She viewed him speculatively. "Name-bearers generally don't, you know. They normally are allowed in afterward when things are tidied up a bit. Most don't have the—you'll pardon the pun—stomach for it."

He made a wincing face at her terrible play on words. "I would like to be there, Green. With you."

He always amazed her. How could she turn down such a heartfelt request? He wanted to see his child come into the world. "We'll call for you when it gets near. As soon as the real pains start, Mathers will induce the neural block. Go get something to eat now while you can." She grinned up at him. "It's bound to get pretty hectic around here, later."

He bent down to brush her lips with his. "Are you excited?" he whispered.

"Oh, yes!" She paused then peered up at him. "What about you?"

The aqua eyes bore into her. "I am excited about a new life, yes."

The rest he left unsaid.

*H*er birthing pains came quickly. Mathers, who had found out about the lack of a methodologist in the region, had wisely brought a neural block. Green was unendingly grateful. Jorlan was called for shortly thereafter, when the birthing was imminent.

Avatar and Mathers stared agog at the Marqueller.

"What is he doing in here, Marquelle?" Avatar bristled. "This is no place for a squeamish man! They haven't the stomach for it!"

Despite her exertions, Green's eyes met Jorlan's in amusement. Avatar had unwittingly reiterated Green's earlier pun.

"Stop your bellytwaddle, Avatar!" Mathers bellowed. "The child comes and I won't have you spoiling the moment!"

Jorlan took Green's hand in his own, bringing it to his lips. He whispered soundlessly against her palm.

Shocked, her gaze flew to him, just as the final contraction took her.

"Look, there it is, now!" Mathers, sash in hand, all but jumped up and down. "The new Tamryn heir!"

Even Avatar looked misty-eyed.

The child entered the world with a lusty bawl, chubby arms and feet kicking furiously.

Jorlan was overcome at witnessing the entrance of a new life into the world. A life he had helped to create. His light eyes filled with moisture. His face shone with joy. "A boy! It is a boy, Green!" An ear-to-ear grin split his face.

Until he looked up and saw the crestfallen expressions of Avatar and Mathers.

The smile died on his face as the true meaning sank in. It was not an heir.

Green lifted herself on her elbows. Her face was aglow with happiness. "A boy? Let me see him, quick, Mathers! Is he beautiful like Jorlan?"

In that moment he loved her more than he could say.

"I think he is beautiful like you, name-giver." He kissed her forehead. "I am sorry I did not give you the heir you hoped for."

Green darted a glance at Avatar. The child was not a daughter. There was no heir to the Tamryn holdings. They would have to face the Septibunal without Tamryn security for the future. Green thought quickly. "Mathers, bring me the sash!"

Avatar sucked in her breath. "No! Green, you cannot!"

"Bring me the sash, Mathers!"

Muttering, Mathers handed her the same sash that had once been draped over Jorlan, claiming him to the House of Tamryn. Green draped it over her newborn squalling son.

Jorlan sucked in his breath. "What are you doing, Green?"

She flicked on the wristview on the bedside table to record the event. "I, Green, fourteenth Marquelle of Tamryn, hereby claim this child, who shall be named"—she glanced to the balcony, seeing the magnificent planet that bound Forus moon as it crested in the sky—"*Arkeus*, heir to my lands and fortunes and all that is Tamryn. He shall be known in his own right as Marqueller. Let it be noted that the deed is witnessed by two women, as is the law."

With that she snapped off the viewer to dead silence in the room. Even little Arkeus, who seemed to understand the importance of the moment, stopped crying for the occasion.

For the first time in Forus recorded history, a male had been named heir to a fortune and to his own title of Marqueller without benefit of a fastening.

"*What kind of a name is Arkeus?!*"

"That's all you have to say?" Green smirked up at Jorlan. He had been saying the same thing repeatedly for three months.

With the birth of Arkeus, Jorlan had changed. It was as if the boy grounded him in some way. There was a completeness to him that had been missing before.

Green had never seen a name-bearer so taken with his child. Jorlan cared for Arkeus and watched over him like an attentive Kloo. A strong bond developed quickly between father and son. Arkeus's eyes began to turn a pale aqua.

Green wondered if her child had inherited his father's abilities. If Arkeus was a Sensitive, he would not grow up in the dark about his traits—Jorlan would be there to guide him.

It was obvious to all who could see that Jorlan loved this child.

As he loved her.

Green viewed him through her lashes as he played with Arkeus on the floor of their chamber. He had spread the coverlet over the flooring and placed the baby on his back, so he could kick hands and feet in a new position.

Jorlan lay on the coverlet facing him, resting his head in his palm as he watched the same four dark spirally hairs on the top of his head.

"I think he has a few more hairs. . . ."

Green tried not to smile. Arkeus was born bald. "He doesn't."

Jorlan looked at her indignantly. "Well, when is he going to get some?"

"Anya sent a message that you were the same way until about six months, and look at how thick your hair is now. Besides, what are you so worried about? He's just a baby. He'll attract plenty of bids, I assure you."

It was the wrong thing to say. Jorlan became very serious as he viewed his son. "He won't need any bids. He'll be his own master."

Green bit her lip. In naming Arkeus her heir, she had given Jorlan a new focus for his cause. "Do not speak that way, Jorlan. You will turn his head."

The aqua eyes narrowed. "I intend to."

She was hurt by his words. "And you are not happy with your fate?"

He rose and walked over to her. "You do not have to ask me that. Not now. You have taken me, you know it."

She did know it. Knew it by what he had whispered in her hand the day their son was born. "Why would you not think Arkeus could be happy with his future, as well?"

"He will be because he will choose it himself."

"Oh, really? And who will produce that miracle of twisting convention?"

"I will."

She just shook her head. In a way, his determination excited her, made her . . . respect him.

A rumble sounded in the distance.

"An arc storm is coming."

"Yes. I must release Shringa from the coop. I will be back soon." He rose to leave.

Green's brow furrowed. "You're sending the Klee out *into* an arc storm?"

"Not exactly." A mysterious smile graced his lips as he left the room, carrying his son in the crook of his arm.

Later, when he hadn't returned, she went to the balcony, out into the perfectly deep-blue evening that seemed to have sprung more from an artist's palette than from nature. There in the distance she spotted her name-bearer.

He was racing arcs with the wild Klee.

And he had Arkeus with him.

"*You* ou take our child on such a dangerous ride, Jorlan?" Green spoke low as Jorlan lifted the coverlet and slipped into bed next to her.

"He was in no danger, I assure you. He was safely cushioned against me and Shringa glided so smoothly—it was almost as if the Klee flew." He gathered her in his arms.

"Flew. In an arc storm." She raised her eyebrow.

His lips twitched. "Yes. Arkeus loved it." His mouth played with her ear. "One day I will take you, lexa. . . ."

"No you will not! I have had quite enough of arc storms to last me for a lifetime."

He chuckled low against her throat. "Do not let one near-incineration color your opinion, name-giver."

She gasped, pulling away from him. "You know about that night? How?"

His teeth gleamed in the dark. "My grandmother told me before our fastening. She said you were so enamored of me that you rode all night into the middle of a storm simply to get that scroll signed. I thought she was trying to impress me with your sincerity. Was it true?" He batted his lashes at her. "Did you ride *all* that way through the arcs simply for me?"

Green crossed her arms over her chest. The snap-branch! Of course he didn't know *why* she had done it, but still . . . it did make her sound rather . . . besotted. "Be still! You have caused enough trouble for one evening! Go to sleep."

Jorlan threw back his head and roared with laughter. "I cannot believe you did that, Green." He grinned at her, baiting.

Green waved her hand as if to say it was unimportant and turned her back on him to go to sleep.

He cuddled up next to her, pulling her close. "Did you ever wonder why the arcs did not hit you?" he whispered, catching her earlobe in his teeth and tugging.

She froze, then looked at him over her shoulder. "I did wonder that, yes."

Aqua eyes pierced her in the darkened room. "What would harm you would harm me," he said enigmatically.

"What does that mea—?"

His mouth covered hers hotly. As did his body.

"*Jorlan . . .*"

"Mmm, I do favor this position, Green. . . ." He sank into her hot and deep. Green moaned in pleasure.

She arched up against him, her hands cupping his shoulders. Whether it was to push him away or bring him closer mattered not.

He initiated whenever he chose.

He made love the way he desired.

Jorlan was in control.

The next day, a stern summons arrived from the Septibunal.

She could delay it no longer.

Green announced that they were leaving that day. No one questioned a Marquelle's prerogative.

Amid a flurry of activity, they prepared for the journey back to Capitol Town. After saying their good-byes to the household, Jorlan released Shringa from her coop. The Klee prawked sadly and raced off to the hills.

"You are not taking Shringa with us?"

"No." He looked thoughtful for a moment. "His place is not with me."

What an odd thing to say. "How do you know that?"

Jorlan grinned at her, revealing two deep dimples. "He told me so. He awaits another, who is coming soon."

"You're making that up."

He smiled at her, left eye flashing with an aqua spark of amusement.

Throughout the first day, far in the distance, Green could see the Klee, following their passage along the rim of the hills.

"Shringa is watching you, you know." Green rode her mount next to Jorlan and Arkeus.

"The Klee watches us to make sure we come to no harm." Jorlan adjusted the sleeping babe in his arms and bent over to pet Kibbee, who in turn tried to take a nip out of his finger. He pulled it back just in time.

"She's angry at you for running off with the foreign Klee. You'll have a time with her now." Green chuckled.

"Hmm. She will forgive me soon, won't you, Kibbee?" He stroked her side feathers. Kibbee spit a huge wad at a jinto leaf they passed. Barely missing his boot.

Green laughed. "Your wiles don't work on everyone, blaze-dragon. Kibbee has much more sense than I do."

Kibbee concurred with a loud prawk.

Jorlan gave her a sultry look through lowered lashes. "Ah, but I so like when you lose your senses—especially when you give them over to me."

Green's mouth formed an O; she quickly turned to see if any of the women overheard, but they were out of earshot. "Mind yourself!"

He shook his head and winked at her. "I have always left that to you."

Her face flushed. She pulled the reins of her Kloo forward and left him to ride with Arkeus and Kibbee. His soft laughter followed her.

Jorlan was coming into his own.

Green was not sure how to handle that.

But she damn well wanted to try. Every wonderful, fascinating, spellbinding thing she had ever seen in him was coming to be.

The journey home took nearly three weeks and was pleasant enough considering what lay before them in Capitol Town.

Under his father's expert care, Arkeus fared the trip exceptionally well. The babe actually seemed to like being out on the land. He even grew a few more curly little hairs on the top of his head, which Jorlan and Mathers pointed out at every opportunity. The two of them had teamed up somewhere along the journey to constantly sing the child's praises.

Of course Green knew her son was exceptional. He was a Tamryn, after all. She spent hours playing with him at night, a complete slave to his drooling grin.

The final night of their journey, as they lay in the sleeper, Green knew she was going to have to tell Jorlan about the Septibunal's summons.

Her lips pressed over his as he rested back on the pallet. "Cover me, Green," he murmured, his mouth moving along the soft, tender skin of her jawline. "The way you did when we were journeying to Tamryn Lane. Do you remember?"

"When I had to seal your mouth with my own to halt your cries of pleasure from being overheard by the women?" She sighed as his arms embraced her.

"Yesss. While I looked up at the stars. I loved that, my name-giver. Love your passion and strength. . . ."

She smiled as she nipped his chin. "Do you? And is that why lately we end up wrestling to see who gets on top?"

He grinned broadly. "It does seem to stimulate you—especially when you are sleepy."

"Really."

"Yes. And the best part of it is, you are never quite sure *how* to react to the situation."

"Really."

"Yes. And that is when I can get you to simply *react*—to me."

"Hmm. I'm not sure I should be allowing that behavior, it—"

He burst out laughing. Green's hand covered his mouth. "Shhh! The women will hear you!" He blinked his jet lashes slowly at her. She pulled her hand away and shook her finger at him.

He stared up into her arresting face. Her auburn hair was framed in the soft glow of flamelight. He did not know how the Top Slice had produced such a woman—courageous, honorable, fair-minded, and free-thinking. Her intelligence, her wit, and her beauty were as unique as the rare blanock song. Her sensuality a constant catalyst to his own sensitivity. "You are everything to me, Green. *I love you.*"

Green's palm cupped his cheek. "Blaze-dragon . . . name-bearers often fall in love with their name-givers."

His hand came over hers. He stared penetratingly into her eyes. "This is different."

She knew that. *Felt it.* The love Jorlan spoke of was of an entirely different depth. He had formed an exclusive connection to her that was as mysterious and complex as the nightsong of Forus. This was not the simple love of name-bearer for name-giver—this was so much more.

Which made what she was to tell him that much more difficult. Green swallowed. "We must stand before the Septibunal tomorrow."

He said nothing, simply waited silently for her to continue.

"They are questioning the validity of our fastening."

"How so?" he asked quietly.

"Evidence has been brought to them that seems to refute your Oath of Proof."

"That's not possible, Green." His fingers delved into her hair at the base of her neck. "My oath was true—as you well know. How could there be evidence to the contrary?"

"I don't know. It was well known that you vehemently opposed the fastening—"

He exhaled his breath. "That is not enough to call both my word and yours into question."

"No, they have something else. . . ." She paused. "My sources tell me it is powerful evidence against a victory."

"I see. So, what does this mean—if they should 'prove' this?"

"Our fastening will be dissolved. Arkeus's position will be precarious, to say the least. Both our houses will have to pay a huge forfeiture. I might lose my titles and lands. You definitely will lose yours. Afterward, you will no longer legally have the protection of the house of Tamryn around you."

His jaw pulsed in barely controlled fury. "I am just to accept this? Is my worth as a human being simply a matter of my veil? We have fewer rights than a Klee! At least a Klee runs free when he wants to—he *owns* his life."

Green hugged him to her. "I agree with you. It is wrong, and if we get through this I will do everything I can to effect changes in the House of She-Lords."

"If we get through this! *What about my son?* What will happen to him?"

"That depends. Normally, he would not be of consequence to the Septibunal, but I have made him my heir. There will be a bitter battle over that, for his inheritance will be safeguarded from any forfeiture I would have to pay."

"What if he weren't your heir?"

Green raised her chin defiantly. "He is my child and a Tamryn! They will never separate me from him—I have given him a birthright."

Jorlan could not help the flash of admiration he felt for her resolve; she was an exceptionally strong woman. "Then what of me, name-giver . . . what shall be my fate if they dissolve this union?"

Her lips trembled slightly but her voice held steady. "You are my name-bearer, Jorlan, and a Tamryn as well. I will never let you forget that—regardless of what the Septibunal decrees."

The hand at the back of her neck roughly pulled her toward him. "Then don't you forget that I am going to hold you to that promise, name-giver."

His mouth seized hers.

He tasted of exotic terms.

*I*t quickly became obvious to every observer in the room just who was behind the charges. Only one person on the floor of the House of She-Lords was viciously slandering the Tamryns, and that was Claudine D'anbere. And while Marquelle Harmone had returned to her seat on the Septibunal, it was plain who was pulling her strings.

When Green and Jorlan entered the room to take their seats in front of the assemblage, silence ruled.

Jorlan brazenly carried his son into the meeting.

As he took his seat, many remarked that the resemblance between father and son was uncanny. The identical pairs of jet-rimmed aqua eyes captivated many a She-Lord. Several members speculated on whether or not the Marquelle would entertain prebids from their daughters. While prebids were not binding, they did hold some favor. Of course all would depend on the outcome today. The poor babe might end up on the Rue de la Nuit.

Along with his gorgeous father.

Duchene Hawke called the session to order with a nod of her head. "Marquelle Tamryn, step forward please."

Chapter Fifteen

reen stood and approached the Septibunal table.

As she walked by, Jorlan gave her a supportive nod.

"A charge has been brought before this assemblage against you that is quite serious in nature. Some of us"—Hawke glanced sternly down the table at Marquelle Harmone—"have reason to believe that you misrepresented the nature of your alliance with the Reynards. Evidence has come to us that, in fact, your name-bearer, Jorlan, was not intact at the time of the Ritual of Proof."

A murmur went through the crowd.

"Furthermore, the question as to whether you knew this at the time and sought to circumvent the law by forswearing the Ritual has also been brought to bear."

"May I answer these charges?" Green stood proudly before them, her voice not wavering in the slightest, despite the inner trepidation she had.

"Before you do, I must warn you that anything you say from this point forward will be Weighed. If you say nothing now, in consideration of your past deeds on this floor and for OneNation, I am prepared to call this a nolocharge and we will convene to decide the appropriate levy."

Duchene Hawke was giving her the chance to retain her title at a heavy monetary loss. Jorlan would of course be forfeit, but her son would remain with her. She turned and looked at Jorlan.

He watched her steadily. Then he surprised her by mouthing "take it."

He loved her that much. A tear formed in her eye. He was willing to sacrifice himself and be taken from his son to protect her. She shook her head no. *I will fight for both of them until the last breath leaves my body.*

Facing the Septibunal once more, she said, "I will speak."

Duchene Hawke raised a brow. "Are you sure, Marquelle?"

Green nodded.

The Duchene clearly did not think she had made a wise choice. She sighed deeply. "Very well. Proceed."

"Jorlan Tamryn was intact the night of our fastening. There was no conspiracy to thwart the Septibunal. These charges are all false. The honor of my house would never let me make a false statement to the governing body I hold so dear, and who my very foremothers helped to create. To impugn my honor in such a way is reprehensible and I call forth the person who would issue such a claim. Let her say these things to my face instead of hiding behind the voices of others." Green pierced Marquelle Harmone with a disgusted look. The woman fidgeted slightly in her seat.

Green's honest and impassioned voice seemed to sway the crowd. Low chatter broke out.

"Silence in the chamber!" Duchene Hawke roared. "Jorlan Tamryn, step forward!"

Jorlan rose with Arkeus in his arms.

As he passed by Claudine D'anbere, she called out, "The child may color the severity of the Septibunal's ruling! His presence sends a sub-liminal message that this man is bound irrevocably to the House of Tamryn."

Duchene Hawke glowered down at Claudine. "Are you saying we cannot be impartial in the presence of a mere babe, She-Count?"

"No. I am saying the child's presence is disruptive; it is an obvious, sympathetic ploy orchestrated by the Tamryns." She reached into her pouch, pulling out a scrolled document. "This is the fastening contract that Anya Reynard was to have signed for me—before Green *coerced* the Duchene's signature onto her scroll!" The audience turned and stared at Green disapprovingly. Claudine, knowing she had significant crowd support now, smugly continued on. "If the Septibunal rules justly today, I will ask for a ruling of Conveyance!"

Green paled. If they lost the ruling, the She-Count was going to ask the council to override Anya's signature and give Jorlan to her as pay-ment for her side of the "insult." Her eyes met Jorlan's and she knew he could read the anguish she had been able to hide from everyone else.

Instead of the apprehension she expected to see, there was a calm resignation to him. A quiet strength. His eyes showed her his love. There was so much emotion contained behind their aqua depths! He patted and rubbed his son's back as he patiently waited for Claudine to finish. In that moment Green knew that the rulings of women could never supersede a spirit that was free.

"So you see, I do have a vested interest here." Claudine went on. "Remove the child!"

Duchene Hawke started to nod to the sentries when Green fore-stalled her. "No. My son has more of a right to be here than She-Count D'anbere does! It is his fate we decide today."

"Isn't that rather dramatic?" Claudine sneered. "No one has an inter-est in that male child. You may keep him, if you wish, but it would seem more of a liability to me. Perhaps you can have him sent to a monkery."

Green flinched at Claudine's callous attitude. Her sweet babe sent to a monkery? Not while she had breath! Her eyes filled with pride as she glanced at his beautiful, dear face. He gave her a tiny smile.

She smiled back. "Arkeus will always be on Tamryn land—*for he is my heir,*" she said softly.

Pandemonium broke out in the courtroom.

"He cannot be your heir! He is male!" Claudine blared.

Green removed her wristview and handed it over to the panel.

They viewed the proof with frowns on their faces.

"It appears that Arkeus Tamryn is the Tamryn heir—*for now.*" She gave Green a stern look. "However, the Septibunal will review this issue with you later, Marquelle Tamryn." She turned her head to address D'anbere. "The child stays in the room."

Anya winked at Green. "Brava, my girl," she mouthed to her.

Although stymied, Claudine recovered quickly. "He may be called the Tamryn heir today, but I have a prior claim on his father! The line is sullied." She sneered at Green.

"My line is not sullied. I will not have the father of my heir impugned!"

"Jorlan Tamryn," Hawke addressed him. "As a Duchene's grandson, you know that the honor of your great house—the house of our Founder—is at stake here. So I ask you just once: How did you go to your fastening bed?"

Jorlan gave them all an insolent, flippant look. It was the very same brash look he had afforded them the last time he stood in front of this governing table.

Green's eyes misted over at his wonderful uniqueness. Jorlan was a handful of trouble and always would be. Another woman might not think fondly of his difficult ways and headstrong attitudes, *but she loved them*. She loved him.

He looked so utterly beautiful standing there, daringly facing them all, his new son in his arms. A son who looked so much like him that Green had already been tentatively approached by a mother interested in becoming friendlier with the Tamryns "for their sake of their children."

Jorlan's low, beguiling voice was strong in the chamber. "I came to my name-giver the way I was supposed to—with the honor of my family intact. And . . ." He paused purposefully.

The members of the Septibunal all leaned forward in their seats, not immune to his charm. "And?"

He smiled rakishly. "And with a slight bit of attitude—but nothing she couldn't handle." The room immediately broke out in raucous laughter.

Jorlan winked at Green.

Duchene Hawke's lips twitched. "Yes, we can imagine."

"Do not let his smooth tongue and handsome face turn your heads!" Marquelle Harmone sternly reminded them. "We have evidence to the contrary."

What evidence could you possibly have? Green wondered.

"Bring the witness in!" Harmone called to one of the sentries.

Two sentries escorted a bedraggled youth into the room.

Green frowned, whispering to Avatar. *"It's that dotty upstairs servant; what was his name . . . ?"*

Green heard Avatar murmur something about him being a snip-butt but that's all.

"Opper," Jorlan supplied under his breath.

"State your name, please," Duchene Hawke commanded.

Opper looked up at the most powerful council on Forus moon and immediately began to preen.

Which did not endear him to these auspicious women in the least.

"I'm Opper."

"And what do you know about this matter?"

"Well, I was a servant for *his-self* in the Marquelle's house. Prepared him that night for . . . *you know* . . . the velvet touch."

Snickers peppered the room.

Hawke rolled her eyes. "Go on."

"Well, he was not too happy about being in the bed straps, you see." Jorlan's face darkened.

"Just get to the point, please," Hawke said.

"So it was my job to ready him, you know, and all. And when I went to put the Tamryn sash on him, I noticed that he didn't have no . . . veil." Opper looked at his toe. "No veil at all."

A buzz of voices started up. He sounded very convincing.

Duchene Hawke asked, "Did you say anything at the time?"

"Of course I did!" Opper noticed that he had the room's attention, so he dove into his role. "I said to hisself, 'You don't have no proper veil!' and he says to me if I ever say anything to anyone he'll make it go bad for me. Then he struck me with his fist. In my face, hard like that!" He made a fist and punched his other hand.

Green glanced at Jorlan. So this was how his cheek had been bruised. This servant had struck him—in her own house! Her eyes narrowed at the orange-haired man. He would pay for that.

"He's a strong one, that velvet petal is." Opper rubbed at an imaginary spot on his cheek. "Hurt me bad, so I kept my mouth shut, as I'm only a servant and all. But when I heard about how there was some questioning of the matter, I did the right thing and came forward." He puffed his chest out and stood straight. It seemed Opper should have been a performer instead of a servant.

The Septibunal seemed to believe him. Green looked at Jorlan in dismay. This was very damaging.

Jorlan spoke low. "How could I have hit him if I was tied into the bed straps."

Duchene Hawke's mouth opened to respond to him, then closed, then opened again. "He's right. How could he hit you if he was tied up?"

"Well, I—I released him because he was making such a row about being tied up."

Ever the stateswoman, Green pounced on *that*. "Why would you release him?"

"He asked me to—for a little bit, and he pretended to be nice and I felt sorry for him."

"You felt sorry for him," Green parroted negatively. "But you did retie him."

"Wh-what do you mean?"

"Well, when I came into the room, he was tied up."

"Yes, well, I had to do that; it was my job."

Green's knowing look met Hawke's. She had just established that Jorlan was definitely tied up when she came into the room. "If he had no veil, why would you retie him into the straps?" she asked softly.

"Because that's my job!" he answered in a frantic whine.

"And he just let you?"

"We had a deal!"

"Before or after he hit you?"

"What difference does that make?"

"You tell me."

Opper put a halt to her interrogation. "I said all that I have to say! I'm not the one without the veil!" He stopped. "Least ways not on my fastening night." Several people chuckled.

"Take him out." Hawke instructed the guards.

"He's lying," Green said to the panel.

"Why would he lie, Marquelle?" Harmone interceded. "He has nothing to gain; whereas, you and Marqueller Tamryn do."

Green was incensed at the insinuation. "You would take the word of a questionable servant over *mine*? A Marquelle who has stood on this very floor and successfully debated the policies of this land?"

"His testimony is disturbing . . ." another member concurred. "What reason would he have to lie? He has no motive."

Green observed Claudine. Even as a child, whenever she had done something underhanded, she never could hide that small smirk of hers. She was gloating. Green knew exactly why Opper had lied. Claudine had either threatened him or paid him off handsomely, or both.

The only problem was she couldn't prove it. Worse, his testimony had obviously swayed several of the members.

There was only one thing left for her to do. Moreover, she had to do it now—before they ruled. She cleared her throat. "Clearly this is a case that cannot be resolved by these means. Therefore, I request that the Septibunal suspend the vote until more evidence can be found, one way or the other."

Hawke raised her eyebrow and gave Green a look that clearly asked what she was doing. They certainly could take a vote.

Claudine was outraged. She was not about to let the satisfaction of a victory slip through her fingers now that it was so close.

Which was what Green had counted on.

"Wait! Before you decide to suspend the vote, I demand satisfaction! I'm the aggrieved party here!" She waved her unsigned scroll in the air.

Anya wrinkled her nose at it.

"What satisfaction might that be?" Hawke asked wearily, knowing the answer.

"I call the Marquelle Tamryn to a Forfeiture duel at dawn to settle this matter, once and for all. It is my right!"

Jorlan's mouth parted in surprise. He had not been expecting this. Green was a stateswoman, not a warrior. He tried to catch his name-giver's eye to tell her not to agree. She would be no match for Claudine.

"I'll do it." Green responded briskly.

Claudine smiled in victory.

"But with one stipulation."

"What is it?"

"If I go to meet you in a duel, you will forever after leave Jorlan alone. If I am victorious, you will forfeit everything to me, Claudine. *Everything.* Your title, your lands, your wealth. Are you willing to risk all that, Claudine? Or shall we end this now and both go to our respective homes and forget this nonsense?"

Jorlan released the breath he had been holding. His shrewd name-giver was trying to maneuver D'anbere into dropping the matter.

Claudine's pupils contracted in evil delight. "I will never back down."

Green's face fell. She had miscalculated. Claudine's insane jealousy surpassed her desire for Jorlan.

Duchene Hawke pounded the table with her fist. "It is done then! The Septibunal agrees. They will duel at dawn to settle the matter. Victor will take all."

"No," Jorlan hissed. "*No.*"

Arkeus began to cry, sensing his father's agitation.

*W*hen they left the chambers, Green instructed Avatar to escort Jorlan and Arkeus straight home. She needed to see her solicitor to put her affairs in order.

She refused to meet Jorlan's questioning eyes as she mounted her Kloo and left them on the street.

Tidying up her affairs took longer than one would think.

The decisions were not simple ones. Making sure loved ones were cared for were never simple decisions. She sighed with regret, but she had done the best she could. Jorlan and Arkeus would be well provided for and Tamryn House would remain their home always.

As she was leaving the solicitor's, she was surprised when a young street spark handed her a note.

She opened it.

Green:
I must see you at once. I realize this is a difficult time, but I would not ask if it were not of the utmost importance.
I'll be waiting for you at the house in the Rue.

RIVER

Green rubbed the bridge of her nose. He would never send a note like this unless he was in trouble. In all the years they had been together, River had never once asked anything of her, always preferring instead to maintain the acceptable behavior of a pleasurer. His situation must be dire.

She would have to help him if she could.

She mounted Kibbee and headed off to the Rue de la Nuit.

"River, are you here?" Green let herself into the house.

"Yes, in the parlor. Why don't you join us?"

Us? Green walked into the room and froze. River had Opper cornered into a chair by the table. "What is this?"

River turned and smiled. "I heard about your troubles, Green. It seems this fellow has not only been throwing lots of touch about the Rue; he's been bragging up an arc storm. He says he has a rich benefactress who has set him up on Pleasure Street. I just wonder who that could be?" He shook Opper by the collar. The orange-haired former servant squeaked.

"I wonder." Green stormed over to the table. "Claudine D'anbere, by chance?"

Opper dug in and grimaced mutinously at her. "I'm not talkin'."

"You seemed more than willing to talk earlier. Well, the damage has been done. You might as well release him, River. Claudine and I are to settle our differences in another way."

"Not yet, Green. I've prepared a written confession on the viewer. At least it will clear Jorlan's name for you."

"I won't sign it!" Opper said.

Green's lips parted. "Why would you do that for Jorlan, River?"

He exhaled slowly. "I think that if a man has stayed true to a veil, he shouldn't be cheated out of his honor by the likes of him." He nodded at Opper.

Green looked at him curiously. Why would a pleasurer care about the honor of houses and veils?

"I also did it for you," he added softly.

"*For me?* Why?"

"Let's just say I owed you for the parting gift you gave me and call it at that."

"You didn't owe me anything for that—I wanted to do it."

"As do I. Now, Opper . . ." He crossed his arms over his chest and gave the orange-haired man a look that clearly stated he was not going to wait too much longer.

"I'm not signing it!"

Green rolled her eyes. "Forget it, River, he—"

River's green eyes flashed in annoyance. He bent over and murmured something low in the man's ear. Opper gulped and hastily placed the tip of his forefinger on the screen for an imprint. "I had no choice! She-Count D'anbere threatened me—said if I didn't go along it would go bad for me."

"She approached you the day of my fastening?" Green asked.

Opper nodded. "Came upstairs and realized I was the one seeing to hisself. I had no choice!"

"There is always a choice," River intoned softly. "You accepted D'anbere's coin and now you are hers. I would not want to be you."

Opper swallowed. "Can I go now?"

River gestured with his hand back and forth as if he were sweeping him out. Opper dashed for the door, slamming it behind him in his haste to leave.

"What did you say to him to make him sign the confession?"

He smiled slowly and shrugged. "That, my Marquelle, is a pleasurer's privileged information."

Green laughed as he handed her the confession. "This will mean a lot to Jorlan and his grandmother. I cannot thank you enough, River."

"Are you still meeting her at dawn?"

She did not ask how he knew. Gossip spread quickly in the Rue.

"Yes. A challenge was issued and met."

He nodded. "I wish you well, then. I hear she is very, very good."

Green looked down. "Yes."

He lifted her chin with his thumb. "Come with me to the Western Region, Green. Bring Jorlan if you wish, we could all start over."

She smiled faintly. "You know I cannot do that."

He cleared his throat. "She is a platinum class warrior, Green."

"I know."

He knew what she could not say. His hand cupped her cheek. "Be careful, will you?"

"Always."

"I'm leaving tonight."

"Not tomorrow?"

"No."

"Is she a danger to you?"

"Yes."

Green nodded in understanding. If she lost the fight with Claudine, River would be defenseless against her. At least Jorlan would be protected by the terms she had forced Claudine to accept. Claudine might very well take her anger out on the man who had been her enemy's pleasurer.

"I'm sorry for that."

"I'm not. I have a whole new life that I am very eagerly looking forward to—thanks to you."

"You'll be all right?"

His green eyes flickered. "Better than you know."

"Good-bye, River. Good way to you."

"And you, Green."

She went to the door and stopped. "I have always felt there is a hidden side of you, River, a side you don't let anyone see."

River's jade eyes glinted through lowered lashes. "Perhaps you just think this side exists, Green. Perhaps I am nothing more than what you see."

"When I was a little girl, I used to think that it was actually Arkeus that revolved around Forus."

The edges of River's sensual mouth curved up secretively. "Interesting concept," he murmured.

"Something tells me I wasn't completely wrong, either." She smiled knowingly and left.

River watched her through the window as she made her way along the street.

Alone, his jade eyes brightened to a most interesting shade of aqua.

"*Y*ou'll tell him I love him?"

Green stood over her sleeping son, her fingers lightly brushing the few hairs on the top of his head.

"Don't do this, Green. Let me go to her. If I give myself to her as forfeit, the Septibunal will dismiss everything, including this insane challenge!"

Green squared her narrow shoulders. "No. I will not do that. How can you even think to go to that monster? You would never survive it, Jorlan."

"I will take my chances!" he all but roared. "I cannot let you do this!"

"*You* cannot let me do this? Do not be foolish, blaze-dragon. This is what a Marquelle does. Now I will speak of it no more."

"It is suicide."

Green notched her chin up. "And what makes you think I cannot take her?"

"Green, I love you and think most highly of all of your abilities but you are not a warrior. She *is*. Be reasonable on this! Let me—"

"No. That is the end of this discussion."

His pale eyes narrowed. "Very well, then, come with me for a ride."

"Now? At this hour?"

"If not now, when?" he spoke softly.

She swallowed at his underlying meaning. This might be their only chance. A soft rumble in the distance seemed to accentuate his request. It brought to mind some of the dangers of the night. "Jorlan, do you mean on your Klee?"

"Yes. Come." He held out his hand to her. "Let me show you a world that you don't know."

Hesitantly, she held out her hand to him. She wanted to experience what he did on these rides.

*D*o you think it wise to go so far out?" Green glanced warily down at Sabir's gently ruffling feathers.

"Do I think it wise?" He smiled enigmatically.

"You know what I mean—safe."

"I would not take you anywhere I did not think was safe. That is not to say it is not dangerous." His lips nibbled the back of her neck.

Green scrunched her shoulders up at the ticklish action. "Now, why did I expect a forthright answer? You never give one—"

"I always give you a forthright answer, lexa. It is just not the answer you expect."

"Nooo—it's not an answer I can decipher."

He chuckled behind her as he nudged Sabir into a faster pace.

Green clutched the Klee's mane. She'd never admit it, but she was more used to Kibee's slower, even trot.

He took her far out onto the back lands, rolling vistas under the wide expanse of night sky. Green had always loved this part of the estate. The indigenous plants had never been tamed back by human hands. It was a primitive Forus vista, alive with the sights and sounds of Forus life. Even though women had colonized this place for over a thousand years, the night remained alien. It became an exotic, mysterious veil that shrouded the senses. Elusive, beckoning. Perhaps even dangerous. She glanced up over her shoulder at Jorlan. *Exactly like her name-bearer.* A shiver trailed down her spine.

She was not surprised that he noticed. Nothing ever got by those penetrating aqua eyes.

In the distance, swirls of vapor spiraled into the sky, rising from the ground in a prelude to the night's enchantment. The air itself seemed to take on a shimmering pattern. Clouds gathered around them. Green blinked, mystified by what she was seeing. "Jorl—"

"Shhh." His arms came around her, bringing her closer to him. "Enjoy the night, Green. There is nothing to harm you here."

Sabir picked up speed. Out of nowhere firewings surrounded them, accompanying them on their journey. Their rapidly beating luminescent wings, fluttering, tiny, bell-like chimes. The small lights glittered over her hair as the long strands trailed into the wind.

A strange, beautiful scent filled the air. Moist with a hint of night tilla. Green inhaled deeply, letting the wonderful aroma tingle down her body. No wonder the Kloo and Klee loved to sleep on the leaves.

She closed her eyes as she exhaled slowly, her entire body coming alive to its potent call. Sometimes dawn, her favorite time, brought with it a special promise of the day. But this was different. "Why have I never felt this before, Jorlan?"

"It is the special song of Forus, Green." His warm breath licked the folds of her ear. "It is opening to you, my love."

As if on some unheard cue, the Klee also inhaled. Sabir filled his intake chambers with the air of night song. A low, warbling sound resonated through his throat. Along the horizon, arcs began to skip from cloud to cloud.

Sabir, fueled, increased his speed across the land, his pace literally taking Green's breath away.

Behind her, Jorlan's solid, warm chest and encircling arms, her only anchor.

"We must go back before the arcs get closer, Jorlan!" she called back to him above the rumblings of the approaching storm.

"That wouldn't make much sense, lexa, as we are heading *into* the storm."

Green struggled in his embrace, trying to turn about. *"Into the storm?* Are you mad? We cannot—"

He brushed his cheek over hers as he leaned forward to speak. "You must trust me, Green . . . as I am about to trust you."

Green opened her mouth to object—then snapped it shut. This may very well be the last time she had a chance to find out what it was that he kept so closely guarded. She was positive that, whatever it was, it held the key to him.

To everything that he was.

She knew that what she was about to witness would change her perceptions forever.

It was dangerous, but she didn't care. She wanted to know.

She needed to share this part of him—even if it meant surrendering herself to his judgment in this. She had sacrificed everything for this man; but there had never been any doubt in her mind that he was worth her faith.

Silently, she nodded.

He exhaled against her throat, a brisk rush of sultry air.

Into the night Sabir raced, surrounded by firewings. Arcs began randomly cascading toward the ground, hitting the ore-rocks with loud, crackling booms. The atmosphere around them became highly charged. Thunder shook the ground.

No . . . not thunder!

Green looked out across the fields to a far rise in the land. There, where night met land, *thousands* of wild Klee gathered! Green's lips parted at the spectacular sight. They were all running in the wind! Their feathery manes were lifted into the sky; they almost seemed to glide through the arcs! Firewings flitted beside them in joyous accompaniment.

"By the Founder!" She whispered, "What are they doing?"

"They are racing the arcs." He bent them farther over Sabir's back. "As we are about to. . . ."

Before Green could respond, Jorlan motioned to the Klee with a flick of the reins and they turned directly into the storm.

A hazy light surrounded them; the firewings increased until there were so many of them, it was like seeing through a curtain of tiny stars. The arcs were fast approaching them.

The air seemed to hum with urgency. The rumbling grew and grew. *Then it was upon them.*

Arcs sizzling, spitting down from the sky around them. The atmosphere ignited. Jagged bolts struck the rocks in deafening crackles of sound. All combined with the hooves of ten thousand Klee racing!

Amid the excitement of the storm, Green noticed something she had never realized before. "They don't break apart," she marveled.

Jorlan smiled mysteriously. "No, they don't."

The arcs came faster and faster. Hitting all around them. The back of Green's neck tingled, both from the electrified air and Jorlan's breath.

The firewings began forming a spark netting around them!

"Are they protecting us from the arcs?"

"Not entirely. You see, they are protecting the arcs from us."

"What do you mean? Tell me what is happening."

"The storms are not what people think."

"What are they?"

"The arcs are conduits of Forus."

Green tried to turn in her seat. "What do you mean, *conduits?*"

He shrugged. "They are the carriers, if you will, of a type of conversation."

"I do not follow you."

"I will explain shortly. For now, enjoy the experience. It will make you feel good."

She did feel good. Unbelievably good.

Suddenly the Klee raised their heads in unison and blared joyously at the sky. The deafening sound rose over the arcs themselves, reverberating across the land. It was an incredible sight. "What are they celebrating?" she yelled over the din.

"Forus life, my name-giver," he called to her, before throwing back his own head to joyfully shout into the night. It was a rejoicing release of strength, a gathering of power, an acknowledgment of respect.

A warm rain began to fall, washing the air clean. Green and Jorlan lifted their faces, letting the balmy water sluice gently over them.

The arcs started to move off to the east.

Most of the Klee scattered, disappearing into the wild as quickly as they had appeared.

As the last of the arcs rumbled past, a few of the younger Klee chased after them.

Firewings flittered lazily about them now, and Sabir slowed his pace to a natural gallop—still swift by anyone's standard.

Jorlan turned Sabir to the west, following an ancient trail into deeper vegetation. Some of the firewings followed them. The brief touches of their wings felt like tiny kisses along Green's arms.

They entered a hidden glade. Arkeus-shine glinted off a cascading waterfall and a small pool. A Dreamtree to the right of the pond was in night bloom. Its long, feather-strands swayed in the crisp after-breeze of the arc storm, creating a peaceful, shushing sound. The top of this Dreamtree was dotted with pale pink blossoms. The fragrant blooms were deep purple in the center and surrounded by the Dreamtree's signature curved leaves. The spicy essence was said to inspire the heart's desire.

It was a beautiful spot. Hidden, lush, mysterious, beckoning.

"A favorite place of mine, since I have come to your lands," Jorlan told her.

She was not surprised. The place was much like him.

He brought Sabir up and dismounted, then offered her a hand down. She refused his help; after all, she was a She-Lord. "I don't need your help; I am an accomplished rider."

His lips curved up as he removed his hand. A stubborn She-Lord.

She swayed dizzily. He righted her, giving her a knowing look. "You have never raced the storms before, lexa. There is a lot of energy. It can be disorienting."

"So I see." She staggered over to a large rock, grabbing the edge of it as she sat down. With a shaky touch, she pushed her hair off her face.

In just a few hours she would be meeting Claudine in a probable death match. She didn't want to think of that now. She didn't want to take one moment from her time with Jorlan.

She patted the rock. "Come, tell me what you will, name-bearer." She smiled slightly. "Tell me how many impossible things you can do before morning." Her nose wrinkled. "My mother used to tell me that—it was part of a story she told me at bedtime I think—something about a girl, an explorer of worlds. She went through a wormhole . . . I can't remember the rest of it, except that someone or something was always late."

Jorlan rested across the top of the flat rock, lying on his side next to her, his bent arm supporting his chin. "Too bad you can't remember more; Arkeus would love it."

Green laughed. "He's not much of a critic; he loves everything."

"That can be a good trait."

"Yes, it can."

A line furrowed the center of his forehead. "It can also cause him severe disillusionment."

Green watched him carefully. "As it did you?"

He observed her silently, the pale color of his eyes shining in the low light. It struck her how close in shade they were to the water that pooled in front of them.

"You will have to make sure he doesn't suffer that, then. You must guide him."

"And how shall I guide him?" he asked seriously.

"Tell him never to lose his love of all things. Tell him to temper this love with the acceptance of the nature of life."

"The nature of life as you see it or as I see it?" He gave her a charming smile.

"Perhaps in essence they are both the same."

"I begin to believe that is true." His hand reached over and cupped her neck, bringing her to him for a brief kiss. He released her. "In any case, you shall be there to guide him, as well."

Green looked away at the waterfall.

Jorlan was silent for several moments.

They both knew that was unlikely.

"Why did you risk everything for me, Green? In the beginning—was it simply honor, the connection of our families?"

"I'm afraid not." She turned back to him. "I wanted you, Jorlan. I always intended to offer for you. In time, I had hoped you would come to me on your own terms. Claudine's interference forced my hand. I had to act quickly."

His fingers stroked down the side of her face. "And look where it has gotten you."

Her hand came over his. "A beautiful son and a name-bearer I am besotted with—a good bargain in any tally." She smiled faintly. "The two of you are a threat to my resolve, although I shouldn't be telling you this. You both thoroughly have me and I fear I shall spoil you both—"

She stopped and swallowed the lump in her throat. She would not be spoiling anyone after the dawn came.

Jorlan squeezed her hand.

"Jorlan, please tell me what you meant earlier when you said that the arcs were a conduit for Forus."

"*Forus is alive, Green.*"

Chapter Sixteen

"Alive . . . ? Of course it is alive. Every planet that supports life—"

"No. I mean that it is truly alive. The arc storms are how Forus 'connects' with itself. The ore-rocks are likened unto children, although it is an alien relationship and difficult to explain. Forus speaks to its children. *All* of its children."

Its children? She sucked in her breath.

Green was thunderstruck by this revelation. "Are you saying the moon itself is some kind of massive life form?"

"Yes. An ancient consciousness."

"But . . . that is impossible. . . . We would have detected intelligence. . . ."

"Not this kind."

"I don't follow you."

"The methodologists consign such intelligence to the simple rhythms of nature. Even Arkeus is part of its cycle."

"Are you mad? That can't be!" And yet she remembered thinking herself that sometimes it seemed that even though the moon revolved around the planet, it was Arkeus that shadowed Forus.

He viewed her sharply. "Do you really think it so strange? How many times have you heard our people say we must live in harmony with our land? Why do you think they feel that way? Intuitively, they have *sensed* it is the right thing to do. How many stories and legends have been passed down—even from Originpoint—about such places . . . ?"

"They are fiction! Stories to stimulate the mind, that is all."

He shook his head. "From such stories reality comes. Isn't that the way of it?"

Horrified, she looked down at the dirt beneath her boots and suddenly lifted her feet up. "Does it think? Is it watching us now?"

Jorlan chuckled. "Nothing like that. Forus *feels*. A cognitive process that is strictly emotive. Perceptions so complex, so sophisticated, so evolved, and so removed from our own that it has a unique cognizance—if that is even what you wish to label it."

"Well, how would you label it?"

"I wouldn't. It is too hard to put into human terms; the nearest I can come is that its consciousness is visual 'awareness.' This is nothing like your emotions. It is not human emotion at all. You must not confuse it with that. It is very different. All of the life forms here, except, for the most part, our kind, are intricately connected to Forus. The blanocks. The firewings. The Klee." He raised an eyebrow teasingly. "Even your precious Kloo, though I hate to admit that."

She had noticed he said *your* emotions—not our emotions. How much of him was connected to this alien life form? From what he was saying, every life form on Forus was symbiotically connected to each other and to the moon. It disturbed her. The concept was so alien; they had lived here for over a thousand years and had been so unaware of it.

"This is difficult to comprehend. How is it that you know all of this, Jorlan?"

He stared at her, waiting for her to make the right connection.

Her lips parted as the answer came to her. *"You are a Sensitive."*

"Yes. I am connected to all things here, as Forus is to me. Just like the jinto and the blanock."

That explained why the blanocks had come to her garden. To be near him. It explained so many other things as well: *I've never seen jinto before, at least not with my eyes.* She remembered his words that day by the river. Green realized there would be layers to him that only he and Forus could share.

"How exactly are you connected, Jorlan?"

"I 'hear' the pictures of our existence. I am part of all that is Forus— yet I am separate. Sometimes I can feel the currents of change."

Some Sensitives had strong magnetic abilities. It seemed Jorlan was one of them. *Maybe not just Jorlan.* She had suspicions, and she had to ask. She swallowed. "Arkeus?"

He inclined his head. "Yes, he is like me."

"Is—is this good, Jorlan?"

His fingers stroked her face tenderly. "It is very good, name-giver. Very good indeed."

"Why?"

"Forus reached out to us, but we did not hear its call. In the way of life, it adapted itself and knew we would adapt to this place over time. Eventually, some were born with a certain disposition that allowed the connection to form. So the link started, and it has continued for seven hundred years. Slowly we changed, understanding more and more. Forus does not interfere with our choices, but the ability to connect with Forus can change our lives. There is a wisdom here, a well to sense, a knowledge to plumb—if you have the ability to translate it to human terms. Such wisdom could be invaluable to us as a species."

Green thought about that. A line of worry creased her forehead. In the wrong hands, such knowledge might also prove too tempting a manipulation. Was their society in danger? As a member of the House of She-Lords, she had a responsibility to protect the colony.

Jorlan sighed. "You worry about the possible threat. I cannot lie and say it does not exist—this is why I have kept the secret to myself, as I assume others do. They probably fear for their own lives and safety should their full gifts become known. Some of us can pinpoint the best places for crops to be planted, for the digging of valuable minerals . . . and much more, Green. The unscrupulous could seek to exploit, others to command."

"Very true. Are you in connection with other Sensitives?"

"No. I have never even known there were others until recently."

She wondered out loud, as so many others had, why the Sensitives were all male.

"I don't know why exactly."

Something else occurred to her. "The meteor-blades! Is this the reason you are able to wield them? Is it somehow part of you being a Sensitive?"

"Partly. You see they are not really meteor-blades, Green. They are *real* razor rock."

Her eyes widened. "That cannot be! Razor rock is deadly! No one can control its response."

"I can. Razor rocks are the true children of Forus. They are not off-world as the methodologists think. They are the by-life of an arc cycle."

"Explain this arc cycle."

He closed up. "It is too complicated to put in words. Suffice it to say that ore rocks are more than they seem."

Green suspected he did not feel comfortable sharing that information just yet.

"Why did you and the Klee yell into the storm?"

He grinned. "We celebrate the static change of existence. Existence is ever changing yet ever constant. The emotive-vision is a Forus gift and brings much joy. The arcs bring a signature. It is Forus's way to . . ."—he hesitated to find the right way to express himself—"to depict a great love of all that is."

Green recalled what she had witnessed. The Klee, beautiful and free, lifting their hearts to sing to the wind. And Jorlan doing the same. She would never forget how his beauty rose from within him. She was so thankful she had been there to witness it—to carry such an awe-inspiring image with her forever.

Forus was more than their home; it was their shelter in the storm. It changed her thinking, somehow. The knowledge she had been given tonight could help her effect widespread changes. *If she lived past the morrow. . . .*

"Tell me more about the razor rocks—how are you able to wield them?"

"I am connected to all things here, as Forus is connected to me. I hear the pictures of our existence—as do these Klee and these firewings. I am part of every movement of this place, and yet I am separate. The meteor-blades respond to my movements; together we create the forms. The movements you call the Gle Kiang-ten. Your masters have intuited the secrets from the land but no synth blade could ever match the power of a real one. You see, the forms and the razor rocks derive from Forus itself."

"How do you do it?"

"I connect directly to the source, so I become its nature."

She viewed him thoughtfully. His words mirrored an almost identical tenet of the Gle Kiang-ten. "Can all Sensitives do this?"

"Some have the ability but . . . one can be more adept than another."

"Why is that?"

"I don't know. I think it has something to do with a manipulation of some kind. . . ." He seemed genuinely puzzled.

Green bit her lip as she watched him obliquely. Manipulation . . .

The Santorinis.

Could it be? In trying to improve their species had Santorini accidentally created a greater, special "link" to this "alien" world that aided their survival? It was true that after Santorini's experiments the colony had begun to thrive. Still, no Santorini Sensitive had ever been discovered.

"Does this manipulation factor you speak of exist now?"

He closed his eyes a moment. "Yes."

"Is it coming from you?" She held her breath as she waited for his answer.

He closed his eyes again for a moment. "No."

"Can you tell me anything else?"

"The source of the manipulation . . . can *manipulate*."

"Is that good or bad?"

"I don't know. Forus does not make these distinctions."

"Have you always known about Forus?"

"Yes, Green. I just did not know about being a Sensitive. When I was young, I intuited my connection. It has always been with me. I never knew one of the by-products of it would turn out to be ultrasensitivity to physical stimulation. Thank you for pointing it out to me in such an enticing way." His teeth flashed white in the darkened night.

She smiled. "My pleasure, blaze-dragon." She glanced up at the stars. "We should be getting back. It's late."

"We have time. Let's stay awhile longer." He rolled over, placing his head on her lap.

Green ran her fingers through his silky hair. She did not want to return yet, either. He gazed up at her, pale eyes luminous against the shadow of his face. Beautiful and so very like the waters of Forus . . .

She shivered. *The connection.* It was there in his eyes and always had been.

Every crew member on board the *NEOFEM* had noted and felt the beauty of this place. Despite this being their adoptive home, they all loved this land. It was not always kind but it was ever complex. And its embrace was pure.

"What is it?" he asked quietly.

"Nothing." Her thumb rubbed a small circle on his temple. Should she tell the Septibunal what he had told her? It was her duty to inform them of this startling revelation. And yet, how would they react?

He seemed to intuit what was bothering her. His long jet lashes flickered, shading his expression for an instant. Then he glanced up at her. "Don't withdraw from me, Green," he whispered. "I could not bear it if you did."

She gazed at him in shock. "Why would you ever think that? I love you, Jorlan. You are a Tamryn and the father to my heir."

His hand reached up to cup behind her neck. He brought her face closer to his. "The Slice might consider us tainted by our abilities to 'see' alien thought forms."

"That's nonsense. Your connection to Forus makes you all the more human. Surely your difference from Forus must be etched inside you— there for you to wrestle with; especially if you feel we, as a race, fall short."

His face displayed admiration for her own astute intelligence. Green had immediately fathomed one of the human difficulties of being in tune with Forus. He lifted his lips to brush her mouth softly with his own. "You are my connection," he mouthed huskily against her lips.

She smiled. "I hardly think so."

His lips twitched. "It's true. When you opened my world to the phys-ical, you truly released my Sensitive nature. Brought it to another level entirely. I had intuited many things, but they did not connect within me until you ignited my desire. I will always be grateful to you for that, Green."

"Grateful," she deadpanned. "Wonderful."

He grinned, showing two deep dimples. "They say that the Dreamtree has the ability to bring forth desire. . . ."

She knew where he was headed. "That is not always the best thing."

"Ah, but sometimes it is." He swung off her lap, to stand before her. "Shall we find out what your desire is?" He held out his hand to her.

"Why me? Why not you?"

"Because we already know what my desire is."

His strong hands went to the collar of her gown, loosening the small ties. It fell to her feet, a pale cloud of material.

He released the clasp that held back her hair. Long strands of auburn cascaded about her shoulders and back, down the form of her body to her waist. Her breasts, which were larger now that Arkeus had been born, lifted against the silken mass. Nipples, pink even in this light, poked through the tresses.

Jorlan stared at her with a look of raw desire, so elemental that there was indeed no doubt as to what his desire was. Her.

He shed his clothes as she watched. When he was naked before her, he wrapped his arms around her and pulled her under the flowing strands of the Dreamtree.

"That is simply a legend, Jorlan."

"Is it?" He bent forward to nibble the edge of her lip. A sweet-musky taste of him to entice her into wanting more.

But she always wanted more of this man.

It was his very difference that attracted her.

And she didn't just mean his sensitivity, for that was only a certain part of him. If was as if they belonged together. As if every particle of her matched up to every particle of him. When they were together, they entwined and connected. *Like arcs to ore.*

The feather-strands swayed over her naked flesh, a thousand tiny strokes of gossamer. With every rustle of the wind, they sifted around her body, making her skin tingle.

Jorlan gathered her close against his heat, against the smooth plane of his torso. They became encased in a world of feather touches, born on the scent of nightsong.

"It feels as if you are caressing me everywhere, Jorlan," she breathed.

"Yes," he whispered, the backs of his fingers sliding down her back, tangling in her hair and the feather-strands.

In the distance a blanock began to sing its rare song.

Green closed her eyes, taking in the night, the sounds, the scent, and the feel of Jorlan around her. "It is Forus, isn't it?" she realized.

"Yes," he murmured. "Tell me, what is your heart's desire, Green?"

"You," she answered unequivocally.

"Then you shall have this desire." He pressed his lips against her forehead. "*Listen . . .*"

He closed his eyes and began swaying with her in his arms, swaying to the gentle wind, swaying with the feather-strands.

His muscular arms tightened about her waist. One of his palms flattened against her buttocks, pulling her into him. The hard length of him, smooth and velvety, slid over her lower stomach. Rolled above the mound. Pulsed against her skin.

His other hand tangled in her hair as his lips skimmed over her neck. He began to hum low in the back of his throat as he swayed them between the wind and feather-strands.

When his fingertips began to slide along her body, so light, so perfectly, she realized that he was *connecting* with the Dreamtree. The motions of the branches in the wind, in the night, became his motions. They were not guided by thought. They were guided by the feel of Forus nightsong.

Each part of her became sensitized to his bare touches, his breezy caresses. Only his manhood pulsed strongly against the underside of her belly. A vibrant link.

The backs of his fingers grazed over her nipples. Green felt her hair slide against the peaks as well. The lengthy strands slithered over his hands. The sight was erotic. Spellbound, she watched him stroke her body with light sweeps of touch.

Firewings, flitting around the Dreamtree, haloed Jorlan from behind. His dark hair slid forward, gleaming blacker than the night. In this magical lighting, his intent, chiseled features were more beautiful than she could ever describe.

She had never seen this expression on him before. He was giving himself completely over to the Sensitive within, allowing the emotion, the connection to overtake him.

His palms dipped down her legs like feather kisses, sweeping up to where he pressed on her.

"You feel like the Dreamtree, Jorlan."

"Do I?" He blew gently on her lips—a temperate breeze, tingling the edges of her mouth.

"Now you feel like the storm, my name-bearer." Green closed her eyes to enjoy the sensations he was giving her.

"And this . . . ?" he drawled close to her mouth.

Green felt the tips of his jet lashes brush her lips. Her mouth parted at the exquisite, delicate touch. "Magnificent," she breathed.

A warm gust of breath exhaled from his nostrils, tickling her neck and collarbone.

Suddenly she felt herself falling backward.

Her eyes snapped open and she clutched Jorlan's shoulders. "What are you doing?"

He chuckled low. "Trust me, name-giver." They fell onto a swirled pile of strands at the base of the tree. The feathery appendages cushioned the fall.

Green sank into bliss.

The cushy mattress cradled them both. The hanging strands continued to sway about them, a curtain of tactile pleasure. Through the filaments, the tiny flickering lights buzzed about.

It was the most perfect night, she thought. The most perfect man.

Jorlan rested full on her, his body at once cool and hot. Cool skin from the breezes, breath hot from desire.

Green felt supple contact everywhere.

Jorlan ran his lashes over her mouth once more, then swept them up her cheeks. She had never realized how unbelievably erotic male lashes could be. He combed them down over her collarbone, over her breasts. Then flickered the peaks of her breasts. Green arched up against him. Moaning quietly, not wanting to disturb the night. The feather-strands rustled.

His lashes tickled over the rounded curve of her stomach. The little sweeps stimulated every nerve ending. He flicked his lashes over the backs of her ankles, and down the arch of her foot. As he did so, he pressed a kiss on the side of her ankle and her instep. His mouth damp, his lashes dry, spiky. Then she felt those feather lashes skittering up the length of her inner thigh like a row of tiny spines. Green discovered that she was highly sensitive to such teasing touches.

She laughed, squirming in his grasp. "You are tickling me, blaze-dragon!"

His teeth caught the tender skin high along her inner thigh. He tugged before slowly releasing the prize catch from his sharp grip. "I want to tickle you . . . and tingle you . . . and . . ." His hot tongue licked at the sensitive area. Quick, tiny, damp flicks.

Green gasped.

"*. . . taste you . . .*"

With tiny laps of his tongue, he feathered her much as he had done with his fingers and lashes. When Green tried to reach out for him, he took the opportunity to wrap some of the feather-strands around her wrists.

Green blinked as she realized that he actually had the audacity to tie her up! A She-Lord!

He gazed down at her, eyes amused, fiery azure slits. Her mortified expression was all too easy to read. "Now this is truly interesting." He chuckled low.

"I think you should—"

"Do this?" He covered her mouth with his own and gave her such a deep, powerful kiss that Green whimpered into the talented mouth.

Then he showed her how a tongue could become like a feathery touch on silk. He laved her body with swirls of the barest touch. The tip of his tongue, fluttering against the peaks of her breasts, insinuating between the Dreamtree feather-strands to wetly tease her nipples. Green cried out, sending a group of firewings into tizzy flight. Over-come by her reaction, he drew the distended peak between his pursed lips and suckled strongly.

Then he went back to his agenda, using only his stroking tongue, scraping across every part of her until she was thrashing against him in the feathery bower. Calling out his name.

Calling out for him to come to her.

And only after he spread her legs and licked long and slow at the center-line of her nether lips, only after he had pushed her over the edge by wiggling the tip of his tongue at the very tip of that line—where he once again pursed his lips and suckled strongly—did he come to her.

He rolled them over in the nest of strands. The feather-strands were all over him, on his back, in his black hair.

But he did not enter with a feathery touch at all.

He entered hard and fast and strong.

And he stayed deep.

Green gasped for breath against him, overcome by the sheer magnitude of his penetration. Overcome by the power of his love.

He hummed low in the back of his throat. That same, raw, husky sound that he had used earlier. Tuning.

Then she felt him *seep* into her. There was no other way to describe it. He was connecting with her. Just as he connected with the Dreamtree, with the Klee, and with Forus itself.

The sensation was overpowering. In the last sane part of her mind, the part that retained her responsibility to her sisters, she wondered if this could be a threat to all women. But the thought did not last long.

Sexual ecstasy of a kind she had never experienced in her life tumbled through her.

It was complete.

It was in every part of her.

It was Jorlan in every essence.

She felt his life, his rhythm, his elemental emotions, his passion.

Green cried out in sheer ecstasy.

Atop her, Jorlan lifted her legs over his shoulders, penetrating her in a position she was sure no She-Lord had ever experienced. He thrust his hips hard against her and ground in, further accentuating her responses. Her nails scored the backs of his arms.

Jorlan moaned low. He had never experienced this kind of connection in his life! Not so complete.

Not so utterly complete!

"Green," he rasped, brokenly, for he could say no more. He threw his hair back off his forehead, catching her in his passion-hazed focus. Sweat dotted his brow.

Green's expression was one of utter amazement. "Did you know it could be like this?"

He nodded. Jaw clenched, he closed his eyes as tremors of awareness skipped through him.

And her.

She felt him in every pore of her body.

"Why didn't you ever tell me?"

"It—was—not—time," he ground out.

"And now it is?" She moaned as he flexed inside her.

"Now it is."

Before she could ask why, he began to move in her. Steady surges, he swept in and out. *Plains dotted with Klee . . . hukka fields bending in the warm rain . . . a screechwing descending for its nightly kill . . . a newborn human taking its first breath . . .*

His shoulder muscles and back muscles rippled with his skillful movements. Forms in and of themselves—not unlike the Gle Kiang-ten in their own way. A cooling breeze suddenly sprung up, covering them in rich chill.

Forus's sigh.

Dreamtree blossoms shook loose, showering them in pink and purple rain. Covering them in spicy salutation.

"I will always love you, Green. Forever."

He burst inside her then. *Arkeus setting in the east . . . a ship landing on a plain . . . jinto leaves floating forever down the river . . .*

And she exploded with him.

Her last image before she dozed was Arkeus in retrograde.

Chapter Seventeen

Twice more during the night, Jorlan unsuccessfully tried to convince Green not to meet Claudine. Exasperated, he had watched her fall into their bed at home for a few hours of rest.

He tried once more just before dawn. "Green—"

"No more! I must do this for you and Arkeus. It is my duty to take care of you. I love you both and must make sure of your welfare."

"And I love you, but would never expect this of you! You cannot face that swagger in a duel—even with a half-blade! Green, you are not skilled. She has named it a duel of weaponry; what if she names the meteor-blade? You have said yourself she is very proficient in it."

"The seconds would have something to say, I imagine. Her honor would suffer irrevocably if she purposely chose a weapon that an opponent might have no expertise in. Most likely she will choose the half-blade." Jorlan was not so sure.

"Are you good with half-blade?"

"I am a stateswoman," she answered vaguely.

He exhaled in frustration. "You won't stand a chance against her!"

Her amber eyes veiled. "Perhaps not. That is not the point to be focused on here."

Jorlan realized then that he could not talk his stubborn name-giver out of this duel. He remembered her words before they left the Dreamtree. "I only wish that I could forever remember every beautiful, loving thing exactly as you have said it to me tonight. I wish that time would never blur its edges or soften its impact."

He had told her, "You will remember all of it for it is inside you, Green, and it has become part of you. Like me."

Jorlan recognized that he could not, *would not* let Green take such a risk. The protective instinct was also male, and he embraced it.

Against her half-hearted objections, he beguiled her into letting him love her again. When she fell into an exhausted slumber, he slipped from their bed.

Donning his clothes, he went over to his wardrobe and silently opened a secret compartment on the bottom.

Slipping his meteor-blade around his waist, he concealed them within his tunic.

He was going to do what any man should have the right to do. He was going to protect his family.

Silently, he closed the door behind him.

*G*reen's lashes flickered slightly as Jorlan strode determinedly to the door.

From beneath their shadows, amber glints flashed knowingly, then drifted shut.

*   *   *

*I*t was pathetically easy to gain access to the D'anbere estate. Apparently the obnoxious She-Count did not think anyone would ever dare to violate her stronghold.

Jorlan was not surprised when he found her in her private study gleefully examining an array of weapons, obviously trying to decide what would be best to use on Green. Something that would be acceptable to the Top Slice, yet advantageous to her skills.

She had strapped on two cross-blades, testing their feel. She was a woman who liked the weight of weapons on her. Jorlan might have admired that, had she been any other woman.

The cross-blades were long, weighty weapons that were designed to be used in close hand-to-hand combat. They were a favorite instrument of the wild Southern tribes, whose women meted out justice swiftly and with no recourse.

She turned at his soft footfall, expecting to see a servant.

"I told you I did not wish to be disturbed! How dare you enter without my—?" She stopped when she recognized Jorlan. Her delicate eyebrow arched speculatively.

Then her cold eyes flared greedily with erroneous assumption. She believed that Green had sent him to pacify her. Silly Marquelle! She would have this velvet petal and still go after Green Tamryn.

Jorlan leaned against her desk and crossed his arms over his black tunic. One booted ankle indolently crossed over the other. Mimicking her, he also arched his eyebrow.

"I suppose I dare much, She-Count."

Claudine threw back her head and laughed. "Dare all you like, Jorlan. I shall find the challenge of subduing you delightful."

Unconcerned, he flicked an imaginary speck of lint off his sleeve. "Actually I had a rather different challenge in mind."

Claudine strolled over to her hameeri cabinet. Lifting a bottle of the liquor, she poured herself a small goblet. "I would offer you one, my brazen petal, but I never drink with the servants."

His lids lowered. "What a shame—for you."

Her nostrils flared. "Say what you have come to say so that we may get on with it. I realize you are going to plead for my mercy with Green and offer yourself up for her. Whatever you have to say will not change my terms. Total surrender to me. Complete compliance to my wishes."

He cocked his head to the side. "Complete compliance?"

She swirled the hameeri around in her goblet, mouth twisted into a licentious smirk.

His face bronzed in rising hatred. Who did this woman think she was? What made her think she had the right to destroy people's lives, simply to get what she wanted at any human cost?

Claudine was the worst example of their society. She had coerced his grandmother, repeatedly tried to ruin Green, and threatened his son. An entitled Lordene, spoiled by her apparent power with no conscience and no accountability.

Tonight she was going to account. *To him.*

He stood away from the desk and began pacing slowly toward her. "Actually, I had something quite different in mind."

"Did you?" Her eyes blatantly devoured him as he came closer. Handsome, muscular and primed. "I'm all . . . ears."

Casually he lifted the edge of his tunic, letting her see the edge of the hammers on the meteor-blade. "My challenge for Green's."

The sight of a meteor-blade on him was so unorthodox that it took a few moments for his outrageous suggestion to sink in.

She snickered.

Like lightening, she was on him. Her arms seized him in a headlock. In the blink of an eye she drew a curved cross-blade from her waistband and held it to his throat.

"Foolish boy; you see how stupid such a challenge is? Already I have you subdued. I am a platinum class warrior! Leave women's matters to women. It would be a pity to waste such a prize piece on such a juvenile notion of devotion."

In a skilled maneuver, Jorlan twisted about, instantly freeing himself from her grip. Grabbing the wrist that held the blade, he quickly spun her around, capturing her in his own hold. Soon Claudine's own cross-blade was at her throat.

Her eyes widened in surprise. "Very good, Jorlan. I see your grandmother has indulged you in many ways. So you have been taught to fight, but wielding the meteor-blade is quite a different matter. Only the most skilled warriors can do it. Think twice about your challenge—you will not survive me."

Jorlan released her abruptly, flinging her from him.

Without taking his eyes off her, he unwrapped the meteor-blade from around his waist. Expertly, he scalloped it about his wrist, letting the hammer swing forward, bringing the rope to the perfect tautness to begin an execution of form. "Think again. It is you who will not survive, Claudine." His aqua eyes narrowed with hatred for every twisted thing she had done. "Believe it."

"No man has spilt blood on Forus for over a thousand years. Would you be the first? Do you really want to attempt to soak the ground with female blood? For if you do, you will not live long to glory in it. The Septibunal would have you executed as a deviant."

"I'm willing to take that risk."

Claudine was no fool. She recognized the skill in his handling of the weapon. Strangely, she was stimulated by the fact that she would have to conquer him to win him. Suddenly she ached to fight him.

For when she was through, she would offer him no quarter. She was sure the release of victory would be as potent as any other.

It always had been.

And after she killed the precious Jorlan, *Green* would come for her. The Marquelle would never allow such an affront to her House to pass. In the past, Green Tamryn's irksome sense of honor had always become the fatal flaw that played perfectly into her plans.

Jorlan would be a convenient diversion.

Her focus had always been Tamryn.

"Shall we?" She unlatched a door that led directly out into the gardens. Meteor-blades were rarely used indoors. Their deadly trajectories required high-speed spins. In combat, a man of Jorlan's height would require a diameter of close to twenty-six feet to properly execute many of the forms. When used in this manner, the meteor-blade duel was a lethal dance of terrifying beauty. Such battles were rare, for few had the skill to enter into such a combat. Reaction would be strictly instinctual; timing precise.

Claudine backed away from him as she began to swing her meteor-blade in the small, circular prelude motions of battle. Her steps were sure on the stone-laid terrace.

"I'll give you first strike, my brazen petal, just to show you how fair I can be." She taunted him, confident in her victory before they had even begun.

"How generous of you, She-Count." Jorlan whipped the meteor-blade over his head in a wide loose arc—an unusual first move.

Yet when he slung his wrist forward, he did not catch her off guard as he had hoped. The orbs zinged through the air only to be brought up short by blades that intersected his throw.

The ropes of their weapons twined together with a shredding force.

Both duelists pulled back on their weapons, expertly untangling them before either took damage. Novitiates often lost the battle in this manner before it had even begun.

Both of them slung the meteor-blades back around and to opposite sides.

"Not bad for a beginner." Claudine sidestepped to the right, dropped to one knee and executed a perfect lateral arc. Her blade sliced in a rapid zigzag pattern directly toward him.

Jorlan immediately rolled to his left. One of the many dangers of fighting with the meteor-blade was its field of damage. Because the reach was so long, an expert bladeswoman could take down nearly anything in her path for a radius equal to more than twice her height.

Of course in the heat of battle, close forms were high strategy.

Jorlan threw his blade on a perpendicular intersect, catching hers. He sharply yanked his wrist back in the hope of wresting the weapon from her. It didn't work; she was too sharp for that. Too skilled. She quickly circled her arm and snapped her blades around his shoulder. One of them grazed his tunic, instantly slicing through the material.

The quick, initially painless slice brought an instant well of blood bubbling up through his clothing. Claudine's eyes gleamed malevolently. "I have always liked the sight of red on black. How about you?"

"I have never much cared for the combination, Lordene." Jorlan dropped to the ground to avoid her blade coming perilously close to his head. He rolled over onto his back and snapped his blade out from ground level. Claudia recognized the intricate form, called *Blanock Lifting*. She wondered how he learned it. The rope snagged one of her knees. She could only watch as it whipped around the back of her leg, slicing into the opposite ankle when he flicked his wrist to release the circumference blades.

The cut was not deep but Jorlan hoped the slick blood would make her footing unsure.

He had no qualms about killing her. As long as she lived, this woman would be a constant threat to Green and to his son.

A highly trained warrior, Claudine rapidly recovered from the hit. She almost caught him in a rebound shot.

"I have to say, Reynard, you have much more life in you than my three past name-bearers combined. What a pity your grandmother didn't honor our contract. We can still remedy that, you know."

She caught his wrist in a superb form known as the *Twine of Night*. Jorlan knew he had but an instant to save his hand. He pushed himself *into* the spin, pulled back on his meteor-blade and engaged the ropes of his own hammers.

The maneuver stopped the damage. Claudine had to retract or be in danger of losing her weapon.

"My name is Tamryn," he hissed back at her. "And ever will be! Your past name-bearers—did they not have such skill with the meteor-blades? Is that how you killed them?" Jorlan felt blood dripping down his arm inside his tunic. It would soon affect his accuracy. A meteor-blade battle was best kept short.

Claudine laughed. "Don't be so mundane. No man would ever fight a woman. No man except *you*. They were quite easy to be rid of, actually. The poor things were so surprised at the final moments. Well, what did they expect?"

"I am surprised you are admitting this." Jorlan angled himself toward the backdrop of foliage. There, his black clothing would make it harder for her to see him.

"You will not live to tell it, my petal. The last one, poor Haringer, literally begged me for his life. I pushed him into a nest of weavermouths. He screamed for hours."

A small gasp of horror came from the bush behind him. Jorlan could not take his eyes off Claudine for even an instant to see what it was.

He was too busy deflecting her rapid strikes. The form known as *Arc Storming* was a difficult one to counterbalance.

"I grow weary of this play, Jorlan. Let us end it."

"You want me to present my neck to you for slicing?"

She grinned evilly. "I promise to be quick."

"Now, why don't I believe that?" He saw a small opening and lunged fast, snapping her meteor-blade from her grip with a powerful twist of his arm.

Claudine staggered back, stunned he had been able to do it.

"As you have said, let us end this now, shall we? I will give you quarter on one condition. . . ."

Claudine smirked. "Aren't you forgetting something?" Her hands went to the curve-blades at her waists, pulling them from their sheaths. "There will be only one left here tonight, my fiery ex-veil. And it will be me."

"Aren't *you* forgetting something?"

Claudine looked puzzled for an instant. Until she saw him tie the meteor-blade he had taken from her around his other wrist.

She snorted. "No one wields two blades! No one except a Golden Master, and they say she is myth; the secret warrior, ultimately wise in the ways of the Gle Kiang-ten!"

"Really." He began to spin the dual blades out, crisscrossing them in the air.

"They say she quietly guides us in *woman wisdom*, that her strength is unmatched for it is a strength born of knowing when to stand down and when to fight. It cannot be you!"

"I never said it was." The hammers snapped and he prepared for his ultimate strike. "Perhaps you thought it would be you?"

He had guessed correctly. Enraged, Claudine lunged toward him with curved blades, dicing a killing path.

She sliced one of his hammers before the second one found its mark and sunk down deep into her back, slicing her open from neck to waist.

Jorlan wrested the other blade from her, catching her in his arms before she fell.

He was not happy in the killing. He was the first male in over a thousand Forus years to spill blood. "What makes you hate Green so?" he whispered more to himself than anything.

With her last bit of strength Claudine D'anbere opened her eyes. Lips curving sardonically, she uttered her final words. *"Hate her? Foolish . . . petal . . . what . . . ever . . . makes . . . you . . . think . . . I . . . hate . . . her?"*

Stunned, Jorlan rested her body on the ground, not even wanting to think of the implications of her words.

A slight rustling behind him caused him to spin on his heels, hand clutching his weapon.

A glow of flamelight illuminated a small face staring silently at the body on the ground.

The girl, a beautiful child of about twelve, with long black hair and gray eyes. *Claudine's daughter.*

She looked at him with luminous gray eyes, eyes that were bright with shock and revulsion. Jorlan swallowed. He hadn't known Claudine had a daughter. The girl had seen her mother die in his arms. He reached out a hand to offer her some comfort.

With a sob, she turned and ran into the night.

His shoulders slumped in sorrow.

The girl had heard her mother's confession, of that he was certain. He remembered her small gasp of horror. She was a witness who would either view this incident as heinous crime or just punishment. What would she do to him?

It didn't matter. Green and Arkeus were safe.

*O*n his return to Tamryn House Jorlan found the leaf of a special plant he had been searching for.

He pressed it under his shirt.

It stopped the flow of blood on his arm almost instantly. By the time he entered his bedchamber, the wound had healed as if it had never been.

Discarding his clothes, he slipped silently between the silken covers. Green was still sound asleep.

Avatar would not be awakening her at dawn. Gathering her close in his arms, he fell into a troubled sleep.

"*D*id you hear about She-Count D'anbere?" Mathers fussed around Jorlan, spooning him a nice cup of snogglehound pudding.

"No, I haven't. Although I know that Green was not called to the duel." His hand covered his name-giver's on the table.

She smiled at him, answering for Mathers. "She was found dead in her gardens. They say there was an eyewitness."

Jorlan swallowed, and softly cleared his throat. "Yes?"

"It seems the She-Count was practicing forms in the garden when the blades snapped back and sliced into her back."

Jorlan tried not to exhale too loudly.

"Nasty things, them meteor-blades. Can't stand them myself." Mathers shuddered.

"Nothing wrong with a good blade!" Avatar harrumphed as she chucked Hugo a clump of pudding. The snogglehound gulped it in midair, doing a stupid little flip of ecstasy. The pudding hadn't been named after them for nothing.

"Tell that to the unfortunate She-Count." Jorlan gazed down at his plate.

"Unfortunate?" Mathers sputtered. "I say it was providence! That hateful snip-butt. I thank the Founder that my Lordene is safe!" Mathers dabbed her eyes with the edge of the table covering causing Avatar to frown.

"I can't say I'm sorry that I don't have to face her," Green said softly. "I suppose I owe that meteor-blade a debt of gratitude for surely, in its action, it protected my family. If someone had actually been wielding the weapon, I would have to thank that person as well for showing such courage."

Jorlan glanced at her out of the corner of his eye but said nothing. He went back to eating his pudding.

"Who's the witness?" Avatar asked.

"D'anbere's own daughter." Mathers answered. She placed a snuffle treat in front of Arkeus, who gurgled gleefully before picking it up and sticking it in his ear.

Frowning at the untimely morning sweet—and wondering how she was going to stop Mathers from ruining her son—Green righted the baby's hand and guided it to his mouth. Aqua eyes rounded as the delicious taste reached his Sensitive senses.

He gurgled appreciatively.

Green chuckled. His father's son, all right.

Avatar choked on her limo juice. "D'anbere's daughter? What a terrible thing for a young woman to witness!"

"Yes, it was. The girl claims the mother got her out of bed to make her watch her practice with her meteor-blade." Mathers shook her head. "They say D'anbere never let up on the poor girl. Now she's disappeared and no one can seem to find her. They think she took off to the Western Regions—a caravan guide claims she saw someone answering the girl's description riding alone and heading west. She thought it was odd and called out to her, but the child ignored her and raced off."

"By herself?" Green frowned. "That's a very dangerous trip for such a young girl."

"For anyone. What's more, the Septibunal received a signed confession this morning from that snip-butt Opper. Seems D'anbere had a hand in that, as well! Horrible business whichever way you look at it. At least her child will be allowed to retain her titles and lands, although there's no telling how she's been affected by all this, or if she'll ever return to claim them." Mathers picked up a tray and bustled out of the room.

Jorlan exhaled a sigh of relief. *The girl did not turn him in.* He owed her for that. He wished there was some way he could repay her—but he knew there was not. Although he had no regrets about what had happened with Claudine, he did regret that the girl had witnessed her mother's confession and death. He prayed she would be all right.

He leaned over and brushed some crumbs off the baby's chin. His son gave him a dreamy look as he valiantly tried to keep his eyes open. Jorlan smiled lovingly at him. Arkeus was about to nod off. Sometimes overstimulation of the senses did that to Sensitives. It appeared the fine taste of snuffle treat was a bit too overwhelming for his newborn palate.

"Well, Marquelle, I think I'll go check out our supplies." Avatar stood. "You never can tell when we'll need something at the marketplace." She winked at Green and left the room.

Green snickered. She knew the old girl was off to meet the Reynard kitchenkeeper again.

Suddenly, the room seemed unnaturally quiet. Green noticed that Arkeus had nodded off abruptly and Jorlan was silently eating his meal.

She spoke into the stillness of the room. "Thank you, my blaze-dragon."

He gazed at her with lids half lowered. "For what?"

She returned his circumspect look with a knowledgeable one of her own. "For who you are. For giving yourself fully to this fastening. For being so much more than just a name-bearer. For your love. And most of all for your strength."

Still, he waited. Waited for something more.

Green reached for his hand, interlocking her fingers with his. "You are truly my other half, Jorlan, and I could never live without you."

At last. With those few words, she had given him the most priceless gift on Forus moon! *An acknowledgment of his equality.*

His aqua eyes shined so brilliantly they lit up her soul.

*G*reen Tamryn moved with controlled precision.

Inner strength guided the secret sequence of her forms, creating a heroic abstraction across paving stone.

The hushed movements in low predawn light mimicked the rustle of wind as everyone in the house lay sleeping.

This was the best time, this quiet time. It was her time to renew vision. It was her time to clear the mind.

It was the best time for reassessments.

With a deadly snap, the dual meteor-blades echoed through the trees. Expertly slung, their fatal trajectories gathered speed and momentum in the classic stance of Gle Kiang-ten. Corded ropes arced and spun out. Like lovers, they moved together as the first rays of day crested the horizon.

The perimeter rustled, sighing to the same pulse-beat. Flora quivered with expectation as dawn approached, heralding the majesty of simply being alive.

Forus Morningsong. Sung with the perfect symmetry of a Golden Master.

She was the shadow.

She was the weapon.

She was the wind that could change.

Over and over the rite went, building into a dance of mortal beauty. Swaying. Dipping. Twirling. Leaping. The expertise had never been simply in the execution of the forms, but in the form of the execution.

She was not connected to Forus, but to a parallel wisdom, springing from its source. Her hidden dance was in the knowledge of when to step and when to pause.

When to fight and when to wait.

And when to let others finish the round for the good of the entire event. All had turned out as she had hoped.

The threat was gone. Passion had been revealed. Pride was restored. A new life had come to bring joy. And, unexpectedly, an ancient love had finally revealed itself to all of its children.

Still, there was another out there, not yet revealed. . . .

And Arkeus was about to rise.

So the Marquelle of Tamryn prepared to listen to this coming aurora, no matter its sound.

For she was a woman first, with a heart of fire and the wisdom to know that the dance we follow is ever our true ritual of proof.

And it can never be held in the court of any land.

Just in the court of our higher selves.

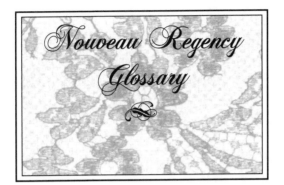

Nouveau Regency Glossary

Afterburn—refers to sexual prowess, i.e., "She has quite an afterburn."

Airscreen—projected real-time holographic screen from a wristview.

AL—after landing; refers to the date, i.e., 318 AL

Almacks, the Later—famous Top Slice club in Capitol Town.

Ancestresses—foremothers.

arc storm—severe Forus electrical storm.

arc-er—slang for arc storm.

arc-it!—screw it.

Arkeus—planet that Forus moon revolves around.

Arkeus Seize—style of furniture, rather ponderous.

Bair-tin—the sixty-three vid-tomes of governing law.

Balinting lace—lace from the Western Colony of Balinting.

balum fruit—a sweet, oval-shaped fruit believed to be an aphrodisiac by the Select Quarter.

Banta psillacyb—hallucinogenic plant.

barboy—male tavern servant.

Baroner—(m) name-bearer of Baronelle.

bed price—the cost to secure a name-bearer.

bed straps—used to secure the name-bearer on the fastening night.

bellytwaddle—complaining.

beta-baize—gamboling game table.

biocrobe—engineered microbe.

bioforms—life form.

Bladeswoman—a female proficient with the meteor-blade.

Blanock Lifting—intricate form of the Gle Kiang-ten.

blanock—multicolored, small Forus creatures. Humans are especially partial to their song.

blaze-dragon—a difficult but beautiful creature of fiery disposition, indigenous to Forus.

bus-bit—response to piece of information that is disbelieved.

by-life—life form that is the by-product of another experiment.

Capitol Town—central city.

Captain, the—also the Founder, Cybella Reynard.

chasing the velvet veil—looking for sex, as in promiscuous, i.e., "She's chasing the velvet veil, isn't she?"

chum-off—bugger off.

cilia twig—fibrous twig.

cit ways—cosmopolitan.

code-sealed—electronically sealed.

coil-winder—poisonous creature.

come-out—a veil who is entering the bid circuit.

coophand—takes care of Kloo and Klee.

coop-keeper—takes care of the coops.

coops—stables for the Kloo and Klee.

crawlsinthedark—a night creature best left unexplained, but which makes a damn good soup.

cross-blades—type of weapon.

cysystem—used by Forus architects to construct single abodes or entire cities.

damselle—young, unfastened female from an aristocratic family.

darkmatter—a man who does not quite fit in, someone who is inscrutable.

dim-bit—a young dim-nit.

dim-nit—a stupid one.

Dreamtree—beautiful plant with colorful night blooms.

emotive vision—a vision that is accompanied by its own unique emotion.

ex-veil—one who is no longer a veil.

fasten—marry.

fasten-off—marry off.

fil-Duchene—son or grandson of a Duchene.

fil-Earlene Shazi—son of Earlene Shazi.

firewings—glowing, small-winged creatures.

first-seasoners—young come-outs in their first season.

flowercream—delicious cream of pressed flowers, has a lovely scent and delicate taste.

foremothers—ancestresses.

Forfeiture duel—the winner takes all.

Forus—moon that revolves around Arkeus.

Founder— Cybella Renard.

fuzzle-muzzle cream—this really is made from fuzzle muzzles.

Gardens, the—a shady part of town.

gen-en—genetical environment.

ginny trail—leads west.

Gle Kiang-ten—a form of martial art practiced on Forus.

glinty—ostentatious.

Golden Master—adept of the Gle Kiang-ten.

good way to you—have a nice day.

grav assists—used to aid handicapped.

Hadley Tip—edge of the Southern Region.

half-blade—small weapon.

hameeri—liquor.

handheld—viewer.

high-held—has airs.

hocked—drunk.

hock-top—drunkard.

hok—the sap from this plant is used in fermenting brew.

holofan—picturesque fan.

Honor Forfeiture—the injured party receives either money or property to assuage their honor.

hormomitor—registers hormonal levels.

House of She-Lords—government arena, where popular issues are debated by the titled women.

hukka—grain crop that must be harvested before it flowers.

Inez ranges—mountains.

insult barter—price paid to injured party when a bed price is reneged on.

jacama—a spice, also a settlement in the west.

jakakoos— hopping critters.

jickne—glutinous critter.

jinto—a plant-life of Forus; the giant leaves are interwoven into Forus myth.

joined septille—a dance.

keeping room—front parlor.

kitchenkeeper—servant responsible for overseeing the kitchens.

Klee—animal native to Forus, noted for its speed and unpredictable nature.

Kloo—fussy sister animal to the Klee, noted for endurance and for being nosy.

Kloo Balcony set—elite, showy group who frequent Almacks, the Later and sit in the choice seats by the mirastone walls. The name derived from the Kloo's well-known love of drama.

Kloo hand—handles Kloo.

Kloo mirrors—ornate mirrors named after the vain Kloo.

kloobroth—gossip, rumor.

lexa beast—a fierce hunter, this animal becomes tame when offered a balum fruit.

lillacia—a flower, lilac hybrid.

limo juice—tart nectar of the limo fruit.

lineage scrolls—carried by Forus females.

link circuit, the—society eligibles.

lumpies—breakfast of champions.

mack-mock—foolish talk.

majordoma—female butler.

Male Tragedy Paradox—(MTP) affliction that befalls an aroused male.

masoglass—hard translucent building material.

mesh-pond—sentient plant system that grows over its own secreted fluid.

meteor-blade—lethal weapon, as potentially dangerous to the wielder as it is to its target.

midwoman—caretaker.

mirastone—reflective surface.

monkery—cloistered place for intractable veils, where they devote their lives to meditation.

name-bearer—fastened male.

name-giver—fastened female.

natal accelerator—taken to speed up gestation.

needlewing—biting, flying creature.

NEOFEM—also called the Seed Ship, this ship transported the women to Forus.

neon night part of town—refers to the Gardens, a racy section.

new-breed—daughter of an aristocrat, who is free to experience the pleasures of the Top Slice.

newi—the bristles of this plant are used for brushes.

nightbloomers—Forus plants that bloom at night.

nightsong—the sound of Forus night.

nod-bod—boring person.

nog-twist—idiot.

nolocharge—no penalty; slate wiped clean.

Number 99 (at the Gardens)—a disreputable club.

Oath of Proof—taken at the Ritual of Proof, given by the potential name-bearer.

on the prime lattice—refers to a veil's potential high worth in a bid, i.e. "He's on the prime lattice." The term originated with Santorini's work on genetic alteration.

OneNation—the largest country on Forus.

ore-rocks—Forus rocks that attract arcs.

Originpoint—Earth.

outwolf—loner, an unflattering term for an unfastened male.

patrona—woman who keeps a pleasurer.

pharmkit—medicine chest, bag.

placardview—flat, envelope viewer.

placed pond—woman-made pond.

plantrooms—conservatory.

plat-coin—currency.

platinum class—refers to expertise of warrior.

pleasurer—male prostitute.

pocket envoy—messaging system.

postfastening—day after the fastening.

prebids—sometimes entertained by mothers, not as binding as a true bid, however prebids guarantee that the actual bid will be given some favor.

primary port (to be of)—refers to a top bloodline, as in "She's primary port."

protector—guard.

psillacyb—hallucinogen.

Ramagi—a silklike material.

razor rock—potentially dangerous life form that protects itself with a circumference of razor-sharp shards.

repairer—medic, engineer, etc.

Ritual of Proof—ceremony of a man's purity.

roseyal—hybrid flower plant.

Rue de la Nuit—section of town where favored pleasurers are housed by their patronas.

ruling of conveyance—verdict by Septibunal in matters of dispute.

rut-bid—epithet, meaning bulls**t.

sam'on talk—used in the western provinces.

Santorini—brilliant geneticist, mother of selective gen-en.

sassbit—a younger person full of fight, who tries to give sass to their elders.

scinose—a male duenna; a dogsbody.

screech wings—carnivorous life-form, flies.

Season, the—the time of year devoted to finding and securing a name-bearer; the Season lasts more than a season.

Seed Ship—NEOFEM.

Select Quarter, the—the top fourth of the aristocracy; descendants of the original bridge crew of the *NEOFEM*.

selective gen-en—sensitive genetical environment; technique developed by Santorini for producing superior male children.

Sensitive—a male who displays heightened awareness.

Septibunal—top governing body.

Septille—a dance.

sheensui bark—placed over fastening beds, it slowly grows and entwines, forming unique patterns.

Shredder—a southern game of chance played with portions of the shredder plant.

sleek-cut—makes a fashion statement.

sleep houses—servants' quarters.

Slice (Top Slice)—the crème de la crème of the aristocracy.

snap-branch—an irritating sassbit.

snip-butt—an upstart.

snob-bobs—underwater creatures, a delicacy coveted by the Slice.

snogglehound pudding—not really made from snogglehounds.

snuffle treat—makes you snuffle, but it tastes good.

spark—young male prostitute.

spirit-law—a higher law.

spleened—vexed.

stateswoman—orator.

sunpods—pods that turn in the direction of moisture.

swaggers—obnoxious, strutting She-Lords.

T9-disc—small disc worn on a chain, usually holds household codes.

tag—punch.

tasteslikerooster—it does.

tight one—someone who is strictly by the book.

tilla—the leaves of this plant are particularly beloved by Kloo and are used for their beds.

Tops—nobs.

Top Slice—the aristocracy.

torque—a tough character who can turn it around.

touch—slang for money and/or sex.

trapper—mouth.

tribeswoman—from the South Region.

Twine of Night—meteor-blade form.

unscrolled child—a bastard.

veils—virgin males.

velvet petal—sexual slang for men, as in "He's a fine velvet petal."

velvet touch—slang for getting sex.

Victorias—rural community in Hadley Tip.

vid-tomes—multimedia, multidimensional books.

visionaries—perched on top of the roofs of houses, these rooms were originally built for defense, but later became places for romantic trysts.

waggering—taking advantage of name-bearing hopefuls, i.e., fornication.

waggers—male hopefuls of the Season.

waistlet—chain worn around the waist that holds T9 discs.

waiting-servants—escort new name-bearer to the fastening chamber.

weavermouth—hideous, evil alien life forms that you never want to invite for lunch.

wilding—an untamed one.

woman of the town—an experienced, well-connected aristocrat, who knows her way.

wristview—great for viewing vid-tomes.

zip—sex, i.e., "getting the zip."